Love & Other Scams

-a novel-

Philip Ellis

G. P. PUTNAM'S SONS
NEW YORK

PUTNAM
— EST. 1838 —

G. P. PUTNAM'S SONS
Publishers Since 1838
An imprint of Penguin Random House LLC
penguinrandomhouse.com

Library of Congress Cataloging-in-Publication Data
has been applied for.
ISBN: 9780593542477 (hc)
ISBN: 9780593542484 (ebook)

Printed in the United States of America
1st Printing

Interior art: Ring © Pitako / Shutterstock.com

BOOK DESIGN BY KRISTIN DEL ROSARIO

For Mum

However far in life I go,
it will be because of everything you gave me.
Thank you for your love, your support,
and most important, your cheekbones.

Love & Other Scams

PART ONE

Just Like
Elizabeth Taylor

One

"You'll be next," says a woman with a tight perm and spinach in her teeth. Coming out of nowhere, this sounds vaguely like a threat, and it takes Cat a moment to realize that the lady—the bride's aunt, she remembers—is probably referring to her presence here on Pluto.

"Fingers crossed!" she replies, smiling. Her cheeks ache like the practiced muscles of an athlete.

The tables are named after celestial bodies. Bridesmaids are seated on Venus, groomsmen on Mars. Johnny and Susie and their respective parents are on planet Earth, because as he said during the speeches, she is his whole world. Mercury is for immediate family, Jupiter for close friends, Saturn and Neptune for the couple's extended circle. Uranus has been omitted, for obvious reasons.

There aren't enough unattached people at this wedding to warrant the traditional singles table, and so Cat finds herself stranded all the way out on Pluto, within arm's reach of the loos, between Auntie Gladys (of the perm) and Greg, a friend of the groom's father who is keen for everybody to know that the Porsche parked outside belongs to him.

Now, as she sits making chitchat while overcooked salmon and room-temperature chardonnay muddle in her stomach, Cat finds herself conducting a mental cost-benefit analysis. The combined train fare and taxi to the scenic country venue were extortionate, and even though the dress she's wearing was off the sale rail and she purchased the cheapest item on Susie and Johnny's gift registry, it's all still more than she can really afford.

She shouldn't have come. She hardly knows anybody here, was not granted a plus-one, and has yet to even speak to the bride. But Cat is here anyway, because she knows this is probably the last time she will ever see Susie and Johnny. Soon they will be moving out of London, and the chances of bumping into them by chance in a pub in Soho will be eliminated. Then, a year from now, they will either get a dog or have a baby—which of the two is immaterial— and their social lives will begin to revolve around Sunday walks and coffee mornings with other parents and/or dog owners. Cat has long stopped keeping track of the times she has watched various other friends and acquaintances approach this tipping point and then vanish onto the other side.

It wasn't such a big deal in her midtwenties, when the circle of single girls she knew was wider and they were all hustling to find that perfect job, perfect flat, perfect man. What she didn't understand until later was that many people move to London only so that they can one day move back out. They do their time, work their way up some ladder or another, either cohabiting with the same boyfriend they've had since school or going on a carousel of dates until they find someone whose aspirations complement their own, and then they set about planning their escape to somewhere else, a commuter town or charming village where they can afford (with an injection of money from at least one set of parents) to buy their dream house.

Cat must have been off sick the day that everybody got that memo. She spent her twenties flitting from one temp job and unserious boyfriend to the next, and only realized everyone else was working to a strict timeline after the fourth engagement announcement.

She's not even especially close to Susie and Johnny. Cat has long harbored some unsettling suspicions about Johnny's politics, which have only been emboldened by what she has seen of his family today, and if Cat's being honest with herself, Susie can be kind of a drip. But Cat feels a sting regardless, because they are going somewhere she cannot follow. That's why she attends the weddings, she supposes. Because when else would she ever actually see any of the women she used to consider her friends?

"Oh, my dear," Gladys coos sympathetically when Cat's eyes fill up, threatening to ruin her mascara.

"I always cry at weddings," she says, and excuses herself.

The bathroom is blissfully empty. Cat locks herself in a stall and retrieves the flask of vodka from her clutch, knocking it back and swishing it like mouthwash to take away the taste of bile. At twenty-nine, she is arguably too old to be sneaking her own booze into events, but the table wine lasted all of half an hour and it's a cash bar, even though she's fairly certain neither the bride's nor the groom's family is exactly poor.

Of course, that's how the loaded stay *loaded*, Cat thinks, popping a Tic Tac into her mouth and refreshing her lipstick. Invite everybody to the poshest hotel in the Home Counties to show off just how bougie you are, but don't actually pay for anything you don't absolutely have to. Oh, and nobody can come unless they bring a gift or envelope full of cash.

Weddings are actually a pretty great scam, now that she thinks about it. The only start-up capital you really need is a willing accomplice. Cat scans the room on her way back to Pluto, identifying at least two single-looking men: one at the bar, another on the dance floor, dutifully swaying with Johnny's grandmother. She imagines approaching one of them and proposing they get engaged, hit up everybody they know for expensive homeware and gift certificates, then divide the spoils and go their separate ways. If she can find a guy who would be up for the idea, it might just end up being her most fruitful relationship to date.

"Did it hurt?" asks Greg when she gets back to the table.

"Did what hurt?" *I swear to god, if the next words out of your mouth are "When you fell from heaven"* . . .

"Your nose stud," Greg says. "I'm always curious when I see people with those things."

"Not really," she tells him. "I mean, yes, it did. But it was so long ago, I hardly remember."

"Like childbirth," he says.

"Sure." Cat nods. "Like childbirth."

There is an awkward lull as the DJ fumbles the transition from one song to another, and then the room is once again filled with the beat of a song from the early 2000s.

"Why aren't you up there shaking your thing?" he asks. "A young filly like you shouldn't be putting herself out to pasture with the likes of us." He jerks his head at Gladys, who wrinkles her nose at being compared to a farm animal. Cat feels a pang of sympathy. She is hardly thrilled by the pastoral metaphor either, but even Greg's fumbled attempt at a compliment hits her ear like a mother tongue after years abroad.

"I'm old-fashioned," she tells him. "Waiting for somebody to ask."

"Well, in that case," he says, grinning and extending his hand, "may I have this dance?"

Greg is easily old enough to be her father, and his skin has a slight sheen to it, like glazed pork. But Cat is single at a wedding, and his eyes have been on her since she first sat down. If nothing else, she thinks, he's probably good for a vodka tonic.

Cat has nothing in her purse but a pack of mints, a crumpled five-pound note, and a blister bandage for shoe emergencies. Her freelance job hasn't been paying much lately, and the last of her money went to the wedding gift and this dress, an aquamarine number which she has to admit looks pretty damn good.

Greg's palm is clammy as he leads her into the crowd, and Cat suspects—for the second or third time today—that it isn't a cold making him sniff and sweat so much. The song is fast, retro, and apparently right up his street. He jerks around like a bargain-basement Mick Jagger while Cat does her best to keep up, shimmying as much as her dress will allow.

"See? There's life in the old dog yet," he shouts proudly.

"I never doubted you!" Cat replies, and surprises herself by laughing. She remembers when she used to love weddings: the drinking, the dancing, the chatting absolute shit with people she's never met before. She can still salvage this evening, she thinks. As long as this corny but pleasant enough man is aware that she will most definitely be leaving alone once the lights come on.

When the music slows down and Whitney starts to sing about how she has nothing, Greg's moist grip tightens on Cat's hand, and she allows herself to be pulled into an awkward half hug.

"We love this one," he says. "My wife, I mean my ex-wife, and I. It was our song."

"It's a good song," she tells him, unsure of what else to say. He seems satisfied with her response, however, and they continue to sway in silence.

She can't remember the last time she slow-danced with somebody. From the way Greg is stepping on her feet, neither can he. Cat rests her head lightly on his shoulder as they each shuffle from side to side, embarrassed by her body's sudden hunger for any form of physical contact. The spell is soon broken, however, when her dance partner's avuncular hands begin to wander.

Handbag vodka or not, Cat suddenly feels as sober as a judge.

"I need the loo again," she says abruptly, pulling away from him just before the song comes to an end.

"Women and their bladders," says Greg, shaking his head in amusement, as if this is some sort of old adage. He makes his way toward the bar, and as soon as he is facing away from her, Cat seeks out the bride and groom to say her goodbyes.

She finds Susie sitting at the top table, dress hiked up around her knees, kneading the sole of her right foot.

"Cat!" Her eyes widen in surprise, and Cat's stomach plummets as she realizes: Susie didn't know she was here. Might have even forgotten they'd invited her in the first place.

"I just wanted to say—" Cat begins, but something catches in her throat. What *does* she want to say?

I paid nearly two hundred pounds to be here and I wish I hadn't bothered.

I just got sexually harassed because you sat me next to some old creep.

We haven't been friends for a long time now, have we?

"I'm off now," she says.

"You're leaving already?" Susie asks. "But we haven't even had a chance to catch up—"

"Congratulations," Cat interrupts. "I'm really happy for you."

It's not true, but she's told bigger and uglier lies than that. She returns to Pluto, grabs her bag off her chair, and gives Gladys a hasty wave before Greg can return, then rushes out of the ballroom and into the hotel lobby, where she asks the man at the front desk to call her a cab.

"They usually get here in around ten minutes," he tells her.

"Thank you," she says. "I'll wait outside."

Pretty soon, Greg will wonder where his wallet is. He will check and double-check his pockets and the floor under Pluto, before asking the DJ to put out an announcement, by which point Cat will be long gone. Not that he would ever suspect her of palming his billfold while he was pawing her buttocks. He was too preoccupied with his own hands to notice what she was doing with hers.

Cat holds the door open for two smokers who are heading back inside.

"Love your dress," one of them says as she passes.

"Thanks," she replies, and her smile this time is genuine. "It has pockets."

Two

The bar at the Oceanic Hotel is quiet when Cat arrives, but she opts for a bar stool rather than a seat at any of the empty tables. Jake is the only one working tonight, and he gives her the same neutral almost-smile in greeting as always. His crisp white shirt seems to glow against his brown skin, and Cat can't help but notice—not for the first time—how snugly it fits his shoulders.

"Nice dress," he says.

"Thanks," she replies. "It's already paid for itself." She retrieves Greg's wallet from the pocket at her hip and places it on the bar triumphantly. It's getting late, and she should have gone straight home, but the siren call of one more drink to celebrate her little win was too tempting to resist, and she requested a new destination as they approached Islington, tipping the driver liberally for his trouble.

"I would love a glass of whiskey," she says. "Something smoky. The pricier the better. And one for you too."

"Very generous." He raises an eyebrow, then turns to the rack behind the bar. A moment later, he places two tumblers of amber liquid on the counter between them.

"Who are these on?" he asks.

"Somebody who deserved it," says Cat. "Trust me."

Another faint smile plays on Jake's lips. He picks up his glass and gently clinks it against hers.

Cat and Jake never talk directly about her hobby. The only reason she is being so brazen now is because she knows Jake won't snitch on her. If he was going to, he would have done it by now.

Cat originally started frequenting the bar as a way of making herself scarce during her housemates' weekly date night. She even anticipated meeting somebody here, a handsome, mysterious stranger who would offer first to buy her a drink and then to sweep her off her feet. But despite its glamourous non sequitur of a name (the Oceanic isn't even within walking distance of the river, let alone the sea), Cat discovered a largely corporate clientele: consultants and conference-goers and the occasional City boy flashing the cash.

In other words, fish in a barrel.

This was a little over a year ago. Three different friends had welcomed their first precious bundles that summer, meaning a spate of baby showers, gender-reveal parties, and christenings. Cat was skint as a result and had an idea she was keen to try out; the Oceanic Bar presented a prime opportunity. She would rock up on a Thursday or Friday night, dressed in a blouse and slacks or shift dress and heels, doing her best impression of somebody who has had a long day at the office and is in need of a stiff drink. She would strike up a conversation with a table nearby or sometimes just wait for them to talk to her. She was, after all, a woman alone at a bar, and groups of men are easier to predict than Hallmark movies. She'd end up joining them at their table, laughing at their jokes and dishing back a little patter, scooting closer in her chair until she was literally rubbing shoulders with at least one of them.

And when she got near enough, her hand would slip into the jacket on the back of the chair. Or she would intentionally knock over a glass, leaving herself free to surreptitiously rifle through a wallet while her new acquaintance busied himself swabbing warm prosecco off his trousers with a napkin. Over the course of an evening, with a little luck, there were potentially hundreds to be made.

She never took huge amounts of money, and she only targeted people who she reckoned either could afford it or wouldn't even notice. And she tried not to make too regular a habit of it. But every couple of months, when freelance graphic design gigs were thin on the ground, when rent was due, on those days when she had to choose between buying food and paying her phone bill on time, Cat knew she could fall back on an evening at the Oceanic.

And she would be lying to herself if she didn't admit, in those unguarded moments when drifting off to sleep after a night grifting at the bar, that she secretly gets a kick out of it. Not the crimes themselves—they're just a means to an end, a product of the financial necessity and borderline desperation that comes with being broke in London—but rather the moment that comes immediately after she has stolen something. That rush. There is no feeling in the world quite like that of breaking the rules, of doing the exact opposite of what a grown woman is supposed to do . . . and getting away with it.

And then Jake clocked her.

It was a busy Thursday. Cat had just relieved a recruitment consultant of thirty quid when she felt his eyes on her. She resisted the urge to tense up or look at him right away, taking a moment to reassert her composure. Then she threw her head back, shaking her scruffy blond bob coquettishly as she laughed at the deeply unfunny comment her new friend the recruiter had made, and used the opportunity to glance toward the bar, where, sure enough, Jake was watching her.

His expression was sphinxlike, his lips pursed in either judgment or mild amusement. It wasn't the kind of gross, obvious stare Cat was used to receiving from men. It didn't feel predatory or intrusive. He just . . . *saw* her. And she knew instantly that somehow, he had figured out what she was up to.

She assumed he would ask her to leave, or worse, call the police. But he didn't. She gave the hotel a wide berth for a while, tried her craft on the punters in a Be At One not far away, but the bouncer made her nervous and she never went back. And when she braved another visit to the Oceanic a few weeks later, Jake greeted her with a nod as if she were a regular.

At first she thought he'd spared her because he fancied her, but he's never made a move. In fact, he barely speaks at all, unless Cat is the one to initiate conversation. She's done so a couple of times, thinking it can't hurt to keep him on her side. The fact that he is gorgeous, with short black curly hair and eyelashes so dark he could almost be wearing eyeliner, is beside the point.

"So where have you been tonight?" Jake asks.

"Wedding."

He takes in her clipped tone—not to mention the fact that she is here in the Oceanic at eleven p.m. rather than catching the bouquet—and nods.

"Weddings are the worst," he says, taking a languorous sip of his whiskey. His tongue darts out to clean the trace of liquor off his bottom lip. Cat's eyes linger on it for perhaps just a second longer than is proper, and she distracts herself with a mouthful of her own drink. Almost instantly, her nostrils start to burn and her eyes threaten to water. This is the *good* stuff?

Cat has always loved the idea of being the kind of girl who can enjoy whiskey. She's not sure where it comes from. The way it seems to be widely seen as the purview of people who are cool and worldly, perhaps. Or maybe it's simply a holdover from the brief time in her early twenties when Cat's efforts went into trying to impress guys, not rip them off. Or, possibly, she is just trying to play Billy Big Bollocks in front of a certain inscrutable bartender.

"That's . . . smooth," she says unconvincingly. She's wincing, she realizes.

Jake laughs. It only lasts a second, but it's the first display of actual emotion Cat has seen from him maybe ever.

"That was my fault," he says. "I poured you the one that our flush guests tend to like. I should've asked you what you *usually* drink."

"My answer would have been . . . vodka."

The edge of Jake's mouth tugs upward into a half smile, and she thinks for a second that he is going to laugh at her again.

"Well, why didn't you say so?" He rolls up his sleeves. "I'll make you a martini instead. Just let me know how you want it." He looks her dead in the eye, and that eyebrow goes up again. "Dirty?"

Oh my god. He's flirting. He's actually, finally flirting. Isn't he?

"Dry," Cat rasps. "With a twist."

"Coming right up."

She pretends to look at her phone while Jake measures vodka and vermouth, the muscles in his forearms tensing as he secures the cap to the cocktail mixer and proceeds to give it a series of vigorous, commanding shakes. Thank god he doesn't make eye contact during this part.

"Dry with a twist," he says a moment later, presenting her with a glass frosted with condensation.

"Perfect," she says after a sip. "Thank you."

He looks like he is about to say something, but his attention is drawn away by three men who have entered the bar, their arrival accompanied by a cloud of cologne and beer sweat.

"Jay!" one of them barks, pointing at Jake. He looks like the drunk captain of his own little ship, catching sight of land.

"What'll it be, lads?" Jake asks, and Cat can practically *see* him dialing up the volume and masculine timbre of his voice. She has a similar trick: lengthening her vowels and projecting poshness when the occasion calls for it.

"Three Peronis. Cheers, Jay," the man says. "I was telling the boys here about your game. Thought I'd give you a chance to win your money back." Then, noticing Cat for the first time: "Hey, beautiful."

Cat sits stirring her martini as Jake attends to his new patrons, pretending she doesn't see their lewd stares. It's no use.

"I'm Hugo, by the way," the man says, suddenly turning to Cat and holding out his hand.

"Hi, Hugo," she replies, eventually taking his hand because he's swaying while holding it out and she fears it may be throwing off his center of gravity. He has extended his left hand, so either he's left-handed, or he simply wants to make sure she notices the

Rolex on his wrist. "I'm . . . Clara." Is she imagining it, or did Jake just smirk?

"That's a beautiful name," he says, voice hitching like he's suppressing a belch. "And is it true what they say?"

"What who say?"

"That blondes have more fun." He cocks his chin.

Not right now, Cat thinks. This, she knows, is the reality versus her earlier fantasy of meeting a handsome stranger at the Oceanic. Any man who walks in here and approaches the petite blonde sitting alone at the bar is likely to be a fuckboy at best, a predator at worst. She's been mistaken for a sex worker on more than one occasion, and it took a *long* time to convince those particular gentlemen that "freelance creative" wasn't code for something else.

That constant feeling of eyes boring into her, needing to play along to get the job done, having to be hyperaware of her surroundings at all times . . . It gets exhausting. It's also what makes it possible for Cat to so easily relieve them of their money: her slight frame, bottle-blond hair, and wide blue eyes mean most men underestimate her. For all the unwanted attention that they shower on the opposite sex, men seem to have no idea just how closely women watch them in return.

"So," says Hugo, turning back to the bar, seemingly bored by her already. "The game?"

"I don't know, Hugo," Jake says, feigning reluctance. "It's late, I should really start closing up . . ."

"No no no! I promised the boys," he pleads in the manner of somebody who is clearly used to getting his own way.

Jake hesitates and then sighs. "Sure," he says. "Fine."

After pouring them each a pint, Jake is finally cajoled into bringing out a pack of playing cards from under the bar and proceeds to explain the rules of something called "Find the Lady." Cat half recognizes it from a fairground her dad took her to once. She wanted to play, but he grabbed her hand tightly and dragged her away to the teacup ride.

"It's simple," Jake says, shuffling the deck rapidly and expertly. Cat watches from the corner of her eye as his fingers dance over the cards, almost appearing to caress them. Then he lays three cards faceup on the counter, like a tarot spread. The ace of clubs, the ten of diamonds, and the queen of hearts.

"Keep your eye on the queen," Jake says as he turns the cards facedown, and then proceeds to slide them around in circles on the bar. "Where is she?"

Hugo taps the card in the middle. "There," he says proudly.

"Are you sure of that?" Jake asks.

"Yeah."

"How sure?"

Hugo reaches into his wallet and throws down a shiny, brand-new twenty-pound note.

Jake reaches under the bar again and pulls out what looks like the tip jar. Cat instantly feels guilty; she can rarely afford to tip as well as she would like. Jake pulls a crumpled twenty from the jar and lays it on the counter next to Hugo's. He then flips the middle card over.

"There she is," he says.

Hugo greedily gathers up both notes while crowing to his friends.

"Okay," one of the others says. "Let me try."

"Sure thing," says Jake. He lays down three more cards. This time, the lady in question is the queen of clubs. Jake's hands move more swiftly over the cards than in the previous round, and Cat thinks that this new player, who introduces himself as Toby, may actually sprain something from concentrating so hard on the rapidly changing configurations.

"There!" he says once Jake has finished, jabbing the card on the left with his forefinger.

"How sure are you?" Jake asks again. Toby reaches into his pocket and retrieves two tens. Jake matches his bet with two notes from the tip jar, then flips each card over. The far left, the one Toby was so certain about, is actually a jack of spades. Jake slides all four notes back across the counter and pockets them.

"You weren't watching closely enough, mate," says the third man. "I *knew* you had that one wrong."

"Well, why didn't you bloody tell me?" his friend protests.

"You're the one who said you were sure," he says. "Right, move aside. Let me show you how it's done."

On and on the game goes. The three boys throw down note after note on bets as they get carried away. Their eyes are unfocused and their speech slurred, and yet Jake seems to lose more rounds than he wins.

"Don't feel too bad," says the leader with a wink, when Jake finally calls time. "You can't win them all."

"Good game, lads," says Jake, gracious in defeat. He gives each of them that blokey, clasped handshake that makes it look like they're about to arm-wrestle across the bar, and then they are gone.

Cat suddenly understands.

"Well played," she says.

"Sorry?" Jake asks. He widens his eyes, assuming a look of innocence, and she marvels again at just how long his lashes are.

"You let them win enough times to make them cocky."

"No idea what you're talking about," he says, picking up a cloth and giving the counter a casual wipe, like he's playing the part of a bartender in a film.

"You should be a magician," she continues. "That sleight of hand."

"It's a game of chance," he insists.

"And the watch?"

Jake's arm ceases its rhythmic motion.

"Watch?" he asks, no longer feigning innocence.

"A shiny Rolex," says Cat. "I could have sworn your favorite customer was wearing one when he came in here earlier. But on his way out, just now . . . I couldn't see it on him."

Jake doesn't say anything. Buoyed by his silence, Cat keeps going.

"That bro handshake," she says. "Was that when you did it?"

"I think you've had one too many," he says. He turns to face her and smiles, but it lacks its usual dazzle.

"No need to gaslight me," she says. "Your secret is safe."

"I don't have a secret," he says, resuming his wiping.

"Sure you don't." She knocks back the remains of her martini and hands him the empty glass. "It just makes so much more sense now. Why you'd still let me in here after you caught me . . . well, you know."

You thought he liked you, but he's just protecting himself.

"You didn't call security because you didn't want anybody paying too much attention to what goes on in here."

Jake appears to think for a long moment and then asks: "So . . . what now?"

"Looks a lot like a stalemate to me," Cat says.

Jake says nothing. Again.

"And as long as this place continues to be big enough for both of us . . ." Cat shrugs.

Jake appears to chew the inside of his cheek, then smiles.

"I honestly thought you were about to blackmail me," he says finally.

"Oh, please, I don't have a leg to stand on," Cat replies. "Which reminds me. My feet are absolutely killing me. These shoes look great but they're actually feeling pretty misogynistic right now." She hops off her stool and begins to gather her things. "Then again, it seems like we have some complementary skills. Between us, we have quite the talent for relieving people of their belongings."

"Thanks, but no." Jake's face grows serious. "I don't do the partner thing."

"Oh. Okay. Cool. I mean, good. That's probably best." Cat nods. "It's not exactly a lifestyle for me. No judgments. I only do it when straits are dire."

"They must be dire pretty regularly," Jake says. "No offense."

"None taken. They are." She smooths down the front of her dress, even more self-conscious now that the subject of money has arisen than she was when Hugo was eyeballing her earlier. "It's funny," she says. "Not funny ha-ha, I mean, just . . . you know. Interesting. Most people I know, if they had cash flow problems, they'd just ring up Mum or Dad, and seconds later they'd have money in their account."

"Sounds pretty good to me," says Jake. "Shame it doesn't work like that for all of us."

Cat nods. She has lost count of the occasions where she picked up the phone to call her dad, to tell him she was in real trouble, only to think better of it. She knows he would remortgage their semidetached in Winsford if it meant being able to help her out, and that is why she never lets on. He can't afford to be generous any more than she can.

That could all change soon, though.

"A partnership probably wouldn't work anyway," she tells Jake. "Chances are, you won't see much more of me. I'm going legit." As if to prove a point, she pulls out her phone and shows him the appointment on the home screen. "Eight o'clock sharp, Monday morning. I've been freelancing for this big fancy PR firm and they want to see me. I think they want to take me full-time."

She says it in a light and breezy tone, like she has other options, when the truth is this is a real Hail Mary. The project she's been brought in to work on with Velocity PR is winding down, so Cat has been keeping her ear to the ground for other opportunities to jump on. She may have even read, in emails not strictly meant for her but that weren't encrypted either, that Mikhail, their CEO, has been considering long-term contracts for freelancers. So when she not-so-casually brought up the possibility of working together again on Friday, she was ecstatic but not surprised when Mikhail said: "Why don't you come in early on Monday; eight sound good? There's something I'd like to chat about with you." She spent the entire journey to the wedding this morning mentally dissecting those words.

"Congratulations," Jake says. "I'm sure you'll be amazing."

"Thank you." She smiles at him, then down at her phone. "Oh, god! It's so late! I should be getting home. What do I owe you for the drinks?"

He fobs her off with a wave of his cloth.

"They're on the house."

Cat thanks him again and totters out of the bar as gracefully as her sore feet will carry her. On the blessedly short walk home, she keeps thinking about eyelashes and forearms, even though she is trying her utmost not to. Along with the vanishing Rolex, Cat couldn't help but notice something else tonight: a gold wedding ring had been impossible to miss as Jake's hands danced over the cards. If Cat had any remaining close female friends, she imagines they would all advise her that it is best to avoid getting involved with a married con artist.

And anyway, the Oceanic has served its purpose. With a bit of luck, Cat will never have to cheat, lie, or steal her way to the end of the month ever again. Is she thrilled at the prospect of designing corporate logos and social media infographics five days a week for the next however many years? Not especially. But the salary and paid leave would make a nice change.

Maybe she'd even get back on the apps and meet someone pleasant and reliable, have one of those Sunday-papers-and-pub-lunch relationships. After years of temping, contracting, and increasingly desperate acts of petty larceny just to scrape by, Cat feels like her real adult life is finally about to begin.

The next morning, Cat questions the wisdom of that last martini while hugging the mattress in an effort to stop the room from spinning. A nightcap wasn't necessary after all that wine at the wedding, she tells herself. Not to mention her flask, currently peeking out from her discarded handbag on the floor next to the bed.

She downs the glass of water on the nightstand, thanking her past self for this small kindness, then hauls herself out of bed. She steps over the tangle of dress and shoes and pulls on a hoodie and leggings before venturing out onto the landing. The house is quiet, and it's still early; if she is quick, she can make it downstairs, make a cup of tea and small mountain of toast, and return to her room before Tom and Alex wake up.

"Good morning!" Tom greets her as she enters the kitchen. Both of Cat's housemates are sitting at the kitchen table, tucking into French toast, crispy bacon, and an assortment of highly Instagrammable berries. Tom Porter is a radio personality who made the jump to television last year with affable segments on the likes of *Sunday Brunch* and *The One Show*, and his boyfriend, Alex Georgiou, is a doctor who went into private practice as swiftly as humanly possible, exchanging emergency medicine for affluent hypochondriacs.

"Hi," Cat croaks, then clears her throat and tries again. "Morning, guys."

"How was the wedding?" Alex asks. "Must have been fun for you to be getting back so late. We appreciate you trying to be quiet."

It's not like Alex to be passive-aggressive. Usually he just prefers to be plain old aggressive, although his five-foot-nine frame and incredibly pretty face often mean that it feels like being scolded by a Chihuahua. Cat once made the mistake of jokingly calling him "Scrappy-Doo" at a party. He did not speak to her for a week.

She searches her memory for any incidents during her return last night. Did she slam the front door by accident? Walk into that inconveniently placed table in the hallway? Trip up the stairs?

"I didn't wake you, did I?" she asks. The last thing she needs is to be in these two's bad books.

"No, no, nothing like that," Tom reassures her. "We were up late, looking at houses online."

"Uh-huh." Cat maneuvers past them in the direction of the kettle. Tea. Toast. These things will solve all of her immediate problems.

"While we've got you, Cat." Tom puts down his knife and fork, and Cat's stomach plummets. Okay, so maybe not *all* of her problems. "We were just wondering how you might be getting on with making arrangements?"

Cat has lived in Tom and Alex's spare room for years now. It started out as temporary, or at least she thought so at the time. Before that, she'd rented with three other girls in Finsbury Park. The three girls had changed over the years, with a cycle of newcomers arriving like Sugababes as housemates left to live with their boyfriends, or move back home, or go traveling. Eventually the landlord bumped up the rent to a level Cat could no longer afford, even split four ways. That was the first time she came close to leaving London—then she found Tom and Alex on some houseshare matchmaking website. A couple with a terrace house in Angel were renting out their spare bedroom for a steal. *This will do for now*, Cat told herself. *Until I get more clients and can afford something better.* That was three years ago. Freelance work continued to only ever come in fits and starts, and dreams of moving into a more central apartment began to fade.

And the truth is, she has enjoyed living with a couple far more than she ever could have anticipated. They made her feel exceptionally welcome when she moved in, and their wine–and–*Drag Race* nights have been a rare highlight in her social calendar. In return, she has done her best to be a quiet, tidy lodger, only working from home when she can't amass enough change for a filter coffee at Starbucks. The setup is not ideal, but Cat can live with it. Story of her life.

Then a few months ago, Tom and Alex sat her down and told her, eyes wide and glassy with tears of joy, that they were planning to start adoption proceedings, but that before they could do so, they wanted to move to a bigger place, a little less central. Cat has been given until September to find alternative accommodation.

"I'm all over it," she tells Tom, flicking the kettle on. "I should hear back about a few places this week, actually."

"That's great!" he says. "Good job."

Okay, so Cat hasn't actually contacted any letting agents yet. So far, she hasn't found a single thing online that isn't either prohibitively expensive or like something out of a horror film. Now they're into July, and she has less than two months to get something sorted. With no money for a deposit and no proof of steady income.

It's enough to make her nostalgic for those early days of sofa-surfing when she first moved to London, when people would think nothing of volunteering their living room for a few days or even weeks when she was between places. Cat happily did the same at the flat in Finsbury Park, when a friend of a friend went through a breakup and needed somewhere to stay. There'd been a real sense of all being in it together, the hustle and grind of making their ways as young professionals in the big city. It was even kind of fun.

There's something vaguely pathetic, however, about asking to crash on a friend's sofa when you're pushing thirty. And even if Cat could work up enough saliva to swallow her pride, she doesn't know that many people who are still in London. Susie and Johnny, maybe? No. Living with a couple is one thing. Living with newlyweds is out of the question.

I really, really don't want to have to call Dad, she thinks. Coming back to him cap in hand would be almost as humiliating as sleeping on her married friends' futon.

It's okay, though. Cat has a plan. She just needs to secure this design job in the meeting tomorrow morning. Negotiate a salary that will afford her a deposit and rent. Then she'll make a more attractive tenant. Then she can find a place where hopefully she'll only have to share with *one* other person. Ideally someone fun. With cool friends. Maybe even some single male acquaintances.

But she's getting ahead of herself. One obstacle at a time. Starting with this hangover.

Three

Cat arrives at the offices of Velocity PR at eight o'clock sharp.
She's been up since six, blow-drying her hair and going over the
list of ideas she prepared to show how much of an asset she can be.
Make yourself indispensable, she thinks. *Show them they can rely
on you.*

Cat isn't stupid; she knew even before she moved to London
that making a living as a professional artist wasn't going to be
feasible at first. So she pivoted to design work, thinking herself
quite industrious, before learning that she wasn't the only young
arts graduate to have that idea. *It's fine*, she thought. *I'll make some
money doing this and work on my sketches in my free time*. It seemed
so simple.

She didn't anticipate still being in the same position nearly a
decade later, pitching for everything from big-brand projects to glo-
rified busywork. Even worse, these days she's competing against
people who are younger, not as jaded, and willing to do it for less.
Today that changes, Cat has decided. She is the mistress of her

own destiny. A go-getter with, as her mum might have said, *gumption*.

Velocity's CEO, Mikhail, is a preternaturally cheerful twenty-five-year-old with a bouncy quiff and narrow lips. He is the kind of man, Cat has often thought, who is just one software upgrade away from being handsome. He is dressed casually this morning, in a hoodie and cuffed jeans, but she knows they probably cost just as much as, if not more than, the burnt-orange power suit she is currently wearing, which she saved up for months to buy and has worn so often the elbows have taken on a slight sheen.

"Kittycat," he says, welcoming her with a hug. "It's been too long since we had you come in. Have you helped yourself to coffee? Green juice? Pastry? Piece of fruit?"

"It's great to be here," she tells him. "And no, I'm fine, thanks." If her sweaty palms and the jittery feeling in her stomach are any indication, Cat has had more than enough coffee already this morning.

"Okey-dokey." Mikhail beams. "Straight to business—that's what I appreciate about you. Shall we take this in my office?"

Once they are both seated, Cat dives into her proposal, listing the many ways in which she is not only willing but *excited* to take on more work, and how it would actually save the company money versus per-hour invoicing if they were to keep her on retainer, or perhaps even bring her in-house on a part-time basis, and—

"I'm going to stop you there," says Mikhail, holding up a finger. "This is all wonderful. You've clearly given this a lot of thought, and I admire your industriousness. I really do, Kittycat. You remind me a lot of me, actually."

Cat smiles, trying not to bristle at the nickname she never vetted or feel condescended to by this man whom she could have babysat not so long ago.

"I'm just afraid we're not at a stage where we'd be considering an in-house position," Mikhail continues.

"Oh," says Cat. "Okay. Never mind. Worth a punt, eh? Let's just talk about this new project, then."

"Project?" Mikhail tilts his head.

"Yes," Cat says. "You know, the reason you wanted to see me today?"

"Ah." His characteristic cheer dampens. "Here's the thing, Cat. We're actually in the process of downsizing temporarily. This climate, you know? People just aren't prioritizing any share of wallet for boutique PR solutions. Which is shortsighted, if you ask me, because what are they going to do when there's an upswing and everybody has forgotten who they are? But anyway. I wanted you to be the first to know that starting this week, we'll be outsourcing a lot of extraneous design work to independent contractors."

"That's great to hear," says Cat. "I—"

"On Tenner," Mikhail adds.

Her first thought is that he's joking. Tenner is, after all, a punch line to any freelancer worth their salt: an app where people can advertise all kinds of creative and digital services—logo design, copywriting, photo shoots, video editing—for ten pounds a pop.

"Are you serious?" she says, incredulous. "Sorry. I mean . . . *Seriously?* What are you thinking?"

"We're *thinking*," Mikhail says, lips tightening into nonexistence, "that this will save the company upward of two hundred thousand pounds in the next six months. Is there anything in your folder, Catherine, that will save the company even half that amount? Because if there is, believe me, I will gladly hear it."

His use of her full name sends Cat's simmering frustration into a boil. The man who dropped the best part of five grand on a 3D printer for a one-off campaign last year, simply because he wanted the shiniest toy, is now demanding she justify the rate she hasn't dared increase in the last two years for fear of this exact outcome.

"This could have been an email," she says, doing her best to keep her tone even.

"I beg your pardon?" Mikhail frowns in confusion.

"I'm just not sure why you had me come in at eight o'clock on a Monday," says Cat, "just to tell me you don't need me anymore. You could have emailed. Or called."

"Oh, no, that wouldn't do," says Mikhail. "That's not how we do things here. We're a family, after all. It was only right to tell you face-to-face. You deserve that much, after being in the trenches with us for so long! It's the kind thing to do."

Appallingly, he seems to really believe it. And yes, Cat supposes they *are* a family of sorts: she's spent more time on the phone with Velocity in the last few weeks than she has with her own father in the last year. Has grown used to receiving emails at all hours of the day and night, and fulfilling unreasonable requests that she never feels able to say no to. She thought, in her own way, that it meant something too. That by showing willingness, being amenable, and suppressing her frustrations, she was demonstrating she was a team player. She realizes now that she's been something else entirely—a mug.

"You won't get work of the same quality on Tenner," she says. "I know that sounds like I'm just tooting my own horn, making a case for myself, but it's true. It's all content farms in Delhi and teenagers in their bedrooms."

She realizes a second too late that she has misspoken. Mikhail, she remembers, told her proudly when they first met that he had started this company at his parents' kitchen table when he was eighteen. He looks at her now with something close to pity, the way you might regard a beloved family pet that can no longer control its own bladder.

"The truth is, Cat," he says, "quality has rather been the issue."

"I don't understand."

"Well, you always fulfill the brief," he says, "but . . ."

"But what?"

"We've had to run some of your recent assignments past another designer to be—how do I say this?—tidied up a little."

"I'm sorry?" Cat says, baffled.

"Oh, I know you are," he continues. "But we haven't been entirely satisfied with the level you're working at for a while. Some of your designs feel phoned in. If I were to hazard a guess, I'd say the issue is passion. Or a lack thereof. This restructuring has come at a fortuitous time."

"It has?"

"Yes! Don't you see? Now you can do what I tell all of my team to do. Chase your real dream!"

"Graphic design is my passion."

"Let me rephrase that, then," Mikhail says. "Find something you enjoy . . . that you're also good at."

Cat doesn't know what to say to that, and is so blindsided by Mikhail's kind assassination of her sole marketable skill that when he indicates the meeting is over and their business concluded, she follows his cue and stands.

"This is going to be an exciting time for you, I can tell," he says, placing his hand on her shoulder. "The world is your oyster. You're so lucky. I'm jealous, if anything!"

She looks down at his hand, still dumbfounded, and perhaps interpreting this as implied impropriety, Mikhail hastily removes it, before wishing her well once again and gently ushering her out of his office.

Cat counts herself lucky in one sense: she doesn't start crying until she is in the lift and the doors have closed behind her. What the hell just *happened*? By the time she reaches the lobby, the first bitter sting of tears has been replaced by fury. If her work was so bad it had to be "tidied up," why did nobody tell her? Why was she given no opportunity to improve, no clarification as to what the client was actually looking for? The answer, she sees now, is simple. Mikhail was lying, or at the very least, obfuscating the truth in order to cast himself as a patient, benevolent employer and expedite an awkward conversation. She has been swindled into placidly accepting her own obsolescence.

And I thought I was the scammer.

Cat pauses in the lobby to check her makeup and is shocked to see there are no outward signs of the seismic shift that has just occurred in her life, leveling her one remaining prospect at legitimacy. She catches the security guard at the front desk eyeing her with suspicion, and she wonders if Mikhail has called down to ensure she leaves the premises without causing a scene. She gives the man her most winning smile, dropping her key card clearly marked "Guest" onto the desk in front of him, then discreetly flips him off as she vanishes into the revolving doors.

She emerges onto a packed street and is almost surprised to find that the city continues to exist just as it did before she entered the building half an hour ago. Hundreds of people rush past her, either staring at or barking into phones, hurrying to make it to their desks by nine o'clock. Insensitive of them, really, to rub it in her face like this. Don't they know how utterly, royally fucked she is?

Cat steps into the human current and allows it to carry her to the nearest Tube station. She swipes her phone against the contactless payment pad at the barrier, wondering how long she has before that stops working, and steps onto the escalator. Almost involuntarily, out of some combination of boredom and habit, she does what no healthy person does when they need cheering up. She opens Instagram.

The app fails to load as she descends beneath the city, several layers of concrete and steel away from the nearest network tower. Probably for the best, she decides. She boards her train and stares down at her screen as it attempts to refresh her feed, that circular arrow inviting her to try again, and again, and again, despite the evident futility. Cat may be in shock, but she's not oblivious to metaphor.

The feed refreshes as the train pulls into a station with public Wi-Fi, but only one photo loads before the carriage's journey resumes and the app freezes again. It is a genre of Instagram post that Cat has become all too familiar with over the last couple of years. She recognizes the hand in the picture before she even sees the name; the tiny scar on her thumb from an errant champagne glass, the nails that would be immaculate even during an apocalypse. And on the third finger, a diamond the likes of which Cat has never seen.

Louisa Vincent is getting married.

As soon as the train reaches its next stop, Cat bolts out of the carriage and makes her way back up toward street level, poking at her screen with an accusatory finger until the escalator brings her high enough that the signal is finally restored. She swipes through the carousel of images to see a close-up of the obscenely large diamond on Louisa's finger, her hand placed delicately, decoratively, over that of her beloved (a man Cat swiftly identifies in the tags as one Stephen St. Aubyn).

No sooner met but they looked; no sooner looked but they loved, the caption reads. Cat recognizes the quote as Shakespeare. Louisa's way of saying it was love at first sight, she supposes. And it must have been. Cat might not have caught up with Louisa in a while, but she sees everything she puts on Instagram, and she would have known if Louisa were dating anybody. This engagement, this guy, that *ring* . . . a veritable whirlwind.

The last time she saw Louisa must have been at Shilpa and Parul's baby-shower-slash-gender-reveal party last summer. They only chatted for five minutes before Louisa had to "bounce," but surely she would have mentioned if she was getting serious with someone. That was about nine or ten months ago. Ten months to land a man and a ring like that? Louisa has always had a talent for getting what she wants, but this is some kind of record.

Cat alights the escalator, scans her way through the barrier, and begins to draft a congratulatory message in the comments. Eyes fixed on the screen, she almost Red Rovers herself over the outstretched arms of a man and woman who are holding hands and walking as slowly as humanly possible. Their affection is blocking the exit.

"Excuse me," Cat mutters impatiently, maneuvering to their left in an attempt to squeeze past them. Oblivious, the man's shoulder jolts against Cat. She watches almost in slow motion as her phone flies out of her hand and hits the ground facedown with a resounding crunch.

"Thanks a lot, guys! Really nice!" Cat hisses, then louder at the offending couple: "Bloody tourists!" But they are already gone, meandering out into the crowd. Cat gingerly picks up the device and turns it over. The screen is a spider's web of jagged, interconnected fractures.

"Perfect," she says to nobody in particular. "Just perfect."

The Monday-morning crowd surges on through the station, the occasional passerby shooting Cat a dirty look for getting in the way, while a blissfully happy Louisa beams up at her through the cracks.

Cat Bellamy first met Louisa Vincent in Introduction to Modern-ism on a humid Wednesday morning in late September. Cat had misjudged the weather that day and, seeing clouds from her bedroom window in halls, worn a soft fuzzy sweater under her pleather jacket. She'd felt like Buffy the Vampire Slayer for the first half of the walk to the lecture theater, but by the time she arrived her back was drenched in sweat. She didn't dare remove her jacket in case the sweater showed patches, and so she sat there, quietly sticky and miserable, waiting for the class to begin.

Uni wasn't anything like she'd expected. The films she had seen about college life were all American, for one, and so she had expected day after day of hanging out on a sunny green quad, not dashing from one class to another on the opposite side of campus in the rain. And she had yet to fall in with a comedically mismatched group of friends. In fact, aside from the girls on her floor, who were all polite enough, making friends was proving hard. Everyone else seemed to have come to Bristol in groups, entire ready-made social circles migrating wholesale from prestigious sixth-form colleges to the university, negating the need to do anything other than exchange small talk with the quiet northern girl who had mistakenly thought dying a pink streak into her mousy hair would be a "conversation starter."

Then in breezed a girl in a belted shirtdress with ice-blue eyes and long, dark, glossy hair pushed back from her porcelain face with a pair of Ray-Bans. She appeared to survey the room for a moment, then her gaze fell on Cat.

"Is anybody sitting here?" the girl asked with cut-glass diction, gesturing to the empty seat next to Cat. Cat shook her head, but the girl had already sat down and dug a Moleskine notebook out of her backpack.

"I'm Louisa," she said, extending a perfectly manicured hand.

"Cat," she replied, shaking Louisa's hand, but not too hard: she looked like an expensive kind of doll that would break easily if mishandled. "I thought I'd met everyone on this module," she added. This was, after all, the third week of the semester. Even the students who were too broken by freshers' week to attend the first class had shown up for the second. "Were you late admission?" Cat asked, and Louisa's eyes widened in horror.

"Nothing so desperate," she said. "There was a slight snafu with my calendar. As in, I read the dates entirely wrong."

Cat had spent the entire summer planning for the move from Winsford to Bristol, in between shifts washing glasses at the Star. She couldn't imagine messing up her schedule so thoroughly that she would arrive three weeks late. Not when she had classes to register for, and that excruciating meeting with the bursar's office during which the terms of her scholarship were explained in detail.

"Keep up your grades, Ms. Bellamy, and we will never have to see each other again after today," the bursar had said to her. Cat had been so transfixed by the matching tufts of hair sprouting from his ears and nostrils that she didn't immediately notice his gaze was fixed squarely on her chest.

"So there I am in Santorini, on this daddy-daughter trip that my father surprised me with as a sendoff before uni," Louisa said, "when we get this call inquiring as to whether I'll be attending this semester!" Louisa laughed and shook her head, as if to say *Isn't that just so me?* Cat had only just met her, and even she was inclined to agree that yes, this was *very* Louisa.

"This was literally *yesterday morning*," Louisa continued. "I didn't even have time to get back to London! We arranged to have all my things from home boxed up and sent straight to my new place, and I caught the first flight I could back to the mainland, then bought a ticket to Bristol. Of course, I had to spend the night in Amsterdam. Bloody KLM. It was quite the ordeal, actually. But! Here I am."

Cat didn't know how to respond. On the one hand, she couldn't quite believe this girl's casual approach to her own education, to her future—or how seamlessly such a profound "snafu" appeared to have been resolved. On the other, she couldn't help but be slightly charmed by Louisa's carefree self-assurance that everything would work out in her favor. It was like encountering a real-life Cher Horowitz.

"Well, it's nice to meet you," Cat said. "If you need any help catching up, I—"

"Would you?" Louisa asked, her hand pressed on Cat's now. "That would be *so* helpful. If I could maybe borrow your notes? Or even better, we could meet up for coffee and you can walk me through everything I've missed while being a complete idiot in the Aegean?"

"Oh," said Cat, taken momentarily aback by how quickly Louisa jumped on the offer before she'd even had time to make it. "Um, sure."

"You have no idea how much you're saving my arse right now," Louisa said. "I'll owe you. Big-time. Whatever you want. Seriously! Name your price. A Tiffany necklace? My firstborn child? It's yours."

Cat laughed. "I don't think that'll be necessary," she said. "Why don't you buy the coffee, and we'll call it even."

Louisa shrugged. "Whatever you say." She smiled at Cat and squeezed her hand. "I love your hair, by the way." Cat smiled back at her. And for the first time since uni had begun, she didn't feel so alone.

Four

Cat has done her best to put Louisa out of her mind since seeing the announcement. She has, after all, had other things to preoccupy her, like the couple who *True Romance*'d her phone, and how exactly she is going to pay to get the screen fixed, and oh yes, where she is going to live if she can't find a job soon. But if there's one thing she should know by now about Louisa Vincent, it is that she is rather hard to ignore, and a week after seeing the engagement post, Cat receives an email from somebody named Darcy Wong inviting her to celebrate Louisa's exciting news over afternoon tea at a place called Wonderkitchen, all one word, on Friday at three p.m.

The excuses make themselves. Anybody with a job would struggle to get Friday afternoon off at such short notice. Cat could easily beg off going—*they* don't know she's currently jobless. Sending her apologies in the form of flowers or a card would be a damn sight less expensive and exhausting.

But she can't deny that she is more than a little intrigued. She hasn't seen Louisa in nearly a year. Louisa was supposed to be at Susie's wedding, although Cat now deduces she was busy getting proposed to in Monaco at the time.

No. As much as she might like to pretend otherwise, Cat is curious. It is this curiosity that brings her to Wonderkitchen on King's Road at three o'clock on the dot. The restaurant's website did not include a dress code but stressed its "hip" and "trendy" credentials, and so she donned the tiny leather jacket that every woman in her late twenties owns, over a Blondie T-shirt and half a dozen necklaces. She already feels herself sticking out like a sore thumb amid the mumsy sheath dresses and shapelessly chic COS ensembles worn by seemingly everyone else here, but she knows better than to try to emulate that style herself.

There was a party at university, not long after they met, when Cat showed up in what she had thought a perfect imitation of the classy, preppy look she'd begun to covet: a secondhand wax jacket that was only slightly too big for her, and an imitation Burberry scarf she'd bought at a market stall.

"Sometimes I think it's almost cooler to not wear a designer label, you know?" Louisa said that night, apropos of nothing. "Honestly, jeans and a T-shirt can look so chic with the right accessories." That was her semidelicate way, Cat realized, of telling her something she might never have figured out for herself: no fake will ever fool somebody who has worn the real thing. It was one of countless times Cat felt that her best simply wasn't good enough, that she would always have to scrimp and save for the kind of clothes that Louisa would only sleep in. She may have misjudged her outfit today, but it would have been more embarrassing to walk into Wonderkitchen wearing something that only further singled her out as a prole.

The hostess leads Cat to a table in a quiet corner near the back of the restaurant, where several other women are already waiting. She recognizes Darcy Wong immediately, having done the usual cursory investigating on Instagram. Darcy is some kind of PR powerhouse based out of Singapore. Extraordinarily pretty: the kind that comes from genetic gifts, a pricey doctor, or both. She rises from the table, beaming, as Cat approaches.

"You must be Cat!" Darcy pulls her into an embrace.

"Guilty as charged," says Cat.

"Louisa isn't here yet, so why don't I introduce you to everybody nice and quick before she arrives?" Darcy takes Cat by the shoulders and physically turns her toward the table, her slender arms deceptively strong—Pilates, maybe—and reels off a list of names and professions like a manic game show host.

There is Olivia Clarke, a beautiful Black woman who Cat learns is a human-rights lawyer; Priya Joshi, a South Asian management consultant who also makes videos on YouTube about how to be a more productive and successful girlboss; and Harper Lawrence, a pale redhead who is in the middle of completing her PhD. It is difficult not to feel three inches tall.

"Everybody, this is Cat," says Darcy. "She's a talented designer and entrepreneur."

So I'm not the only one who's partial to lurking on the internet, Cat thinks. She gives the other women a pathetic wave and sinks into the nearest empty seat.

"So," Cat says, keen to take the attention off herself, "how does everybody know Louisa?"

"We're besties-in-law," Darcy tells her, as if that is a term people use frequently. "My husband, Evan, he and Stephen have been friends for years, and they've just launched this fund together. The number of nights Stephen slept in our guest room while they were developing the business! He's practically family, the sweetheart. Anyway, once he told us things were getting serious with Louisa, we knew we just had to meet her, and, well . . ." She lets the sentence trail off with a flourish of the wrist.

"I knew her at boarding school," says Priya. "Nothing bonds two people like doing time together." Darcy and Harper both nod knowingly.

"I met her through Habitat for Humanity," says Olivia.

"You met her building *houses*?" Cat asks, incredulous.

"Oh god, no!" Olivia almost cackles. "It was a *fundraiser* for Habitat for Humanity. An art consultation with Louisa was one of the items on the silent auction."

"That . . . makes more sense," says Cat. She doesn't add that the thought of refugees or disaster survivors living in a house built by Louisa Vincent fills her with horror. As if the poor souls, imaginary or not, haven't been through enough.

"What about you?" Cat asks, turning to Harper, who appears to have become momentarily distracted by her inverted reflection in a dessert spoon.

"She's my cousin, but not?" Harper says, raising one shoulder in a nonchalant shrug. She doesn't speak like the others. They're all English cut glass, fine crystal. Harper's mid-Atlantic drawl is like the expensive spirit you pour into the crystal.

"Our parents are friends," Harper explains. "And so I always called her mom *Auntie*, that kind of thing, but there's no actual relation there. At least, I don't *think* so. Anyway, we spent every winter break together in Whistler as kids. I just happened to be spending some time in London this summer before I go back to Berkeley to finish my thesis." She runs a hand through her thick russet curls and shrugs again. "And I'd never had a real English high tea, so . . . here I am."

Cat intuits that Darcy must have procured everybody's contact information from Louisa herself in order to gather them here. Olivia and Priya make sense; they are from the same world. Harper is family, or close enough. But why was Cat invited? They may have gone to art school together, but their trajectories have diverged significantly in the intervening years. While Cat lives on Pot Noodle and anxiety, Louisa makes bank as an art consultant, advising wealthy clients on what kind of abstract paintings to hang in the guest loo. Cat is still pondering the reason for her presence here when the woman of the hour walks in.

Louisa enters every room as if she owns it. And, knowing who her father is, Cat doesn't always rule that out as a possibility. She remembers that morning in the lecture hall, the way she envied Louisa's easy grace and charisma. At first she had assumed that kind of elegant self-assurance came from moving through life having never encountered an obstacle. It took her a while to figure out just how much work went into cultivating so effortless an air.

Louisa tilts her head as she approaches the table, feigning surprise, and her hair, black as wet ink, flows off her shoulders like she's being shot in a slow-motion music video.

"You didn't," she says to Darcy in an accusatory tone. "You naughty thing! I thought it was just the two of us having a bite!"

"I did!" Darcy is practically glowing. Cat knows what it's like to have Louisa's attention on you. It's like standing in the sun—before you get burned.

Louisa does a clockwise lap of the table, hugging and kissing each of the women without ever actually making physical contact. When she finally reaches Cat, she places a hand over her heart and blinks away tears that may or may not actually be there.

"Darling," she says. "I'm so glad you're here."

Despite herself, Cat feels that familiar warm glow returning.

"I wouldn't have missed it," she says, even though this is only the first of what will doubtlessly be multiple prenuptial celebrations. "And congratulations!" she adds, remembering why they are all here.

"Thanks, babe," Louisa replies, already breezing back up to the head of the table. Darcy plops herself down in the chair next to her, comfortably falling into the role of lieutenant now that the real general is here.

As soon as they are all seated, two waiters sweep into the room and begin to lay out the makings of their afternoon tea: silver stands laden with finger sandwiches, salmon blinis, intricate pastries with feta and mint, tiny oatcakes topped with whipped goat cheese, pistachio macarons, warm cherry scones, and an ice bucket with a bottle of champagne.

"Sorry we're having to rough it," says Darcy, in full earshot of one of the waiters. "I called Claridge's, but it was just too short notice."

Roughing it? This is the best-looking lunch Cat has seen since she can't even remember when.

"Did you speak to Anders?" Louisa asks. "You should have asked for Anders. He loves me. There was one night there, maybe it was my birthday, where I got so tiddly on champagne, I . . ." She puts her hand over her mouth coyly. "Let's just say I've never been turned away from Claridge's since."

"I'll remember that for next time," Darcy says meekly. "Try the salmon! It's what they're known for here."

"Oh my gosh, Darce." Louisa laughs, and claps her hand over Darcy's. "No need to be so on edge! You're making me feel like bridezilla already. This is perfectly fine."

Cat clearly isn't the only person at the table who can tell that things are not perfectly fine, because Priya cuts in.

"I think a toast is in order," she says, raising her glass. "To Louisa!"

"And Stephen, right?" adds Olivia.

"Right! Louisa and Stephen!"

They all clumsily extend their arms and clink glasses over the heavily laden table.

"I needed this." Louisa exhales after taking a sip and meticulously returning a single stray strand of hair to its proper place. "Traffic today was just hell."

"Totally," says Cat, who had noted the congestion while walking here.

"Where have you come in from?" Harper asks.

"Islington," Cat answers.

"You know . . . I immediately regret asking," the American admits. "I always think I know London better than I actually do."

"Our first house was in Islington," says Olivia. "Before Primrose. Charming part of the city."

It dawns on Cat that they think she owns a place, like the rest of them.

"It's all right," she says, not exactly disabusing them of the notion. "I'm actually looking for a new—" But the conversation has already moved on to Louisa's living situation. She is temporarily staying in her mother's Sloane Square town house ahead of relocating to Singapore, a decision that surprises Cat, who has actually met Louisa's mother.

"Stephen wanted me to live with him at his apartment in Fulham, of course," says Louisa, "but it just felt right, residing separately until we're married."

"That is so bloody romantic," sighs Priya. "Meanwhile, the last guy I dated never even invited me back to his place once, because his condo association was really strict and didn't allow overnight guests. I told him he was within his rights to contest that rule, maybe petition the board—"

"Oh, babe." Olivia puts one hand over Priya's and reaches for the champagne bottle with the other.

"Anyway, it doesn't matter," Priya continues. "He must have lost his phone or something, because he stopped answering my texts. Or maybe there was some problem with the network. That can happen, you know. I've had an email to Gwyneth Paltrow bounce back three times now."

On Priya's left, Harper takes her other hand and shakes her head kindly.

"Oh, babe," she echoes.

Cat can sympathize with Priya's plight to a degree: dating in London can feel like a humiliating game show that is so fast and loud you're never really sure if you've understood the rules, or even know what you're playing for. But sooner or later you've got to catch up or you'll find yourself falling through a trapdoor or covered in slime.

Priya wants the fairy tale. Cat gets that. But what she knows and Priya doesn't, it seems, is that the original version of every fairy tale is a gory horror show that usually ends in a woman getting her toes chopped off or eyes pecked out.

"I have to ask, sweetie," Olivia says to Louisa. "Why the cloak and dagger? I must admit I was a little shocked to read you were engaged on Insta and not in *Tatler*."

"I think it's romantic," says Priya. "They're flouting convention."

Yeah. Because an engagement post on social media is practically punk.

"Stephen's parents would certainly rather we had done it that way," says Louisa. "They'd probably rather we had not got engaged so quickly full stop. But what can I say? When it's right, it's right. And I was just so excited, I wanted to tell the world there and then."

It sounds exactly like something a newly engaged, hopelessly-in-love woman might say. But Louisa never does anything without a very specific reason. No amount of mushy feelings would have deterred the woman Cat knows from engineering a public, grandiose proposal. Where was the flash mob Louisa once fantasized about?

"Besides," Louisa continues, "a press thing wouldn't have worked with our timeline. We missed the deadline for *Tatler*'s print issue, and I needed to let people know now, because . . . well . . ."

She glances at Darcy, who practically fizzes with happiness at being in the know.

"Stephen needs to be in Singapore by Q3 so that he and Evan can take their business global," Louisa says. "And the whole emigrating thing is so much easier if you're a married couple, so . . ."

"No . . . ," gasps Priya.

"No!" yells Olivia.

"Huh?" asks Harper.

"What?" echoes an equally confused Cat.

Louisa smiles coquettishly and nods. "The wedding is in a month and a half," she announces. "You are all cordially invited to join us on August twenty-eighth."

"You're mad!" Olivia shrieks. "Positively mad! That's not enough time! August next year, maybe, at a push!"

"That's what wedding planners are for," Louisa says with a shrug. "It helps that I have an absolute guardian angel for a matron of honor." She nods to her left, in the direction of Darcy, who almost purrs at the compliment. From the corner of her eye, Cat could swear she sees Priya tense. As the high school friend, she must have thought she had the role of head bridesmaid in the bag. Unofficial cousin Harper, on the other hand, seems more occupied with applying as much clotted cream to her scone as possible.

"Actually," Louisa says, her lips widening into a sly smile, "I wasn't going to do this just yet, but given the timeline, and the fact I have you all here . . ."

She holds out her hands to either side of her and indicates for them all to do the same. A moment later they have formed a circle around the table, as if they are about to say grace or attempt a séance.

"Ladies," says Louisa, "would you do me the honor of being my bridal squad?"

Priya's grip on Cat's fingers becomes viselike, and she is the first to gasp an excited "Yes!" followed shortly by the others, until their shared acceptance of Louisa's impromptu proposal is a cacophony of ecstatic squealing.

Cat, whose heart rate has been steadily rising, waits until it is polite to excuse herself and practically sprints to the ladies' room. Once safely ensconced in a stall, certain she is alone, she allows herself to start spiraling.

Her mind was already whirring with the cost of this tea, not to mention the inevitable, expensive carousel of events that precedes a wedding. The gifts, the clothes, the meals, the hotels. It is all happening again, and this time, it might just ruin her.

She is intimately familiar with the financial logic of weddings.

It's an inverse equation of sorts: the wealthier the people getting married, the more it seems to cost the guests. Not to mention the hen weekend. Long gone is the night out in Brighton or even Dublin, replaced by long weekends in boutique Alpine spas or villas on the Amalfi Coast. A normal person's highest aspiration is a rich person's basest expectation. Even before knowing any of the details of the imminent nuptials, Cat knows she would have struggled to afford to attend with a whole year's notice to save up. With barely seven weeks, she has no hope of going. Not when she's just lost her sole legitimate source of income.

"Fucking fuck," she whispers, then clamps her hand over her mouth when she hears somebody else enter the bathroom. She tears off some toilet roll and reaches under her T-shirt to dab beneath her arms, before opening the stall door, walking over to the sink, and holding both of her wrists under the cold tap. A moment later, Harper emerges from one of the other stalls, and they smile politely at each other in the mirror.

"Wild, right?" Harper says. "All of this?"

"Totally," Cat agrees.

"But also . . . very Louisa," Harper adds.

"Very." Cat nods. Harper nods too, like they've just come to some kind of understanding, then dries her hands and holds open the door in a manner almost chivalrous.

Harper follows her back to the table, and as Cat takes in the group anew, she realizes why she is here, why Louisa would include her in this. The old schoolmate, the family friend, the fellow career woman. Together, they tell the story of the bride. Cat represents Louisa's time at university, the first-class degree of which she is so proud.

Cat will have to say she is too busy to go to the wedding, that it is simply too short notice, and she will be unable to fulfill her bridesmaid duties to the level that will surely be expected. Louisa will be disappointed, or at least pretend to be, but she'll get over it quickly enough. Theirs has never been the kind of friendship where either party really knows how to give the other what they need, anyway.

Five

By the time Cat and Harper have retaken their seats, the conversation has moved on from the venue to the proposal. Specifically, the enormous rock with which Stephen pledged his troth and that now adorns Louisa's finger.

"It's called the Tsarina," she tells them. "According to family legend, the diamond comes from a tiara worn by the empress herself before the revolution. Apparently it was somehow smuggled out of Russia after the royal family died, and Stephen's great-grandfather acquired it at Christie's a decade later."

Horseshit, Cat thinks. Louisa should know better than to believe a tale like that. She realizes a moment later that of course Louisa *does* know better. She knows her history and would be well aware that the Romanov crown jewels are currently intact and in the Kremlin. But it certainly lends a romantic grandness to the ring—and by extension to the woman who wears it. Cat wonders whether the St. Aubyns themselves are prone to such embellishments, or if Louisa is simply spinning a yarn for the benefit of the women at this table.

One thing is for certain: wherever this diamond actually came from, it is guaranteed to be worth a fortune. Cat is no jeweler, but even compared to the engagement rings sported by both Darcy and Olivia, it's *huge*: a glittering teardrop the size of a cocktail olive.

"You really can tell it's something special," says Priya. "I mean, sheer size aside. The color, the clarity. Exquisite." Darcy nods and says something about carats. Cat realizes she is with a panel of armchair diamond experts—yet another subject she would fail at in a pub quiz.

"Well, *actually* . . ." Louisa tucks a lock of hair behind her ear in mock bashfulness, and Cat can sense all eyes follow the movement of the ring as she does so. "Can I tell you girls a secret? And I mean a *secret*. It cannot leave this table."

Once she has secured their silence, she lowers her voice and says in a stage whisper: "This isn't actually the real ring."

The party exchanges yet more confused looks, and Louisa is "forced" to elaborate.

"The real thing is worth a literal fortune, and it's damn near impossible to insure," she explains. "So Stephen, the absolute love, had this made for me. It's a perfect replica of the Tsarina, but I can wear it to Fortnum's without being terrified I'll lose it."

"Just like Elizabeth Taylor," Darcy simpers.

"Elizabeth Taylor went one extra, didn't she?" Cat hears Harper say. "She hired security guards even when she was wearing paste, so people would *think* she was wearing the real jewels."

"That's right," says Louisa, somehow looking even more thrilled with herself than she already was. She subtly tips her head backward, and everyone at the table turns, peering toward the front of the restaurant, where a handsome, bearded man in a black suit sits with a newspaper and a cup of coffee.

"Who's that guy?" asks Cat.

"Elijah," says Louisa. "My . . . driver." She winks.

"Oh my god," says Olivia. "Louisa has a bodyguard. That is so hot."

"Wait," Cat says. "So you have personal security for a piece of jewelry you're not even wearing?"

"Stephen's folks insisted," Louisa says, and Cat could swear she actually *preens*. "It's not just the ring. There are all sorts of horrible people out there who don't like the St. Aubyns. They get all sorts of beastly correspondence, you know. Stephen's dad said that as I'm going to be family soon, I'll need protection. You can never be too careful."

The St. Aubyns are Britain's answer to the Murdochs. Cat has gone for job interviews at companies owned by them, read magazines published by those companies, expressed her moral outrage on social media at divisive articles published by tabloids that are just other arms of those companies. At least one of Stephen's grandparents, Cat knows, has a knighthood. Louisa might not have bagged Prince Harry like she once dreamed, but she's marrying into a kind of royalty all the same.

"So do you ever actually get to wear it?" asks Harper. "The real diamond?"

"Well . . ." Louisa lowers her voice to another conspiratorial whisper. "Stephen does like it when I wear it to bed sometimes."

Darcy and Priya gasp and then giggle, scandalized. Olivia's laugh is throatier, more knowing. Cat, on the other hand, is thinking of poor Elijah, stationed faithfully outside the bedroom door while Louisa and her new fiancé go at it.

"And of course, I'll wear the Tsarina on the big day," Louisa adds. "I'm not going to wear any other jewelry on my hands or wrists, and then Stephen is going to put it on my finger along with the wedding band during the vows." She waggles her digits to illustrate her point.

It figures. For most couples, the ceremony is about declaring their love and fidelity in front of everyone they know. For Louisa, it's a chance to show off her enormous diamond to everyone she knows.

Conversation soon moves on to the many other wedding-related questions. Where will they honeymoon? How many guests are they having? Who is designing the dress at such short notice? Positano. A modest hundred and fifty. Stella McCartney.

"Stell's a dear family friend," Louisa can't help saying.

Cat tunes in and out for the remainder of the meal, oohing and aahing when required, and trying to surreptitiously move as many of the delicious finger sandwiches and little cakes as possible onto her plate, figuring she might not be able to afford to eat again today after this.

Louisa is eating like a dainty little bird, and Cat would suspect that she is trying to lose weight before the wedding, had she not already nobly declared she will be doing no such thing, as an act of body positivity. It is, of course, easy to be positive about your body when you've been a sample-size clotheshorse since you were a teenager, all cheekbones and clavicles.

"We should probably get the check soon," says Harper. "I have a video chat with my PhD supervisor this afternoon and I'll probably need to allow an extra half an hour to coach her through how to unmute her mic." The others nod and hum in agreement. Never mind that a second bottle of recently opened champagne sits untouched in the bucket at the end of the table. Cat's eye nearly twitches at the waste.

"This will be our treat," Darcy tells Louisa on behalf of the group, waving at one of the waiters, and Cat wishes she had known that this would be part of the arrangement before she showed up. There it is again: that itchy, all-too-familiar tightness in her chest. The elevator music of her life, the nagging feeling she can put off but never fully ignore, like a toothache or tinnitus. In this moment, Cat might as well be the only person at the table. She is never lonelier than when she is forced to worry about money.

She does some cigarette-packet sums in her head, pretty certain that the website said afternoon tea was fifty pounds per person. But that was before the champagne. And Louisa's share. A decent portion of this month's rent will be going to a glass of fizz and some sandwiches. Cat could kick herself. She can't bring herself to regret the sandwiches, though. They performed their duties admirably.

On the edge of her vision, she sees somebody approaching the table, and with a heavy heart she reaches into her pocket for her bruised credit card, already resigning herself to another evening scamming wankers at the Oceanic.

"Hello, ladies," the man says, and Cat realizes he is not the waiter. Not unless Wonderkitchen gets its uniforms from Savile Row and its staff from a modeling agency.

"Baby!" Louisa squeals in delight, jumping up and throwing her arms around the newcomer. The elusive Stephen St. Aubyn, Cat presumes. Once again, she cannot fault Louisa's taste. With his square jaw, flawless teeth, and perfectly coiffed hair, the man looks like bloody Henry Cavill.

"Sorry to interrupt," Stephen says once they have all been introduced, "but I was rather hoping I could steal Wee away from you now."

Wee? The old Louisa would never have approved that nickname. It must be true love.

"What are you on about, darling?" Louisa asks.

"How do you feel about a weekend in Cannes?" Stephen says, gazing down at her adoringly, one arm hooked around her lower back, pulling her close as if he's a ballroom dancer about to dip her.

"I feel rather positive about that," Louisa replies, turning briefly to the girls and widening her eyes as if to say, *What is this man of mine like?*

"Wonderful." He breaks into a grin straight out of a toothpaste ad. "I've packed you a bag; it's in the car."

Darcy, Priya, and Olivia let out a shared "Aww!" and Stephen turns his smile in their direction. "Lovely to meet you all, truly," he says. "I've taken care of the bill. It's the least I can do, considering I'm absconding with the lady of the hour. Oh." He snaps his fingers as if remembering one more thing. "Keep your calendars clear two weeks from tomorrow. We're having a little engagement party."

Louisa flutters her fingers at them briefly, giving them one last glinting look at the surprisingly convincing fake diamond, and then they are both gone.

"Wow," says Harper. "He's quite the whirlwind, huh?"

"Isn't he, though?" says Darcy dreamily.

"He seems nice," Cat adds, thankful at least for not having to pay for lunch.

"This was divine," says Olivia, "but I really have to run. It's technically Magdalena's day off, so I suppose I should go and take Oscar off her hands."

"And I desperately need to find an outfit for this Women in

Leadership event tonight," Priya says, rising from her seat. It's as if all the oxygen left the room with the happy couple, and now everyone is desperate to get back to the fresh air of their own lives.

"It was really cool to meet you all," Harper says, but Olivia is already halfway to the door, and Darcy and Priya are both checking their phones.

"My Uber is here," Darcy announces, blowing a collective kiss and vanishing.

"Mine too!" Priya smiles, waves, and follows her.

"It was nice to meet you too," Cat says to Harper, fumbling with her own phone, pretending to hail a ride. She already knows the exact timetable of the bus stop around the corner.

"I guess I'll see you at the engagement party," Harper says, pulling on an oversized blazer and then scooping her genuinely massive hair out from under the lapels.

"Can't wait!" Cat says, hating that being fake becomes second nature after five minutes in the same room as Louisa and her posh friends. "Uber is still connecting me to a driver," she fibs, pointing redundantly to her phone.

"Okay," says Harper cheerfully. "Bye!" She shoves her hands in her blazer pockets and ambles out of the restaurant. Once Cat has watched her disappear across the street and out of view through the window, she turns her attention back to the table. She shrugs off her leather jacket, throws it over her arm, then swipes the full bottle of champagne from the ice bucket, obscures it with her jacket, and hotfoots it out of the place before anyone can return to clear the table. Outside, the afternoon air is misted with a fine drizzle, but Cat keeps her jacket exactly where it is as she briskly heads three streets over and taps onto the bus with her free hand.

"You have got to be joking," says Jake when he sees her walk in. Cat, to her credit, has some idea of how she must look, stomping into an empty bar in the middle of the afternoon, tipsy and brandishing a stolen bottle of champagne like a trophy.

"I'll share," she tells him. Jake looks at her with what Cat now thinks of as his trademark unreadable expression, and she begins to think she has seriously misjudged the situation. The last time they saw each other, he rejected her tacit invitation to collaborate on a criminal enterprise and she told him she would probably never return. Why, exactly, did it seem like such a good idea to come here? Then Jake makes an exasperated sound, halfway between a sigh and a growl.

"Give it here," he says. "I'll hide it behind the bar. Unless your goal is to get me sacked."

"Can you even get sacked?" Cat asks. "I thought you were the manager."

"Whatever gave you that impression?"

"You're the only person I ever actually see working here."

"Shannen is the manager," he says, and an image comes to Cat from her first or second time here: a woman with a face like vinegar and that day's race cards sticking out of her back pocket. No wonder they've been able to get away with so much here.

Jake reaches out to her across the counter. Cat hands the champagne over, and he grimaces. "This is warm as piss! Where did you bring it from?"

"Chelsea."

"It's the good stuff," he says, examining the label. "Better than anything we have here, anyway. Why do I get the feeling there's a story behind this questionable life choice?" He ducks under the bar for a second, then reappears with two glasses straight from the freezer. They're the sort that modern myth says are modeled after Marie Antoinette's left boob.

"We use these for porn star martinis," Jake says, filling them both. "I'd say leave it to chill for a moment, but those bubbles look like they're on their last legs."

"They stayed valiant on the bus here," Cat says. "Cheers!" She empties the shallow glass in three gulps, and he refills it before placing the bottle out of sight.

"So," he says. "The story?"

Cat groans. "I don't want to talk about it." Jake nods and sips his share of the loot. "Fine," she huffs. "So I have this friend Louisa . . ."

She finds herself spilling the whole sorry tale to Jake over the rest of the ill-gotten bubbly. How she has been driven to near-destitution by the hen weekends, destination weddings, baby showers, and gender reveals. Her recent unemployment and looming deadline to find a new place to live. And Louisa's sudden reappearance in her life, bringing with her a whole host of poorly timed expensive social obligations.

"Here's a thought," Jake says once she has concluded her litany of woes. "Don't go to the wedding."

"You really don't know a lot about women, do you?"

"Enlighten me."

"It's not just about the wedding," Cat explains. "It's everything that surrounds it. The engagement party, the bridal shower, the bachelorette party. When you become friends with someone like Louisa, you sign a social contract. If I opt out of any of these things, I'm breaking that contract."

"Would that really be so bad?" Jake asks.

"Louisa would blacklist me. And even if I *had* other friends . . ."

Cat can hear the whine in her own voice and clears her throat. "I'm just not in a position right now to alienate the only well-connected people I know," she says.

"Forgive me. I didn't realize your social life was authored by Jane Austen and that skipping the wedding of a woman you clearly don't even like very much would *ruin* you."

Once upon a time, Cat would have rushed to deny Jake's allegation. *Louisa is my best friend*, she would have said. But at some point, and not even particularly recently, that ceased to be even remotely true. A best friend is someone you can confide in, right? Share anything with? Cat tries to imagine telling Louisa about her money troubles, tries even harder to envision Louisa's understanding, and soon gives up. Turns out she doesn't have a best friend after all. Maybe she never did.

"It's like we're from different planets," she says, more to herself than to Jake. "I spent years learning her alien ways, studying the culture and the language, like one of those boffins in onesies from *Star Trek*."

"And let me guess. She never returned that courtesy."

"I don't think she'd even know how. I'm fluent in Louisa, but she wouldn't even be able to get through a conversation if I didn't hurry to meet her where she is. I don't know. Maybe being brought up that spoiled does something to your brain. Rewires it somehow. Any time something incredible happens, she acts like it's no more than what she is due. Getting whisked away to the Riviera for a weekend. And god, that *diamond* . . ."

"I don't follow," says Jake.

"She has this priceless diamond engagement ring that may or may not be from imperial Russia, right? It's so valuable that she can't even wear it in public. She's only going to wear it on her actual wedding day. And that's practically *normal* for her. To own something so expensive she can't even take it out of its box. Meanwhile I'm out here saving my charity shop tops for best."

"It's a very cool top," Jake says gallantly. "Blondie are awesome."

"It's like rich people don't even know what that kind of money can do," Cat continues. "Just a *chip* of that rock would solve all of my problems."

"Isn't it a pity, then," says Jake, gazing down into his glass, "that you're so hell-bent on going straight." Jake's eyes slowly swivel to meet hers.

"What do you mean?" she asks, even though she is fairly certain she knows *exactly* what he means. It's precisely the same thing that first occurred to her the moment she saw the ring. She's beginning to think this might make her a terrible person. But that didn't stop her from daydreaming about how she might do it on her way over here.

"I mean, you have a knack for this kind of thing," Jake says.

"Hardly," she says ruefully, idly tapping the stem of her glass with a fingernail. "Ripping off drunk idiots isn't exactly the calling card of a criminal mastermind. What *you* do, on the other hand—that takes finesse."

"Stop. You're making me blush."

"Seriously, though." Cat looks up intently into his eyes, wanting him to know she meant the compliment. "If you were going to, you know . . . How would you do it?"

He raises an eyebrow.

"Hypothetically," she adds.

"You're not wearing a wire, are you?"

"Is that your way of asking what's under my top?" *Remember: he's married.* "Sorry," she says, cutting herself off, cheeks burning. "Forget I said that. But yeah. The diamond. Just as a . . . What do you call it? A thought exercise. How might you do it?"

Jake leans back against the rear bar and crosses his arms over his broad chest, staring into space as he considers her question.

"First," he says, "I would rappel down the side of this rich family's house and go into the father's office via the window. Presumably that's where the safe is, right? At night, of course. Then I'd crack the safe and secure the ring."

"No! Really?" Cat leans forward, chin resting on her hand, rather taken by the image of Jake scaling a mansion. Then Jake bursts out laughing, and she knows she's been had.

"Con man," she mutters.

"Go on, then," Jake says. He is no longer laughing, but a mirthful crease remains around his eyes. "How would the Cat burglar do it?"

I'd snap it right off of Louisa's bony finger if it got me that kind of money, she thinks, and says: "Well, obviously I'd assemble a ragtag team of masters of disguise, tech geniuses, and acrobats who can do cartwheels."

"That's the spirit."

Their hypothetical schemes only get more ridiculously farfetched from there, and Jake opens another bottle—"cheap stuff this time, sorry"—as they exchange ideas. One scenario involves descending on a wire into a room full of lasers à la Tom Cruise in *Mission: Impossible*. "You'd have to do that part," Cat tells Jake. "I have a feeling you're more coordinated." In another, they hire an actress to gatecrash the ceremony, claiming to be pregnant with the handsome Stephen's love child, prompting Louisa to hurl the ring at him in rage, leaving Cat and Jake to retrieve it from the floor amid the ensuing chaos. "A lot of moving parts on that one," Jake says. "Surely the best plan is a *simple* one."

"What counts as simple?" Cat asks. "You and me team up to

steal the ring, just the two of us? A bartender and his favorite customer?" She scoffs.

Jake frowns. "I don't recall ever telling you you're my favorite."

"So you admit it!" She points at him in victory, and his face becomes suddenly impassive once more.

"See, that, right there," she says. "You're able to just switch gears, keep your cool. I just know I'd freak out in the middle of a job that big. I'd need someone like you as backup."

She laughs again, but Jake remains stoic. Fine, Cat gets the message, he doesn't want to talk about this anymore. It's a weird kind of small talk to make anyway; she's surprised he has indulged her this far. He probably wants to get on with his shift and then back home to his wife.

"I should go," she says. "Thanks for the drink. And the company. You've helped me salvage a pretty crappy day."

She rises from her bar stool and is about to leave when she feels his hand on her elbow. It is cool from handling the chilled bottle and glasses, and Cat feels a shock of something like goose bumps rush up her arm. She looks back to him; a tiny line has formed between his eyes, like he's deep in thought. Or angry.

"Give me your phone," he says.

"Are you for real?" Cat rolls her eyes. "I thought that was a joke. Mate, I *told* you I'm not wearing a wire, and I am definitely not recording anything on my phone if that's what you're worried about—"

"I know." Jake releases her arm and holds out his palm, beckoning with his fingers. Whatever. Her phone is still smashed to buggery anyway. Cat retrieves it from her bag, unlocks it, and hands it over. Jake taps something into the screen, then gives it back to her. She isn't even sure what has just happened until she is at the door a moment later, when she gets a message. From Jake. He must have called his own phone from hers so he'd have her number.

> If you're serious about this, call me when you're sober. We can talk about it properly. J.

Cat looks up from her screen to Jake, but he has already disappeared into the back of the bar.

Six

In the days leading up to her thirtieth, Cat receives more bills than she does birthday cards. She thought she'd managed to buy herself some time with the money she took from Greg at the wedding, paying off her outstanding phone balance and distributing just enough across her various credit accounts to keep them off her back a while longer. There had even been enough left to finally have her first dentist checkup in two years and get her roots done.

But on the morning of her birthday, along with a card from her grandmother, Cat finds a final notice on the doormat from a company whose name she doesn't even recognize: some financial behemoth that has absorbed the debt from an ill-advised payday loan she took out several months ago in a moment of desperation. This new organization has instituted a strict policy of progressing cases to collections in the event of late payment. Haunted by the image of a bailiff showing up at the house, Cat finally, reluctantly opens her banking app and cancels the monthly donation of ten pounds to the breast cancer charity she has been making ever since she started her first Saturday job at fifteen.

She comes downstairs from showering to find Tom and Alex putting the finishing touches to a platter of birthday pancakes, complete with a giant, looping "30" spelled out in chocolate chips. It is such a sweet gesture that Alex, sensing Cat might be about to tear up, barks: "They're from a mix. I need to get to work."

"So," Tom says once Alex has left and the two of them are polishing off the final few pancakes, "got any exciting plans for the day?"

He doesn't know, of course, what a loaded question that is. Couldn't know that Cat sent out messages months prior to check people's availability for a bottomless brunch or a dinner somewhere, and received nothing but a handful of lukewarm "maybes" in response. *People are busy,* she told herself. *That's London for you.* She has been trying her best not to think of every birthday she trekked across the city to attend, or of how Olivia, Priya, and the others were able to drop everything when Louisa snapped her fingers the week before. If people weren't fussed about coming, it would be downright humiliating to press them on it, so Cat dropped the matter entirely.

"My dad is coming into town," she tells Tom with a smile. "I'm meeting him off the train in an hour."

Her dad was the one to suggest a visit, asserting that a day trip to London sounded like fun. Cat didn't exactly believe him—this being the man who whistled through his teeth at the prospect of paying more than four quid for a pint—but was pleased to be relieved of the pressure to make other plans and told him she would clear her calendar for the entire afternoon. On the Tube to meet him, the thought crosses her mind that there may be an envelope of money in her near future. It *is* a milestone birthday.

You are a terrible person, she informs herself.

Euston is fairly quiet for a Saturday, and Cat spots him the second he comes through the barrier, wearing the black overcoat he usually reserves for funerals and that would make him look like a bouncer were it not for the Man City scarf wrapped tightly under his chin despite the mild morning. It is a sight so familiar Cat could draw it from memory, though she would sketch him with fewer lines and slightly rounder cheeks. His hair has been mostly gray for years, but she doesn't remember it being so wispy. She knows, rationally, that he is nearly sixty. Still, though. When did her father start to look so *old*?

"How was the journey?" she asks, stepping forward and letting herself be scooped up into a swaying embrace. At least he smells the same: stale coffee and Old Spice.

"It were all right," he says. "Had to change trains in Birmingham. Twenty-minute wait, not too bad. Station used to be a right shithole there, but they've done it up nicely, fair play to them. I got myself a latte. Happy birthday, love."

Cat takes him to Carnaby Street, thinking that he will enjoy the street art and sixties nostalgia, and then suggests they have lunch at a dumpling place nearby.

"It's your day," he says. "Lead on."

The dumpling place, it turns out, has a queue that starts at the door and snakes all the way around the corner.

"Didn't you book a table?" Dad asks.

"It's not that kind of restaurant," Cat says, feeling stupid for bringing him here on a Saturday. "You just show up and hope for the best. It's fine; we can go somewhere else."

"No, it's your day." Dad stuffs his hands into his pockets, as if mentally and physically preparing to stand there for the foreseeable future. "If you want to eat here, we'll eat here."

"Thanks." Cat smiles and knocks his elbow with her own. "I think you'll really like it."

Ten minutes later, the line has not so much as budged, and Cat relents.

"Let's go somewhere else," she says.

"I thought you had your heart set on this," Dad says, nodding skeptically toward the restaurant.

"I'm more interested in not dying of starvation on my birthday," she tells him. "Come on, let's see what else there is." She loops her arm through his and off they go. Half an hour later they're sitting in a blissfully warm booth, tucking into mediocre cheeseburgers and washing them down with a couple of beers. They don't talk while they eat, and it is almost like being back at home, sitting down to have tea at the table together with the radio on in the background.

"How's work?" he asks, dabbing the corners of his mouth with a napkin.

"It's good, thanks. I have some exciting stuff coming up." The lie is so familiar it tells itself. The truth is that just yesterday Cat received a form rejection for a barista position because she lacked the requisite two years' practical experience. Even the creepy-old-man pub at the bottom of her road, which smells like the carpets haven't been cleaned since the smoking ban of 2007, isn't hiring. Picking up some shifts waiting tables or pulling pints has always been a backup plan Cat assumed she would never need, but she naively expected it would be incredibly easy if she ever did.

"I nearly forgot," Dad says once the waitress has cleared their plates. "Your present."

Please be cash, she thinks, and immediately feels ashamed when he pushes a small box across the table. It is wrapped in newspaper, something her mum did each Christmas when she ran out of gift wrap. Cat tears off what looks like a page from the *Middlewich Guardian* and opens the box. Her breath catches in her throat at the sight of the brooch inside: a gold silhouette of a horse's head with a tiny emerald for the eye. She spent her entire childhood looking up into that beautiful green dot.

"I can't," she says. "I can't take this."

"Who else is supposed to have it?" Dad says. "You always liked it, didn't you?"

"Of course. But—"

"You're turning the big three-oh, Cat. I think you're finally old enough to be trusted." He gives her a tight-lipped smile, and his voice grows thick. "Besides, I think she'd like the thought of . . . of you wearing it."

"Thank you," she says, closing the box reverently and pretending not to see him wipe his left eye while signaling for the bill.

"I should be getting back to the station soon," he says. "My ticket's only valid at certain times. And then you can go and get ready for whatever wild night out you've got planned with your mates."

Cat doesn't have the heart to tell him that her birthday plans start and end according to his train timetable, and instead she simply nods and accompanies him back to Euston, then to the ticket barrier. She kisses him on the cheek, getting another jolt of Old Spice tempered with gherkin. He hugs her tightly, but when he goes to pull away, Cat holds on for a second too long and he fixes her with a concerned look.

"You *are* all right." He says it as more of a statement than a question.

"I'm great." Cat puts on her best grin. "Now bugger off, so I can go get drunk."

She doesn't know if he believes her or if he just wants to, but either way he smiles and she is off the hook.

"Have fun," he says. "Here." He pushes a ten-pound note into her hand, and before she can even pretend to refuse it he turns and marches toward his train, ticket in hand, where she cannot follow.

Cat decides to save on fare and walk home. It is still early, and all around her the city hums with the promise of a Saturday afternoon on the cusp of becoming Saturday night. She passes group after group of people drinking and smoking on patios outside bars, the women all dressed to the nines, most of the men in jeans and T-shirts. A group of lads in their early twenties fall out of a taxi on the opposite side of the road, a day of indulging already catching up to them before the sun calls it a day. Other women her age might be at pre-drinks already, doing their makeup together on bedroom floors surrounded by wineglasses and hair dryer cables, cackling and gossiping and singing along tipsily to Taylor Swift. In some other universe, Cat might even be one of them, being spoiled by her closest girl friends for her birthday.

You bitches are the best, she would say. *I love you so much.*

Halfway back to Islington she stops at a small shopfront where *Cash 4 Gold* scrolls across a digitized sign in the window. The owner shows no indication of recognizing her, although this is not her first visit.

"Fifty quid," he says when she shows him the brooch.

"We both know it's worth at least four hundred," she counters.

He just shrugs. "Sixty. Final offer."

"Give me two hundred for it."

If time were on her side, she could find a buyer willing to pay more online. But time is yet another asset she doesn't have. The owner clicks his tongue in thought, looking down at the horse and then back up at Cat.

"Fine," he says. She pushes the box across the counter toward him with a violent jerk of the arm and snatches the cash and receipt from his hands before the reality of what she is doing can sink in and change her mind.

She doesn't remember the rest of the walk home. The next thing she knows she is back in her bedroom, folding the two hundred pounds (along with the tenner her dad gave her) into the envelope the credit card bill came in, ready to be paid into the bank first thing Monday morning. Then she climbs into bed and pulls the covers over her head, fully intending to cry herself to sleep despite the early hour.

Neither sleep nor tears are forthcoming, just a horrible sort of numbness. Still shrouded in the duvet, Cat reaches for her phone. As if of their own accord, she watches as her fingers type two words into the search engine: *Tsarina diamond*. She scrolls and scrolls, and the more she reads, the more she feels as if she is coming back into her own body. Her heart quickens and her pupils dilate as a joke turns over in her mind, solidifying like dough into an idea.

Cat opens a new tab in her browser and types five words: *Jake, Oceanic Hotel bar, Islington.*

Seven

On Monday morning in a small café around the corner from the Oceanic Hotel, Cat and Jake make labored small talk. He said to call him when she was sober if she was serious, and sober she was when she asked him to meet her here. Wild and wired, maybe even a little bit manic, but sober.

The air between them is thick with the knowledge they are stepping away from their safe existing dynamic, possibly for good. It is the first time she has spoken with him outside of the bar, something made all the more noticeable by the fact Jake is not wearing the crisp white shirt she has come to associate with him, but a black T-shirt that hugs his biceps, which are just as impressive as the forearms Cat spends a great deal of her time trying not to think about.

"So," she says finally, working up the courage to broach the subject of why they are both here.

"I'm sorry," he says before she can continue. "I think I got a bit carried away the other day. All that talk of diamonds. It was a fun way to spend the afternoon, don't get me wrong, but . . . I should never have suggested we talk about it for real."

"Oh." Cat feels like she's being given the brush-off after a one-night stand. "I'm not sure I get it."

"It's not you; it's me," he tells her. Okay, she has *definitely* heard this speech before. "I just prefer to work alone," he clarifies. "A partner . . . It complicates things."

"Yeah, you said. And I hear you. It adds more moving parts to the equation. And it's true that we don't really know each other." It is not for want of trying on Cat's part: the man in front of her keeps a pretty bare presence online. Even discovering his full name in a lifestyle blogger's two-year-old write-up of cocktails at the Oceanic felt like unearthing a treasure.

Jake Marlowe.

That had helped Cat find him on Instagram, Facebook, Twitter, even LinkedIn, but even after a night of stalking—due diligence, really—she feels she still only knows the bare minimum about him. He mainly shares posts from mixology accounts and rarely posts himself, just the occasional photo of him and a striking, proud-looking woman she assumes is his mother.

"This whole proposition is mad—please don't think I'm not aware," Cat says. "Under any other circumstances, I'd be saying exactly what you're saying. But, Jake, here's the thing." She digs into her pocket for a printout and lays it flat on the table between them.

"I did some googling," she says. "And this is how much money you and I could stand to make if we are able to get our hands on the Tsarina."

She was shocked to learn that Louisa hadn't been lying. At least, not entirely. The Tsarina *is* a real diamond, a quite famous one, actually, and while accounts of its origin as a Romanov crown jewel seem spurious to say the least, the stone's quality speaks for itself, regardless of its provenance. Cat hasn't ever seen that many zeros lined up together other than the few times she's played the lottery. She's willing to bet Jake hasn't either, because his resolve appears to soften before her, and that little frown appears between his eyebrows again.

"This is worth more than the ring Kanye gave Kim," he whispers. "By a *lot*." So he's been doing his research too. Interesting.

"I'm telling you," she says. "I really think we can do this."

Jake says nothing for a moment, just stares down at the big, *big* number and the black-and-white photograph of the diamond. He absentmindedly twists and turns the foil top from his can of San Pellegrino over in his hands until it resembles a tiny silver spear.

"How?" he asks.

"Simple," she says. "We play to our strengths."

"I lift watches and wallets," he says. "This is—"

"Exactly the same, in principle," she interrupts. "It's just higher risk and higher reward, that's all. And out of the two of us, you're the one with the magic touch needed to get hold of the ring without anyone noticing. I get us access to the ring, you get us the ring, boom."

"In theory." He appears to give it some real thought. "I mean, if I were able to slip the ring off the bride's finger, which I *might* be able to do . . ."

"I know you can."

"A rock that size? That weight? She's going to notice immediately. We'd never make it to the exit." He frowns even deeper, and then the line disappears. "Unless . . ."

"Yes?" Cat watches him carefully, as if he could fly away at any moment.

"You told me Louisa wears a fake, right?"

"She does."

"A fake realistic enough to pass for the genuine article?"

Cat smiles and nods, as if to finally welcome Jake onto the page where she's been waiting for him.

"If we can get our hands on the *pretend* diamond," she says, "we'd be able to steal the Tsarina . . ."

". . . and replace it with the decoy before anyone suspects a thing!" Jake finally stops fidgeting with the foil in his hands and gives Cat a look so intense it feels as if it will leave a mark.

"Let me ask you again." Cat leans forward over the table. "How would you do it?"

A light is dancing in Jake's eyes that wasn't there a moment ago.

"All I would need," he says slowly, "is five seconds, congratulating Louisa on her special day." He reaches out and takes Cat's hand, clasping it between his. "I would keep her eyes on me, tell her how radiant she looks. Maybe get a little bit emotional, the way people do at weddings. I might even pull her into a hug, and then . . . voilà."

He draws his hands away, and the first thing Cat notices is how cool the air feels on her skin after being wrapped in his warmth. The second thing she notices brings another huge smile to her lips.

"Oh, shit," she says. "You're *good*."

He held her hand for a matter of seconds. And, okay, she may have allowed herself to get slightly distracted by his touch and intent gaze, but it is with a slight thrill that she sees, wrapped around her own ring finger, a deftly fashioned loop of silver foil. She glances up at Jake. He still has that look in his eyes.

"Did you really come here just to tell me no?" she asks.

"I really did," he says. "You came into my bar day-drunk and pitched a spectacularly bad idea. And you're right, I don't really know you. This could end a million bad ways. But . . ."

"But what?"

"It's a thief thing, isn't it?" He smirks. "We're a curious lot. Once you told me about the diamond, I couldn't stop thinking about the ways we might be able to pull this off." He prods the sheet of paper on the table. "And this is a *lot* of money."

Cat wonders, again, about Jake's situation. Whether his small cons at the hotel are just to supplement his income, like tips, or acts of financial desperation. Whether the prospect of the mind-boggling number on that paper is enough to get him on board with this frankly ridiculous plan she has cobbled together.

"So . . ." She lets the word hang in the air.

Jake exhales slowly, his eyes still on the piece of paper. Then he smiles and tells her: "We can do this."

He looks like he is about to say something else, but Cat is already on her phone, excitedly scrolling through her contacts. She planned this next step the other night too, in a feverish haze.

"Who are you—" he begins, but she shushes him.

"It's ringing!" she whispers. Then, a second later: "Louisa, hi!"

"Cat? What a surprise! Lucky *me*!" Jake looks at Cat like she's lost her mind, but she forges ahead before her nerve can fail her.

"So sorry to hassle," she says, "I just wanted to ask something super quick." She doesn't even allow Louisa to respond before continuing: "I can't tell you how much I'm looking forward to celebrating your good news this weekend. Would it be all right if I brought Jake along to the engagement party?"

"Who's Jake?" Louisa asks, while the man in question visibly blanches across the table.

"He's my boyfriend," Cat says. Jake's expression is uncharacteristically readable now, and it appears to be saying: *What the fuck?* She can practically hear Louisa's ears pricking up on the other end of the line.

"You have a boyfriend?" Louisa asks. "You never said! Oh, you sneaky thing, you! Well, yes, naturally he's invited."

"Fab," Cat says. "I can't wait for you to meet him. You're going to love him."

After she hangs up, Jake leans forward in his seat and says: "Are you going to let your *boyfriend* in on what just happened?"

"It's simple," she says, twisting the foil around her finger. "You've got the talents we need to make the switch, and I'm your way into the wedding. Our only problem is, I've been invited to a dozen or so weddings in the last three years and as the single friend, I never get the option to bring a guest. You need to be a part of the equation. If we can make a convincing enough couple at the engagement party next week, then Louisa and Stephen will be more inclined to give me a plus-one so you can come along. Then, I know I can get you close enough to the diamond."

The smile returns to Jake's full mouth.

"That's genius, actually," he says.

"Isn't it?" She grins. "So you'll come as my date to the engagement party, charm the socks off Louisa and Stephen, and we're in."

"Sounds straightforward enough," he says. "I *can* be very charming."

Oh, I know, she thinks.

"I suppose, if we're going to pretend to be the perfect couple"— Jake clasps his hands together on the table and leans forward— "we should actually get to know each other better."

Cat nods. "We're off to a decent start already," she says. "We already know about each other's secret life of crime."

"And I know how you like your martini." He sits back in his chair, as if to get a better look at her. "I can infer all kinds of things from that."

"What, pray tell, can you glean from that?" she asks.

"You know what you want," he says. "Or at the very least, you know what you *don't* want. You have little patience for other people's bullshit. You're driven but not uptight, and you probably surprise men with how you tend to take charge in bed."

Cat simply stares, agog. Jake smirks.

"Or," he adds, "you just don't waste time diluting your spirits."

"You might as well have just called me a typical Cancer," Cat says.

"So I was right, then?"

"Maybe. On a few counts. Although that bedroom comment was . . ."

"A little forward, I know. Sorry. I just figure, since you've now promoted me to pretend boyfriend, we should probably get used to talking intimately if we're going to convince anyone we're actually together."

"I suppose you're right." She narrows her eyes. "Did you really just get all of that from my drink order? Or do you have some kind of secret body-language trick? You know, like how fortune-tellers will cold-read people and tell them what they want to hear."

"I'm just a really good bartender," he says with a grin.

"If you say so," she says, unconvinced. "Anyway. What about you?"

"What would you like to know?"

"Do you have any brothers or sisters?"

"No. Just me."

"Same. Are your parents still together?"

"My dad bounced years ago. It's been me and my mum ever since. What about you? I'm picturing an idyllic childhood somewhere green up north. Yorkshire? The Peaks?"

"Cheshire, actually. And it was . . . okay."

"Wait a minute. So what you're saying is . . ." He raises his voice just enough to be heard over Cat's grunt of displeasure: "You're a Cheshire Cat?"

"Congratulations," she says, "on making the same joke I've been hearing since I was in primary school."

"Your parents must have thought that would be adorable."

"It gets worse," she says. "My mum's name was Alice."

Jake laughs, but she sees a flicker of something cross his face as he registers her use of the past tense. She's used to this reaction. Thirty is still remarkably young to not have a mother. All through school and university, people would coo and fuss when they found out, telling her how sorry they were, as if her mother had just that minute died. Then the conversation would falter, or fizzle out entirely, and afterward Cat started to suspect people found her hard to talk to or considered her to be bad luck. All of which is to say, she is grateful when Jake tells her he has an even more important question.

"Bourbons or custard creams?"

"That's easy." She relaxes a little. "Custard creams."

"Correct answer," he says. "Thank god. I think this fake relationship has legs."

"You know what?" She twists the foil ring around her finger. "I think so too."

It is only later, as Cat is scanning her Oyster card against the barrier in the Tube station, that she notices she is still wearing it. And in remembering the way Jake's hands felt on hers, she realizes something else: he wasn't wearing his wedding ring.

PART TWO

The Great Pretenders

Eight

"Hot date tonight?" Alex asks, passing Cat on the landing as she exits her bedroom.

"Not exactly," she says distractedly, checking the contents of her handbag.

"You certainly *look* like you're going on a date." Alex eyes her artfully messy hair, short silver dress, and peep-toe shoes with something vaguely resembling approval.

"Who's going on a date?" Tom shouts from the bottom of the stairs.

"Seeing as you vetoed an open relationship, it's not me!" Alex calls back down. "It's Cat. She's all dressed up, but she says it's 'not exactly' a date, whatever that means."

"Not exactly?" Tom peers up at them, his befuddled expression clear as day from their vantage point. "Surely it either is a date or it isn't."

"You know, I do not miss the apps," says Alex smugly. "I mean, sure, there's something to be said for being able to schedule a dick appointment at three o'clock on a Tuesday afternoon like a manicure, but ultimately they make it far too easy to avoid committing."

"You shouldn't be going on dates with anyone who isn't willing to *call* it a date," Tom admonishes her. He might as well add a "young lady."

Cat rolls her eyes. It's an unfortunate symptom of living with such a settled, mature, some might say *boring* couple. From time to time, they can't help acting like they're her parents. She doesn't even think they know they're doing it. Even worse, on such occasions, Cat feels herself slipping into the role of stroppy teenage daughter.

"Guys, it's fine," she tells them, hoping to cut this entire conversation short with a thin slice of truth. The less either of them knows about her real life, the better. "I'm going to a friend's engagement party, and I happen to be going with a guy," she continues. "It's honestly no big deal."

"That certainly sounds like a date to me," Alex sniffs.

"Who's the guy?" Tom inquires as Cat carefully descends the staircase.

"A man I met online who says he has a van full of puppies and sweets he'd like to show me," Cat replies, her hand already reaching for the front door. "Don't wait up."

The South Bank is teeming with life as Cat crosses the Golden Jubilee Bridge. She and Jake agreed to meet outside the Southbank Centre before the party, so they can arrive at the venue together, and she heads there now. The sun is low and blinding, bathing everything in the kind of warm light that seems to erase imperfections, be they skin blemishes or overflowing trash bins. Cat feels a sudden, potent surge of affection for this city and the electric, urgent sensation that first drew her here—the irresistible notion that in a place like this, on a night like tonight, anything could happen.

Cat shimmies through the winding queue for the London Eye, her mood so bolstered she doesn't even resent the omnipresent tourists, and sees him first, before he can turn to find her in the crowd.

He stands in front of the shaded skate park directly under the Southbank Centre, watching a group of kids egg each other on as they perform tricks on their boards. As a teenager, Cat wasn't immune to the skater-boy thing. She can't help but wonder if Jake ever went through that particular phase.

He is wearing a cornflower-blue shirt tucked into dark jeans that hug legs Cat realizes she has never actually paid attention to before. They are thicker, stronger looking than his tall, lean frame would suggest. Cat reminds herself why they are both here—this is far from a real date, whatever Tom and Alex think—and waves, catching his eye as she closes the distance between them.

"Hi," she says.

"Hi," he says back, and are those *nerves* she detects? "Sorry, I got distracted." He gestures to the skateboarders. "You look . . ." He trails off as he takes in her dress. "Amazing," he finishes. *Two for two*, she thinks. It's a Reiss number she found in a charity shop last year and has reserved for first dates ever since. It hit her earlier, as she hung it up in the bathroom to steam out the creases while she showered, that this was to be the garment's first outing in some time.

"Thanks," she says, grinning as she takes in the familiar-looking Rolex on his wrist. "You too. Perfect Tory drag. They're going to love you."

"I thought you'd approve. It felt apt." The corner of his mouth twitches upward, and they both glance to the Houses of Parliament, just visible over the river. "Shall we?"

They begin their walk up the bank, and it is not long before they are passing the outdoor bookstall on the river's edge opposite the National Theatre.

"I should probably know your favorite book," she says. "In case anybody asks."

"That's . . . specific. How intense *are* your friends' interrogations, exactly?" Jake asks. "Is it likely to come up?"

"Your favorite *author*, at least. I'd be a terrible pretend girlfriend if I didn't at least know that."

Jake nods, then thinks about it for a moment.

"You're going to think me a philistine," he says.

"Well, now you *have* to tell me."

"Fine." He takes a deep breath, then blurts out: "John Grisham."

"Wow." Cat snorts. "Were you raised in an airport?"

"They're really good!" he protests. "Fine. Who is *your* favorite author?"

Cat briefly consults the mental list of important feminist writers that populate her bookshelf, whose words changed the world and adorned every tote bag she has ever misplaced. Sylvia Plath. Toni Morrison. Margaret Atwood.

"Jilly Cooper," she finally confesses. "There was always a stack of them on the porch when I was growing up. They were my mum's. I remember sneaking one off the pile when I was about eleven and being absolutely hooked. She never seemed to mind that I was reading books with so much bonking in them. I think she figured as long as I was reading, it was a good thing."

Jake grins. "And there I was, thinking you were so high-minded," he says, "when it turns out we're both literary dirtbags."

"If anyone asks," Cat says, "my favorite book is *The Color Purple*."

"Your secret's safe with me," Jake says with a wink.

They continue their walk, passing a busker singing a Lewis

Capaldi song (in fact, Cat can't be entirely sure it isn't actually Lewis Capaldi) and a group of young women in neon-tinted helmets and kneepads twirling and swerving gracefully through the crowds outside the Tate on Rollerblades. They stop briefly to take in a guerrilla performance of *Romeo and Juliet* outside the Globe: a man with enviably silky long hair delivers Juliet's famous balcony monologue from a perch on the railing, while his Romeo, a girl with a buzz cut and a melodic Irish accent, sings the male lines back up to the gathering audience from the narrow beach below.

They see a couple of mudlarkers down there too, carefully parsing the narrow shingle with their metal detectors and grabbing canes for fragments of glass, pottery, and tin. God, this city! Cat almost wishes they could just spend the rest of their evening right here, but her phone informs her the party is only two minutes away.

The morning after her tea with Louisa and the others, a card came through the door. Because Louisa's mother would never allow even a small, last-minute party to be thrown without official invitations. The note bore the time and date of the function, and in lieu of an address, simply the name of the venue—"The Maiden"—and a set of coordinates. Cat imagined it was supposed to be cute as she typed them into Google Maps.

When she and Jake arrive at their destination, she scans the signage on the buildings, then double-checks the map on her screen.

"I don't see a bar called the Maiden," she says. "But I'm sure we're in the right place. Hold on, I'll call Louisa. I wouldn't be surprised if she got those coordinates wrong. So typical of her. I mean, the Shard is right there. I bet that's where we need to be."

Before she can dial, she feels the weight of Jake's hands on both of her shoulders, and he gently steers her around until she is facing the waterfront.

"Might this be it?" he asks, and even though she can't see his face, she can practically *hear* his raised eyebrow. The *Maiden*, it transpires, is a boat. Because of course it is. A very big boat, as it happens, moored at Bankside Pier, with a flowered arch over the walkway that connects it to the quay. At the top of the narrow bridge, Louisa waves down at them.

"I was wrong," Cat mutters through a polite smile. "*This* is so typical of her."

Nine

"Welcome aboard!" Louisa trills when Cat and Jake reach the top of the narrow walkway. Her gown looks as if it has been spun from gossamer or possibly sprayed directly onto her body. Just a few feet away, Elijah stands guard in the same black suit he wore last week, holding Louisa's sparkly gold clutch.

Louisa hugs Cat, then immediately turns to Jake.

"And who do we have here?" she asks.

Jake holds out his hand and introduces himself. "Delighted to meet you," he says, his voice doing that mimic thing Cat has observed in the bar. "And congratulations on your engagement."

Louisa looks at him like he is a mouthwatering forkful of filet mignon, then returns her attention to Cat.

"Where have you been hiding this one?" she asks, as if this week doesn't mark the most time Cat has spent in Louisa's company since university. Then, without waiting for an answer, she moves aside, revealing an anxious-looking young man in a waistcoat holding a tray of champagne flutes.

"Almost everyone is here," she says, handing them each a glass and ushering them onward toward the main deck, where a few dozen people are gathered. "If you'll excuse me, I need to pop to the ladies' room before we set sail."

"Set sail?" Cat inquires, incredulous, but Louisa has already gone, Elijah following closely in her wake.

"Are we being taken hostage?" Jake leans in and asks. "Isn't this how most Bond movies end?"

They head into the party, and upon catching sight of them, Stephen detaches himself from a group of men sporting strikingly similar haircuts and blue suits to come and greet them.

"Cat, so good to see you again," he says, kissing her on the cheek. His perfect teeth are practically luminescent in the golden-hour light. "And you must be Jake. Pleased to meet you."

"Likewise," Jake says, shaking his hand casually but firmly. "It looks like it's going to be quite a night."

"Just something we threw together," says Stephen. "We're lucky that Uncle Jonty was in the country and the *Maiden* was available. She's his pride and joy."

"I can see why," Jake says, proceeding to ask some question or other about boats, to which Stephen responds with evident glee. Their exchange has the agreeable hue of male bonding to it, Cat decides, so she takes a moment to glance around at the other guests. Louisa's parents are at port and starboard, respectively, appearing to keep as much of the ship between them as possible, which makes sense. The divorce happened after uni ended and Cat and Louisa were no longer in regular contact, but she has heard secondhand that it was brutal. She recognizes Stephen's parents, Jolyon and Matilda, from various magazine articles. Darcy is here, of course, as are Olivia and Priya. She spies Harper's wild curls over the top of a tray of canapés, and they share a brief wave.

"What line of work are you in, Jake?" she hears Stephen ask, bringing her back to the conversation with a jolt.

"Hotels," says Jake with a bland smile. He and Cat agreed earlier this week to keep their cover story vague and short. In other words, less likely to trip either of them up or come back to bite them in the behind later on. Cat has told enough face-saving half-truths in her time that this part comes quite naturally.

"I hear you have plans to expand your business," Jake says. "Very impressive."

Deflection is another tactic with which she is intimately familiar. In the vast majority of cases, people only ask you about your life in order to then have the opportunity to talk about their own. Stephen, it seems, is no exception, launching into a well-rehearsed spiel about his company—although even after his soliloquy Cat has no idea what he actually *does*. She suspects his clients aren't 100 percent sure either.

"Tobin, mate," a cherubic-looking blond man says, clapping Stephen on the shoulder. "I think you're wanted."

"Who's Tobin?" asks Cat.

"I am," says Stephen brightly, and excuses himself, dashing across the deck to join Louisa.

"Oh, I get it," says Jake. "Tobin. As in, St. Aubyn."

"Yeah!" The blond guy nods enthusiastically, every part of him bobbing and bouncing almost independently, more marionette than man, then holds out his hand. "Freddie Meriweather. Best man."

"Jake. This is Cat."

"What is it with men and calling each other by their surnames?" Cat asks.

Freddie turns his attention to her and tucks his head backward, momentarily confused.

"Guys are always calling each other Smithy or Jonesy," she continues. "I don't think I've ever heard a woman do it."

"How funny!" Freddie says. "I can't say I've ever noticed. It's just been that way since school. Nobody's ever done it with me. Do you suppose I should be insulted that they haven't? Then again, Meriweather is rather a lot of syllables, isn't it, as opposed to just Freddie, or even Fred, although nobody has ever called me that on account of there being my uncle Fred, who was a ghastly man by all accounts, although he *was* always very kind to his dogs, too kind if anything, the way my cousin tells it he used to have Cook prepare better meals for the dog than his own—"

"And where did you go to school?" Cat cuts in, regretting this line of inquiry and eager to bring his train of thought to a halt. Freddie gives her a horrified look, as if the answer to her question is obvious.

"Eton?" Jake ventures hesitantly. Freddie's mortification intensifies for a second, and then he throws back his head and laughs, blond hair flopping in every direction.

"Eton!" he wheezes. "Oh, Jake, you're a card. *Eton.* The very idea. No offense to Eton boys, of course. Damn fine lot, for the most part. Except for out on the cricket green, of course." He wipes a tear from the corner of his eye and shakes his head as he saunters away, murmuring: "Eton. Marvelous."

Cat and Jake are exchanging equally baffled looks when the music is lowered and everybody's attention is drawn to the newly engaged couple on the other side of the deck.

"Firstly, thank you all for coming," says Stephen in a voice that seems made for public speaking. "I suppose you'll be hearing me say exactly the same thing in a matter of weeks!" Gentle murmurs of polite laughter hum through the party. "I'll keep this nice and quick," Stephen continues, to which Freddie yells: "That's what he'll be telling *Louisa* in a matter of weeks!"

At this, the younger-skewing portion of the group erupts in

genuine, braying laughter, and Cat can't help but giggle a little too. That's one great equalizer, she supposes. It doesn't matter how lofty or privileged your station in life: your best man will always take you down a peg or two.

"All right, all right," says Stephen with a self-deprecating, remarkably good-natured smile. On reflection, Cat revises her theory: she imagines that being as rich and handsome as Stephen St. Aubyn makes you rather impervious to jokes about your sexual performance.

"We're just so thrilled that you can be here to celebrate with us," says Louisa. "And, well . . . that's it! Let's get this show on the road!" She throws out her arms like a magician's assistant, and Cat realizes with a lurch in her stomach that they are moving. At some point, the *Maiden* detached from its moorings, and it's now gliding down the Thames.

"So eat, drink, be merry," says Louisa benignly.

"And if you get too merry, the loos are downstairs, not overboard!" Stephen points his glass at Freddie, who holds up his hands and mouths "mea culpa." Stephen looks as if he is about to say something else, then he pauses, hand reaching into his jacket pocket. "Apologies." He gives the crowd that megawatt smile one more time, then strides away, vibrating phone already pressed firmly to his ear.

The music resumes and Cat notices, for the first time, the string quartet on one corner of the deck. Heaven forbid Louisa hire anything as gauche as a DJ for her engagement party. What is she going to have at the wedding, a full orchestra?

"She's a stunner, isn't she?" says a man to their left. He is a ruddy-faced, middle-aged gentleman wearing a yellow bow tie, navy blazer, and bright red trousers.

"She'll make a beautiful bride, for sure," says Cat.

"Bride?" The man looks at her as if she has just sprouted a second head. "I think you'll find she intends to remain the *Maiden*."

"You must be Stephen's uncle Jonty," Jake interjects, shaking his hand and introducing both himself and Cat. "You're right, she's a real beauty."

Jonty clasps both hands around Jake's, evidently touched by his words.

"Thank you," he says. "Now, please allow me to introduce the other lady in my life—Saf? Saf, darling?"

A young woman whom Cat had assumed to be one of Stephen's or Louisa's younger cousins turns to them and artfully places her arm on Jonty's shoulder. He introduces her as Saffron.

"Charmed," she says, somehow without moving a single facial muscle.

"I've had rotten luck with women in the past," Jonty explains. "Well, anyone here can tell you about my gold-digging harpy of an ex-wife—good riddance to bad rubbish indeed! But Saf, here, she's been my saving grace these last three weeks." He looks at her, moony-eyed, and her immobile expression ekes out a small smile.

"Tell me, Kate," Jonty says, and she feels her hackles rise. "What does your father do?"

Not *What do you do*, or even *What does Jake here do*, but *What does your father do*. As if no woman could exist in the context of herself alone. Cat is unsure whether this is a posh thing, a patriarchy thing, or some ugly combination of the two flavors.

"He's a union rep," Cat replies, and then before Jonty can issue any follow-up questions, asks: "What do *you* do, Saffron?"

"I'm a dancer," she says, elongating the "a" into an extra syllable.

"I should have guessed," Cat says. "I mean, that *figure*. I'm raging, frankly." Saffron gives another coy smile, while Jonty huffs silently next to her, as Cat thought he might. Men like Jonty never like it when someone would rather talk to the woman next to him, especially when they only brought said woman along as a desperate ploy to illustrate their own masculine prowess.

Fuck the halo effect, Cat thinks, clocking the dancer's sapphire earrings. *Work, girl.* Jonty soon moves on, Saffron in tow, keen to show off his prize to everybody else in attendance now that it's clear this particular audience is not sufficiently impressed by his trophy.

"Would you look at that," Cat says quietly. "We're not even the first scammers at this party."

"I feel quite cheap," Jake replies with mock chagrin.

They watch as Jonty introduces Saffron to one guest after another.

"Poor guy," Jake says. "Should somebody tell him?"

"Poor guy, my arse," Cat says. "Don't tell me you feel sorry for him."

"The boat-owning toff?" He clasps his chest. "Not even a little bit. It just seems so easy. It's like she's taking candy from a baby."

"I assure you, he knows what this is, deep down," Cat says. "And you know what? Good for her."

"To Saffron," Jake says, and they clink their glasses together.

"Cat, hi!" Darcy appears at her elbow, grinning so widely it must surely be causing her physical pain. "Is this the famous Jake?"

"Hi there," Jake says, slipping into his cordial mode once again. "Nice to meet you . . . ?"

Right. I'm his girlfriend. I should be doing this part.

"Sorry!" Cat exclaims. "Jake, this is Darcy Wong, a dear friend of Louisa's. And, Darcy, this is—"

"Your beau, yes I know," she says. "Oh! And apparently I'm a poet who doesn't know it." She titters. "The group chat has been absolutely *agog* in anticipation, Jake. Louisa was telling us what awful luck Cat here used to have in men, but clearly she was exaggerating!"

"Pardon?" Cat wrinkles her nose.

"Oh, no." Darcy's smile literally turns upside down. "Forget I said anything, please. It's just, well, the party was last-minute enough as it is, then you call Louisa asking to add some random guy to the guest list, which turned out to be *perfectly fine*, she's being ever so chill for somebody getting married in a matter of weeks, and, well . . . All she said was she's sure that Jake will be an improvement on the kind of guys you dated in uni."

"The guys *I* dated? What about—" Cat feels Jake's hand on the small of her back, and she stops to take a breath. They're here to pose as the perfect couple, to guarantee they get into the wedding next month, not to retaliate against Louisa's queen-bee bullshit by dredging up *her* various youthful misadventures. Cat amuses herself momentarily by imagining the kind of speech she'd give if *she* were Louisa's chief bridesmaid.

"That was all a long, long time ago," Cat says through gritted teeth.

"Of course." Darcy smiles again, but it's the kind of smile you give to a child who still believes in the Tooth Fairy.

"Is your other half here?" Jake asks, clearly trying to break the tension. "He's Stephen's business partner, isn't he?"

"My *husband*," Darcy says, "couldn't make it, I'm afraid. Evan is still in Singapore, busy busy! But he's flying over in a week or so. He wouldn't miss Stephen's stag weekend. You know what *men* are like. Am I right, Cat?" She nudges Cat with her elbow, eager to foster some sentiment of sisterhood after putting her Jimmy Choo in her mouth.

"Apparently I do," Cat says. Jake's hand presses more firmly against her back, presumably his way of letting her know she needs to rein in the attitude. But all she can think about is how warm his touch feels now that they're out on the water and a cool breeze is ruffling everybody's clothes.

"But what about you, Jake?" Darcy asks. "How did you and the lovely Cat here meet?"

Jake's hand seems to tense. Or maybe it is Cat's entire spine that has suddenly frozen.

How did they meet? How *did* they meet? Cat can't believe they quizzed each other on cookies and books but didn't think to come up with a plausible story of how they met that doesn't involve petty theft.

"It's the oldest story," Jake says. "A boy, a girl, a bar . . ." He turns to look down at Cat, and she returns his gaze, doing her very best impression of a smitten kitten. She might even flutter her eyelashes a little. "I just knew she was the one for me," he says, his eyes still on hers.

"Me too," Cat says, but it comes out as more of a squeak.

"That is beautiful," says Darcy. "Girls! *Girls!*" She beckons over Priya and Olivia, both of whom look like they've already made a decent go of the open bar. "Jake is just telling me all about how he wooed Cat," she says.

"Aww!" says Priya, whom Cat remembers as being the group's resident romantic.

"Wooing? What is this, medieval times?" Olivia slurs, pulling a stray lock of hair from where it has become stuck to her lip gloss. "Did she let down her hair so he could climb up her tower?"

"Nothing so cliché," Cat says, starting to enjoy herself. She's never had the opportunity to do this ridiculous kind of showing off before, has never even *wanted* to. But just because she and Jake aren't actually together doesn't mean she can't have a little bit of fun.

"First, he took me for martinis," Cat says, figuring this part is still technically true.

"Dry, with a twist," Jake adds in that supplementary-information way that Cat guesses boyfriends do.

"And he showed up with a gift," she says. "A first edition of my favorite book."

"*The Color Purple*," he supplies helpfully to the group.

"And then . . . ," Cat says. Somehow, knowing all of this fake romance stuff will undoubtedly get back to Louisa gives her a sick sense of pleasure.

"And then," Jake picks up, like a good improv partner, "we went to an outdoor production of *Romeo and Juliet*."

He drops his hand from her back and entwines his fingers with hers, raising their joined fists to kiss the back of her knuckles gently. Damn, he's good. And correct, in a way. After all, this *is* technically their first date.

Fuck it, she thinks. *In for a penny . . .*

She shifts her body slightly so that she's facing him head-on and rises on her tiptoes slowly, giving him plenty of time to figure out what's about to happen. It's still his call. He can kiss her forehead or give her a cutesy peck on the cheek. Just something to complete this Oscar-worthy performance.

Instead, he uses his free hand to cup her chin gently. He tilts her face ever so slightly upward. He bows his head. And brushes his lips against hers so softly, it takes a second for her body to recognize what's happening and for her heartbeat to quicken. Her eyes drift closed, and she kisses him back, pushing her lips against his with more force for just a second before Jake's grip on her hand tightens as if to signal *enough*.

"There's nothing like that honeymoon period," Darcy sighs.

"You guys are the *cutest*," Priya says.

"Get a room," Olivia says, then hiccups.

"Your glass is empty," Jake says. "Let me take care of that for you." He relieves Cat of the empty flute, nods graciously at the bridesmaids, and heads off in search of the bar, leaving her to flush and try to pretend that this was *not* just the first time Jake Marlowe ever kissed her.

"God, he's a bit perfect, isn't he?" Priya muses.

"If they seem too good to be true," Olivia says, "they usually are."

She has no idea how right she is, of course. None of this is true. All the same, Cat can't deny that she's enjoying soaking up this unique brand of female attention. But just as quickly as it came, that glow departs and Cat's warm blood turns to ice as two things hit her.

Louisa is watching her keenly from across the party.

And Cat just kissed a married man.

Ten

"We should probably get a new group chat going, right?" Darcy suggests, jolting Cat back into the conversation. "For all things wedding?"

"That's a great idea," says Priya.

"Okay, one sec . . ." Darcy digs around in her bag, retrieves her phone, then waves for Harper to join them. "Bridesmaids, assemble!" she exclaims. Harper saunters over in a sequined, psychedelic jumpsuit that breaks pretty much any rules Cat has ever learned about color stories, her hair teased into an even bigger cascade of curls. She should stick out like a sore thumb amid the pastels and jewel tones of the rest of Louisa's milieu, but somehow the whole look works.

"Hey, girls," Harper says, "what's up?"

"Bridesmaid admin," Cat tells her. "Darcy thinks we need a group chat."

"No doubt." Harper nods, seeming more at ease than the first time they met. Cat realizes she's a little stoned and feels a sting of envy. A concerto of pings sounds from their respective pockets and purses as Darcy activates the WhatsApp group.

"Even more notifications—amazing," Olivia drawls. "I need to pee," she adds, and begins to stagger off. Darcy and Priya follow, each of them taking one of her elbows and helping her course-correct when she veers dangerously close to the chocolate fountain.

"Is she okay?" Cat asks. "She seems . . ."

"I know," Harper says, nodding. "From what I can gather, she and her husband aren't in a great place. Hence the rum and Cokes and occasional outbursts."

Cat is surprised, then realizes she shouldn't be. Olivia and her husband might earn a small fortune between them and be raising their son in a Victorian terrace in Primrose Hill, but anyone whose life looks that perfect . . . Well. Olivia said it herself.

"Too good to be true," Cat murmurs.

"I tried to suggest she talk to someone about it," Harper says. "But then she called me a mollycoddled, over-therapized Yank who doesn't know what she's talking about or when to shut up."

"Yikes," Cat says. "Bit harsh."

"Eh." Harper shrugs. "She's hurting. Besides, I've been called worse. *Much* worse. And even an insult sounds kind of charming in that British accent, you know?"

"Oh my god," Cat says with a grin. "You fancy her."

"The domineering high-powered attorney who looks like she just stepped off the set of *Suits*?" Harper feigns confusion. "Yeah, there's absolutely nothing of appeal there."

"Oh, she's fit, for sure," Cat agrees. "But also kind of . . ."

"Mean?" Harper shrugs again. "Never let it be said that Harper Lawrence doesn't have a type. Don't worry, though. Chasing un-available straight women hasn't been a hobby of mine for at least two years. And besides, I'm not about to start any drama at Lou-isa's wedding by seducing one of my fellow bridesmaids. I swear she thinks lesbians are like piranhas or something. When I tell you it took me *forever* to convince that girl I wasn't attracted to her after I came out . . ."

"I thought you were practically raised as family?" she says. "Wouldn't that border on truly creepy?"

"Try telling her that."

Cat remembers the way Louisa used to be at uni: resolute in her belief that everybody, barring gay men and the very elderly, was obsessed with her. Even more annoyingly, she was often proven correct.

"When I finally got through to her, I actually think she was more offended than relieved." Harper snorts.

"That makes you a rarity!" Cat says. "You're one of the only people in the world to ever reject Louisa Vincent."

"Ha! Forget my academic career; maybe *that* will be my legacy."

"I'll make sure that they engrave it on your tombstone," Cat tells her.

"Thanks. You're a real pal." Harper smiles, and a comfortable silence ensues as they just stand there, taking in the party. It doesn't escape Cat that this is the first function she has attended in a long time where she hasn't arrived alone, then sat or stood on the edge of the proceedings, waiting for enough time to elapse that she could acceptably leave. When did her life become such a Smiths song?

As if reading her mind, Harper inquires: "Didn't you come with somebody?"

"Yeah," she says. "My boyfriend, Jake." She tries as hard as she can not to focus on how good that sounds coming out of her mouth.

"Where is he?" Harper asks with what seems like genuine curiosity, not the pointed quizzing Cat has become used to at these kinds of things. "I feel like it's bad etiquette to leave your girlfriend alone at a party. Especially when there are lesbians circling like sharks."

"I thought you were like piranhas."

Harper tosses her wild hair dramatically and says: "I am an entire ocean, honey."

It has the effect of sounding both profound and deeply stupid, and Cat is still laughing as she goes on a lap of the deck in search of Jake. She has barely made it half a dozen steps before a familiar voice calls her name. It is, with the exception of herself, Jake, and Harper, the only accent she has heard tonight not shaped by years of private school.

"Cat? Is that you?" Ronan McCann ambles over, one hand in his pocket, the other clutching a tumbler of whiskey.

Cat feels as if the deck has opened up right underneath her and she has been dropped into another time entirely. For a split second, she is no longer on a boat on the Thames. She is not a thirty-year-old woman. She is nineteen, smoking a roll-up in bed with her first boyfriend. The air is thick with smoke and still-wet paint and sweat. The sensation only lasts a moment, but it rattles her. People who think time travel is the stuff of science fiction have evidently never run into an ex.

"Ronan."

"It *is* you." He throws his whiskey-holding hand around her shoulder, narrowly avoiding soaking her back. His coppery hair falls over his eyes, and he shakes it away. That move used to melt Cat's knees; she always thought it made him look like the unkempt romantic hero of a Gothic novel. She has since read *Wuthering Heights* and knows what a fuckboy Heathcliff actually was.

It never occurred to Cat that she would see Ronan here. Sure, he was at uni with Louisa too, but Cat was the common denominator.

She had no idea the two of them were still in touch. "How've you been?" she asks.

"Honestly? Pretty fucking good," he says.

"I heard you had a big gallery show recently," Cat says. "I'm so happy for you."

"Oh, you know how it is," he says, swilling his whiskey. "You have to play the game. Be a show pony. I hate it." Cat highly doubts that. His shirt, which unless she is mistaken comes from Paul Smith, is unbuttoned to his solar plexus. She is starting to figure out why he's here after all. Louisa, upon learning that one of the scruffy boys she used to know is on the rise in the art world, would be keen to reintegrate him into her milieu, to use his ascendancy to bolster her own credentials. Even if she *has* reportedly been shit-talking Cat's exes to the others. And Ronan, however above all of that he might claim to be, isn't so proud that he'd turn down an invitation to mingle with the type of collectors who undoubtedly make up a good portion of the crowd tonight.

"What about you?" he asks. "It's been ages, la. Catch me up." He sounds even more Scouse than he did ten years ago. Is it possible that while Cat lengthened her flat vowels and recalibrated her vocabulary at Bristol, training herself to call dinner "lunch" and tea "dinner," funneling her broad accent into received pronunciation, Ronan has spent the last decade doing the exact opposite? She's read the occasional profile of him: the bold, exciting painter who is proud to hail from Liverpool. One or two journalists mistakenly described him as working-class. Funny how even a moneyed accent can bamboozle people if it comes from anywhere north of High Wycombe.

"Not much to tell," she says. "I'm a graphic designer, mostly freelance—"

"You know what's funny?" he interrupts, leaning into her as if he's about to share a confidence. "I was just thinking about you the other day."

"Really?" Oh, this rings a bell. Ronan's way of appearing so curious, so *interested*. It's a pity he never got the hang of actually listening to the answers to the questions he asks.

"Yeah." He sips his whiskey. "Do you remember that night in final year when you posed for me?"

Cat suppresses a grimace. "How could I forget."

He promised it would be just between the two of them; he needed to practice, and he found life drawing so sterile. Fast-forward to the end of the semester, and there was Cat's naked body in oil on canvas for all the world—okay, all of uni—to see at Ronan's showcase.

"That painting was when I first really started getting to grips with my style, my point of view, what I want to *say* with my work," Ronan tells her now. His hand comes out of his pocket and caresses her cheek. "You always were my muse."

One of the great gifts of turning thirty is acquiring a certain level of immunity to the bullshit that would have affected you very differently at twenty. Like surviving an infection and developing antibodies. Cat almost flinches away from the touch that once upon a time would have had her telling Ronan she didn't mind if he didn't have a condom, and she fixes him with a polite but tight-lipped smile.

"I need to go find my boyfriend," she says. "It was good to see you, Ro."

Ronan blinks in surprise, clearly having expected their conversation to go in a more predictable direction based on every precedent Cat has ever set. She manages to restrain herself from punching the air, *Breakfast Club* style, as she brushes past the man who broke her heart in search of the man currently pretending to have stolen it. She spots the boy with the tray of drinks first and begins to make a beeline for him, then stops in her tracks when she sees who he is talking to. Or rather, who is talking *at* him.

Julia Vincent, aka the mother of the bride.

Cat would not describe herself as being genuinely intimidated by many people—her side hustle relies on her being able to approach pretty much anyone—but every time she meets Louisa's mother, she gets the distinct impression that she has been thoroughly evaluated, like an antique or a racehorse, and deemed to be an unworthy investment.

Julia appears to be berating the poor young man for some slight or other, although any casual observer might assume she is simply asking for the time. It is only Cat's wealth of experience with this particular family that leads her to believe otherwise. Appearances are everything to the Vincents. It would never do for the matriarch to lose her temper at her daughter's engagement party. But Julia is *also* not the sort to let any kind of misdeed go unpunished, no matter how minor.

The poor thing. He only looks about eighteen. Cat remembers the nightmare customers she had to put up with in her first waitressing job and can't quite decide which she would rather serve less—rowdy older men trying to look down her top, or Julia Vincent, looking down at her full stop.

She should intervene, really. Try to distract the monster so the terrified young villager can flee. Or she could turn around and just try to find the bar. She isn't here to make waves, after all. Maybe drawing less attention to herself is the right idea. But before Cat can decide on her next move, somebody else steps into her eye line toward Julia and the waiter.

It's Jake.

No! she almost exclaims. *You don't know what you're getting yourself into!*

She hoped to make it through the gauntlet of prewedding celebrations without having to face Julia, but she isn't about to throw Jake to the wolves after he just proved so game a partner. Not that he looks like he's in any immediate danger. In the handful of seconds it takes Cat to close the remaining distance between them, Jake appears to have introduced himself and kissed Julia's cheek. More shockingly, she has *let* him. And the young waiter has seized his moment to retreat.

"No," says Jake as Cat reaches them, a shocked expression on his face. "I genuinely thought you were Louisa's sister." Julia giggles coquettishly.

"Cat!" Julia says in greeting, in a tone almost bordering on genial. "I believe this tall drink of water is yours?" She pats Jake's forearm with an air of approval, then lets her hand linger there.

Thirsty old mare, Cat thinks, smiling and confirming that yes, the charming young gentleman is with her. Julia's hand doesn't stray from Jake's arm. In fact, she is now giving his muscles a light squeeze, like she's picking out fruit in a supermarket. Jake's smile remains as genteel as ever, but Cat is sure his eyes are screaming *Help me*.

"It's lovely to see you again, Julia," she says. "I was sorry to hear about you and Mr. Vincent." While Louisa has called her mother by her first name for as long as Cat has known her, she only ever refers to her father as "Daddy," and Cat is still uncertain as to his actual first name.

"These things happen," says Julia, her smile tightening.

"Of course," says Cat. "It's no reflection on you at all. I just wanted to say that I think you're conducting yourself with remarkable grace."

"I beg your pardon?"

"Well, I just mean that if *my* ex were bragging about his new girlfriend at a party where I was in attendance," Cat ventures, "I would be livid. You're a better woman than me!"

"New girlfriend." Julia says this as a statement, not a question. All warmth has left her face now, and as Cat predicted (or more truthfully, as she *hoped*), she lets go of Jake's arm. "Cat," she says by way of farewell, and stalks away, waving a bejeweled hand to catch the attention of some family friend or other.

"That'll keep her occupied for a while," Cat says.

"Hunting down her ex-husband's new sweetheart?" Jake asks.

"Finding out that no such sweetheart exists," she clarifies. "At least, not to my knowledge. But Julia will spend the rest of the night interrogating her and Mr. Vincent's shared acquaintances, convinced that they're covering for him. It should keep her off our backs until we are safely back on dry land."

"You are incurably dishonest," Jake says. "I love it."

"I think myself more of a knight in shining armor," she protests. "Did I or did I not just rescue you from a dragon?"

"And I am truly thankful."

"Nah, it was the least I could do. You threw yourself on her sword so that harangued waiter could live."

"I thought she was a dragon."

"Dragons can have swords, Jake. And piranhas can be sharks."

"I believe you. I think." He shakes his head. "I just can't stand the way rich people talk to others. Like if you're wearing a uniform, you hardly even count as a human being."

"Whatever she was scolding him for probably wasn't even his fault," Cat says. "I imagine anyone in a waistcoat holding a tray looks exactly the same to her. I'm sorry you have to be here."

Jake puts his hands in his pockets and holds his head back as if to get a proper look at her.

"What?" she says.

"Nothing." He removes one hand from his jeans and offers her his arm. "I just remembered I owe you a drink."

"All right then." She links her arm around his, and they walk in unison toward the bar. "Just . . . No more champagne."

"Fine by me. I've never really cared for the stuff."

"You could have fooled me the other day," she says. "I believe you were the one to open that second bottle."

"Would you have preferred I let you drink alone?" He frowns down at her. "That would have been downright unchivalrous."

Cat leans into him for a second, little more than a playful nudge, then freezes. Jake takes another step, then lurches back, anchored to the spot by her arm still entangled in his.

"What is it?" he asks.

You're married, that's what.

Cat wants desperately to ask him what his wife thinks of their arrangement, if his wife even *knows* about what they're planning. But then one question leads to another, and another. Does she know about his sideline at the hotel, or is she blissfully ignorant of how he makes money? What does *she* do for a living? What's she like? Is she pretty? Or funny? Cat hopes, at the very least, she is kind.

There is so much she wants to ask Jake, but this is hardly the time or place, and so she forces her questions back down before they can bubble up of their own accord.

"Nothing," she says. "Still getting my sea legs."

They haven't quite reached the bar when they are intercepted by Louisa.

"There you are!" she exclaims, grabbing Cat by the arm and dragging her—and by extension, Jake—inside, where Darcy, Harper, and a rather worse-for-wear Olivia are already gathered. Stephen appears a moment later with Freddie.

"We have some exciting news," Louisa tells them. "Just for the inner circle."

The fact that Louisa refers to her bridal party as if it is some kind of secret society or the upper echelon of a cult doesn't even strike Cat as strange.

"*Another* speech?" Jake says under his breath, so that only Cat can hear.

"Think of it as endurance training," Cat whispers. "For the wedding."

"Oh my god," Olivia slurs. "You're pregnant."

Louisa fixes her with an ice-cold shut-the-fuck-up stare, but it's too late—the small group is already vibrating with potential energy.

"For real?" Harper asks.

"Is that the reason for the short engagement?" says Priya.

"You don't waste any time, mate!" Freddie claps Stephen on the back.

"I am *not pregnant*," Louisa hisses, and they fall silent. She exhales slowly, and the sudden, angry flush of red leaves her high, delicate cheeks as quickly as it appeared.

"We wanted to tell you we found a venue," Stephen chimes in rather lamely.

"Yes," Louisa says coolly. "Thanks for ruining the announcement, Liv."

Olivia has the good sense to look sheepish, and she mimes zipping her mouth closed.

"Where did you manage to get at such short notice?" Priya asks, her fairy-tale enthusiasm waning for the first time.

"Yeah, where are we talking?" Harper asks. "The Ritz? The Shard?"

"God, can you *imagine?*" Louisa snorts. "No. We've managed to get something a little more on-brand."

Puzzled looks are exchanged.

"You all know art is my truest passion," Louisa says. "Well," she adds, looking at Stephen, "a close second." This, at least, Cat can corroborate. When Louisa actually bothered to show up for her classes at uni, she was one of the most knowledgeable, engaged students. She might have cribbed every talking point from Cat's notes, but she made them her own, like an actress taking her turn as Medea or Clytemnestra.

"Anyway, the venue will reflect that," Louisa says. "And blow every other summer wedding out of the proverbial water, if I do say so myself."

"Oh my god, will you just *tell* us," says Cat more harshly than intended. Louisa has always had this tendency to pontificate. Fortunately, Louisa interprets her impatience as enthusiasm, leaning in and waiting for the others to do the same before finally saying: "The National Gallery."

Priya and Olivia gasp. Harper utters a muted, Keanu-esque "Whoa." Darcy squeals and clutches Louisa's hand.

"You got it?" she asks. "Last time we spoke you said it wasn't a done deal yet."

"My father had to take somebody to lunch," Stephen says, "but yes! It's ours."

"Brilliant! Just brilliant." Freddie pats Stephen on the back so vigorously he winds him. "Which one's that, again?"

"That's . . ." Cat searches for words. Where did they all go? "Unbelievable," she finally manages.

"Right?" Louisa says. "Isn't it just so perfect?"

Cat, stunned, can only nod, then, amid the cooing, excuses herself and practically sprints out onto the deck. She turns away from the crowded prow, making her way around the side of the boat until she is far enough away from the music and the people that she can be certain she is alone. She grabs on to the railing and leans out over the water, letting the brisk breeze whistle in her ears and cool her burning forehead. Before her, the city twinkles as they glide past, windows and streetlights gleaming like fireflies against the darkening blue of the summer dusk.

"Fuck *you*," she says to all of London, and to one person in particular.

Eleven

Cat didn't date much at uni. There were plenty of guys who expressed interest, partly because she was friends with Louisa, and partly because heterosexual twenty-year-old boys will ask out any girl who stands in front of them for longer than ten seconds. But Cat had a scholarship that depended on her maintaining excellent grades, and so if it came to choosing between a night of pound party shots and dancing to Tinchy Stryder, and staying home with a biography of Francis Bacon, well, in her mind, there was no choice.

The one exception came in second year, when Ronan approached her after a seminar and asked her if she'd like to go for a pint sometime. Cat had been about to decline, when Louisa interjected and accepted on her behalf.

"You're living like a nun and it's getting a bit weird, darling," she said. "Besides. He's fit, don't you think?"

He was, as it happened. Tall and lanky but in a way that suggested his body under those baggy, artsy sweaters would be firm with lean muscle. His hair flopped like something out of a nineties romantic comedy. He smoked rollies, which Cat found kind of gross and appealing at the same time, and he held very strong opinions about Cubism. He was pretentious but cute, and she would later learn he had a birthmark shaped like an eyebrow on his inner thigh. She would nickname it Frida.

The night of their first date, after who-knows-how-many hours drinking cider and talking about the kind of shit that second-year art students think deeply profound, Ronan insisted on walking Cat home. When they reached her front door, he kissed her until her face felt slightly singed from his stubble, then winked, said, "To be continued," and sauntered off. He seemed awfully pleased with himself, Cat thought. Then again, she did find her knees a little shaky as she unlocked the front door, so perhaps some of that cockiness was justified.

"You dirty stopout!" Louisa exclaimed from the kitchen the second she entered the hallway. "Just one drink, she said! I'll be back in an hour, she said!" Cat groaned. "Tea?" Louisa continued. "I want all the gory details. Usual spot, I take it."

At the start of term they had opted out of student housing and moved in together with another girl, Karolina, in a terrace house off campus. Louisa took the master bedroom, of course, and Karolina slept in the roomy attic conversion, leaving Cat with the bedroom at the back of the house. It got next to no light during the day, but the window frame *was* wide and broad enough to sit in, and Cat whiled away countless afternoons in that drafty nook, blanket over her shoulders, a mug of tea cradled in her hands, book laid open on the sill in front of her.

It was to this window that Louisa followed her now, carrying two steaming cups, a packet of custard creams nestled under her arm. Louisa's room might have been the social hub of the house, the place where they drank wine and put on makeup and watched *Sex and the City*, but every now and then Louisa would venture to "the slums," as she called it, and no matter how ridiculously small the gesture, Cat appreciated it.

"So," said Louisa, folding her willowy limbs in on themselves until she was squeezed onto the opposite end of the window seat, "is it love?" Before Cat could answer, Louisa dug a packet of menthols and a lighter out of her pocket and gestured for her to open the window. This was another marker of Louisa's visits to the rear of the house. She never smoked in her own room.

"He's nice," Cat said. "He kept calling himself a Tracey Emin fanboy, which I think means he wanted to let me know he respects women, but hers was the one female artist's name he could come up with on the spot."

"I'm just happy to see you venturing out of hibernation and engaging in the local ecosystem's dating rituals," Louisa said between puffs. "I was starting to think you were a lesbian. Or even worse, celibate." Cat wrinkled her nose at this casual homophobia—it would be another couple of years before Louisa started acquiring followers on Instagram and began editing the thoughts that made it out of her mouth.

"Well, I don't think I'll end up marrying Ronan, but a second date isn't out of the question," Cat said. "He's *tall*, isn't he? Makes you wonder if everything is . . ."

"Proportionate?"

"Exactly."

"I support this," Louisa declared. "We're not the sort to marry the first guy we meet at uni, darling. I mean, if Prince Harry went here, it might be a different story."

"We're nineteen—that's too young to be talking about marriage full stop," Cat said, blowing on her tea.

"You're the one who brought it up!"

"Barely." Cat frowned. "I just don't understand how so many

girls our age are already thinking about what they'll be doing ten, twenty years from now."

"Oh, come on. Be honest. We've all been thinking about our wedding day since we were a *lot* younger than we are now."

"Sure, when you're seven and you're wearing a veil made from loo roll and marrying your poster of Jeff Buckley."

"Who?"

"But it just feels silly now that we're practically adults to be planning a wedding to somebody you haven't met yet."

Louisa's brow furrowed as she neared the end of her cigarette. She swiftly removed another from the pack, lighting it using the embers from the first, then tossing the butt out of the window. "Are you saying you haven't given any thought to it? At all?"

Cat gazed resolutely out of the window, and Louisa reached across to slap her on the knee.

"I knew it! You *have*!"

"Hardly. Not really."

Louisa fixed her with an imperious look, and Cat knew she had strayed into conversational territory where one of them held seniority.

"Indulge me," Louisa said. "I know you were practically raised by wolves, but just imagine, if you can, your dream wedding. You know mine would be at the Wolseley. Where would yours be?"

"I—"

"Close your eyes and visualize it," Louisa said, squeezing her own shut. "Anywhere in the world. Anywhere at all. Where is it?"

Cat didn't have to close her eyes. She knew.

"The National Gallery," she said quietly.

Louisa's eyes popped open in surprise. "That's certainly grander than I was expecting," she said, impressed. "I thought you'd say the Yorkshire moors or something."

"I'm from Cheshire," Cat said, correcting her for the hun-dredth time, "not Yorkshire."

"Why the gallery?"

Cat fixed her stare out of the window again before speaking.

"My mum used to take me there," she said. "Each year, we'd go on a day trip to London during the summer holidays. Get on a coach at the crack of dawn, arrive in time for breakfast. We always went to the National Gallery. The Portrait Gallery too. At first, I loved it because it was so exciting, so different from home. Then I started properly paying attention. Really *saw* the art, the million and one ways these people had found to show how the world looked through their eyes. That was the place where I first realized I wanted to be an artist, that it was even possible. And . . . it was the last place we went together, Mum and me, after her diagnosis. It was one of the last good days she had."

Louisa reached out again, only this time her touch on Cat's knee was gentle. "What a perfect way to honor her," she said. "Just perfect."

Twelve

Cat doesn't know how long she has been standing alone watching the water rush by below, or if she is shaking from rage or from the cold. She isn't even here, not really. She's curled up in a window ten years ago, sharing something precious against her better judgment. And she is so, so angry. Not at Louisa, but at herself, for caring so much. Cat has no plans to get married. It's not like men are queuing up to ask her. And she could never afford the National Gallery even if a wedding *were* in her future. Why does it hurt so badly to know that Louisa, who always gets what she wants, is getting this one additional thing? A thing Cat isn't certain she even wants in the first place?

She doesn't hear Jake approach over the roaring of the Thames. She just feels the comfortable, warm weight of a jacket being laid over her trembling shoulders.

"You all right?" he asks. "You did quite the vanishing act there."

"Oh, shit." Cat turns and leans back against the high railing so she is facing him. "I'm sorry. I didn't mean to leave you with them like that."

"That's not what I meant," he says. "I'm a big boy, Cat. I can handle making small talk with tipsy party guests. That's literally my job. I just wanted to make sure you're okay. What happened?"

Cat can't think of a way to explain it to him that won't make her sound stupid, or petty, or both.

"I just needed some air," she says. She can tell right away from the look he gives her that he isn't buying it, but he doesn't press her.

"How's this for an idea?" he says, putting his hands on the railing next to her. "We stay here, out of everybody's way, until the boat docks, or moors, or whatever it is that boats do."

"That is a capital idea," Cat says. "And then we make a run for it?"

"I don't think that would fly with Louisa," he says. "We'll thank her, ever so graciously, for a killer party. And then we will disembark."

"And *then* run."

"Sure." He smiles out at the water. "Just let me stretch first. I've seen how fast you can move."

"Hardly."

"You positively *scarpered*, Cat. Still. I suppose it's good to know you can make a quick getaway."

"What kind of master criminal would I be otherwise?" she asks, and he turns his smile on her, and for a moment the warmth from the blazer around her shoulders seems to extend into the depths of her stomach, where it sputters and glows like the remains of an untended fire. Then, because she doesn't trust herself to say anything, she forces herself to turn back around to watch the city as it goes by, and Jake does the same.

A little over an hour later, the *Maiden* deposits Stephen and Louisa's guests back onto the length of the South Bank from which they departed. All warmth and light have gone now, and Cat slides her arms down into the sleeves of the blue jacket as she and Jake stroll eastward. Their comfortable silence lasts for three whole minutes before Cat can take it no longer.

"Can I ask you something?" she says. "Something a bit personal?"

"Ask away." Jake holds his hands out, as if to indicate that he has nothing to hide.

"What does she think of all this?"

Jake's brows rise up in the middle. "She?"

"Yes."

"She . . . who?"

Is this guy serious? Cat rolls her eyes and reaches out to grab Jake's left hand.

"Your wife," she says. "What will she say when you come home tonight, not wearing your wedding ring?"

Jake's confusion intensifies momentarily, then realization seems to dawn, and he laughs.

"Oh, *that*," he says. "I wouldn't sweat it."

"Not exactly the reassurance I was after, if I'm being honest," Cat says more primly than she would like. "I just know that if *my* husband were running around town hatching schemes with another woman, I wouldn't be too happy about it."

"'Running around town'? 'Hatching schemes'?" Jake smirks. "What is this, *Bugsy Malone*?"

He sees she is unamused, and he stops and turns to her, his expression becoming earnest.

"Look," he says. "There is no *she*. I just wear a wedding ring at work to ward off drunk older ladies at the bar who try to give me their room keys. I honestly forget I have it on half the time. I should have expected you to clock it. I should have explained."

"Oh." Cat narrows her eyes. "So you're really not married?"

"If I had a wife at home," he says, "I would never have kissed you. Sorry about that, by the way. We were just doing such a great job improvising, bouncing off each other . . . I got carried away. It definitely helped sell our story, but it won't happen again."

"Well. All right then," Cat says, processing all of this information as quickly as her spinning head will allow. And now Jake is *smirking* at her again.

"What?" she demands.

"Nothing," he says. "Just . . . A bit presumptuous, isn't it? Assuming my nonexistent wife would feel threatened by you. You're not half full of yourself, Cat Bellamy." His use of her full name stokes the fire Cat has been ignoring since they left the boat.

"Says the man who kissed *me*," she shoots back. "The man who is apparently *so* desirable he has to fake a marriage just so the cougars will give him some breathing room."

"Two words," he says. "Julia. Vincent."

"Ugh." She rolls her eyes again. "Fine. Touché."

"But just for the record," he says, "the only fake relationship I'm in right now is with you."

"And don't you forget it."

A moment later they reach Waterloo Tube station and pause in the entrance.

"Oh, bugger, sorry," she says, starting to shrug out of the comically large jacket. "You must be freezing. Let me give you this back."

He looks at her quizzically, then laughs.

"Don't worry about it," he says. "It's not mine."

Cat thinks back, with more clarity than she should, given the amount of wine she and Jake kept sneaking back onto their quiet side of the boat, to when they met on the South Bank earlier tonight. How the blue of Jake's shirt highlighted the smooth richness of his dark skin. The open collar, the rolled-up sleeves, the

Rolex. Of course he wasn't wearing a suit jacket. A warm evening had been forecast (on dry land, anyway). It was Stephen and Freddie and their cohort who were decked out in near-identical royal blue.

"You *didn't*," she says accusingly but also with delight in her voice.

"You looked cold" is Jake's only response.

After a moment's thought, Cat begins to rifle through the jacket's pockets.

"Uncle Jonty is not going to be amused," she says, holding up a driving license. Then she opens up the soft, supple leather wallet and a familiar thrill reverberates through her. There is easily three hundred quid in cash here.

"Looks like this partnership is already bearing fruit," Jake observes.

"It would seem so," she agrees.

"Speaking of which . . ."

Cat lets him continue, still pretending to count the money in her hands, unsure of what exactly he might be about to say on the subject of this little double act of theirs. Probably something along the lines of: *That kiss wasn't really necessary.* Or: *Louisa is very beautiful, isn't she?*

"I have a better plan," he says.

Cat looks up at him.

"Excuse me?"

"For the job," he adds. "Well, more of an amendment to the original plan. Which is still a *great* plan. No offense intended."

"Oh, out with it." She bats his arm lightly and then slips half of Jonty's cash into his hand. She keeps her expression neutral, withdrawing her fingers from his the moment he takes it.

"I was thinking," Jake says. "There's a lower-risk way of doing this."

"I'm all for reducing risk," Cat says. In addition to researching the value of the Tsarina online, she may also have looked up the maximum sentence that a crime like this can incur in the United Kingdom. On the bright side, should things go sideways, she wouldn't have to worry about finding a place to live for a very, very long time.

"It's that Elijah," Jake continues. "He never leaves Louisa's side. Looks like he's probably killed at least one person and knows a hundred other ways to do it. If there's even a chance of him catching us in the act . . ."

"We knew Louisa had security," Cat replies. "And you're *good*. You told me you could do this."

"I'm good, but I'm also trying to be smart."

"Fine. So what's your amendment?"

"Just something that occurred to me tonight. About weddings. What usually happens on the big day."

Cat stops and grabs Jake's wrist. "Freddie!" She almost yells it.

Jake grins. "Exactly. The best man always holds on to the rings before the ceremony, right? And no offense to dear Freddie, but . . ."

"But he's as thick as mince."

"He makes an easier mark than the bride, in any event. Fewer eyes on him."

Cat is annoyed she didn't think of it herself sooner. Freddie is cut from the same expensive cloth as the lads she saw Jake conning at the hotel: cushioned from life's hardships and all the more trusting for it.

"You're right," she says. "It's the smarter play."

"And to think, you only brought me tonight to look pretty."

"Okay, you can stop being *quite* so pleased with yourself. We still have a lot of work to do. Did you get a look at the ring?"

"I did." Jake pulls his phone out of his pocket and shows Cat an array of surreptitiously but competently captured, surprisingly high-resolution photos of Louisa's left hand. The plan already underwent an amendment before they boarded the boat; they agreed that stealing the false Tsarina prior to the wedding would place Louisa on high alert. An alternative approach is required.

"These, along with everything she put on Instagram, will be enough for us to create a replica of our own," he says. "The only question now is, how exactly do we manage that?"

"About that," Cat says, pulling the pilfered jacket closer around her. "I think I have an idea."

Thirteen

A few days later, Cat strides into the foyer of Velocity PR's offices. It is barely nine a.m., but she already feels a warm prickle against the back of her neck and the beginnings of perspiration under her cheerful floral blouse. It is the heat, she tells herself, and the exertion from carrying this box. It is most definitely *not* nerves.

As she walks toward the front desk, she hears a second set of footsteps echoing behind her: Jake, emerging from the revolving doors far enough behind her that no onlooker would think they are together. She sees him in the mirror that spans the rear wall of the foyer. He is dressed unseasonably in a buttoned-up peacoat and carries a leather weekend bag.

"Good morning!" she says brightly to the security guard behind the desk. She lets him take in the baby-pink cardboard box in her arms. It is roughly the size and shape of the television she had in her bedroom as a teenager, a cube that is more awkward than heavy.

"Treats," Cat says by way of explanation. "I have a meeting with Velocity on floor ten." He nods, then wearily drags himself up from his seat and out from behind the desk, still holding his polystyrene cup of coffee, and indicates for her to follow him to a set of turnstiles between the lobby and the lifts, similar to the ones at Tube stations. Cat used to be able to swipe herself in using her guest pass, but no more.

The guard scans his keycard and the gates slide open. Cat thanks him and walks toward the lift, stooping slightly to punch the call button with her elbow. The guard begins to walk sullenly back toward his desk, where Cat suspects he is watching Netflix, but Jake bumps straight into him. Tepid coffee splashes all over both of them.

"Sorry, man!" Jake says, holding the guard by one shoulder to steady him. "That was totally my fault. Wasn't looking where I was going."

The guard huffs, dabbing uselessly at the damp brown stain on the front of his shirt, and looks like he is about to berate Jake. Then he takes in the chic coat, the leather bag, and seems to think better of it. Jake looks like one of those dressed-down CEOs heading off somewhere expensive for the weekend, and the guard no doubt is calculating what might happen if he were to yell at one of the people who pays rent on the pricey offices upstairs.

"It's fine," he eventually grumbles. He digs a tissue from his pocket and continues to swab at his ruined uniform, while Jake scans himself through the barrier with the keycard he just lifted right out of the guard's hand. The second he is through, he drops the card and, with a discreet nudge of his foot, sends it sliding back across the glossy lobby floor, where it comes to a stop under the guard's shoe. The guard, assuming he dropped it in the kerfuffle, hastily stoops to retrieve it.

The entire operation takes a matter of seconds, and Jake joins

Cat in the elevator just before a soft *ding* signals the doors are about to close.

"Not bad," she says once they are alone, faintly smiling at him in the reflective surface of the doors in front of them. "Not bad at all."

"The coffee was a stroke of luck," Jake says, unbuttoning his coat. "It distracted him." He takes the peacoat off, folds it quickly, and stashes it in the holdall.

It hits Cat now more than it has before exactly what they are doing. The ruse, the disguise—they are about to attempt their first job together. A bona fide *heist*. This is a step up from shell games and picking pockets. Cat rubs the back of her neck, trying to dispel the anxious itch she still feels there.

"Hey," Jake says, catching her eye in the metallic mirror of the lift doors. "Breathe. You've got this."

"Is it that obvious I'm freaking out?" she asks.

"If you told me you weren't at least a little bit nervous, I'd think you were lying. This is a little out of both our comfort zones."

"Are *you* nervous?"

Jake purses his lips for a moment before answering.

"Every single time," he admits. "There's always a millisecond when part of me thinks, *This is all going to go horribly wrong*, or *They're going to find you out*. And every time, it's my job to ignore that voice. To convince myself that it's going to go exactly as planned."

"A confidence man who believes his own tricks? Sounds dangerous."

Jake smiles ruefully. "A good con artist's first mark is always himself."

They say nothing else for a moment, simply look at each other in the mirrored doors, until they reach the fifth floor, and their reflections split apart.

"My stop," Jake says. He steps out of the lift, turns back, and says: "Break a leg."

The last thing Cat sees before the doors shut again is Jake's smile, and then she is moving again, up to the tenth floor.

"Cat!" Mikhail greets her as she steps out of the lift, bounding as always, and appears genuinely thrilled to see her. It's almost as if he *didn't* fire her the last time they saw each other.

"Hi! So good to see you!" Cat beams. She called to set up this meeting earlier in the week. Mikhail believes her to have taken a freelance design gig with Tatin, an extremely popular new bakery in Soho that always has a queue out the door. Cat insinuated that her new client might be in need of PR representation and that she would be more than happy to set up a meeting.

"Unfortunately there was some flour-based emergency this morning," she says apologetically, "so Tatin has sent me in their stead. With Cronuts!" She holds up the pastel-colored box, which she stood in line for and spent a good portion of Uncle Jonty's money on first thing this morning.

"Oh, that's a pity," says Mikhail, visibly crestfallen for a second before adopting his usual wide-eyed smile. "Still, what a pleasure to have you back in the fold! Let's . . ." He trails off, gesturing for her to follow him into the open-plan office, where she deposits the box of baked goods in the kitchen area.

"I've had Charmaine working on pitches," Mikhail continues eagerly. "I suppose we could always run them past you, and you can relay them on to your friends at Tatin." He snaps his fingers and beckons Charmaine, an impeccably groomed blonde who looks like she belongs on *Selling Sunset*, to join them.

"Of course," Cat says. "Although, it seems only fair to tell you, they're rather enamored of another agency at present."

"Oh?" If Mikhail's aura is usually that of a golden retriever, at present that dog has just been kicked.

"Yeah," she says, drawing out the single, breathy syllable. "Darcy Wong." She lowers her voice to a conspiratorial tone. "They *really* like the idea of going with her. She's a dear friend of mine, actually, and *very* good at what she does. But I told them, I said I worked with Velocity for years and they are the best of the best, trust me, you're going to want to give them this contract."

She's playing with Mikhail. He's on the hook and has no idea that there is no trendy, buzzy client at the end of this conversation. That these are all just distraction tactics, while Jake seeks out what they're really here for. The fact that Cat gets to turn the tables on their last conversation is just sweetener.

As if on cue, the lift doors open and Cat sees Jake enter the office in full caretaker drag—dark blue jumpsuit, cap pulled low over his face—pushing the cleaning trolley he found on the fifth floor, where all of the janitorial supplies are kept and the CCTV has been broken for weeks. Somewhat predictably—depressingly so, in fact—nobody in the office pays him any mind as he begins to empty wastepaper baskets into the bin bag on the cart. What he said on the boat was right. Put somebody in the right kind of uniform and they might as well be invisible.

"Well, of course, I mean, yes," Mikhail stammers. "Robust competition is what drives all innovation, after all. It's just . . . you *did* rather lead me to believe that Velocity was a shoo-in."

"I apologize if I gave you that impression," says Cat, who has never felt less sorry about anything in her life. From the corner of her eye, she sees Jake slip into the storage room at the end of the office, unobserved by any of what Mikhail refers to as his "Ve-lociteers."

"Oh, it's quite all right," he says, the idiotic grin returning. "In fact, can I take a moment to say, it's lovely to see you taking such initiative. Bagging a new freelance gig in such a short time and using your new connections to help out your old family here at Big V . . ." He places a hand earnestly over his heart. "I'm proud of you."

I am five years older and a good inch taller than you, you conde-scending squirt, she thinks, bowing her head graciously.

"I have to say," he adds, "it's a pleasant surprise. I'll admit, I was slightly worried when we let you go. Part of me thought you might give up the freelance creative game altogether and the next time I saw you would be across the counter at Starbucks."

Cat doesn't know which she finds more repellent—that this man-child presumes to know her or that he thinks a job in the service industry is humiliating.

"You know what, Mikhail?" she says. "Screw you."

"Pardon?" Mikhail genuinely looks like nobody has ever spo-ken to him this way, which is just going to make it all the more enjoyable.

"Screw. You." Cat raises her voice so the rest of the office can hear. "Do you have *any* idea how many times you have been truly, outrageously rude and patronizing to me? To everybody here? You are a privileged little twerp whose entire business empire was possible only because your rich parents gave you some seed money to get you out of the house. You're about as self-made as a ham sandwich."

This is not strictly part of the plan she and Jake put together. But now that she's started, Cat doesn't know how to stop. She real-izes she has been storing up every criticism and condescending remark Mikhail ever cast her way, letting them ferment. Given the chance to spit them back at him, she can't help herself.

"Cat," he says in a low voice, smile rigidly plastered on, "I think that's about enough."

"Oh really?" she says, gathering steam. "Do you want to know what *I* think is enough? How about paying your freelancers a half-decent rate instead of farming work out to content farms on Tenner? How about setting appropriate office hours instead of emailing people at midnight and expecting them to reply? How about dressing like a *grown-up*"—she jabs a finger in the direction of his millennial-pink hoodie—"instead of coming into the office decked out like a teenager and expecting anybody to respect you?"

She doesn't even stand behind that last point, but she's been holding on to this anger so tightly that now it's unspooling too fast and she can barely keep up. More and more people are looking up from their desks and turning toward her, eyes widening. Good! Let them stare. This is her "I'm mad as hell, and I'm not going to take it anymore" moment. With a bit of luck, this is *all* they will remember about today.

"Cat," Mikhail says, his tone careful, like he's talking somebody down from a ledge, "I'm sensing a lot of unresolved resentment. Why don't we step into my office and we can—"

"No!" Cat grabs the box of Cronuts from the counter and upends it, sending an avalanche of pastries tumbling out onto the carpet, from which a small mushroom cloud of powdered sugar then rises. "I *won't* go with you! I *refuse* to be silenced!"

Mikhail, Charmaine, and the rest of the Velocity team are all regarding her, and the scene she is making, in silent horror. Behind them, she sees Jake return from the storeroom and roll his cart briskly back down the hallway to the elevators.

"Okay," she says, her voice returning to a normal pitch. "Good talk."

And she marches out of the office for what she can safely assume is the last time, an empty pink cardboard box dangling from her right hand. The atmosphere in the room is charged as she makes her exit, turning the corner to where Jake is holding the lift, and she allows herself to fantasize that at least one disgruntled employee will admire her candor.

"What the hell was that?" Jake asks as soon as the doors close. For a split second, the strained sound of his voice makes her think he is angry, but when she looks up at him, she sees the tensed chin and realizes he is trying to keep himself from laughing.

"We agreed that my role was to create a diversion," she says breathlessly. Her voice will probably be quite hoarse tomorrow, but it will have been worth it.

"You played your role to perfection," Jake informs her. "I didn't know you were such a good actress."

"That was all real," says Cat. She feels light, giddy even, as she turns her gaze on the cart. "Did you get it?"

"Sure did." Jake unhooks the refuse sack from the trolley and pulls down the sides, revealing the bulky, heavy item resting on the base of the cart. Between the two of them, they transfer it into the pink Cronut box, and Jake rapidly changes out of his overalls, donning the peacoat and finally placing the box in the hardy leather bag.

They planned this next part ahead of time too. They can't be seen leaving together, so Jake stays in the lift when Cat gets out at ground level, where the increasingly tetchy guard escorts her out of the building. It turns out Mikhail *did* call down to make sure she goes quietly this time.

Once out of the lobby, Cat pretends to storm off, and the security guard watches her go through the glass frontage. When she is out of sight, she takes a left, and then another, until she is in the alley standing in front of the ramp that leads to the building's underground car park. Any second now, Jake will be getting out of the lift at the parking level and making his way out to meet her.

Any. Second. Now.

When one minute passes, and then another, a small niggle of doubt begins to burrow into Cat's chest. The questions she's been trying not to ask, about how well she really knows Jake and if she can trust a man she met through mutual thievery in a bar.

"Ignore that voice," she reminds herself out loud. "Everything is going to be fine. It's all going to turn out exactly as we planned."

When Jake appears out of the shadows of the car park a moment later, she feels a rush of relief and can't resist throwing her arms around him in excitement.

"We did it!" she says.

"We did it!" he agrees. "And you are *strong*."

"Sorry." She lets go, looks to her left and then her right, and adds: "Might I suggest we get the hell out of here?"

"I know a spot we can hide," Jake says, grabbing her hand and pulling her along with him.

The Oceanic is as dead as always when they arrive, barreling through the lounge area, around the bar, and into the room at the back, where they inspect their newly stolen goods. It is a state-of-the-art 3D printer, purchased by Mikhail on a whim for a client project a year ago and promptly forgotten about. The fine layer of dust on its glossy black casing leads Cat to believe that it will be weeks if not months before anyone at Velocity notices it is missing, by which point enough time will have elapsed that nobody will make a connection between a stolen piece of equipment and her little outburst.

"And you know your way around this thing?" Jake asks, looking at her uncertainly.

"I'm one of the only people at that place who ever used it," she says.

"All right then." He grins, and Cat could swear his eyes actually *twinkle*. "Let's make a diamond."

Fourteen

"I thought you said you knew how this thing works."

"I *do* know how it works. Just . . . don't rush me."

Getting the 3D printer out of Velocity, it turns out, was the easy part. Cat reminds Jake that there's more to making an indistinguishable replica of a priceless diamond than simply feeding some photos into a computer program. She is just having some issues remembering the complete process, if the constant beeping and flashing "input error" is any indication.

"Why does a PR agency have pricey tech like this just lying around gathering dust, anyway?" Jake asks as Cat fiddles with the virtual model of the ring she has created on her laptop.

"Three-D printing was going to change the world a couple of years ago," she says. "I suppose it still is; I mean, you see the occasional headline about geniuses creating new organs for transplants or printing meat that vegans can eat. Mikhail insisted that the agency invest in the most advanced unit out there, only to immediately consign it to the cupboard of forgotten gadgets. But for that one project, I was the one who got training." Cat finishes putting in the new specifications and exports the job wirelessly to the printer.

Beep! Input error.

"It shows," says Jake.

She scowls at him and tries again.

"What are your plans after this?" he asks.

"After I get this thing to work?" She shrugs. "Probably go get a falafel."

"No," Jake says, "after the job, I mean. What are you going to do when we've got the diamond and you're a millionaire?"

"Well, we need to find a way of actually selling the thing first," she says, crouching and squinting at the printer display.

"I'm looking into that," says Jake. "Just think hypothetically. We've pulled off the job, we've moved the ring, we're both rich. What do you do?"

Cat rests on her haunches and thinks about it for a moment.

"I don't know," she says. "Relax on an island somewhere, enjoying my wealth, probably."

"An island? Really?"

"Sure. I feel like most heist stories end with cocktails on a white-sanded beach, usually somewhere near the equator with no extradition treaty."

Jake doesn't say anything.

"What?" she asks. "My post-jewel-theft retirement plans aren't up to your standards?"

"It's not that," he says. "I just can't quite picture a version of you that knows how to relax."

"Should I be offended by that?" Cat frowns. "I get the distinct impression I should be offended by that. And I hardly think that's true. I mean, how many nights have I spent sitting at your bar with a martini?"

"Yes, while swindling customers or planning this job. Face it, Cat. You're a workaholic."

Beep! Input error.

Cat scoffs and turns her attention back to her laptop on the floor next to her, determined to get it right this time.

"You don't know what you're talking about," she mutters.

Except. Well. Cat tries to cast her mind back to the last time she wasn't preoccupied by rent, or work, or her increasingly felonious side hustle, and draws a blank.

If Cat no longer had to scrape and claw her way into freelance gigs, if for the first time in her life she didn't have to worry about money, what would she do instead? What could her life look like? She realizes, with some consternation, that she has not actually thought this far ahead. If she had to think of an answer on the spot, she supposes she would finally have time to paint. But when was the last time she even opened her sketchpad?

Beep! Input accepted.

"Well, thank fuck for that," she whispers, then looks triumphantly up at Jake. "See? I told you I knew how to work this thing."

Jake helps her to her feet. "I never doubted you," he says as the printer whirs to life, and the upper section of the device lowers into the vat of frankly gross-looking resin that fills the glass tray, and production begins on their faux Tsarina. The Tsarinot, as they have already started calling it.

"And you?" Cat asks. "What are your grand plans?"

"I'd like to get my mum into a bigger house," he says. "Although part of me suspects she'd rather just buy the one she has. The landlord died a while back and left it to his absolute shit of a son, who keeps ratcheting up the rent."

"Mummy's boy!" Cat teases.

"Fine, I'll splurge on a Lamborghini and a lobster dinner."

"That's the spirit. What else?"

Jake crosses his arms. "I imagine I'd want to find a person who could help me spend the rest."

"Not me," Cat says, clearing her throat. "Desert island notwithstanding, I think I could quite easily find ways to spend it all by myself."

"Such as?"

"A small castle, maybe. You know. Something tasteful."

They stand there for what feels like an eternity but is probably closer to a quarter of an hour, listing the ridiculous things they will be able to buy that neither of them remotely wants, while an ultraviolet laser shapes their future. When the machine gives one final victorious beep, Cat carefully extracts the tray, upon which is a row of four gooey, slightly misshapen approximations of the Tsarina.

"Decoy diamonds," she declares with as much enthusiasm as she can muster.

"That should be the name of our covers band," Jake states, his expression growing skeptical as he peers at them more closely. "These are . . ."

"A first draft," Cat finishes for him. "We have plenty of time to perfect it."

"So what do we do with these, exactly?"

"Maybe they'll look better with a bit of sanding down and polishing?" Cat suggests. She's being optimistic, she knows. None of these would pass for the real thing for more than a second. "Although it will probably be worth trying another batch." *Or twenty*, she adds silently.

"I'd best go out for supplies then," Jake says, heading for the door back into the bar.

"Good idea." Cat scrolls through her phone for the list she prepared earlier. "Some sandpaper would be useful, and some rubbing alcohol."

"I was actually thinking about falafel," Jake says. "And maybe some donuts. But I can pick up that stuff too. Then we can get to work on these rough diamonds."

"Now, *that* should be the name of our covers band," says Cat. "Seeing as I can't sing to save my life."

Jake lingers in the doorway for a second.

"Luckily for you," he says seriously, "I have the voice of an angel."

Fifteen

Liberty London looms so high over Great Marlborough Street that its iconic Tudor façade appears to be on the verge of tilting forward the closer she gets. All around her, shoppers in Balenciaga trainers and Gucci coats filter in and out of the front doors, oblivious to the ceaselessly polite requests for change from the man sitting cross-legged on a square of cardboard just feet away.

Despite having lived in the city for a decade, Cat has never before been to Liberty. She always used to think of vast department stores like this as being more akin to museums than shops, full of priceless exhibits to be admired but never touched. She is so taken by the beauty of the landmark emporium when she first walks in, the architecture of the central atrium so like a cathedral or throne room with its mezzanines and high, ornate rafters, that she forgets herself momentarily.

Her outfit today is a carefully careless affair: oversized chambray shirt, loose jeans, and a pair of platform espadrilles. Her hair, purposely tousled, is held back from her face with an enormous pair of sunglasses. She looks like the disheveled daughter of a banker who has just rolled out of bed and has never had to worry about making a good first impression. Wandering around the store, she has seen women her age and younger in similar states of disarray, shuffling aimlessly, no doubt hoping to spend their way out of their respective hangovers. No amount of unbrushed hair and croaky voices, however, can distract Cat from the fact that the bracelets glittering at their wrists are Cartier, their handbags Mulberry.

"Can I help you with anything, madam?" a clerk politely asks one of them, a wan, waifish thing swaddled in a tan poncho who is inspecting the scented candles, raising them to her sculpted nose one by one. "The Faraway Palm is a very popular choice."

"It smells wretched," she replies calmly, placing it back onto the display. "Oud gives me a headache. You should really put a warning on those things; you may very well end up killing somebody."

"Oh. Erm . . . right," the sales assistant stammers. "I'll . . . look into that. Is there anything else I can—"

"No, I'm quite all right, thank you so *muuuch*."

Bingo, Cat thinks.

"Millie!" she exclaims, stepping into the young woman's path as the salesgirl takes the opportunity to scurry away.

"Pardon?" the woman asks, jolted from whatever consumerist haze in which she may have been immersed.

"Millie Coutes, yeah?" Cat speaks through her sinuses as much as she can without bursting into giggles. "It's me, Flossy!"

The girl wrinkles her nose as if she has just stepped in something. "I rather think you've got me mixed up with someone else," she rasps. "My name is not Millie; it's Zara."

Cat tilts her head, pretending to reexamine her. "Are you sure?" she asks. "I could have sworn we were at St. George's together. The year below Eugenie, remember?"

"I went to school in Switzerland," the girl icily informs her. "Now, if you'll excuse me—"

"And who is *this* little fellow?" Cat says, changing tack and stooping to address the long-haired Chihuahua who has chosen this very moment to peek out from Zara's designer tote. "Why, if he is not just the most precious thing!"

Zara sighs, perhaps resigning herself to the knowledge that this interaction won't be over until she has fulfilled her end, and scratches the tiny dog's head.

"This is Napoleon," she says. "He's my world. Please don't stroke him," she adds hastily, but he has already snapped at Cat's outstretched hand, an act of aggression he follows with a series of high-pitched yaps. "He's highly sensitive. He doesn't take quickly or kindly to people with whom he is not familiar."

In other words, he's a snob, Cat thinks, wiping her hand on her jeans. *Or you just couldn't be arsed to train your animal properly.* The bite didn't hurt—Napoleon's size and proportionate strength negated that possibility—and she feels a pang of near-sympathy for this creature who likely spends most of his day sitting and shitting in a purse.

"Well, sorry for the crossed wires," Cat says, rising to her feet again. "It was nice to meet you."

"Sure," Zara says, already moving on. Cat watches her head back down toward the ground floor and the exit, feeling more than seeing Jake move away in the opposite direction. He was able to swiftly liberate a gold bangle from Zara's wrist and a small wad of cash from Napoleon's handbag house while Cat gamely diverted the attention of both parties. Now they make their way to another of the many chambers within the vast store like bees in a hive, keeping their distance so as not to arouse suspicion but each keenly aware of the other.

They select their targets with care, avoiding wide-eyed tourists and harangued families on day trips to the city. In the jewelry department, Jake strikes up a conversation with a lady in her fifties they overheard berating her housekeeper over the phone. He asks her opinion on a necklace he is thinking of buying for his fiancée—"I could do with a female perspective and you seem like you have impeccable taste," he says earnestly, at which she beams—while Cat slips the Hermès scarf from where it hangs out of her raincoat and stuffs it into her own back pocket.

In women's wear, Cat advises a woman against trying on an Issey Miyake dress, telling her that geometric prints can be unforgiving and she would look so much younger in this floral maxi. The woman bats her eyes in disbelief at this intrusion, then confides in Cat that she was thinking the same thing.

"I have to fire somebody tomorrow and the optics are probably better if I don't look so severe," she says. "You're sure the flowers aren't too chintzy?"

"I'd call them timeless," Cat tells her, and the woman expresses her gratitude before carrying the frock to the nearest sales desk, where she will add to the growing collection of shopping bags hanging from her left hand, unaware the Dior perfume she purchased earlier has gone missing.

Cat pauses to admire an emerald-green jersey dress, which she imagines, just for a second, styling with her faithful knackered leather jacket and a pair of boots. But dresses she can't afford are the reason for her visit to Liberty in the first place, she reminds herself, walking away from the mannequin without checking the price tag.

She has at least been spared the ordeal of attending a group visit to the bridal shop; the truncated timeline of Louisa's engagement rendered this particular ritual moot. Instead, Darcy sent her a link to the exact dress she was to reserve online. It is a soft, muted pink, the color of a naked lip ("vagina pink," Alex said when she showed him a picture), in a draped Grecian style that will complement all of the bridesmaids' figures.

She felt grateful in that regard, having previously forced herself into some truly hideous and ill-fitting garments in the name of duty, but her relief was short-lived. Because she knows that kind of flattering fit doesn't come cheap.

"How much are we talking here?" Jake asked her when she rang him in frustration.

"The website said *price available upon request*," Cat said. "*Price available upon request*, Jake."

"Oh. Shit."

"Yeah."

And so here they are, raising some much-needed capital for the dress, the wedding gift, the flight to the as-yet-unannounced hen destination, by picking the pockets of affluent Londoners who have come to kill an hour before their lunches of salads and pinot gris.

They never speak, never even make direct eye contact with each other, and yet a game forms between Cat and Jake as they stalk their prey, listening acutely to find the best—that is to say, worst—candidates and then closing in, sharing an unspoken understanding of what needs to be done. Cat has never been so conscious of her own surroundings, and a thrill runs down her spine each time they check off another mark, each time she or Jake succeeds in procuring an object without getting caught in the act. It is like the Velocity job unlocked something and now they are both tuned into a frequency only the two of them can hear: Cat is filled with the kind of giddy pleasure she remembers feeling when playing tag or hide-and-seek.

"Jesus," she says breathlessly as they step back out of the air-conditioned sanctuary into the muggy morning, her pockets laden and heart still pounding.

"You were great in there," he tells her.

"I was just trying to keep up."

"No, you're *good*."

Cat feels a small, unfamiliar swell of pride at the idea of Jake's being even remotely impressed by her talents. Then he adds: "Flossy," with a smirk.

"Shut up," she says with a grin, discreetly fishing a loose twenty from her haul and handing it to the gentleman on the pavement.

"Ta, darling," he says.

"Have a good one," Cat says.

"Can I tempt you to lunch?" Jake asks as they turn the corner onto Regent Street.

"You certainly can," she replies. "I've worked up quite an appetite."

They split a bottle of cheap rosé in the kind of French brasserie that can be found on any corner in this stretch of the city. They dine on minute steak and French fries for twelve pounds apiece, old habits dying hard, then leave a tip double the value of the bill.

Sixteen

"Oh, for fuck's *sake*."

"Pardon?!" two voices gasp in unison. Tom and Alex are in the middle of preparing their dinner; Cat's profanity cut through both the tranquil evening mood and Jessie Ware playing on the Amazon Echo. She doesn't get how cooking together is supposed to be romantic. The heat, dependence on following instructions, and proximity to knives all make it sound like a recipe for disaster.

"Sorry, I didn't mean you," Cat says. "This old thing just keeps freezing. Makes it impossible to get anything done."

She gestures to her intrepid setup: laptop propped open on the kitchen table, in proximity to the house's unreliable internet router. Cat has thrown herself into job hunting with gusto over the last couple of days, tarting up her CV as much as possible without being outright fraudulent. Okay, fine, so she may not have worked for *Harper's Bazaar*'s digital team. But she subcontracted for a client who did, and doesn't that amount to the same thing? Everybody fibs on their résumé a *tiny* bit, she reasons.

All being well, the Tsarina will yield the most financial security she's ever known, but until that happens, she still has a hefty credit card payment to somehow conjure out of her overdraft. The jaunt to Liberty helped to cover the ridiculously expensive brides-maid dress and wedding gift—a set of eye-wateringly priced linen napkins that were still the cheapest thing on the registry—but people just aren't carrying as much cash around as they used to, and Cat reasons it can't hurt to have a backup plan, if for whatever reason her partnership with Jake ends up hitting a dead end.

Maybe she shouldn't be thinking this way. Cat has read the foreword to enough self-help books and empowering memoirs on Amazon to know that negativity begets negativity, but she's also lived long enough to be a realist. Even simple plans can go awry, and not everybody gets the outcome they want, no matter how well they prepare or how hard they work for it. And if the heist doesn't come off, Cat will still need a place to live. Finding honest work and going straight are still an option. Even if that means feeling her soul corrode away as she scours the internet for a free-lance gig that pays in actual currency, not "exposure" and "free snacks."

Her phone rings, and for a moment she allows herself to think it is somebody responding promptly to one of the countless inqui-ries she has sent out into the ether, although she knows better than to expect that too.

"Darling, I have an emergency."

Not ever the words you want to hear when answering the phone, least of all when they're coming from Louisa Vincent.

"What's going on?" Cat asks.

"Canapés!" Louisa shrieks.

Cat relaxes, her sudden terror that the wedding might be off abating.

"Tell me about the canapés," she says slowly. "Are they safe? In good emotional health?"

"You've always thought you were funnier than you are," says Louisa, but Cat can tell this isn't being said with any real spite—Louisa's ire is clearly occupied elsewhere. "I just can't handle all these *opinions*. Mention you're getting married and suddenly the world and its valet have a hot take. On the dress, the venue, the flowers. All of which are impeccable, might I add. But Christ, the food!"

"Let me guess," Cat ventures. "A bunch of your pals are vegan or gluten-free."

"Oh, I can handle all that," says Louisa, almost growling in irritation. "You know I haven't eaten bread since 2012. No, it's the ones with no taste whatsoever who are just doing my head in. Victoria Parker suggested we have pork chops! I *mean*."

"How dare she," says Cat drily.

"You have no idea the kind of pressure I'm under," Louisa continues. "I like to think I've shown remarkable grace under fire in putting this whole thing together in a matter of weeks, but bloody *hell*, Cat, this menu! How am I supposed to cater to a hundred people who think that *pork chops* are a suitable wedding breakfast? I might as well just plate up a bunch of Big Macs and be done with it."

"Why don't you ask Darcy to help you?" Cat asks. "Isn't this peak matron of honor stuff?"

"Oh, Darcy is sweet," Louisa says, "but I'm starting to think I may have made an error in appointing her. She's not exactly one of life's leaders, you know?"

Cat does not mention that Darcy has shown leadership skills aplenty on the bridesmaids' group chat, primarily in the form of issuing proclamations and then following up with frequent reminders to ensure they all remain "on plan." Instead she simply asks: "Do you need me to come over?"

"Oh, no, that's fine," Louisa says, the trembling falsetto gone from her voice. "I've got a friend of Julia's coming over with some canapé samples. Stephen and I are going to try them together. I just needed to rant." Cat doesn't know whether to feel oddly touched that Louisa is so comfortable being honest for once, or annoyed that she has yet again been recruited for emotional labor.

"Anyway," Louisa carries on breathlessly, "what's new with you? Have you called Ronan yet? He's been asking after you."

Blissfully, a doorbell rings in the background before Cat has to respond.

"That must be Nigella with the Brie!" Louisa exclaims, and the line goes dead.

"Of course it is," Cat mutters, flinging her phone onto the table and returning her attention to her laptop. A moment later, her phone rings again. This time, it's Jake.

"Someone's popular," Alex remarks as she picks up. She rolls her eyes at him.

"Hi," she says.

"Are you free tomorrow?"

"Well, it's not like I have a job to get to."

"Tomorrow is Sunday, Cat."

"Oh. Then yes, I am free tomorrow."

"Feel like coming east with me?"

"What for?"

"I might have a solution to our little problem of how exactly we go about selling a priceless and famous diamond."

Cat lowers her voice, conscious of Tom's and Alex's pricked ears. "I'm listening."

"I know somebody, or rather, somebody I *know* knows somebody who can link us up with a buyer."

"One of your . . . friends?"

Jake hesitates before answering. "Something like that."

They arrange to meet at noon the following day and hang up. Alex whispers something to Tom, who turns to Cat with an apologetic expression. Dinner is ready, and they only made enough for two.

Cat imagines a rendezvous in an abandoned warehouse, or a car park overlooking the river, and is surprised when instead, Jake leads her off the Tube and through a series of perfectly normal-looking streets in Barking, each lined with narrow, squat, semi-identical terrace houses. She feels like she's on her way to visit someone's nan, not a fence. (She looked up the word "fence" before leaving the house to be sure she knew how to use it correctly.) Eventually, Jake stops them at a house with a bright yellow front door, flanked by distinctly phallic sculptures wrought from copper.

"I should tell you," he says, hand brushing her lower back, "before we go in—"

The door flies open, cutting his sentence short.

"Do you make a habit of loitering in doorways?" asks the stern, frankly Amazonian woman standing on the threshold. Her curly black hair is clipped close to her scalp, and she wears a black T-shirt and jeans. The only flashes of color are a pair of enormous gold hoops in her ears, a bold red lip, and her nails, which are painted a bright turquoise and instantly draw Cat's eye. Then she grins, and it is as if a different person entirely is standing before them. "Are you going to introduce the strange woman, Jacob, or did you lose your manners as well as your key?" It is not immediately clear to Cat which of them she is referring to as strange.

"Cat Bellamy," Jake says with an air of unfamiliar formality, "this is Vivi Marlowe. My mum." He smiles, and shrugs, and has the decency to look sheepish as hell.

"Your mum," Cat says, wondering if she has misheard him. Except of course she hasn't, because *look* at them both. The resemblance couldn't be clearer. The arch of the brows, the full mouth. They even appear to share the same ears. This is unmistakably the woman she saw on Jake's Instagram while scrolling like a crazy person.

Jake has brought Cat to his *mother's house*. Without telling her, or giving her the chance to put on a different, more meeting-the-parents-appropriate outfit than the ripped jeans and Iggy Pop T-shirt she is currently wearing. There's usually a specific kind of impression one wants to make on the mother of their boyfriend, fake or otherwise, and showing up empty-handed with "I Wanna Be Your Dog" emblazoned across her chest is not it.

"Let me guess," Vivi says, ushering them inside. "He didn't tell you that's who you were coming to meet today."

"I . . . he . . . no."

Vivi shoots Jake a look that clearly has years of meaning behind it as they follow her down the narrow hallway and into the small kitchen, which is filled with the warming aroma of roasting chicken.

"You must think I'm some kind of Joan Crawford nightmare," she says to Cat. Then, to Jake, she adds: "Go and give your brother a kiss."

"Brother?" Cat turns to Jake. "I thought you said you were an only child."

"I *am*," Jake says. "That's just how Mum talks about Raymond."

At the sound of his name, an ancient, slobbery black Labrador appears from beneath the kitchen table.

"Raymond, I presume," Cat says. Raymond does a careful lap

of the kitchen, looking up first at her, then Jake, then returns to the doggy bed under the table, his curiosity seemingly satisfied, leaving a trail of saliva in his wake.

"Lunch will be about half an hour," Vivi says. "Cat, I assume you know your way around a potato peeler?"

"I do," says Cat, and Vivi promptly hands her one.

"I was going to do roasties but ran out of time," says Vivi, "so we'll have to have mash instead." She points Cat toward a bag of potatoes on the counter. "Jacob, be a love and take your brother for a walk?"

"He's fine," Jake protests.

"I won't ask twice," says Vivi. "His lead is under the stairs." Jake relents and, with the air of a mildly disgruntled teenager, goes to fetch it.

What the bloody hell is happening? Cat thinks.

"Did you manage to get in touch with Uncle Sid?" Jake asks as he loops the lead onto Raymond's collar.

"One thing at a time" is Vivi's response.

"Uncle Sid?" Cat asks.

Jake sighs impatiently. "I told you I knew someone who might be able to help us find a buyer," he says. Cat feels her entire body tense up. He's going to talk about their plans in front of his mother?

"He failed to tell you that *I'm* the one with the contact, not him," says Vivi, rustling around in a cupboard and emerging victorious with a box of stuffing mix. "And *I* told *him* that I wouldn't set up a meeting with Sid until I had met you and heard more about this job you're planning."

"You know?" Cat gulps.

Vivi laughs and starts pouring the stuffing mix into a bowl. "I'm his mother, dear," she says. "I know *everything*."

Cat looks to Jake, who mouths "I'm sorry" before leaving with Raymond.

"You look a bit flummoxed, love," says Vivi. "Tell you what. You peel, I'll talk."

"All right," says Cat. She picks up a potato and gets to work.

"I'm going to hazard a guess that my Jake hasn't given you much of an idea of how he grew up," Vivi says, stirring first hot water and then butter into the stuffing mix. "The short version is this. His dad, Billy, was smooth as silk and twice as slippery. I was nineteen when I met him, he was twenty-six. That alone would probably be a red flag these days, but I thought I knew my own mind, and he seemed to be going places. Had ambition. Not for anything legal, mind you, but that didn't bother me much. He was fun, you see. My parents weren't much for fun. Naturally I ran off with him, and within a year we were married, and not long after I was pregnant with Jake. And then . . ." She smiles. "You can probably guess the next part."

"He left."

"Tale as old as time, isn't it? A confidence man and a gullible mark."

"What did you do?"

"There I was, twenty-one with a baby and nobody else in the world, just another one of those Black single mothers that the newspapers kept warning everybody was coming for earnest tax-payers' money. My parents didn't want a thing to do with me by then, of course. I'd shamed them both, running away with a man like that. And even though Jake was legitimate, conceived in love and more importantly in wedlock, they still saw him as . . . Oh, I don't know, proof of my disgrace, I suppose."

Vivi places the stuffing in the oven and takes the potatoes, which Cat has peeled and roughly chopped. She tips them into a pot, fills it with water, and places it on the stove.

"Billy's friends saved us. Sid, Lenny, Maggie, Kathleen, Kevin. None of them knew where he'd gone, just that he'd borrowed money off all of them right before he legged it. When they first showed up at my door, I thought they'd come to collect. But instead . . ."

She pauses for a moment.

"'You don't double-cross your own, and you certainly don't run out on them.' That's what they said to me. And then they just came in, weighed down with bags of food and nappies and a bunch of things it hadn't even occurred to me that I couldn't afford yet. They told me that Billy might have proven worthless, but that they'd always do right by me. That I was family. I don't think they knew quite what that meant to a scared girl whose own parents wouldn't have her."

"Honor among thieves," Cat murmurs.

"Ha! Oh, I like that," says Vivi. "Anyway, the rest is fairly simple. They were always there, from that day on, and I've been there for them in any way I can too. I didn't have a clue about half of the dodgy stuff they got up to at first, but I soon learned. Turns out I'm a whiz with numbers, although my old math teacher would gladly tell you otherwise. I'd help out with some creative book-keeping, make sure nobody went over budget when they were planning a job, that kind of thing. And Jake had a dozen aunties and uncles who were happy to babysit when I needed to work. I don't think Jake ever felt he missed out on having a dad. He never knew the man, would likely have found him quite disappointing, and besides, he almost always got his way with his aunties. He was such a charmer, even as a little boy."

"I can well imagine," Cat says, thinking of Julia, and Jake's insistence that older women find him simply delightful.

"And I'm not blind or stupid. I know they were teaching him other things too. The kind of skills not covered by your GCSEs. I suppose he inherited his father's gift, if a knack for nicking can be considered genetic. But I made sure he finished school. I thought at least if he had some grades to his name, he could always get a normal job. That he could do anything he wanted, that he wouldn't be bound to the life."

Cat feels a spark of recognition at Vivi's pragmatism, her knowledge that things can fall to pieces and you need to plan accordingly. She's been following that same impulse for as long as she can remember.

"He makes a mean martini," Cat says. "That's how we met, actually. At his work." She knows that this is where Vivi's entire story has been leading. Nobody offers up her life story to somebody she just met unless she's either a pathological narcissist or expecting information in return. Cat is betting strongly on the latter.

"Which begs the question," Vivi says. "What are your intentions with my son?" She must spot the look of sheer terror on Cat's face, because she waves one of her hands and says: "Don't worry, I'm not asking you about your dowry. Jake tells me this entire courtship is a ruse, and I believe him, although you are pretty and not his usual type—which is a compliment, believe me." Cat doesn't even have time to blush before Vivi continues: "But don't let it go to your head. What I meant to ask is this: what, exactly, are you getting Jake into?"

Cat gives her an abridged version of the job. The diamond, her and Jake's agreement to pose as a couple to get into the wedding, their plans to switch the Tsarina with the dupe.

"You understand now, I'm sure, why I insisted on meeting you," says Vivi. "Jake has always had a talent for the grift, but he's never attempted something like this before. And from what I can gather, neither have you."

"You wanted to assess the potential risk," says Cat. "I get it. Really."

"That's part of it. I also wanted to meet the girl who is so willing to rob her own friend blind. Forgive me, that just seems a bit . . . heartless."

"You haven't met Louisa."

"True enough. But how can I trust that you won't screw over my Jake the same way you are this Louisa?"

"I would never betray Jake," says Cat, unaware until the moment the words leave her mouth of just how true that is.

"That's very nice, dear, but I've heard it before." Vivi's tone is still kind, but there is no missing the steel behind what she is saying. "There's a reason he sticks to his own little grifts, you know. He tried a job with a partner once before. Got double-crossed, nearly went to jail. So you can appreciate my reticence."

That would explain his early insistence on working alone. Cat thinks of the Jake she met at the Oceanic Hotel, the keen clarity with which he seemed to look straight through her, the effortless way he swindled those men at the bar that night. She can't imagine anybody ever getting the better of a man like that.

"You're right," Cat says eventually. "I'm out of my depth here. I can only do this with Jake's help. We have to have each other's backs. I don't know how I can prove to you, exactly, that I'm trustworthy. I guess I'll just have to ask you to believe in me. I give you my word, whatever that might be worth."

Vivi stares intently at Cat for what feels like an age, clearly trying to make up her mind. Cat does her best to return the even look and not to cringe or squirm under such scrutiny. Then a smile plays on Vivi's lips, and for a second it is as if Jake is in the room with them.

"Honor among thieves, was it?" Vivi says. "I do like that. I suppose I will have to wait and see."

They both turn at the sound of the front door opening and closing. Shortly after, an exhausted-looking Raymond lurches into the kitchen and promptly flops down in the middle of the floor. The room is so small that he is quite literally under their feet. With a single practiced movement, Vivi hooks her foot under the dog's belly and slides him to one side, clearing a path into the hallway and the equally tiny dining room beyond.

"Everything all right?" Jake asks from the hall, hanging the dog's lead back up in the cupboard under the stairs.

"Put it this way, my love," Vivi says. "Cat here will be staying for lunch."

Jake leans against the doorway, and when he hears this, he breaks into a grin and shines it in Cat's direction. If this was all a test, it seems she has passed at least the first round. She smiles back at Jake briefly, then Vivi points the potato masher to a cupboard to the left of the cooker, directing Cat to where the plates are kept.

"I'll take over here," Jake says, stepping into Cat's place in the narrow kitchen. "Why don't you go set the table and we'll be right through?" Cat exits the kitchen but lingers in the hallway, taking in the practiced ease with which Jake and Vivi move around each other as the chicken, redolent of rosemary, comes out of the oven, as Vivi lays into the potatoes with the masher like they owe her money, as the green beans are sprinkled with pepper.

My dad bounced. It's been me and my mum ever since. That's what Jake told her. But seeing it is something different altogether.

The way they clearly adore each other, even though Jake seems deeply embarrassed by having to bring Cat here for appraisal. It sends a peculiar sensation through Cat, like feeling a cold draft when you thought all of the windows were secured.

Cat has never really understood the Great British Obsession with roast dinners, thinking it a curious mix of nostalgia for a childhood that never existed and a fixation on the idea that this country created at least one piece of cuisine that wasn't a result of colonialism. They were never really a thing in her house growing up, and from what she has gathered of them since, far too many roasts are dry, and the rest tend to overcorrect and end up swimming in gravy. That said, had Cat grown up eating Vivi's cooking, she might have a greater affinity for the tradition.

The chicken is the best thing she has tasted in weeks, moist and rich and comforting. The mashed potatoes warm her from the inside out, and she has never thought green beans so capable of flavor. (Vivi's secret, when asked: "Butter and salt. More of each than any cookbook or doctor would advise.") For the most part, Cat still lives on student fare like pesto pasta and cheese toasties. And while she's had her share of fancy dinners in her time, courtesy of client lunches and countless weddings, she'd all but forgotten the simple pleasure of a home-cooked meal.

"How are you not the size of a house?" she asks Jake, once she has cleaned her plate and can finally speak without her mouth full.

"If your plan to get me on your side includes flattery," says Vivi, "I want you to know . . . I am perfectly fine with that."

"In that case," Cat continues, "I couldn't help but admire those interesting sculptures outside your front door. They're very . . ."—*phallic, priapic, penile*—"unusual," she musters. "Where did you get them?"

Vivi smiles and leans forward in her seat, elbows planted on the table, hands clasped together elegantly under her chin. "I made them," she says. "I'm a bit of an amateur artist. When I have time, like."

"No!" Cat gasps. "Me too! I mean, I studied to be an artist. I always thought I was going to be."

"Jake mentioned something along those lines," Vivi says. "Of course, he doesn't approve of my pieces. He says they all come out looking like willies." She gestures to a pair of glazed cylindrical pots functioning as bookends to a stack of novels by Marian Keyes and Lee Child on a shelf on the opposite wall. "But I tell him, art is *subjective*. That's what I love about it! Jake peaked with his finger paintings, bless him. They were really good, mind you. A touch derivative of Van Gogh, but good all the same. We hung them in the Louvre."

"The Louvre?" Cat looks to Jake, confused.

"That's what we used to call the fridge," Jake explains.

"I see." Cat smiles, tickled by the image of a miniature Jake daubing paper with his own *Sunflowers* or *Starry Night*.

"He soon moved on to magic tricks," Vivi says. "Our Kevin, he went through a stint as a magician, doing shows at working-men's clubs. To this day, I don't know how he did half the things he did. My Jake, though—he wouldn't stop pestering the poor bloke until he disclosed his secrets. Of course, that's not the done thing, is it? So . . ." She emits a low tut of laughter. "Kevin made Jake his *assistant*. And taught him everything he knew. I thought of it as a passing fascination, and in a way it was. Jake got older, and he wasn't interested in magic tricks anymore. But the cards, the sleight of hand . . ."

"I used to spend hours in my room, practicing getting better with the deck in front of the mirror," Jake says, smiling at the memory.

"Naturally, I thought he was doing something else by that point," Vivi interjects. "He'd got to that age, you know."

"Oh my *god*, Mum!" Jake grumbles.

Cat giggles and places a hand on Jake's shoulder. She thinks often of how different her childhood was from Louisa's, but Jake's feels equally distant. To grow up surrounded by paint and clay and magic, with an entire cabal of people who were no blood relation but who *chose* to love you. Learning all of this helps to explain what she knows of Jake, and yet she feels she has a million more questions.

"Jake, please," says Vivi. "If I wanted to really embarrass you, I'd get out the baby photos."

"There are baby photos?" Cat's smile becomes a hopeful grin, and she turns to catch his eye.

"Next time," Vivi promises. "Jake, would you mind clearing the table? Cat will wash up." She rises from her seat. "I have a call to make before pudding."

"There's *pudding*? Okay, I am never leaving."

Vivi laughs and cups Cat's chin gently for a second. "It's only walnut cake, love. Homemade, but still. Why do I get the feeling you're a bit of a waif?" Before Cat can even begin to fathom how to answer such a question, Vivi adds: "Oh, and, Jake, you might as well fetch the brandy from the cupboard in the living room. Four glasses."

"Four?" Jake pauses, an empty plate in each hand. "You mean . . . ?"

Vivi opens a small cabinet under the bookshelf and digs out a small flip-phone that might technically qualify as an antique. "I'll see if Sid is in the mood for some cake and brandy," she says, squinting as she examines the small screen. "I just hope he's on the

same number. And in the country. And not presently locked up."
She peers up at them, thumb hovering over the dial button. "Some
privacy, if you please? Cat, the rubber gloves are that way."

Sid, it turns out, *is* still using his old number, and is neither
abroad nor incarcerated. Vivi ascertains all of this in a private
phone conversation while Cat and Jake do the washing up. They
are unable to avoid bumping into each other as they stand side by
side in the close quarters of the kitchen: it is an image of cozy
domesticity the likes of which could be found in a Norman Rock-
well painting, and Cat has to remind herself she and Jake are not
playing their roles today. They have barely finished drying the
dishes and putting them away when there is a sharp staccato knock
at the front door, and a man lets himself in. She rushes to the
kitchen door to get a look at him but he is already barreling forward to envelop Jake in what can only be described as a bear hug.

"Look at you!" he rasps, hands on Jake's cheeks. "Are you even
taller?"

"I'm thirty-two," Jake tells him with evident affection. "I think
it's safe to say I stopped growing."

"I must be shrinking, then," Sid says with a wink. He *is* a slight
man, to be fair, although there is a certain robustness to him. His
white hair is slicked back, and his startlingly blue eyes practically
sparkle against his weathered, tanned skin. A small silver cross
dangles from his left ear, a red bandanna is knotted around his
neck, and his battered leather jacket genuinely looks older than
Cat. Here is somebody who has not changed their look since the
mideighties. On somebody else, that might be slightly sad, but it
suits Sid down to the ground.

"I thought you were living on that riverboat," says Jake.

"That was *last* year," says Sid. "There's been a commune and a caravan since then."

"Where have you come from today?" Cat asks. "That was an awfully quick commute."

"Crashing with Maggie and Lenny around the corner," Sid replies. "You must be Cat." For a second Cat thinks he is going to pull her into a rigorously ursine embrace as well, but instead he gives her hand a single shake, his grip gentle, the motion firm.

"You're here! I thought I heard the door." Vivi descends the stairs and links arms with Sid as they all file into the living room, where the brandy and cake are laid out on the coffee table. Unless Cat is very much mistaken, while she and Jake were doing the dishes, Vivi took the opportunity to visit the powder room and freshen her lipstick. Sid and Vivi sit side by side on the two-seater settee, while Cat and Jake each take an armchair. She has never felt more like she is Meeting the Parents.

"Right, what's this about a diamond?" Sid asks, taking a generous bite of the cake. Cat and Jake fill him in on the Tsarina, the Tsarinot, and their quest for a buyer.

"What do you think?" Jake asks. "Will you be able to help us?"

"What do I think?" Sid leans back on the sofa and regards Jake with a look that can only be described as misty-eyed. "I think I'm bloody proud, that's what. Sure, I might have expected a call sooner, might have assumed you'd need my help as more than just a fence, but it sounds like you've got quite the capable accomplice here."

Cat is so pleased that she has been using the term "fence" correctly that she almost misses the clear compliment from Sid. She smiles bashfully around a mouthful of cake.

"How do you two know each other anyway?" Sid asks. "Are you—"

"They're just working together, Sid," Vivi interrupts.

"Hmm." Sid polishes off his cake and mumbles something like "Can't have everything."

"And a buyer?" Jake asks again.

"Piece of piss," Sid says. "You're forgetting who you're talking to, lad. I lined up buyers for the Hatton lot in 2015, didn't I?"

"The Hatton Garden heist, you mean?" Cat leans forward in her seat. "Wait, that was *you*?"

"Maybe," says Sid, suddenly coy.

"But I saw the men who did that in all the papers," Cat says. "They were all arrested."

"The ones who got caught were, for sure." Sid winks. "I don't suppose you've got a photo of the ice, have you?"

"We've got something even better," says Jake, reaching into his pocket and bringing out a recently buffed Tsarinot. Cat and Jake have been working on polishing their coarse counterfeit gems for over a week, and this one now catches the light like a prism. Jake holds it out to Sid, who tilts his head and leans forward in his seat to examine it keenly without actually touching it. Vivi exhibits less restraint, plucking it from Jake's fingers and looking at it from multiple angles, making an array of appreciative noises before looking to Sid, whose eyes are in danger of filling up again. Something unknowable passes between them, and then Sid gives Vivi the tiniest of nods. Vivi's eyes go to her son, and then to Cat. She places the fake diamond on the coffee table, picks up her snifter of brandy, and points it in Cat's direction.

"Welcome to the family," she says.

Seventeen

After some additional discussion of the job, and another slice of cake, Jake and Cat say their goodbyes. This time, Cat gets a hug from both Vivi and Sid.

"That was . . . ," she begins, as they walk back to the station.

"I know." Jake winces. "I'm sorry. I should have warned you before we came that you'd be meeting my mum. But I didn't know how to do that without bringing up our family's whole situation, and that you needed to meet her for us to get in touch with Sid, and then she told me she'd explain it all to you if I brought you for lunch."

"I was going to say that was fun," Cat says. "But you're right—some warning might have been nice! I'd have brought flowers or something."

"You would?"

"I believe that's the appropriate gift when meeting your pretend boyfriend's crime-boss mother."

"She is *not* a crime boss."

"Maybe not. But she's definitely a *boss*. And a talented artist to boot."

"Those sculptures!" He smacks his forehead. "I can't believe you saw the house of dicks!"

"They are only phallic if you interpret them that way," she says.

"A single-celled organism without eyes would interpret them that way."

"Maybe so. But answer me this."

"What?"

"You've known Sid your entire life. He clearly thinks the sun shines out of you. And yet . . . you don't have his phone number?"

Jake smiles ruefully. "It's his way," he says. "I could have tried to get in touch with him directly. Make some inquiries, find out where he's living these days, track down somebody who knows his number. But if he got wind that I was contacting him about a job this big without my mum's knowledge or her blessing? He wouldn't help. End of story."

That, Cat can believe. Vivi might not be the codependent toxic smother monster that single mums of grown men are so often made out to be, but it is still obvious how protective she is.

"Sid and your mum," she remarks. "Are they . . ."

"Oh god, no way." Jake shakes his head emphatically. "Why? Did you get a vibe?"

I didn't not *get a vibe*, Cat thinks. "No, just curious," she says. She doesn't have the heart to tell Jake that his mum and Sid are almost *definitely* hooking up, and that Sid's current residence is in all likelihood Vivi's bedroom. It's not Cat's place to speak on Jake's mum's love life, nor is it any of her business. She wonders, though, if Jake would be genuinely shocked to learn that the man who clearly adores his mother has actually acted on those feelings at some point in the last thirty or so years. For someone who she has come to know is adept at reading people, he has failed to interpret any of the signs.

"You know," she says, deciding a slight subject change is in order, "you really are one hundred percent Mummy's boy. Certified, authenticated."

Jake laughs. "But not creepy, right?" He frowns. "Not in an Oedipal red-flag way?"

Cat ponders his question for a moment, then another moment, because she enjoys how his frown is pulling his eyebrows downward and even making him pout a little. Finally, she proclaims: "It would be a way bigger red flag if you *didn't* adore your mum. She's amazing."

Jake smiles, puts his hands in his pockets, and watches his feet as they walk for a moment. Then he asks: "What was your mum like?"

The question shouldn't catch her off guard. She has spent the last few hours in Jake's childhood home, met his family, heard what he was like as a little boy. But even all these years later, Cat feels like she needs advance warning when talking about her mother. Like all of those memories are in a locked leaden box at the bottom of a pond, and she has to wade down to it with the key in her hand.

"She was . . . curious," she says. "Some people would probably call that nosy, but she was actually just interested, which was frustrating at times, when she'd get talking to somebody at the bus stop or in the supermarket and not let them go until she'd heard their life story. I guess I learned a thing or two from her about how to get people to talk about themselves, which has come in handy. She was never a gossip, though. She didn't trade in other people's secrets. She was funny too. I mean, it's probably not hard to make a child laugh, but *I* thought she was hilarious."

"I still think the Cheshire Cat thing is a cute gag," Jake says.

"Yeah." Cat smiles. "I never really minded it, either. And god, my dad loved her. They were so into each other, which even then I knew not everyone's parents were. It was pretty gross to me at the time, actually. Mum would be cooking tea and then he'd just walk up behind her and put his arms around her waist and give her these fast little kisses on the cheek like a woodpecker.

"And then she was ill. And she was still all of those things, but more and more, she was mostly just ill. And after that she was gone."

Cat feels Jake's hand slide into hers as they walk. She is taken aback by how much she welcomes the feeling of his fingers laced between hers and swings their arms between them childishly, keeping her eyes on the pavement.

"Dad was, well, I don't even know what he was. If there's a word for it. She was his world. And then he lost her, and it was just the two of us, and I realize now how much he must have been freaking out at the thought of raising this twelve-year-old girl by himself."

"I can't imagine," Jake says. "I mean, my dad was a shit who left, and I don't think it took my mum long to figure out she was better shot of him. To lose someone like that, though. And you . . . I didn't know you were so young."

"Yeah, I was a real hit when I went up to big school that autumn," Cat laughs bitterly. "'Hi, I'm Cat Bellamy, I love Paramore, and my mum just died.'"

"You mean the other kids weren't lining up to be your pal? But they're so famously empathetic!"

"I know, right?"

"I'm sorry. It must have been hard for you. You *and* your dad."

"He did his best," she says. "Made sure I was wearing clean

clothes and eating three square meals a day. I don't think any other child has eaten more beans on toast than I did. He'd fix my bike, take me to the seaside for day trips in the summer when he had time. But the talking stuff didn't come naturally to either of us; that was Mum's thing. I kind of got used to making do on my own, taking care of myself. I wanted to help him out.

"I studied hard and got good grades, because if he thought I was doing well at school, then maybe he would believe that I was well-adjusted and not sad anymore. It made more sense to me back then. But then later on, those grades meant I was able to get a scholarship for uni, which meant he wouldn't have to worry so much about helping me pay for everything. And that's how it's been with us ever since. I just want him to think that he did a good job raising me, and that I'm not a total screwup who can't take care of herself."

"I get it," says Jake. "That feeling when it's just the two of you. You're a kid, but you're also their ally, right? Their buddy. They lean on you too, even if they don't mean to. So you become like a little adult."

"Exactly."

"But, Cat . . ." He turns to look down at her. "You're *not* a screwup."

Cat smiles and shrugs, and they continue walking in silence, until a lone magpie skips across their path. It looks like it's playing hopscotch.

"Afternoon, Mr. Magpie," Cat says. "Love to the wife and kids."

She doesn't have to even turn and look to know that Jake is baffled.

"What was *that*?" he asks.

"Don't tell me nobody does this around here," Cat replies. "You have to greet a lone magpie; it's bad luck otherwise. One for sorrow, Jake!"

"You are mad."

"Maybe I am," she says. "But better safe than sorry." She can't even remember who first taught her this odd rule, whether it was her mum or her dad or just something she picked up in a book. She just knows that whenever a magpie flew into their tiny back garden, or they passed one on the side of the road in the car, she and her parents, and then just she and her dad, would give it a little salute.

"How do you know the magpie is a boy?" Jake asks her as they turn the corner and the Tube station comes into sight. "What if the magpie was a girl?"

"Are you out-feministing me?"

"Totally." He smirks. "I personally think that bird we just saw was a strong-willed single mother who, frankly, does not appreciate being misgendered and patronized."

"Oh, hark at him," Cat says. "Such an ally! Piss off."

"Don't be sour, or I'll cancel you," he teases. She pretends to pout and sulk for a moment, but then while she is fumbling in her pocket for her card to scan through the barrier, he mutters: "Still into you."

"What?" Cat turns to face him so quickly she ends up getting whipped in the eye by her own hair.

"That's my favorite Paramore song," he says, as if his meaning was obvious. "'Still Into You.'"

"You were a Paramore fan?" Cat looks up at him in wonder. "Just when I think I have you figured out."

A thought occurs to her on the Tube, and she insists they get off at Charing Cross. Trafalgar Square is rammed with tourists, predictably for a Sunday. Families with selfie sticks taking clumsy group shots in front of the fountains, groups following guides holding brightly colored balloons and umbrellas. Londoners, too: arguing couples, gaggles of laughing teenagers, a lone intrepid drunk sitting astride one of the enormous lions. Cat zigzags through them all, Jake close behind her, and she feels more than hears his amusement as he swiftly realizes their destination.

There has never been any reason for them to visit the National Gallery together: the plan is to take the ring from Freddie prior to the church ceremony, long before the reception. But it occurs to Cat now that plans can go awry, and they would be pretty poor thieves if they didn't do any reconnaissance of both proposed venues. Now, Cat figures, is as good a time as any.

They file through the portico entrance, between the enormous Corinthian columns, and into the main foyer. This is where the main reception will take place. Cat remembers thinking, the first time her mum brought her here as a child, how it more closely resembled a palace from a fairy tale than it did a museum, with its mosaiced floors, grand staircase, and domed ceiling. She grasped her mother's hand, uncertain why even as she did so. Was she frightened of getting swept away by the crowds? Or did she just feel so proud, so grown-up, that her mother wished to share all of this with her?

"This place is beyond extra," says Jake.

"Wait. Have you never been here before?"

"What can I say? I'm a typical Londoner. I've not done half the stuff that everyone comes here to do. The Dungeons, the Eye, all that."

"In that case"—Cat beckons him to follow her up the stairs— "let me show you my favorite paintings."

She takes him to the Da Vinci sketches first, although they have a little difficulty locating the shadowy vestibule where they reside like relics in a shrine, and get distracted by Hendrick ter Brugghen's *Man Playing a Lute*.

"He looks like the kind of guy who'd start playing 'Wonderwall' at a house party even though nobody asked," remarks Jake.

They move from the Renaissance to the Baroque, and while standing in front of *Samson and Delilah* by Rubens, Cat offhandedly remarks that Samson looks more than a little like Elijah.

Jake scoffs. "He's not *that* fit."

"Oh, he's not my type at all," Cat says, mildly amused by Jake's defensiveness. "When somebody is that shredded, it's because they wake up at five a.m. every day to work out, and they haven't touched a lick of alcohol since 2011. Sure, it looks great in photos, but it gets boring fast. You might as well try to bang Michelangelo's *David*. You'd get more warmth. And personality."

"Why do I get the feeling you're speaking from experience?"

"I may have very briefly dated a personal trainer when I first moved here," Cat says, her eyes fixed on the dome above them. "It was fun for about five minutes, then he kept trying to wake me up on Sunday mornings to go the gym. The *gym*, Jake."

"Sounds terrible," he says, and Cat can't help but notice that he squares his shoulders back and pulls himself up to his full height as they continue around the gallery. That she manages to hold in her giggle makes her think she could have a future in this confidence trickster thing after all.

"That was nothing," she says, leading him into another hall. "Then there was the massage therapist who was really into wild swimming."

"Wild swimming?"

Cat gestures to Seurat's *Bathers at Asnières*. "It's where you flop around in a freezing-cold pond at the crack of dawn and then talk about it for the rest of the day."

"You've been through the wringer then, I take it."

"Those guys were actually the nice ones. They didn't sneak off to the loo to do coke and think I didn't notice."

"You're having me on now."

"Are you seriously telling me you don't have any horror stories from your love life?"

Jake pauses before responding, just long enough that Cat can tell he was about to say one thing and then thought better of it.

"Not in front of the art," he says finally, with a wink.

She doesn't force the question, instead continuing to show him more of Seurat, then Van Gogh's *Sunflowers*, all the hits, reciting what she can remember of their backstory from art school.

"They always reminded me of those Magic Eye pictures that were everywhere in the nineties," Cat says as they stand in front of Monet's *Water-Lilies*. "You know, how you can be looking at it and see one thing, then if you just unfocus your eyes or change the angle you're looking from, it can turn into something else entirely. Almost as if it's in disguise or something."

"A painting that pretends," Jake muses. "Kind of like us."

"I suppose." Cat ducks her head, aware for the first time of how much she's been rambling. She used to loathe when Ronan stated commonly known trivia or widely held observations about art as if they were profound insights. Is she doing the same now? Assuming Jake knows nothing and pontificating when really she knows little more than what is already offered by the information panels beside each painting?

Jake sidles closer and says: "I like you here. The way you talk about all of this. It's like I'm seeing young, art-nerd Cat come to life."

She smiles. "It was always my favorite place to visit, before I moved here."

He leans in even farther and whispers in her ear: "The security here isn't as mad as I expected, either. A guard per room, if that. And cameras, obviously, but . . ."

"The paintings are all alarmed," Cat whispers back, unable to stop her eyes from tracing the geometry of his jaw from this new angle and proximity. The last time they stood this close, he kissed her. "If you tried to lift anything off the walls, it would raise hell."

"Luckily for us, we have no intention of stealing the *art*," Jake says.

"Exactly."

They make their way back through the rabbit warren of adjoining halls toward the main staircase, walking close together, their voices low enough that no details of the plan will echo out across the labyrinthine walls. To any casual onlooker, they are simply a couple taking in some culture before the weekend comes to a close. They bear left as they exit the gallery and cross the road, neither of them having to voice their next destination: St. Martin-in-the-Fields, the historic church on Trafalgar Square where Louisa and Stephen will be tying the knot in just a few short weeks. Sunday service has long since let out and their footsteps echo once they cross the threshold, like the building has dozed off and been suddenly awoken again at new signs of life.

How many christenings, weddings, funerals has this place seen over the years? Cat wonders. She tries to imagine the sheer volume of blissful couples who have made their vows under that vaulted ceiling, bathed in pearlescent light from the tall windows behind the altar. How could so many people be so absolutely certain they were doing the right thing?

"Not to sound superstitious . . . ," Jake begins, and Cat finishes for him:

"It would feel like bad luck, wouldn't it? Stealing in a church."

"We'll make the switch outside," Jake agrees. "Before the ceremony."

They have wandered up the aisle and are standing before the altar.

"Tell me," she says, "how you see us doing this."

"I'll make sure I'm here early," Jake says. "I can pretend I got the time wrong or something, so that I'm around before the other guests, before you and the other bridesmaids. When Stephen and his groomsmen show up, I'll congratulate him again, make small talk, ask about the stag. I'll clap Freddie hard on the back, say I'm sure he gave the groom a grand last day of freedom."

She can almost picture the scenario as Jake describes it to her: A hungover Freddie almost heaving as Jake boisterously grabs his shoulder, talking loudly to distract him as he swipes the ring from his suit pocket. The way Jake will blather on to kill time as he discreetly pockets the small box, then deftly opens it and exchanges the Tsarina for the Tsarinot by touch alone, before returning it to the best man and sending him on his way into the church none the wiser.

"We'll have to wait before making our getaway," Cat reminds him. "I'm a bridesmaid. It will look odd if I vanish so early. Suspicious, even. Shouldn't we wait until later in the evening to take the Tsarina, when we're more able to leg it?"

"We could. But the longer we wait—"

"The likelier it is that Elijah the *Men's Health* cover model will take custody of the ring again."

"Keep on talking like that, and your fake boyfriend will end up doing a very good impersonation of somebody who is jealous."

Cat snorts, and they turn to head back down the aisle toward the exit. They pass a middle-aged lady holding a stack of hymn sheets as they go, and she greets them warmly.

"Are you here for the Evensong?" she asks. "You're a tad early; it starts at five."

"No, thank you," Jake tells her. "We were just looking around."

She beams. "It's a beautiful place, isn't it?" Her eyes flit between the two of them. "Perfect for a wedding."

Cat returns her smile. "I couldn't agree more," she says.

Eighteen

Clouds have gathered outside, but the afternoon is still warm so they carry on walking, talking about the job, and the diamond, but also nothing in particular, easy in each other's company. They stroll down the Mall, swept up in the tide of tourists, and pause perfunctorily at Buckingham Palace, remarking aloud, as is tradition, "I wonder if they're home," before wandering into Green Park and up to Piccadilly.

It is the kind of Sunday in the city that Cat used to always daydream she would have before she moved here. But then, to save things from becoming more idyllic than she would know what to do with, the leaden sky cracks open like an egg and within seconds, torrential rain is rebounding off the pavement.

Jake pulls Cat into the doorway of a nearby gift shop for shelter from the sudden downpour, and they simply stand there at first, half-laughing at how quickly they have become drenched, before venturing inside. It is the kind of establishment that pops up every few yards in Central London, like recycled background scenery in a *Scooby-Doo* cartoon, that caters exclusively to souvenir-seeking tourists and always smells vaguely like licorice.

"Well, *hi* there," comes a familiar voice. It's Harper, arms laden with tea cozies, miniature teddy bears dressed as Beefeaters, and all manner of other commemorative tat. Spotting their confused looks, she glances down at her haul and says, by way of explanation: "I have a nephew."

"How old?" asks Jake, and Harper eagerly tells them that he is three.

"Isn't three a little bit young for a key ring?" Cat asks. Admittedly, she doesn't know a great deal about children, but she is certain that if a toddler has the means of letting himself in and out of the house, somebody should probably be called.

"Oh, no, *that* is for one of my roommates back in Berkeley," Harper says. "Isn't it amazing? And by 'amazing,' I of course mean"—she lowers her voice, so as not to offend the establishment's proprietor—"the ugliest little tchotchke you've ever seen?"

Cat laughs and agrees that the enamel fob, crudely printed with a dubious, cross-eyed likeness of Princess Diana, is in questionable taste at best.

"We have this ongoing competition," Harper explains, "to see who can bring back the tackiest gift from a trip. Last year, she came back from New Orleans and burdened me with a sculpture of a woman flashing her boobs for Mardi Gras beads. It's spectacular. I keep her on my nightstand. It's basically a full-blown gift war at this point."

"I think it's a war you have a fair chance of winning," Jake says, gesturing at the commemorative Charles and Camilla tea towels currently draped over her shoulder.

Harper beams. "I think so too," she says proudly. Then, as though it's just occurring to her: "Hey! Why don't I go pay for these and then buy you both a drink?"

Cat is tempted to say yes. She likes Harper, who is a damn sight more fun than the rest of Louisa's posh milieu. But it seems prudent to limit socializing to official wedding-related activities. She isn't quite sure how well her and Jake's pretext will hold up under extended scrutiny and fully expects him to agree.

"We'd love that," Jake tells Harper, putting his hand around Cat's shoulder. Clearly she doesn't know her fake boyfriend *that* well.

We'd love that. As if they are a real, ordinary couple who have just had the good fortune of running into a friend on a Sunday afternoon after one of them has just met the other's parents. Cat refuses to dwell on how agreeable it all feels and says: "The pubs around here are all terrible tourist traps, though."

"Perfect," Harper says before wandering off in search of the till.

Less than ten minutes later, following Harper's impromptu purchase of a golf umbrella emblazoned with the Union flag, the three of them are stationed on tall stools around a high, wobbly table, drinking overpriced lager out of pint glasses with handles while "London Bridge" by Fergie plays loudly over the sound system.

"God, doesn't this song remind you of being in high school?" Harper muses, holding her beer with both hands like it is a soothing mug of tea.

"I haven't heard it in years," says Cat. "Did you know the whole thing is wrong, though?"

"How so?"

"In the music video, London Bridge never actually appears," Cat says, assuming the tone she has heard in TED Talks. "It's actually Tower Bridge."

"You don't say!" Harper looks genuinely outraged. "I can't believe Fergie would lie to us like that."

"It was a huge scandal at the time," Jake adds in a similarly instructional voice.

"There was almost an international incident," Cat says.

LOVE & OTHER SCAMS · 179

"I seem to recall some talk of throwing her in the Tower of London," Jake says.

Harper shakes her head. "I'm learning more in this pub than I did on the entire open-top bus tour I took this morning."

"Stick with us, kid," Cat says, clinking her pint against Harper's and wondering when, exactly, she and Jake became an "us."

They soon empty their tankards and, against their better judgment, order another round. The music in the pub, at least, improves slightly. After "London Calling" by the Clash, "West End Girls" by Pet Shop Boys, and "LDN" by Lily Allen, the playlist sticks less religiously to its theme and starts churning out the greatest hits of Queen. Harper stuns them both by singing along, word-perfect, to all six minutes of "Bohemian Rhapsody"—*Wayne's World* was my favorite movie as a kid," she tells them—and then Jake admits, with some discomfort, that his first kiss was to "We Are the Champions."

"School disco, 2002," he says. "Jenny Smith. Prettiest girl in the year."

"Are you trying to make me jealous?" Cat asks playfully, because it strikes her as the kind of thing that someone's girlfriend might say. Pretending to be in a relationship, she is learning, is a lot easier than the real thing. Jake puts his hand over hers on the tabletop and leaves it there. Its weight sits comfortable and warm, like a blanket.

"You have got absolutely nothing to worry about," he says, before turning to Harper. "I loved *Wayne's World* too."

"Excellent, excellent!" Harper grins, tossing her wild curls around in a tipsy imitation of headbanging.

"I don't think I've ever seen it," Cat says, and both Jake and Harper look at her as if she has just confessed to owning a coat made from the fur of Dalmatian puppies.

"It is," Harper says, "and I cannot stress this enough, a modern classic of American cinema. At least, that's what my older brother used to say when we were kids, and *he* always had control of the VCR."

"Tia Carrere was my first love. And you never forget your first." She points at Jake with her tankard. "Speaking of which, you'll have to do more than change the subject to get out of telling the rest of that story! Jenny Smith. Prettiest girl in school. Go."

Jake shrugs. "There's not that much more to tell. I was thirteen, she was fifteen—"

"A cougar!" Harper interjects, and Cat snorts.

"We snogged on the dance floor, and I thought that meant we were boyfriend and girlfriend."

"A fair assumption," Cat says. "For a thirteen-year-old, anyway."

Harper clicks her tongue in disagreement. "If you'll allow me to live the liberal feminist cliché for just a moment," she says, "a reciprocal, egalitarian relationship ideally requires vocal, informed consent from both parties. A verbal contract, if you will."

Kind of like what Jake and I have, Cat thinks. *We both know exactly what kind of relationship we're* not *in.*

"Not such a feminist ally now, are you?" she whispers with impish glee.

"Long story short," Jake plows on, "Jenny Smith did *not* vocally consent to being my girlfriend and ended up going out with this lad called Dave, and as far as I'm aware, they are still together to this day."

Harper clutches her chest, feminist resolve seemingly softened by this development. "Childhood sweethearts," she says. "That is so adorable."

"Who am I to stand in the way of true love?" Jake says, finishing his beer.

"You did the mature thing," says Harper, shuffling down from her seat. "Okay, I am going to get us all another beer, no arguments, and then I want to hear about *your* first kiss." She nudges Cat with her elbow as she strides off in the direction of the bar.

"Is this okay?" Jake asks, once she is out of earshot.

"That you got jilted by your first kiss? Of course it's okay," Cat replies, patting his arm sympathetically. "You have nothing to be ashamed of."

Jake rolls his eyes. "No, I mean being here with a friend of the bride," he says. "I realize I didn't check with you before agreeing to come along for drinks."

Cat considers the unusual scenario for a moment. "I suppose we're helping flesh out our cover story," she says. "And . . ."

"And what?"

"I'm having a good time. Aren't you?"

"I am," he concedes. "She's not like the others we met at the party."

"She certainly is not." A thought occurs to her. "Unless Louisa is onto us, and she's sent one of her spies to get us drunk, loosen us up, and pump us for information."

"And how, exactly, would my embarrassing first kiss shed any light on our cunning scheme?"

He's right. Of all the people in Louisa's orbit, Cat's money would be on Elijah as the most natural-born interrogator. Harper, with her easy charm and slightly dorky sense of humor, just seems genuinely interested in other people. She is, Cat realizes, almost as poor a fit in Louisa's world as herself.

"So something crazy happened on the way back from the bar,"

she hears Harper say behind her. When Cat pivots in her chair, she sees Harper is holding a tray containing three shots of Jäger alongside their beers. "These just magically appeared in my hands," Harper says, her eyes wide with faux bemusement.

"No offense, Cat," Jake says with mock seriousness, "but I'm leaving you for Harper."

"Leave this girl and I'll go *Kill Bill* on your ass," Harper says, carefully placing the tray down on the table without spilling a drop. "And in case it wasn't already abundantly clear . . . Men are not exactly my cup of tea. Even the ones as sweet as yourself." She hands Cat a shot, then Jake. "Now. Bottoms up!"

"All this talk of first kisses," says Cat, once she has knocked back her shot and licked the tarlike residue from her teeth. "Who was yours, Harper?"

Harper sighs and gazes off into the middle distance. "Eliza Kaspersky," she says dreamily. "I mean, if you want to get technical, it was Josh Wyatt in ninth grade, but I don't count him, so you shouldn't either."

"And when was Eliza?" Jake asks.

"My first semester at Yale," says Harper. "I know, it's such a *trope*, right? The nerd goes to college and discovers the joys of womanist literature and homosexuality."

"I mainly discovered Super Noodles and *Jeremy Kyle*," says Cat, "but I can imagine."

"So, yeah. Eliza was my gateway drug. And now I'm all about that lifestyle. It's a wonder my parents haven't disowned me yet."

"For being a lesbian?" Cat asks, aghast.

"For being an academic," Harper says, and lets out a hoot of laughter at Cat's and Jake's horrified expressions. "They're both venture capitalists and hoped I would pursue something equally . . . well, capitalist. They're chill with me being queer but expected me to grow out of my literary theory phase after I graduated. I think a daughter in her thirties who's on her third degree and hasn't figured out what she wants to do for the rest of her life is the modern equivalent of one of those spinsters that parents are always trying to marry off in old novels."

"So you're still taking withdrawals from the bank of Mum and Dad?" Jake asks. Cat very nearly kicks him under the table.

"Nah. I gleaned some funding and live with three girls in Berkeley. I get by. But to my parents it's *beyond* bohemian. You would think I'd run away from home to be a courtesan and live in an opium den, the way they talk about it."

Cat isn't entirely sure what to say. For all the times she has resented Louisa's money and connections, it has never crossed her mind that somebody might *not* use such advantages if they had them. Still, she imagines it makes for one hell of a safety net.

"Well," Jake says, raising his pint, "here's to Eliza Kaspersky."

Cat doesn't know if all Americans are lightweights or just this one in particular, but it's not long after that she and Jake are bundling a sleepy-yet-giggly Harper into an Uber.

"You two are the best," she sighs, and extends her arms to hug them both, dropping her bags and spilling her phone, wallet, and all manner of ugly little keepsakes onto the concrete. Jake drops to a crouch and begins retrieving the detritus while Cat guides Harper into the car. When she turns back to Jake, he is still on the ground, Harper's wallet in his hand. Before she can say anything, he returns it to her handbag and offers up the haul to Cat.

"Text me when you get back," Cat instructs her once Harper is strapped in with all of her belongings.

"I promise." Harper nods before turning to the driver and bellowing: "Home, James, and don't spare the horses!"

Cat closes the car door, and she and Jake both stand there on the pavement, watching the car sidle into traffic.

"You didn't . . . ," Cat begins.

"Hmm?"

"You didn't take anything," she says. "From Harper, I mean."

"Is that a statement or a question?"

"A question, I suppose. She was an easy target."

Jake shrugs. "I like her," he says. "Although I *was* tempted to pinch that Diana key ring."

Cat isn't sure why she feels relieved. Maybe stealing from a drunk woman's purse feels like crossing a line. Or maybe it's because unlike everyone else Cat has met lately, Harper actually works for what she wants.

"No boyfriend of mine, pretend or otherwise, would be allowed to keep something that tacky," she tells him.

He smirks, and they say nothing again for a moment, watching after Harper's car even though it has long since disappeared.

"Are you hungry?" Jake asks finally. "I'm hungry."

Cat nods, famished, the roast chicken and walnut cake from earlier forgotten following the consumption of about a week's worth of alcohol.

"I know a decent chippy around the corner," Jake says. "Well, decent-ish."

"By all means, lead on."

The rain has slowed to a drizzle, but once they're inside it starts up again, hammering against the glass as they shuffle into chairs on either side of a bright yellow Formica table under a neon sign advertising the best chips in London. After just two bites of her cod supper, Cat has some serious doubts about the veracity of Jake's claim, but she is too hungry to care.

"I love hearing the rain when I'm inside," she says absentmindedly, drowning another chip in ketchup and popping it into her mouth. "There's something inherently cozy about it."

Jake chews thoughtfully, swallows, and says: "You never shared with the class."

"Hmm?"

"Your first kiss."

"Oh. Right. Yeah."

"Well?"

"David Drysdale. Very good-looking, but boring as sin. And a terrible kisser! I picked him at Vanessa Price's house party because he'd got off with *tons* of girls, and I thought, *Well, if I'm going to get this over and done with, it might as well be with the most experienced lad in our year.*"

"'Over and done with'? You old romantic." Jake grins.

"I was about to go into Year Eleven without ever kissing anyone. I wasn't going to let that be my narrative, so I weighed up my options and made an informed decision. Sadly, my data was flawed. Poor David was a fan of the old washing machine maneuver."

Jake frowns. "The what?"

"You know, when someone just rolls their tongue around your mouth like they're on a slow spin cycle. I expected more from the Casanova of Christleton High School."

"I'm sorry you were so disappointed."

"Meh. It is what it is." Cat shrugs. "We can't all have a Jenny Smith as our first kiss."

"Well, now I'm paranoid that I was on a slow spin cycle and didn't even know it," Jake says, mortified.

"You definitely don't need to worry about that," says Cat, without thinking.

Jake smiles and raises an eyebrow. "Is that so?"

She resists the pull of the memory of that night on the boat. The way his lips felt brushing against hers. The warmth of him.

"I just mean . . . ," she says, shaking her head to try to clear her thoughts—but what *is* it that she means? She doesn't even know she is drumming her fingers restlessly against the plastic countertop until Jake reaches out and places his hand on hers, stilling her.

"What are you doing?" she asks.

"Nothing," he says. "You just seemed tense for some reason."

"There's nobody around," she says. "You don't need to pretend."

He withdraws his hand. "I wasn't pretending," he says.

"Then why were you doing it?" she asks, hating herself for saying it, hating the line of plausible deniability that is about to be crossed. She can sense, like a coming storm, the inevitability of her least favorite thing: an honest adult conversation.

"I don't know," says Jake, confused. "I suppose I wanted to. Didn't you?"

I did. Of course I did.

"I'm sorry if I overstepped," he continues. "I genuinely thought—"

"I just think it's better if we don't blur any lines, you know?" she says, completely unaware that she thought this until she hears herself.

"Oh. Okay," says Jake, and a look crosses his face, before he returns to that skillful impassivity that lets Cat know she's hurt him.

"There's so much at stake," she says, unable to stop herself from talking. "We've both got so much riding on this. Isn't it better to keep things professional?"

She has the opportunity to change her life with the Tsarina. She can't afford to lose sight of her goal, not now. That's what this is about, she decides. It has nothing to do with being welcomed into someone's home, with Sunday lunch, with daytime drinks and stupid music and a familiar touch on her shoulder, her hip, her hand. Nothing at all to do with how it feels, even for a second, even if it's all just pretend, to be part of a "we."

"You're right," says Jake, his voice cool. "You're right. The job comes first."

Cat eats another chip before she can say anything else that will damage their partnership, that will endanger the job she has placed above all else. It tastes even worse than before.

"I should go," Jake says, rising from his seat.

"Okay," Cat says, unable to meet his eye. "I'll call you? About those ring settings."

"Sure," he says. A second later he is out the door. Cat watches him walk away through the window and then sits bathed in neon, her gaze idly following strangers as they pass in and out of the sickly yellow light. When she finally checks her phone for the first time since this morning, she sees a missed call from her dad and pushes her chips away, all appetite gone.

At least the rain has stopped, she thinks. That's something.

Nineteen

The package sits in the hall for a full day before Cat even notices it is addressed to her. Tom and Alex have been ordering so many parenting books on Amazon, she just assumed that the relatively flat parcel, encased in brown paper and measuring about two feet by one, was for them. Then she trips over the bloody thing on her way back in from a half-arsed, short-lived attempt at jogging, which she had hoped would clear her head, and finally sees her own name—and recognizes the scratchy handwriting. Ronan.

Cat briefly wonders if he has seen sense and mailed over the nude he painted of her when they were twenty, but she doesn't recognize the piece when she tears the brown wrapping away. It's more abstract than his usual oeuvre and depicts a woman in silhouette, standing on what could be a beach or a rock face, gazing out at the sunset. She looks like she is either contemplating the meaning of life or plucking up the courage to off herself. Taped to the back of the canvas are two notes. The first is in Louisa's flowing, looping script:

Just a small token of my gratitude and eternal friendship. L. x

The second is Ronan's still-familiar scrawl:

My Cat,

Louisa commissioned five original paintings as gifts for her bridesmaids. She wanted work that celebrated female power and mystique. I gave special consideration to the piece that would be yours. I call her Calliope. It is my hope that, each time you look at it, you will think of me.

Your Ronan

Calliope. One of the Greek muses. Cute.

"That is so romantic," Tom says after she carries it into the kitchen and props it up on the windowsill.

"Was he too busy to deliver it himself?" Alex asks.

"It was a paying job," Cat tells them. "If Ronan was nursing tender feelings for anyone while he made this, it was himself."

"You can be so harsh," says Tom. "Your ex has just sent you a painting. And a beautiful note. Can't you enjoy that for even a moment?" Alex beckons for her to show him the note and frowns in disdain as he takes in Ronan's pretty words.

"It doesn't even sound like him," says Cat. "It's too overblown, too grand. Not to mention inappropriate. He *knows* I have a boyfriend. I—"

Tom's and Alex's heads both shoot up so quickly they are in danger of whiplash.

"Boyfriend?" Alex asks. "Since when? Who is he?"

"And why haven't we met him?" asks Tom.

Right. That is another part of her plan. Keeping Jake a secret from Tom and Alex. They're a part of her real everyday life. Even if they *are* kicking her out of the house in the near future. Lying to them about her arrangement with Jake would feel wrong, somehow. Too close to home.

"It's very new," she says. "I suppose I just didn't want to jinx things by introducing him to all of my friends." *Only the ones I'm trying to con*, she thinks.

"This is huge," says Tom. "I don't think I've ever heard you use the B word in the entire time you've lived here."

"That's ridiculous," says Cat.

It is also, she thinks, undeniably true. She's dated plenty, had her share of fun—and less fun—encounters with men, like any woman who spent her twenties single in London. But whoever the guy, there was always something that didn't quite fit. He'd be too busy to see her, or she'd be too broke for the activity he suggested, or, more often than not, one of them would simply ghost the other. Dating in the city felt like playing Tetris: with each passing year, the pace of the game sped up and the pressure to make all of the pieces slot together increased. Any incongruities that arose on the first date usually negated the need for a second, until Cat eventually recused herself from the game entirely. Prior to Jake, she hadn't been on a date for nearly a year.

"So you've got one man sending you gifts," muses Alex, "and another who we didn't even know existed."

"You're making it sound far more scandalous than it really is," Tom chides. "She's only got the *one* man on the go. The other one is just . . . a backup, right?" He looks at Cat expectantly.

"Ronan can back up into oncoming traffic for all I care," she says. "Now if you'll excuse me, I have a CV to send out that will no doubt go straight into several people's spam folders."

She turns to leave the kitchen. Two seconds later, she doubles back to grab the painting. It really is a lovely piece, even if it was painted by a bit of an arsehole. And Cat didn't do a fine art degree just to leave an original painting to molder next to the kettle. If everything Ronan said about his rising stock in the art world was true, this could be worth something someday. Maybe even someday soon.

Group: BRIDESMAIDS ASSEMBLE

DARCY: Hi ladies! So I'm sure by now you're all wondering where we're taking Louisa for her hen weekend.

HARPER: Hen?

CAT: Weekend??

DARCY: @Harper I think you guys call it a bachelorette.

DARCY: And yes, @Cat, of course, a weekend! We need to make sure our girl gets a chance to celebrate her last few days of freedom ;)

OLIVIA: A woman I knew tried to strongarm a load of us into a hen WEEK last year. She's dead to me. A weekend is fine. But I need dates stat, @Darcy.

PRIYA: Oh yayyy I love a good hen! @Darcy where are we going?

DARCY: That's the energy I was looking for, thanks @Priya! So. Without any further ado . . .

DARCY: We're going to Palermo!

OLIVIA: Gorg. I love Sicily. But @Darcy, I'm not kidding, I need those dates. I have a law firm to run.

OLIVIA: And a child.

OLIVIA: And a husband.

DARCY: It's three weeks from today, Wednesday morning to Friday evening. Right before the wedding on Monday.

PRIYA: No problem!

OLIVIA: I'm sure that'll be fine. I'll have my PA move some things around.

HARPER: How fun, I've never been to Italy.

DARCY: Sicily, babe.

HARPER: Is that different?

CAT: How much is this going to cost?

DARCY: Don't worry about a thing. Louisa and Stephen know it's a lot, packing all of these wedding celebrations into such a short space of time, so they're taking care of everything. Stephen is covering the BA flights (Heathrow, btw, 7 a.m.) and we'll be using his family's apartment in a stunning palazzo, free of charge.

CAT: Oh

CAT: Cool

CAT: Count me in!

DARCY: And are you all ready for the really exciting part?

PRIYA: There's more??

DARCY: Stephen and his stags will be flying out with us!

DARCY: They'll be golfing on the other side of the island, and then Stephen and Louisa have decided it would be so fun to get the two groups together and round off the weekend with a big group dinner before catching our flight back!

> **DARCY:** @Cat, could you text me Jake's number? Louisa said Stephen wants to invite him along with the boys.

> **CAT:** Wait

> **CAT:** What?

It's been three days since their intensely awkward conversation in the fish-and-chip shop, and she's been avoiding contacting him, but after sending Darcy his number, Cat knows that she owes Jake a heads-up on the invitation he is about to receive. Meeting face-to-face to clear the air would be best. A phone call, at the very least.

She takes the coward's way out and sends him a text.

> Hi. Hope you're good. Just FYI: Stephen is going to invite you on his stag weekend. You must have made quite the impression on him.

She throws her phone down on the sofa next to her, like she's afraid it will bite her if she holds on to it, and tries to focus on the task at hand: shuffling cards. The plan is still for Jake to be the one to lift the Tsarina when the time comes—Cat has far too heavy a touch—but she figures that it wouldn't hurt to improve her own dexterity for the future. You never know when it might come in handy, after all.

So this morning she searched every cupboard in the house, finding a set of dominoes, a battle-scarred Monopoly board, and two travel editions of Scrabble, but not a single pack of playing cards. Eventually, under her bed, she rediscovered the gift bag she'd brought home from a female empowerment event she attended last year. The event wasn't her kind of thing at all—in fact, she suspected at the time that it might be some sort of cult—but Cat isn't the sort to turn down a free glass of white wine or merch that can be resold on eBay.

The goodie bag had yielded little in the way of resellables: a rose-quartz crystal, a small soy candle purporting to smell like a woman's privates, and a deck of tarot cards, which Cat now sits hunched over, thumbs and forefingers aching, frustration growing. *How does Jake make it look so easy?* she keeps asking herself, and then the answer pops into her mind—*Hours and hours of practice, Vivi said*—and the cycle of trying and failing continues, until Cat finally flicks the cards in a temper, sending them sliding across the coffee table.

"Calm down, Mystic Meg," says Alex, walking into the living room with a mug in either hand. "You'll anger the spirits if you treat your cards like that."

He places a tea on the lacquered wood in front of her. Tom is pathological about coasters, which for Alex seems to be enough reason not to use them. Cat doesn't even pretend to understand it.

"I didn't know you were into this stuff," Alex says, shooing her farther up the sofa so he can take a seat next to her.

"I'm not," she says. "Not really. I was just practicing."

"Practicing what?"

"Shuffling," she says honestly. Then, less honestly: "There was some talk of visiting a casino on this hen weekend I'm going on."

"Babe, I don't gamble much but even I know that they have people to shuffle the cards *for* you in a casino." Alex looks at her like she's stupid and takes a sip of his tea. Cat doesn't take it personally. For a doctor, he knows bugger-all about how to sugar a pill. She can only imagine that his rich, predominantly female patients enjoy being sassed by a caustic but handsome young doctor with olive skin and green eyes. It certainly seems to work for Tom.

"So are you going to give me a reading or not?" he asks, looking at the haphazard spread of cards, then back at her.

"I wouldn't know how," Cat says. "Like I said, it's not really my—"

"Fine, I'll just pick one and you tell me what it means," he says, leaning forward and selecting one of the cards closest to him. He flips it over and inspects it. "The Wheel of Fortune." He squints at her, as if his choice of card is her fault. "Isn't that a TV show?"

"Yes," says Cat.

"And it signifies what, exactly?"

Cat's phone vibrates loudly from where it has fallen between the seat cushions, and she gives Alex an apologetic smile before pulling it out.

> He just called me to invite me. I said yes. I hope that's okay.

Jake's tone is curt. At least, she thinks it is. Can you ever really tell somebody's tone in a message? She tries not to read into the subtext of Jake's short, to-the-point sentences and sends her reply.

> This could be great, actually. Anything that gets us closer to the happy couple, right?

Three animated dots appear, indicating that Jake is typing. Then they vanish and reappear. Finally, Jake's response comes through.

Right.

It's official. He's still angry with her. Cat is about to turn to Alex, to ask him if he can explain men as a concept to her, when she remembers that if anything, Jake is the emotionally articulate one out of the two of them, which makes this not-quite-radio-silence all the more maddening.

Cat finds herself wishing, for the second or third time, that she could talk with someone about the whole Jake situation. Her first instinct is to text Harper, which is ridiculous. Cat has no doubt Harper would be great at supportive relationship chat, but telling her anything about the true nature of her and Jake's non-relationship is out of the question.

Alex loudly slurps on his tea next to her, and Cat is tempted to use him as a sounding board. He has proven on more than one occasion that he loves mess, and she doubts he actually cares enough about her to go to the effort of getting her in trouble. But no. That would be too risky as well. Best to do things the Bellamy way. Cat might be a terrible pretend girlfriend, and an undexterous thief, but when it comes to keeping it all on the inside, she is an old pro.

"Let's try again," she says to Alex. "Pick a card, any card."

"Yes, witch!" Alex's tone is light, but she can tell from the way that he hems and haws over the deck, brow furrowed, fingertips hovering close to making a choice only to then twitch away like the cards themselves are hot, that a part of him is taking this seriously.

She has a fairly decent idea of the picture in his mind, the future he has already conjured up but would like written in stone: a bigger house with a garden, and a child to play in it.

She isn't the only one under this roof standing on the brink of a different life. She just has a lot less of hers planned out.

Alex continues to prevaricate until she finally chides him into making a decision, and he hurriedly turns over a card near the end.

"Death?" His pretty eyes bulge at the skeletal figure depicted on the coffee table. "Are you fucking kidding me?"

"Calm down," Cat says. "Even I know about this one: it's not as bad as it looks. It's a metaphor. It means a big life change is coming. A new direction, either career-wise or personally. That's good, right?"

But Alex has already stood up and is marching his tea back to the kitchen, his superstitious side seemingly restored. "I would stick to Rummy if I were you," he says. From the hallway, he calls over his shoulder: "By the way, don't forget the agent is coming to take photos of the house tomorrow. Could you make sure your room is nice and tidy?"

"Sure thing, Dad!" she yells back, sinking deeper into the sofa.

Twenty

After another three days of noncommunication, Jake sends a message summoning Cat to the bar. She arrives five minutes earlier than the time he suggested, and rather than simply breezing into the Oceanic like she has so many times before, instead she walks the full length of the street and back, then lets out a long exhale and walks inside.

It's the middle of the day and the bar is, predictably, empty. Cat doesn't know how this place makes money outside of the after-work Friday crowd. Jake gives her a nod as she approaches, and then a small smile as she gets closer. The nerves she's been swallowing like bile for the last hour abate a little as she follows him through into the back room.

"I got you something," he tells her, and it takes a moment for Cat to fully understand what is happening when he casually hands her a glossy, brand-new iPhone. It's the latest model, the kind that takes almost an entire handspan to comfortably hold, with the equivalent computing power of a small Hadron Collider.

Jake simply shrugs. "Watching you use that smashed one was stressing me out."

These things cost at least a grand, she thinks, and asks: "Where did you get it?"

"Don't worry about it." His tone is nonchalant, but she still spies that glint in his eye.

"Oh. Right. Of course. Thank you." She places the device in her bag next to the old one. "Is that why you texted me?"

"No. Not the only reason. My guy came through." Jake starts rummaging in a drawer in an old filing cabinet. "I showed them the specs, and they were able to create an exact copy of the ring setting to go with our dupe diamond, for the fee we agreed."

"That's great," Cat says weakly. This *is* good news. The plan would immediately fall apart if they were to leave Louisa with a ring that looks nothing like the one they're planning to steal.

"It gets better," Jake continues, finally retrieving a small box from the cabinet. "Sid has found a buyer."

"No," Cat says. "I mean, yes! Oh my god, thank you, Sid!" She didn't even realize how much she was holding her breath over this part. "And he's still okay with the ten percent cut we agreed on?"

"More than okay," Jake says. "I think if he were a slightly less practical man, he'd offer to set it all up for free. He's just bloody thrilled to be involved in a job this big."

The thought warms Cat. She has no doubt that Sid has seen all kinds of stuff in his life. For him to be so excited by something that was her idea feels like the validation she never even knew she was looking for.

Jake opens the box so that it's facing Cat.

"Wow," she says. The ring in front of her looks *exactly* like the one that adorns Louisa's finger, the one she has seen in a dozen or so Instagram photos by now. For a split second, Cat wonders if Jake has just robbed the bride already.

He takes the diamond out of its velvet niche and holds it out to Cat.

"Go on," he says, offering it to her.

"Go on . . . what?" she asks.

"Try it on." He reaches forward as if to take her hand, then stops himself. Oh. Right. Those boundaries she was so eager to lecture him about. Cat dodges his gaze, instead looking at the Tsarinot.

She reminds herself that it is fake. It is a lump of resin, sculpted by a laser and polished over many hours in the back room of a hotel bar, sitting on a cheap imitation of the platinum ring Louisa wears. Jake is not standing here offering her a diamond ring. So why, for a second, does she feel butterflies as she reaches out and takes it? And why does she continue to avoid eye contact when she feels how warm it is from his fingers?

Cat almost puts it on the ring finger of her left hand, then something stops her. Call it superstition. She switches and instead slides it onto the third finger of her right hand, then holds it up.

"How does it look?" she asks.

Jake says nothing at first and Cat's stomach drops. It's an obvious fake. Anyone who sees this on Louisa's hand will immediately be able to tell it isn't the real McCoy. What was she even thinking? They never stood a chance of pulling this off.

Then Jake clears his throat and says: "Perfect."

"Thank god," she whispers.

"Thank Mikhail," says Jake, and she laughs.

"Serves him right for all those invoices he took his sweet time paying," she says, shaking her hair out of her eyes.

"You're right." Jake smirks. "He should *totally* have seen something like this coming."

"I should team up with other disgruntled freelancers," she muses, "and set up some kind of extralegal retribution agency."

"I can see it now!" Jake looks into the middle distance. "Cat Bellamy and her band of merry men, stealing from unscrupulous clients and giving to London's underclass of copywriters, designers, and photographers."

"Joke all you want," Cat says with a mock scowl. "If creatives actually had time and resources, they could come up with some truly ingenious schemes."

"A lack of resources doesn't seem to have presented much of an obstacle to you," says Jake, taking a step forward. "I mean, look around. You've planned an entire heist with nothing more than a cracked iPhone and a grudge."

"Just imagine what I could do with a costume department and a proper night's sleep."

"You don't strike me as the kind of person who ever has trouble sleeping."

"You'd be surprised." Cat shrugs.

Jake steps even closer, so that he is now towering over her.

"What keeps you up at night?" he asks. She can feel the warmth of his breath on her face. "Go on. Tell me."

The way he's looking at her, gazing down, Cat's first thought is that he's going to kiss her again. A jumble of protestations rises up in her throat, haughty words like "boundaries" and "the job." She tries to remember what she said to him in the chip shop, but all that comes to her is the way his hand felt on hers.

Jake steps away without her saying anything, as if he's read her mind. He smiles, looks *extra* pleased with himself, and Cat can't for the life of her figure out why—until he raises his right hand. There, between his thumb and forefinger, is the Tsarinot. He plucked it straight off her finger, and she didn't feel a thing.

"Oh," she gasps. "You *arse*."

The intense eye contact! The physical proximity! That thing he said about keeping her *up at night*! All distractions. Cat is furious. And fascinated.

"Can you teach me how to do that?" she asks.

"Maybe. Why?"

"It can't hurt to have a plan B," she says. "What if you can't get the diamond off Freddie outside the church?"

"Your confidence in me is staggering."

"Shit goes wrong all the time is all I'm saying."

Jake purses his lips, giving her words thought. "You're right," he says. "But learning this . . . it takes a lot of practice. Maybe we should start with some card hustles."

"I'm getting quite good at those," Cat lies. "I can hide the lady just fine."

"Is that right?" His lips twitch into another smirk. What she wouldn't give to wipe it right off his face. What she wouldn't do to—Cat promptly cuts herself off from that line of thought.

"Try and take it again," she says, holding out her hand for the ring. "I want to see how you do it." She puts the Tsarinot back on her finger. "Pretend I'm Louisa. It's the wedding; we're surrounded by people. Go."

"Okay." Jake closes his eyes, inhales and exhales deeply in some approximation of a serious thespian centering themselves, and then opens them again, his entire face lighting up as he takes her in.

"Louisa," he says. "You look stunning." He draws her into an embrace, and it is almost a relief to no longer be in the path of his gaze. "I can't tell you how great it's been," he continues, "meeting my darling Cat's friends."

My darling Cat. Something inside her ripples in pleasure at the words, and she pushes down on it like she's trying to smother it.

Jake withdraws from the embrace, his hands gliding down her arms and brushing against her hands as their bodies part. She curls her right hand into a fist, catching hold of the ends of Jake's fingers.

"Gotcha," she breathes. She turns his hand upward, and they both look down at the ring held between his thumb and forefinger.

"Nice catch."

"I'm a fast learner."

"All right." Jake reaches into his jeans pocket and pulls out the gold wedding band she first noticed all those nights ago. She hasn't seen it in a while. It makes sense that Jake would take it off while posing as her boyfriend, but she can't remember the last time she saw him wearing it at the bar. *Maybe all the cougars have gone into hibernation*, she thinks.

He slides it onto his finger and then beckons her.

"Your turn," he says. "Try me."

An hour later, she has foiled the majority of Jake's attempts to lift the Tsarinot, but try as she might, she is unable to take the gold ring from him: each time her fingers close around the metal, he playfully bats her hand away.

"You keep looking down," he says. "Keep your eyes on mine. Find it by touch."

It's no use. The longer they go on, the warmer Cat's hand becomes from the sustained skin-on-skin contact, her clammy fingers failing to find purchase in any remotely subtle way.

"Damn it," she groans after her hundredth aborted attempt. "So much for a backup plan."

"You *are* getting better," Jake says, pocketing the ring. Cat flushes at the praise and hates herself for it. Then her phone vibrates in her pocket, and she's brought back to the moment.

"If this is the bloody bridesmaids group chat again . . . ," she mutters, but it's not. It's an incoming call. From her dad.

"Do you need to take that?" Jake asks. "I can step out."

"No, it's fine," says Cat, watching the shattered screen until the buzzing stops and is replaced by a *Missed Call* notification. "I'll ring him back later." *When I have good news*, she thinks. *When I have money, and my own place, and can tell him he can finally stop worrying about me.*

Jake looks at her like he's going to say something else, but then he appears to think better of it. She's glad. For all of the inherent dodginess of his adopted extended family, Jake's home life seems incredibly well-adjusted. Cat doesn't feel like fielding any unsolicited questions or advice about her own situation right now.

"So, Palermo," she says. When in doubt, change the subject.

"Not long now." Jake rocks on his heels.

"Think you can handle two days of golfing with Stephen and his Bullingdon Club lost boys?"

"My swing is on the rusty side," he says, stretching out his shoulders so that Cat is unable to ignore just how *broad* they are. "But a free trip to Sicily? I'm down. Maybe we should befriend these people for real and reap the benefits instead of just staging a one-off job."

"Believe me, it is *not* worth it," Cat assures him. "I'm over ten years deep with Louisa, remember?"

"This Stephen seems like an all-right guy, though," Jake says. "I mean, relatively speaking. For a rich white boy who has had every opportunity in life handed to him on a silver platter. Scrap that; the platter was probably solid gold."

"I have to admit, she seems to have done well for herself," Cat says. "He's a bona fide Prince Charming, which instantly makes me wonder what he's like when nobody is watching."

"You think he's got a mean streak?"

"Doesn't everybody?"

Jake gives her that look again: like he wants to say something but knows it would be overstepping.

"What?" she asks.

"I just wonder, sometimes," he says.

"You wonder . . . ?"

"Who hurt you?"

The question sounds like such a cliché that Cat can't help blurting out a laugh.

"I'll tell you mine if you tell me yours," she says.

His brow furrows slightly. "Mine?"

"Vivi told me you got double-crossed on a job a while ago. Don't tell me that didn't make you a little bit gun-shy."

She says it glibly, perhaps a little too much so. Jake's shoulders tense, and it takes a second longer than usual for his expression to resume its forced neutrality.

"I didn't know she told you about that," he says. "She shouldn't have."

"I don't know any of the specifics; she didn't go into details," Cat says, keen to let him know this wasn't a betrayal on his mother's part. "But I understand. You start to think the worst of people, don't you? And for the most part . . . you tend to be right."

"Not always," Jake says. "I've never thought the worst of you."

"Maybe you should," Cat fires back. "I was committing a literal crime when we met."

"True. But you always tipped well with your ill-gotten gains." He smiles. "And once again, you have dodged the original question. Unsuccessfully, I might add."

"Are you my therapist now?" Cat says sullenly, walking out of the storeroom. Jake follows her back into the bar.

"Therapists are for rich people," Jake says. "Talking is free. As is the next round, if you answer my question."

"That's blackmail."

"It's bribery, actually." He rests his forearms on the counter as she files around it and takes a seat on the other side. "I just want to get to know my partner better. Is that so wrong?"

Yes, Cat thinks. *Because once you see beneath the snarky exterior, you'll realize there's nothing under it. You'll wonder what the hell you were doing trying to get close to me.*

"Let's start with the easy part," Jake says, reading her silence as acquiescence. "Why don't you tell me his name."

Cat lets out a long exhale.

"Ronan McCann," she says.

"Sounds like a prick," Jake responds automatically. "Where did you meet him?"

"At uni," she says. "I wasn't that fussed about him to begin with. I thought we were just having a laugh. Louisa seemed more invested in it than me, if anything. She always found it odd that I spent so much time by myself. He was kind of intense, and at first I found it all a bit cringe. He would text me at all hours, telling me he was thinking about me; he'd wait for me outside lectures."

"Was he your boyfriend or your stalker?" Jake asks, pouring vodka directly into a shaker without measuring.

"That's what I said!" Cat replies, the words coming more freely now. "But Louisa said that I just didn't know anything about romance or how relationships work."

"So what happened then?"

"I suppose I got used to the attention," she says. "Found it flattering, even. And I stopped being quite so standoffish with him, and then he eased up a bit on the incredibly full-on gestures, and we kind of found a middle ground that worked for both of us. We were together for two years."

She pauses for a moment, taking in the rhythmic rattle of the cocktail shaker.

"In final year, he couldn't stop talking about our future," she continues. "He had all these plans for what our lives would look like when we moved to London. And then we graduated, and . . ."

Jake slides the martini across the bar toward her.

"He had a change of heart?" he asks.

"He told me that things were moving way too fast between us," she says. She feels that same sting of humiliation now that she did then, when Ronan looked at her as if she were trying to force him down the aisle with a shotgun. "'We've had a great time,' he said. 'But we never agreed that we'd be moving to London *together*.'

"I never even wanted a serious relationship in the first place; he was the one who couldn't help acting like we were Tristan and Isolde or something. And all of a sudden, *I* was the one trying to trap *him*, like some kind of commitment-crazed bunny boiler."

"That must have hurt," Jake says.

"Hurt? Forget hurt," Cat says, picking up her drink. "I was *embarrassed*. Like he won when he finally got me to agree to be his girlfriend, and then he won again by being the one to dump me." She takes a long, bitter sip of vodka and vermouth while Jake grapples with this new emotional calculus. "I'm not saying I'm still sore over something that happened at uni," she adds hastily. "I guess that just set the tone for a decade of serial dating in London with one self-absorbed sociopath after another. And then I bumped into him on that bloody boat and now I'm like, *Oh right, that's where my run of bad luck began*."

"I'm still not sure I understand you," Jake says finally. "But I think I understand men like that even less."

"You can ask him all about *his* feelings soon enough," Cat says, swirling the olive around her glass and then popping it into her mouth. "I'm fairly certain he's going to be at the wedding."

"Well," Jake says, leaning on the bar and looking Cat so keenly in the eye that she nearly slips off her stool, "all the more reason to convince everyone there that I make you blissfully happy."

Twenty-one

Cat and Jake agree that on the morning of the flight to Palermo, they should arrive at the airport together, to keep up their pretense. It is a simple enough idea, but as it is such a lengthy journey on the Tube, and an early morning Uber with two pickups would be nothing short of a "ball-ache"—Jake's word, not hers—they decide that it will be easier if they simply sleep in the same location the night before.

"I live out east," Jake says. "It'll be a trek, but it's doable."

"I suppose the hotel would frown upon us helping ourselves to a couple of rooms?" Cat asks.

"Given what we've both gotten away with there, I wouldn't push our luck any farther," Jake says, and she's inclined to agree.

"It's fine," she says. "You can just stay at my place. Tom and Alex are away for a few days." Jake, ever the gentleman, wouldn't dream of ousting Cat from her own bed and says he will gladly make do on the sofa. And so it is settled, and Cat doesn't give it another thought. Her mind does not linger, even for a minute, on the idea of Jake sleeping under the same roof as her. She does not speculate about what he wears to bed or what his hair might look like first thing in the morning when he wakes up. Does he rub his eyes groggily and then turn his face back toward the pillow, or is he one of those people who greets the day with a deep breath and a long, satisfying stretch? She is not curious at all. Besides, it's not as if she will have the opportunity to find out; they will be sleeping, and waking, in separate rooms.

Or at least so she thinks, until she gets back to the house on Tuesday night from buying last-minute travel miniatures to find Tom and Alex on the sofa, having renounced their plans for a midweek getaway to Birmingham to visit Tom's mother and look at houses.

"She's under the weather," Tom informs Cat.

"She's a hypochondriac," Alex butts in. "I should know—they're my bread and butter."

"That's a pity," Cat says, barely listening, mind racing. "Why don't you guys go out for a nice dinner or something instead?"

"Ugh, no," says Alex. "Work's been a nightmare lately; I just want to open a bottle of wine and watch *The Crown*."

"I thought we were going to finally start *Elite*," Tom says, frowning.

"If you think I'm going to spend my free time reading subtitles just so you can see some Spanish twinks showering together, you have another thing coming," Alex informs him. His Greek accent intensifies, an affectation that Cat has come to know means he will fight if necessary. He was born in Bethnal Green.

Tom throws up his hands. "Whatever," he says, standing up. "I'll get the merlot."

"Malbec," Alex says, correcting him, as he walks out into the hallway. The doorbell rings. Jake is right on time, but his timing could not be worse. Cat hurriedly follows Tom out, but he has already opened the front door to a slightly confused-looking Jake.

"I think I might have the wrong house," he begins.

"No! You don't! I'm here!" Cat waves at him from behind Tom's six-foot-three frame like a terrier jumping for attention. "Jake, this is Tom. One of my housemates."

Realization dawns on Jake's face, followed swiftly by recognition.

"You're Tom Porter," he says. "My mum loves you."

Tom smiles graciously and extends a hand. Other broadcasters might fear that such a comment would render them uncool, but Tom Porter is under no illusions about his career having been built on the affection of the mums, aunties, and nanas of the United Kingdom. Cat tries to picture Vivi Marlowe sitting down to watch Tom interview a reality TV personality about their new book and suppresses an absurd giggle. The mental image expands to include itinerant criminal Sid on the sofa next to Vivi, watching intently as Tom attempts an obstacle course in aid of promoting exercise to the over-fifties, and she nearly loses her shit altogether.

"Wait a minute," Tom says, pivoting slightly to allow Jake into the house. "That must make you . . ."

"Cat's new boyfriend?" Alex appears in the living room doorway like a puppy that has just heard the rattle of food in its bowl.

"That's me," says Jake, reaching out to shake Alex's hand. "It's so nice to meet you both. Cat has told me all about you."

"None of it's true," says Tom jovially, at the precise same time that Alex says: "Funny, she's told us almost nothing about you."

"Jake," Cat butts in. "Why don't you come through to the kitchen, and I'll get us both a drink."

"And a bottle of malbec while you're at it," Alex adds, before Tom bundles him back into the living room apologetically.

"I thought they said they were going away," Jake says once they are ensconced in the galley kitchen.

"They also said they'd never move out of London," Cat mutters.

"What?"

"Nothing." She runs her hands through her hair and takes a deep breath.

"I can go," says Jake, "if this is too much. I mean, I can't sleep on the sofa while they're both, you know, *on it*. We can meet at the airport."

"Don't be silly," she says. "You're here now. We can just . . ."

"Hide in your room until they go to sleep?"

"Well?" That was exactly what Cat was planning to say, but coming out of Jake's mouth, Cat hears how silly it sounds.

"Then I can sneak downstairs, nice and quiet, and just pray that neither of them wakes up in the mood for a snack or a glass of water."

The kitchen door opens abruptly, and they are both confronted by Tom's grinning face.

"Jake," he says, "I couldn't help but notice you have an overnight bag."

"Oh, right." Jake looks down at the leather holdall as if he forgot he was holding it. "We have a flight first thing in the morning."

"You're going to Sicily with Cat? Oh, così romantico!" Tom claps his hands. "Well. Seeing as you're staying the night, you get a vote. *The Crown* or *Elite*?"

"Pardon?"

"Follow me," Tom says, beckoning Jake down the hallway and into the living room. "You can leave your bag at the foot of the stairs for now. Oh, and, Cat?" he calls back to her. "You choose the wine."

After three hours, two bottles of wine, and a "compromise"

that somehow ends in their all watching *The Devil Wears Prada*—Alex's favorite film—Cat is able to drag Jake away from Tom and Alex, who have chosen tonight of all nights to resume their interest in being welcoming hosts, plying Jake with red wine and cashews and questions about his and Cat's relationship.

"Do you pick up many girls in that bar, Jake?" Tom inquires in a manner almost threatening.

"Where do you live, again?" Alex asks, clearly envisioning a future in which Cat moves in with Jake and they are saved the awkwardness and the fuss of having to evict her.

Jake answers all of their questions with relative honesty, only omitting any details that pertain to the job.

"I can understand you being so protective of Cat," he says, reaching his arm over her shoulder and pulling her closer to him on the sofa. "She's special."

Cat, for her part, takes a slug of wine and snuggles into him, enjoying the not-so-subtle look of pleasant surprise exchanged by her housemates. *Maybe I should go into acting*, she thinks. *Because that's totally what this is. Acting.*

"They seem nice," Jake says now, in the privacy of Cat's bedroom.

"They're terrorists," she says. "But . . . yeah. They're not so bad."

"You seemed a bit frazzled when I first got here. Is everything okay?"

"Fine. I just—I hadn't planned on them meeting you."

"I'll try not to take that personally," Jake says, lowering his bag onto the floor and looking around at his surroundings. Cat is suddenly acutely aware of just how infrequently she dusts in here, of the untidy stacks of books and sketchpads and old *Friends* DVDs she has been mainlining since having to cancel her Netflix account. She nudges a discarded bra under the bed with the side of her foot before he can see it.

"I thought it would complicate things," she says, "if even the guys I live with were part of this lie we're telling."

Jake slowly paces the length of her room, a process that takes all of two seconds, and then turns back to her.

"I get that." He nods. "I would feel like shit if my mum thought me and you were a real couple."

Cat thinks back to the long, piercing look Vivi gave her at the house and pities any genuine girlfriend Jake might have taken home.

"Pretending is fun when you can close the door on it at the end of the day," she says.

"I'm sorry." Jake takes to pacing again. "I thought I was doing the right thing, but I should have checked with you before jumping into boyfriend mode tonight."

"I should have texted you some warning," she tells him, thinking: *But I love it when you jump into boyfriend mode. Even if we have to spend the night watching rom-coms with wine. Especially then.*

"No, I should have known better," he says. "I'll give it half an hour, and we can try the creeping-downstairs thing."

"Don't be daft. I'm really not in the mood to explain to my housemates why my new boyfriend is spending the night on the sofa."

"Fine. I'll sleep on the floor." The second he says it, one of the floorboards gives a deeply unpleasant creak beneath his pacing feet. "Looks comfy," he adds, and they both laugh. Cat is surprised by how amusing she finds it—how appealing, even—to see Jake at his least slick. She is reminded of the way he was at Vivi's place, the awkward, embarrassed teenager he reverted to.

"I just don't want to fuck this up," he says.

It is this earnestness, she thinks later, that leads to everything that comes after. Cat is no stranger to a smooth criminal, but every time Jake lets even a glimpse of imperfection show beneath that seemingly effortlessly charming veneer, all she wants to do is grab on to the front of his shirt and pull him closer, to kiss him for real.

She shouldn't, of course. It would be breaking the very rules *she* laid down. She promised not to get distracted by this double act of theirs, never to lose sight of the bigger picture. But right now, as Jake Marlowe stands in front of her, she finds she can't see anything else.

Cat steps toward him. Watches him take in the movement, sees a glimmer of something in his eyes as he tries to determine what she's doing. She takes another step, until there is barely a foot between them and she can feel the heat radiating off him.

He stands perfectly still, his hands at his sides. A gentleman.

"Screw it," Cat whispers, and closes the distance between them.

His chest is solid against her hands, his skin almost burning through his shirt, and she could swear she actually feels his heartbeat quicken in the instant that their lips touch. His arms encircle her, as if on instinct, and he returns the kiss, gently at first but then fiercely, his tongue forcing her lips open.

Cat is so fucking glad that people kiss with their eyes closed so she doesn't have to overthink this moment, so she can just revel in the sensation of Jake's hands on her back, his tongue massaging hers, the way they are both becoming short of breath.

"I thought," Jake mumbles, "that you wanted boundaries."

"I did," she says with a nod that turns into her nuzzling the side of his neck, inhaling him. What kind of man smells this good?

"And now?" He holds her by the arms and forces her away from him, looking down at her in utter seriousness. And she is so breathless, so entirely out of her own head and in her own body for once, that she doesn't have it in her to obfuscate.

"I got scared, okay?" she says. "Because I've wanted to do this for a while."

"You have? Are you having an actual laugh?" His concerned expression becomes one of exasperation. "Cat, I have been flirting with you from the day we *met*."

"You could have fooled me!" She slaps his chest. "Honestly, mate, try telling your face sometime."

"I held your hand."

"We were *pretending*."

"I kissed you at that party."

"In front of everyone! To convince them!"

"I stopped wearing that stupid wedding ring."

"I thought that was part of the act!"

"I took you to meet my *mother*."

"You . . . you did." *Fuck. He really did give me all the signs, didn't he?*

"So what changed?" he asks.

What *did* change? Cat gazes up at her pretend boyfriend and places her hands on his shoulders.

"I'm a bloody good liar," she says. "I think I'm just sick of lying to myself. Especially when it comes to the things I want." She traces her hands down his chest, then dares herself to go farther and—oh god, are those actually *abs*?

"And I want this," she says, pushing him backward, down onto the bed. He props himself up on his elbows, and she lowers herself over him, straddling him. He grins and lifts his face to the ceiling, his entire body shaking beneath her in silent laughter.

"What's so funny?" she demands. Of all the reactions she might like to elicit from Jake in this moment, mirth is most definitely not one of them.

"I was right," he says proudly.

"You were?"

"That martini," he teases. "You can tell a lot about a girl."

She remembers now. God, what was it he said? *You probably surprise men with how you tend to take charge in bed.*

"Is this not . . . okay?" she asks. She feels like she is holding this moment carefully in her hands, like something precious and in danger of slipping through her fingers.

"Cat." His tone brings her eyes back up to his. "Believe me. It's more than okay."

She can feel the warmth of him. That warmth floods now through the rest of her, and she says playfully: "Do you mean to tell me I have your vocal, informed consent?"

Jake bucks his hips so she can feel *all* of him.

"What the hell do you think?" he whispers. His hands slide down from her waist to her hips, the firmness of his touch enough to make her breath catch in her throat, then he grasps the backs of her thighs and, in one deft motion, flips her over onto her back. Cat just has time to yelp in surprise and delight before he covers her mouth with his own.

PART THREE

A Girl's Best Friend

Twenty-two

In the early hours of Wednesday morning, Cat's suspicions are confirmed: Jake looks nothing short of adorable when he first wakes up. His cheeks are flushed, his eyes heavy-lidded. His arm is thrown over his head on the pillow, and a tattoo is just visible on the inside of his left bicep: an infinity sign that looks as if it was drawn wrong at first and had to be corrected. She cannot wait to tease him about this.

"Hi," Cat says. "How did you slee—" He pulls her close to him, eyes still closed, and kisses first her nose and then her chin before finally finding her mouth.

"*Mrnng*," he grunts, his forehead hot against hers. A moment later, his breathing becomes slow and deep again, and Cat is tempted to close her eyes and let herself drift back off to sleep in Jake's arms. But there's no time for that.

"Come on," she says, propping herself up on one arm and rubbing Jake's earlobe between her thumb and forefinger. It is so soft she could die. "We have a flight to catch."

"Five more minutes," he protests, eyes still firmly shut.

"Not a morning person, I take it?" she asks, and teasingly blows in his ear. Jake grunts again, lower this time, and opens his eyes.

"Not until now," he murmurs. "I'm amazed you can even speak, the noise you were making last night."

"Oh god." Cat's voice drops to a stage whisper. "Was I really that . . . loud?"

"Let's just say if Tom and Alex didn't believe we were a couple before, they will now," Jake says. His smile is pure devilry. Cat caresses his jaw and kisses him again. His breath is sour from sleep, and she imagines hers is the same.

"Maybe we kiss on an in breath," he says quietly, and Cat pushes his face away in mock displeasure.

"I shall go and brush my teeth," she says. "We have a flight, remember?"

She begins to raise herself off the bed, but he pulls her back down, snaking a leg around hers so that she is pinned to the mattress—where she can feel one vital part of Jake waking up.

"Five more minutes," she says.

They are an hour late to the airport.

Cat has done the last-minute, heart-pounding race through security before, but she finds that she is in no huge hurry to see the others just yet. Instead, she takes great pleasure in seeing the smooth, practiced movement with which Jake removes his shoes and belt, the meticulously efficient way he has packed his travel miniatures. When they finally reach the British Airways business-class lounge, Jake's left hand is casually slung over her shoulder and teasing the collar of her shirt, while a weekend bag hangs from his right. Cat's right hand is in his back pocket while her left drags a small wheeled suitcase behind her. She can't help thinking that they look every bit the young couple reveling in that first rush of each other—and then remembers immediately afterward that they are no longer pretending and has to suppress a giddy laugh.

"There you are!" Darcy's tone is cheerful but strained, and Cat begins to suspect that for all her careful planning, the chief bridesmaid failed to allow for the possibility that their entire party might not be sufficiently prompt in their arrival at the terminal.

"Sorry we're late," says Cat, but she can feel the obnoxious grin on her own face even as she says it.

"Never mind," says a haughty Darcy, "you're here now." She looks at Jake. "The boys are through there." She points to where the lounge, which overlooks the tarmac, turns a corner, from which the faint sound of braying laughter makes its way to Cat's ears.

"I guess this is where I leave you," says Jake, turning to face Cat so that his arm snakes up her shoulder and cradles the back of her neck. "See you on the other side." He kisses her, despite the fact her lips are still stretched in an idiotic grin, and heads in the direction of the stag party.

"Where are the girls?" Cat asks, once she has recovered her breath and remembered that Darcy is standing less than two feet away from her with one hand on her hip like a highly strung, incredibly toned teapot. Darcy simply jerks her head behind her as if to say *This way*, and then Cat sees them toward the back of the room, sprawled across a couple of enormous plush couches. It is barely six a.m. and they are all dressed for the world's bougiest bottomless brunch.

"You pair are too much," says Priya dreamily as Cat and Darcy approach. Cat realizes she and Jake have been observed from afar and is filled with a sense of, if not quite pride, then satisfaction.

She tells herself it is good for the job, but a less evolved part of her knows that she has just walked into the room with one of the most handsome men these women have ever seen. She hates that she wants their approval for this, and loves that she has gotten it.

Under normal circumstances, now that she is just with the girls, Cat might be unable to stop gushing about last night's exciting development. Not the gory details, of course, but the gist of it at least. Except she can't, because everybody here believes she and Jake have been together for months. So instead, she smiles coyly into the Bloody Mary that Harper has just handed her.

"They take these gendered rituals very seriously," Harper observes quietly, with the fascination of an anthropologist. "Priya and I were the only ones who didn't have a male partner removed like a mole when we got here."

"So Olivia's husband came, then?" Cat asks. "I thought—"

"I've seen more warmth between the ice cream and the emergency blunt I keep in my freezer," Harper says. "Not that it's any of my business."

"Harper Lawrence!" Cat hisses. "I do believe spending time with these posh women has turned you into something of a gossip."

Harper's mouth drops in shock and glee. "Do you think so? How fun! I'll have to work on my accent next."

"One step at a time," Cat tells her.

"What are you two whispering about?" Louisa asks. "Cat, good of you to join us."

She can't have had more than a few hours' sleep, and yet the skin beneath Louisa's eyes is as clear and dewy as ever. Cat adds it to the very, very long list of reasons why stealing the Tsarina will feel so good.

"I'm here now," she says, raising her Bloody Mary. "And I'm ready to party!"

Her phone vibrates in her back pocket. She knows even before she picks it up who the message will be from.

They're talking about polo. Rescue me?

That grin returns, and inevitably, the girls spot it.

"Bloody hell," says Olivia. "He's been gone five seconds—what could he possibly want?"

"I think it's sweet," says Priya. "Does he miss you already, Cat?"

"Something like that," she says.

"I remember when Evan and I were like that," says Darcy wistfully. "He's still a hopeless romantic," she adds hastily. "When the business allows. He is just so busy."

"That's the price we pay for falling in love with such ambitious men," Louisa says, linking arms with Darcy. Cat gets the feeling she is about to be tackled by the pair of them. "We have to share them with their work."

"Says the girl who got whisked away to Cannes, just because," Harper reminds her.

Louisa beams, because of course she has not forgotten. "It's true," she says. "And he is so attentive to my needs, you know? I swear. There's nothing like a modern gentleman."

Odd, Cat thinks. *That was never her type before.*

There was a Saturday morning, not long before the end of university, when Cat awoke to Louisa's knocking frantically on her bedroom door and, when she wasn't immediately met with a response, letting herself in without permission. Her eyes darted around the room. Once she was satisfied that Ronan was not there, as he so often was, she closed the door behind her.

"Darling," she said, "I have a little bit of a situation."

"I'm not going to get the morning-after pill for you again," Cat groaned. "Those chats they make you have are humiliating."

"What? Oh. No, it's not that. At least, that's not the most pressing concern."

Cat shuffled upward in bed, and Louisa perched next to her on the mattress.

"So Gavin came back with me last night," she said. "And we—"

"Yes, I know," Cat interrupted, less groggy now. "Thin walls."

Louisa's boyfriend, Spencer, was reading law up at Saint Andrews. Gavin, the sports science student Louisa had been hooking up with there in Bristol all semester, didn't know Spencer existed.

"Oops! Sorry." Louisa wasted no time in looking sorry before getting on with business. "Anyway. You know what these Welsh boys are like—they drink like killer whales. And now, well . . . I can't wake him."

Cat sat even more upright. "Louisa," she whispered. "Are you trying to tell me there's a dead man in your bed?"

"God, no! He's definitely breathing. Snoring, even. He just won't wake up. I've seen him like this before, almost every time we've had a big night out. It's like he goes into hibernation so the hangover can't get him."

"So what's the problem?" Cat snuggled back down into her pillow. "It's Saturday morning."

"Yes, it *is* Saturday," Louisa said, eyes boring into Cat. "Saturday the tenth, to be exact. And it's nearly eleven o'clock."

"Oh." Cat's voice sharpened. "Oh shit."

"Precisely!"

Today had been marked in the Cath Kidston calendar in their kitchen for weeks: Louisa was expecting a rare visit from her parents. This might not have constituted a crisis for some people, but Louisa's mother wasn't one to simply show up at the front door and whisk her daughter off to lunch. She had the habit of inspecting the house during her visits, to confirm that Louisa wasn't wallowing in squalor on her dime. That included seeing Louisa's room. Why Louisa had chosen last night of all nights to get steaming with her secret boyfriend and then bring him back here was beyond Cat.

Gavin was a decent enough guy, if a little rough around the edges—the latest in a series of dalliances Louisa had with men who were as far from the moneyed, plum-voiced boys she'd dated at home as possible—and the prospect of Julia's finding out about him was out of the question. He played rugby, which Cat had thought of as a posh sport, but when she'd voiced that to Louisa, she had been met with a look of derision.

"What do you propose we do, exactly?" Cat asked. "Carry him downstairs and out the back door? Hide him behind the wheelie bin?"

"No time for that," Louisa said seriously. "They're going to be here any minute. Besides, he's too heavy to carry all that way."

"Then I think you're screwed, love."

Louisa just looked at her meaningfully, as if waiting for her to catch up. And then she did.

"Absolutely not," Cat said.

"Please! Cat. I will owe you *big*-time. You have no idea."

Cat sighed. It had been three years, but she had yet to figure out a foolproof way of saying no to Louisa, which was how she came to find herself in her best friend's bedroom, standing over an unconscious, very large, *very* naked man. Splayed out on top of the duvet in flaccid repose beneath Louisa's framed print of the *Rokeby Venus*, he looked like something from a painting himself.

"You take his arms," Louisa instructed. "I'll get his legs."

"Can we not put some boxers on him first?" Cat gestured vaguely at Gavin's penis. She tried her best to have some propriety by looking away, but it was so large it kept creeping into her eye line.

"We don't have time," said Louisa. "Now, come on. One, two, three . . ."

Both girls grunted in exertion as they hoisted Gavin up and off the bed.

"Is that a tattoo?" Cat asked, edging toward the door. "Is . . . is that an *L*?"

"No idea," Louisa said between heavy breaths. "I think it's a rugby thing. Careful!"

Cat winced, having swung Gavin's arms too hard, resulting in his head's ricocheting off the door frame.

"Sorry!" she whispered.

"He'll be fine," Louisa assured her as they crossed the threshold onto the landing. "Almost there!"

With some awkward pivoting that felt more akin to moving a sofa than moving a human being, they safely deposited Gavin in Cat's room. Cat gently laid down her half on the rug just as the doorbell rang, and Louisa dropped Gavin's lower half.

"They're here!" she yelped, dashing out onto the landing and down the stairs.

Uncertain of what she was expected to do now that she was alone with him, Cat carefully tilted Gavin's head to the side in her best recollection of the recovery position, threw a blanket over his middle, and then followed Louisa out, shutting the bedroom door firmly behind her.

"Good morning, Mr. and Mrs. Vincent," she called, making her way down the stairs.

"Please, how many times, call me Julia," said Louisa's mother. "After all, why stand on ceremony when still wearing one's pajamas in the middle of the day?"

Ah, there it was. The closest thing Cat had to a source of maternal affection these days. She thought for the umpteenth time, as Julia informed her only daughter that she was looking a little ruddy and could do with cutting back on the junk food, that Louisa's mother was one of the few things she had never envied about her friend's life.

"Leave the girls alone, Ju," said Louisa's father jovially. "We both remember what it's like in digs. Well, actually, I got up to so many shenanigans it's a wonder I remember anything!" He winked emphatically at Louisa and Cat, who both laughed on cue. It was a variation of the same joke he made each time they came.

"Daddy, you're terrible," Louisa chuckled, batting his arm playfully before adding with an air of utter insouciance: "Ready for brunch?"

"Are you not going to at least offer us a cup of tea first?" Julia asked.

"We're all out," Cat said on impulse. "Sorry."

Julia flared her nostrils and smoothed down the front of her blouse. "Fine," she said. "But, Louisa, really. Leggings? A hoodie? Go and change into something you wouldn't find on a juvenile delinquent."

Louisa hurried upstairs to get changed, and Cat spent an interminable five minutes making small talk with the pair of them regarding their journey there and their plans for a getaway to Grasse next weekend. When Louisa returned, house keys and mobile phone in hand, Cat finally began to relax. Mere seconds and they'd be out the door, and she could spend the rest of the morning watching telly in the living room while she waited for Gavin to surface.

"Have a lovely brunch," Cat said, walking them all to the door.

"Won't you join us?" asked Mr. Vincent. He turned to Julia. "Doesn't she always join us?"

It was a tempting offer—the Vincents always paid—but Cat didn't exactly relish the idea of going upstairs and getting dressed with Gavin there.

"I'd love to," she said, "but I have a headache." To illustrate her point, she rubbed her forehead grimly.

"Pity," said Julia.

"Get well soon!" Louisa said, ushering her parents out. She shot Cat a look of gratitude and had just reached to pull the front door closed when a sonorous, croaking voice called down the stairs.

"Princess?"

Cat turned back into the hallway, and sure enough, there at the top of the stairs was a very confused, still very naked Gavin. The Vincents stood framed in the doorway, aghast at the scene laid out before them. Louisa froze, blinking furiously at Cat in what looked like Morse code. Cat sighed deeply and replied loudly, "Here, my love!" buying Louisa precious seconds to shoo her scandalized parents out.

"I am *so* sorry about her," Louisa said primly before the door finally slammed shut.

The hallway was silent for a moment in their absence, and Cat heard the distinct sound of Gavin scratching his privates. Then, finally waking up to where he was, he sheepishly covered himself with his hands.

"She won't be back for a while," Cat said.

"Oh. Right." The look on his face was like that of a little boy who had just learned the truth about Father Christmas and was trying to be brave. She sighed again.

"Put some clothes on," she said. "I'll make tea."

Twenty-three

Due to an extremely delayed connection in Rome involving fatigue and vodka-related tears and recriminations, they arrive at the palazzo late. Cat and the others barely have the energy to marvel at how beautiful the place is before filing off to their respective bedrooms—assigned to them on the Google Doc that Darcy shared ahead of time—and collapsing into their enormous, luxuriously comfortable beds. It feels like vanishing into one of the puffy white clouds they flew over before they finally touched down in Palermo, where Elijah was waiting with a minivan. Cat has a great many criticisms of the rich, but after a full day of sitting in the same increasingly stale clothing, she can't deny that she appreciates being able to skip the bus for once and get chauffeured directly to her destination.

When she wakes the next morning, sweaty and disoriented, at first she thinks the noise is the alarm clock on her phone. Except she forgot to set one before passing out.

Cat raises her head from the (still unbelievably comfortable) pillow, double-checks her phone, and then realizes that the infernal beeping sound is actually coming from the next room. She glances over at the bed on the other side of the room, which she vaguely recalls having been assigned to Harper. It is empty. With great reluctance, she throws back the duvet, pulls on an oversized T-shirt, and ventures out to investigate.

The apartment's central living area is open plan, with the spacious lounge leading out onto a terrace on the right and straight into a kitchen on the left. It is to the kitchen that Cat follows the noise—and the unmistakable smell of smoke.

Harper is standing on a stool in basketball shorts and a UC Berkeley jersey, fanning at the smoke alarm with a tea towel. An acrid black cloud lingers over the electric hob, and Cat sees that a skillet of something that might once have been generously described as scrambled eggs has been hastily dumped in the sink.

The beeping finally ceases, and with a deep sigh of relief, Harper steps down from the stool, taking Cat's hand to steady herself.

"I thought I'd make breakfast for everybody," she says loudly, making herself jump. "But it didn't go according to plan," she adds, at a more appropriate volume.

"It's the thought that counts," Cat assures her, although she can't help but feel a tiny swell of gratitude at being spared having to eat whatever caused such a smell.

"What happened?" asks Olivia, striding into the communal area in a silk robe, a towel wrapped expertly into a turban. "I was in the shower and it sounded like an air-raid warning."

"Eggs," Harper says simply. Darcy and Priya tiptoe out of their bedrooms a moment later, the former in a silk slip, the latter in fuzzy pajamas. Cat suspects they were hiding until the alarm abated, lest they be required to help.

"Ooh, are we having Benedict?" Priya asks. "Could I have mine with avocado instead of ham, please? Unless there's smoked salmon on offer."

"The eggs were scrambled," Harper says. "But they didn't make it."

Priya looks crestfallen, but not for long. No sooner has Harper confirmed the untimely demise of their breakfast than they all hear the heavy front door to the apartment creak open and lean over the kitchen island to get a look. Louisa stands in the doorway, looking pleasantly dewy from a morning run in bright yellow athleisure that Cat would have to sell a kidney to afford. An incredibly tall woman with a dark bob stands beside her, wearing a man's white shirt tucked into jeans with Doc Martens. A canvas tote laden with fruit and pastries hangs from one broad shoulder.

"Morning, girls," Louisa says brightly, before erupting into dramatic coughs as soon as she crosses the threshold. "This is Giovanna," she continues, once she has recovered. "I bumped into her downstairs."

"I manage the property," Giovanna says in beautifully accented English. "I thought you might like a light breakfast." She holds out the bag.

"You are an angel," Harper says, reaching out to accept it. "Like, my actual hero. You have no idea."

She keeps her hand on the strap but doesn't move away immediately. *Flirting, Harper? Before nine a.m.? Go for it, girl.*

"Actually, I do," Giovanna chuckles, reaching into her back pocket for her phone and showing it to them all. "The fire alarm sent an alert to my app here. I stopped to pick up the sfogliatelle on my way once I checked the CCTV feed and knew there was no emergency."

"CCTV?" Cat's eyes dart in every direction before landing on the camera positioned near the front door. Giovanna taps a button on her phone, and it rotates: on her screen, the view pans across the entire central space, from the entrance to the kitchen to the sofas.

"It's the only one," Giovanna says. "For security, insurance—that sort of thing. I promise, nobody is watching you ladies in the bathroom."

"Did you say sfogliatella?" Olivia grabs the tote from Harper and starts decanting its contents onto the kitchen island. "I'll get all of this plated up," she says, "and then we can eat out on the terrace while the smoke in here clears. Could somebody put on a pot of coffee?"

Cat starts to wonder if Darcy's being chosen as the bride's second-in-command was a tough call; Olivia is so clearly one of life's natural-born bosses, she could easily have nabbed the gig.

"Do you live nearby?" Harper asks Giovanna while the others are busy preparing a breakfast spread. "I mean, you must—you came so quickly."

Cat shoots her a withering look; that kind of innuendo barely counts as a *single* entendre. Surely somebody with two degrees in English literature should be able to come up with better?

"Not far," Giovanna replies, maintaining cool, consistent eye contact with Harper. She tucks a lock of hair behind her ear. "Not far at all."

Both women seem to have forgotten that there is anybody else in the room; Cat could brain herself with the skillet of cursed eggs and she doubts either of them would notice.

"Cool," says Harper. "No doubt, no doubt."

Cat tears herself away from this McConaugheyan chat-up line and goes in search of sustenance. Out on the balcony, Darcy is reminding everybody of the itinerary for the day: a hike up Mount

Pellegrino, a tour of the royal tombs beneath the cathedral, a traditional Sicilian puppet show at the Cuticchio theater, and finally, some time for browsing at the street markets before dinner.

"That all sounds amazing, Darce," says Louisa. "Except for the puppet show, which sounds mildly traumatic. But here's the thing. I didn't pack for hiking."

"Me neither," Priya chimes in.

"And, while I appreciate how much effort you went to in organizing all of these activities," Louisa continues, "I kind of just want to relax. Organizing a wedding in less than two months has wiped me out, you know?"

Darcy looks at Louisa like she has been promised a puppy for Christmas, only to be told "Just kidding," before plastering on a smile and nodding enthusiastically.

"Totally!" she says. "I just wanted us to have options. But a relaxing weekend sounds great. *Better*, even."

"Smashing," says Olivia around a mouthful of pastry. "We'll put our bathing suits on and go down to Mondello Beach. I for one would love an ice cream."

"I read that ice cream was invented here," says Cat.

"It was," says Giovanna, who has followed Harper out onto the balcony. "We are known for a lot of things. For instance, Palermo is actually the most conquered city in the world." She says it with something not unlike pride. "Sicilia is the largest island in the Mediterranean, and its position meant a strategic advantage for whoever controlled its shores," she continues. "But do you want to know what I think? I think that anyone who sailed remotely near the island found that they were simply unable to tear themselves away from her beauty and had to have her." She fixes her stare on Harper.

Well, damn. *That's* how you flirt.

"It's settled, then," says Louisa. "Beach trip! I think I'll skip the ice cream, though. I might not be dieting for the wedding, but I don't want to tempt fate either."

Darcy and Priya are both so quick to leap in with protestations about how thin she is that the result is harmonized sycophancy, but Louisa has already reentered the apartment to get ready.

Cat grabs a banana and follows her back inside, leaving Olivia and Priya to demolish the pastries and Harper to gaze with ever-decreasing subtlety at Giovanna, and walks straight into Elijah. Either he's been working out, or his suits are getting even tighter; the material strains over his barrel chest.

"Sorry, I didn't see you there," she says. "Wait a minute. Were you here all night?"

"Yes, miss," he says.

"But . . . where did you sleep?" She does a quick mental survey of the space. "There are only five rooms, and Harper and I doubled up."

"I don't sleep, miss," Elijah says, his expression stony.

"Oh really. That's some trick you learned in the SAS, I suppose?"

"I suppose, miss."

She realizes then that he is having her on, and she likes him a little more for it.

"There's a small apartment across the hall," he says. "I slept there."

Servants' quarters. That tracks.

"Well, we all feel safer for having you here," Cat says, clapping him on the side of the arm as she heads in to shower. It is, she cannot help noticing, a *very* thick and solid arm. She wouldn't be surprised if Elijah spent his free time bench-pressing cars or making some extra dosh as one of those mercenaries you see in action films.

"He's quite buff, isn't he?" Olivia says of him a little later, as they are all heading down to the beach in sundresses and sarongs. "I can see why Louisa likes keeping him around. Although I have a harder time believing that Stephen would select such a fine specimen to take care of his bride-to-be."

Cat was thinking something very similar but pretends to be shocked at Olivia's thirsty remarks.

"Louisa is in love," Cat says. "She's not the sort to even look at another man when she's in a relationship." Of all the lies she has ever told, this one feels like it stretches credulity the most, but it seems to satisfy Olivia, who simply slides her enormous sunglasses down her nose so she can take in the view again.

"Must he wear a suit to the beach, though?" she sighs. "Whatever's wrong with a Speedo? Surely he could strap a gun to his thigh or something. I mean, *what* thighs."

"You're incorrigible," Priya informs her, although Cat notices that her gaze is firmly set in the bodyguard's direction as well. "Sorry, Harper, I know we must be boring you," she adds somewhat slyly. Cat fixes her with a look that could turn milk.

"On the contrary," Harper says, either unaware of Priya's tone or choosing to ignore it. "I dated a woman who looked rather a lot like Elijah once. Legs like tree trunks. Soul of a poet."

Priya says nothing in response, suitably cowed now that her attempt at catty behavior has failed to land. Cat finds herself forgetting Priya is the same age as her; she is so eager to cement her role in the group she comes across as much younger.

When they arrive at Mondello Beach, the majority of the group is appalled by how far removed the beauteous stretch of sand is from its Instagram presence, so crowded is it with tourists. Cat doesn't think it's too bad but knows better than to voice this opinion.

"Can't anything ever go right?" Louisa asks, her voice teetering on petulant. She turns to a hopeless-looking Darcy, as if to say *Do something!*

"It's fine. I'll sort it," says Olivia, reaching into the depths of her canvas tote for her phone and dialing. "Mateo?" She laughs throatily. "Sì, sono Olivia." That is all Cat can make out before she plunges into fluent Italian. Moments later, Olivia throws her phone back into her bag and turns to address the others.

"My friend is coming to pick us up," she informs them. "He's a member of a private beach club a little farther up the coast."

"Liv, you angel!" Louisa sings. Cat dares not even look at Darcy; she can feel the impotent rage coming off her in waves.

"He'll be here in fifteen," Olivia says. "Just enough time for us to get some gelato."

"Sounds good," says Cat, relieved that a meltdown has been averted. She wonders if, for all his military training, Elijah has any skill in resolving inter-hen conflicts. Best to not find out, she thinks.

"I can see a stand over there." Priya points to a vendor a hundred yards or so away on the waterfront, and they begin to walk over.

"My treat," Harper says before falling into step beside Olivia and asking: "Is there any chance you could possibly teach me a couple of Italian phrases . . . ?"

Twenty-four

As loath as Cat is to admit it, she has been on much worse hens. Incidents involving group activities as wide-ranging as paint-balling, pottery, life drawing, master classes in calligraphy, and cupcake-decorating and cocktails, each of which ended in at least one woman's exploding in tears or vomit. She senses a similar relief in the others as they spend most of the afternoon basking in the Sicilian sunshine, liberated from the threat of organized fun, the only demands on their time and mental acuity being whether they would like an Aperol spritz next or would rather switch to a negroni.

She is beginning to hope that dinner might be an equally chill affair, enjoyed in a charming trattoria overlooking a piazza just lousy with fountains and tanned beautiful people, but then Darcy informs the group that she has arranged a surprise back at the apartment. She might puff her chest as she says this, wresting back her standing as the savior of the day from Olivia, but Cat could be imagining it.

They are each given an hour to do with as they please before their evening begins, the way a teacher might dispense leisure time on a school trip, and Cat decides that yes, Darcy is taking her quest to reclaim authority a little too seriously. But the prospect of a long shower in one of the palazzo's three bathrooms to blast away the layer of sunscreen and day-drinking fogginess is not one she's going to turn down.

She begins to rummage through her suitcase, cursing herself for not hanging up her clothes when they landed. It's fine; she'll hang her outfit over the shower rail and the steam will smooth out the wrinkles. A pathological aversion to ironing is something she and Louisa have had in common since they lived together.

Cat tugs out the black polka-dot playsuit in a series of clown-like handfuls and is about to go claim a bathroom before the others can nab them, when she spots something else at the bottom of the case. Shimmering viscose fabric in a rich bottle green. She lifts it from beneath her spare pair of shorts, and the material flows like liquid between her fingers. No creases here. *I suppose you really do get what you pay for*, Cat thinks, remembering the price tag she was too afraid to even look at.

She is caught for a second in an absurd delusion. Has she started sleepwalking? Did she go back to Liberty and buy the dress while in some kind of fugue state? Did she steal the dress on her outing there with Jake and promptly forget about it?

Jake.

Of course it was Jake. She didn't even realize he'd seen her admiring the dress. He must have snuck it into her bag before their flight.

"What are you *playing* at," she says, forgetting Harper is on the opposite bed, lying on her front, legs kicking absentmindedly in the air, as she pores over an iPad like a teenage girl writing in her diary.

"My citations are a mess," Harper says in reply. "I'm just trying to extinguish the worst of the dumpster fire before we eat."

Cat leaves her to it, grabbing her phone and her bag of toiletries and absconding to the bathroom, slipping through the door, and swiftly locking it, pretending not to have seen Priya on the same trajectory.

She almost calls Jake, but ringing her boyfriend, or fake boyfriend, or whatever the hell he is now, while she's on a hen and he's on a stag feels far too needy, so she settles for a text. Perched on the edge of the bath, she composes six, then seven, then eight drafts, before returning to her first.

I just found a stowaway.

She hits send, then hastily strips and jumps in the shower, where she can't check her phone for replies. She walks back to the bedroom in a towel and dries her hair. Applies moisturizer to shoulders that are tight and red after a day in the sun. Does her makeup. Her phone vibrates as she is standing over the bed, the dress splayed out before her.

Thought it would look good on you.

It is sweet, and more or less what Cat expected Jake to say. So why does the room feel impossibly hot all of a sudden? First a brand-new iPhone, now a designer dress: whether he paid for these things or not, it all suddenly feels too extravagant. Too much like . . . not like he wants something in return, exactly—if that's what he's after, Cat has already given it to him, gladly, twice—but still. This seems like he just took a step into unfamiliar territory, and she isn't sure whether or not she should follow, or if she even knows how to. She almost misses the days when she had no idea what Jake was thinking, when his face was an uncrackable safe.

She leaves her phone on the bed next to the dress, steps into the wrinkled polka-dot romper, and joins the others in the living room. It has been transformed into a banquet hall, and with a dramatic, excited flourish, Darcy introduces their "surprise": a middle-aged man with a salt-and-pepper beard named Enzo, who has prepared a feast for them this evening.

"Ciao bella," he sings, clasping and then kissing each of their hands in an avuncular, if somewhat overfamiliar, greeting. "Ciao bella, ciao bella, ciao bella."

Cat attended one hen night where the guests were waited on by a butler-in-the-buff: a swole tattooed lunk of a man wearing nothing but a tiny apron to preserve his modesty, supplementing his income as a personal trainer or fitness model by subjecting himself to the increasingly feral attentions of a pack of women drunk on rosé and the freedom of a night away from their husbands and children. A private chef who is old enough to be the bride's father and who keeps his clothes on makes for a refreshing change.

They take their seats around a table so large that Cat has several questions about how it was maneuvered through the front door, and Enzo brings out their antipasto on platters: caprese salad, the colors of the Italian flag remixed in spirals of tomato, mozzarella, and basil, and fresh focaccia with whole sprigs of rosemary and pitted black olives baked into the crust. Louisa surveys it from behind a glass of ice water, then turns to Darcy.

"Your big surprise just days before my wedding was . . . carbs?"

Darcy's expectant smile freezes into a kind of stricken grimace. "I . . . I . . . ," she stammers. "I thought—"

"I'm *kidding*!" Louisa snorts. "Seriously, Darcy, you need to chill out. This all looks phenomenal."

At first they pick delicately at the bread and salad, but by the time Enzo returns with the primo—lobster ravioli in a cream and saffron sauce—they are tearing into everything, the effects of the day's boozing and sunbathing making themselves known. Two bottles of exquisite Chianti are placed on the table to accompany their secondo: a thick-based Sicilian pizza with anchovies, onions, and caciocavallo.

Once the plates have been cleared and replaced by a selection of local cheese and fruit, Darcy clears her throat.

"Ladies?" she says, and all knowing their cue, they leave the table, retreating to their rooms and reappearing bearing gifts. In addition to the expectation that each wedding guest buy something from the registry, Darcy suggested on the group chat that it might be "an adorable touch" if each of the bridesmaids also presented Louisa with a "small token of their affection" after dinner.

Darcy insists on going first, and Louisa makes appropriately appreciative noises over a gift certificate for a Michelin-starred restaurant in Singapore.

"We can go for a girls' night," Darcy says. "Just the two of us."

Priya is next, and Louisa looks confused for a moment as she holds up a circlet of cerulean lace on the end of one finger.

"It can be your something blue!" Priya announces.

"That's so *sweet*," Louisa says. "But if I wore a garter, it would ruin the line of my dress. I could swear I told you that already?"

"Oh." Priya blinks several times in a row.

"Still. It's the thought that counts! This is so *fun*. Who's next?"

Olivia gives Louisa a bottle of Chanel No. 5, which Cat suspects she sent her assistant out to buy at the last minute, and Harper elicits genuine screams of glee from the entire table with her contribution: a video message via Cameo from a nineties heartthrob whose posters, Harper claims, used to be all over the adolescent Louisa's bedroom walls.

The last course—a rich, layered chocolate-and-cream cake called savoia—is brought out, and finally, all eyes turn to her. Cat's funds didn't extend to a second gift, even after her endeavors in Liberty, and so the day before the flight, she dug out her sketchbook for the first time in longer than she cared to remember.

It is a minimalist likeness of the bride, drawn in simple, clean lines. Cat worked from a photo she found deep in the bowels of Facebook: second year, some costume party thrown by the drama students who lived next door, Louisa wearing a negligee as a dress and plastic flowers in her hair. Cat christened her "pound-shop Titania" that night, and Louisa downed so many Malibu and Cokes she didn't even mind. Her smile in the picture, captured midlaugh, is wide and girlish. Cat wonders if Louisa ever laughs like that now, instead of the rehearsed way she throws back her head and actually says the word "Ha!"

"I'm sorry it's not in a frame," she says, "only I—"

"I love it," Louisa says quietly. "It's . . . it's me, isn't it?" She holds the sketch up so the other bridesmaids can see.

"Aww!" Darcy trills, in a manner that stops just shy of condescending.

"I wish *I* could draw," says Priya somewhat petulantly.

"It's beautiful," says Olivia. "Damn it. You win, Cat."

"Ladies." Louisa beams. "It's not a competition!"

"Could you do one of me?" Harper asks Cat, who feels herself starting to blush and is thankful when Louisa clears her throat and refocuses the table's attention back on her, where it belongs.

Twenty-five

Afterward, while Enzo clears all of their dishes and a team of his nephews transports the table back from whence it came, the women bring blankets and cushions out onto the balcony so they can enjoy the cool night breeze. Olivia pours them all shots of limoncello, and they toast the bride's health. Louisa practically glows in the moonlight. Beneath them, the rhythm of the tide sounds like the island itself is breathing deeply, slowly, and contentedly.

A low, sonorous snore disrupts the calm. It comes from Darcy, who has been on the verge of dozing ever since supper, and the sound of her own stertor is enough to jolt her awake. The balcony erupts in giggles, and she excuses herself to go to bed. Once their laughter has died down following Darcy's abashed exit, the evening is signaled to be over, and one by one, they each head inside, to skin-care routines and sleep, until just Cat and Louisa are left on the terrace.

"This is nice," says Cat. She gathers a blanket around her like a cloak and sinks deeper into her seat. Louisa says nothing, and at first Cat believes that to be a product of similar satisfaction. Then she glances over and sees the way Louisa is staring out into the night, eyes wide and unblinking. If Cat were given to cliché, she'd say Louisa has just seen a ghost.

"What's the matter?" she asks.

"Nothing." Louisa keeps looking out at something only she can see, then turns abruptly to Cat. "Do you think I'm making a mistake?"

"What?"

"Marrying Stephen. Am I doing the right thing?" Her face is still strangely blank, like she can't trust herself to express an emotion while having this conversation. It's a trick with which Cat is intimately familiar. She practically invented it.

"I mean, it's certainly . . . quick," says Cat. "But that doesn't necessarily mean it's a mistake."

"Would you go through with it? If you were me?"

"I'm not you," Cat tells her. "Lou, where is this coming from?"

"God, you know I hate it when you call me Lou. I'm not a toilet, Cat."

Your fiancé called you Wee in front of all of us, Cat thinks, but Louisa speaks again before she can respond.

"I just keep thinking, I always expected to be engaged for at least a year. Enough time to plan a *proper* wedding and to decide if I was sure or not. Then Stephen proposed, and this *deadline* came up, and all of a sudden I'm getting hitched in three fucking days."

If Louisa were anybody else, Cat would counsel caution. She would urge her to put herself first, to never let any man make her feel pressured into making the wrong decision. She would tell her that marriage, like motherhood, is not what makes you a woman. She would sit and listen without judgment to every last hope and fear until three o'clock in the damned morning.

But if Louisa were anybody else, Cat's entire future would not be riding on this wedding's going ahead, and she might be able to be a better friend. All she can see is the precarity of this moment and the path things might take if she says the wrong thing. And so instead, she examines this conversation through the lens of how to best serve herself, aware that it is exactly what Louisa would do.

"It's a lot," Cat says, trying to figure out exactly how much force to apply here. Louisa *has* to get married, or the job is off. "But . . . you love him, don't you?"

Louisa nods timidly. "I do."

"And he loves you?"

"Ugh. *So* much."

"Well, there you have it."

"Is it really that simple?" Louisa asks.

"I don't see why not," Cat says. "Sure, getting married is a big decision. But overthinking things isn't exactly romantic, is it?"

"I guess not." Louisa runs a hand through her hair. "I'm just scared of making a mistake."

"What if not getting married is the mistake?"

Louisa looks at her. "I've never thought of it like that."

Cat pours them both another shot of limoncello and hands one to Louisa, as if to signal that the matter is closed.

"I suppose," Louisa says as they clink their glasses together, "if it doesn't work out, there's always divorce."

"Then you and your mother would finally have something in common," Cat says, and Louisa howls with laughter.

"You witch!" she yells. "You absolute shrew!" She knocks back the bright yellow liquid and licks her lips. "She never did like you, you know."

"Well, you can tell her I'm a *huge* fan." Cat winks at her and feels a pang of familiarity.

The nights they spent on the windowsill of her room, smoking and drinking cheap gin and chatting shit. They were real friends, once upon a time. And she can't escape the feeling that she has just given her onetime bestie some terrible advice, simply for her own ends.

"I'm knackered," Cat announces, getting up. She bends to kiss Louisa lightly on the head as she passes her on the way inside. *No*, she thinks. *The show has to go on. Otherwise, what was all of this for?*

Harper is busy stuffing clothes into her backpack when Cat returns to their room. Luggage costs were not an issue, but she only brought the one compact bag. Cat has never met a woman who travels so light.

"Going somewhere?" Cat asks. At the same moment, Harper's phone dings, and when she checks it, a broad smile blooms on her face. "Let me guess," Cat says. "Giovanna."

"She's waiting downstairs," Harper says. "She wants to show me her place."

"I bet she does." Cat raises an eyebrow.

"Oh, I know," Harper says, running a hand through her wild hair. "She probably spins the same old lines to every wide-eyed tourist, week in, week out. But . . . I don't care?" She looks around the room to make sure she has everything.

"You *are* coming back, right?" Cat eyes her up nervously. "You're not eloping or something?"

"I'm totally coming back." Harper grins. "Or . . . I'll meet you guys at the airport tomorrow night."

"Louisa is going to be fuming."

"Louisa can think back to the time she skipped out on my eighteenth-birthday party to go backstage with the Kooks," Harper says. "Although if her mom tells my mom . . ." She stands with one hand on her hip, weighing up the consequences.

"Fine," Cat groans. "I'll cover for you. I'll tell them you're hungover tomorrow and need to sleep it off."

"Kinda hurts my street cred, no?"

"Harper. You cannot hold your drink, and you know it. Don't think I didn't see you switch to sparkling water this afternoon."

"Fine." Harper shrugs. "Thanks. You're a pal."

Outside, a tiny horn honks. Cat walks to the window and glances down. A familiarly strong frame sits astride a Vespa on the street below.

"Looks like your chariot awaits," she remarks.

"They say lesbians bring a U-Haul on the first date," Harper quips, slinging her rucksack over her shoulder. "Look at me, defying the cliché. You could barely fit two cats in this thing."

"Have fun," Cat says through a cackle. "Be safe."

"Thanks, Mom." Harper pulls Cat into a quick one-armed hug, and then she is gone.

Cat brushes her teeth, lobs on some moisturizer to counteract the warm tightness she feels after an afternoon in the sun, and collapses into bed. She is rereading the first page of an Elena Ferrante novel she found in the living room earlier when her phone vibrates on the dresser next to her. It's Jake.

"Mr. Marlowe," she says coyly upon answering. "I'm sure it is quite improper for you to be calling so late. Are you inebriated?"

"Hardly," he says. "Okay, maybe a bit. These boys do like their whiskey."

"So you're drunk-dialing me? How flattering."

"I just wanted to hear your voice."

Cat closes her eyes and imagines how Jake must look right now. The top few buttons of his shirt undone, his cheeks flushed, those curls disheveled. His eyes, she decides, would be pure mischief.

"It's good to hear yours too," she says.

"Was I right?" he asks.

"About what?"

"The dress. Did it look good on you?"

Whatever reservations she may have felt earlier tumble away at the sound of his voice.

"I'm saving it for tomorrow," she tells him. "So you can see for yourself."

"Can't wait." He breathes out, slowly, and she knows then that he is in bed. "I keep thinking about the night before the flight," he says. "How it was so . . ."

"I know." A giddiness creeps over Cat, even though she is lying down.

"The way it felt," Jake says. "How do you *do* that?"

Cat sinks lower into her pillow.

"I'll tell you, if you like," she says.

Cat is woken by a notification on her phone containing three words nobody wants to read first thing in the morning, especially after drinking.

      Is this you?

The message is on the bridesmaids group chat, sent from Olivia and accompanied by a link. Cat sits upright in bed, wide awake with a sudden, ice-cold knot in the pit of her stomach, and her finger hovers over the phone screen for almost a full minute before finally, with a gulp, she hits the link.

It leads to a video. Cat immediately recognizes its setting, but it is a couple of seconds before everything else falls into place and she begins to swear under her breath. The footage, captured at Velocity HQ, is of a woman in a colorful blouse with short, wavy blond hair, filmed from the side so you can't see her entire face. Cat turns up the volume, already knowing exactly what she's going to hear.

"*You are a privileged little twerp . . . ,*" the phone speaker recites back to her. "*You're about as self-made as a ham sandwich.*"

Somebody in the office was recording her little rant. And because no moment can go uncommented upon, and because people are the worst, whoever it was has uploaded it to the internet, where it appears to be going semi-viral.

"Fuck," Cat whispers, her mind racing. "Fucking *fuck.*"

Okay. Think. *Think.* Cat reviews the clip again. Her hair partially covers her face, and the video isn't especially high-quality, which means her voice is slightly distorted. She could lean into plausible deniability and claim this isn't her. More important, whichever little toad was filming her was facing away from the storage rooms *and* the lifts: Jake is nowhere to be seen in the background of the shot. If anyone were to identify Cat from this, they'd have no reason to link her to a missing piece of expensive equipment.

Once she has quelled that sense of panic, Cat considers the immediate practicalities. Olivia has seen this. Which means it's safe to assume the other bridesmaids have too. Cat examines the social media post that the video is attached to. It's from a bland meme account, captioned "Who is this woman?? She is NOT here for your bullshit," followed by an entire row of crying-laughing emojis. Churning nausea worsening, she scrolls down the list of accounts that have shared the video until she sees a familiar name, at which point she very nearly throws up.

@LIVELAUGHLOUISA: This is my dear friend Cat Bellamy. To anybody making fun of her, I say shame on

you. I personally couldn't be prouder of her for standing by her principles and speaking truth to power, even if it means threatening her own career prospects. I've met my fair share of male chauvinist pigs in the art world (you know who you are!!) and I think we could all stand to be more like her. #BeMoreCat #BraveWomen #GirlBoss #TimesUp

Classic. Even when Louisa is coming to Cat's defense, she still manages to make it about herself.

The others are already gathered around the enormous kitchen island when Cat comes out of her bedroom. They are speaking in low voices but all stop when she walks in. No prizes for guessing what they were talking about. It's like sixth form all over again. Priya looks at her with the same mix of pity and quiet horror that Cat became so inured to in the months after her mum died. Olivia and Louisa keep their eyes fixed on the marble counter.

"This is awkward," Cat announces in her boldest voice. "I was actually hoping to break the internet by finally coming up with the right order to put jam and cream on a scone."

"Are you okay?" asks Priya in the kind of careful whisper that suggests she is fearful Cat will erupt into another meltdown at the slightest provocation. Behind those earnest doe eyes, she can actually see Priya making a mental note to retract the invitation to be a guest on her YouTube channel.

"I'm fine," Cat says. "I just wish that someone had told me my business was all over Twitter instead of just sharing it for clout."

Louisa finally looks up at her, eyes widening.

"You're angry at *me*?" she asks. "I was *helping* you."

"Helping?" Cat forces herself to keep her voice even.

"I have a bigger platform than you," Louisa protests, "and I believe it's important to champion women, especially in the male-dominated workplace."

She rattles off the words with such ease, Cat can tell she's said them a number of times before. Probably as a guest speaker at seminars for other posh, pretty white women working in fine art.

"I just wish you'd said something first," Cat says.

She actually wishes she didn't have to hold her tongue so much, but attacking the bride just days before the wedding is not a good look. Even if she currently believes with every fiber of her being that Louisa's lustrous dark hair would look better hanging in clumps from Cat's clenched fist.

"I'm not the one who lost her mind and went all *Lemonade* on her boss," says Louisa, shrugging insouciantly. "I support taking up space and speaking your mind, but that was kind of . . . shrill, babe."

An ache pierces Cat's fingers, and she realizes she has been gripping the edge of one of the tall chairs at the kitchen island increasingly tighter. She lets go, and relief floods through her knuckles.

"Fuck 'em," Olivia says suddenly. "The guy seemed like an arsehole. Typical entitled man."

Cat gives her a grateful smile and confirms that Mikhail *is*, in fact, a complete arsehole. She is about to change the subject entirely and inquire after coffee and paracetamol when Olivia abruptly bursts into tears. Cat is taken aback, especially after that expression of solidarity: Olivia doesn't exactly seem the sort of woman who would express any remorse at stirring shit in the group chat. But she's glad, at least, that they now have something else to give their collective attention to. Priya and Louisa stroke Olivia's right and left shoulders, respectively, while a bemused Darcy pulls a ream of kitchen towel off the roll and hands it over.

"Harrison and I," Olivia says between chest-heaving sobs, "are getting a di-di-divorce."

The kitchen is immediately filled with an a cappella chorus of surprise and commiseration while Olivia fights to catch her breath again.

"What *happened*?" asks Priya. "You guys are so perfect!" Cat thinks that this is probably the worst possible thing to say, but what does she know?

"He said it's my career," Olivia wheezes. "Apparently he feels emasculated being married to a woman who makes more money than him. He also hates that I'm so busy, and he's left at home with Oscar so much, even though that was the arrangement we agreed on after he was born. And Harrison never seemed to have an issue with my salary when he was taking his sabbaticals, or going part-time at the university, or writing his bloody *book*."

"Men always say they love a strong woman," Louisa muses. "Until they don't."

"It's *perverse*," says Olivia. "My job paid for the house we live in, the wine cellar Harrison is so fond of, the nanny who takes care of our son. But now all of a sudden he decides that I've been wearing his balls as earrings all these years, and he would like them back."

She tilts her head toward the ceiling, blinking away her remaining tears, and a familiar steely resolve smooths out the mask of anguish that was there just seconds before.

"If he thinks he is getting a penny from me, from that career he resents so much," she declares, "he has got another thing fucking coming."

"Good for you," Cat says, both impressed and slightly disturbed by Olivia's rapid emotional transformation. She's no stranger to compartmentalizing; she's just never seen it happen quite so quickly and neatly before. It's like watching a curtain fall over a stage.

"Hold on . . ." Up until now, Darcy has been watching Olivia's tears in silent mortification, as if the woman just soiled her pants instead of simply expressing an inconvenient emotion, but now she leans forward to catch Olivia's eye. "When did all of this happen, exactly?"

What an odd, intrusive thing to ask, Cat thinks. Might Darcy suspect foul play on Harrison's part? Is she somehow privy to a piece of evidence that seemed innocent enough before but now points to possible infidelity?

"A few days ago," says Olivia. "I wasn't going to mention it during the trip; I didn't want to kill the mood." She turns to Louisa. "Sorry, sweetie."

"But what about the seating plan?" Darcy exclaims, and Cat promptly shelves her theory. "We're going to have to—"

She catches Cat's intense *shut-up-now-for-the-love-of-god-what-is-wrong-with-you* stare and stops midsentence.

"Actually, it's fine," says Louisa magnanimously. "I needed to redo the chart anyway. Cat here threw us a curveball by actually having a plus-one for the first time in, well, ever. Oh!" Her face lights up. "I'll just move you to the singles table, Liv, and then Cat and Jake can take your and Harrison's seats. Crisis averted!"

She claps her hands delicately, seemingly forgetting that her seating plan was *not* the original crisis, and occupies herself with selecting the perfect nectarine from the fruit bowl on the island, either oblivious or immune to the disbelief and fury radiating off of Cat and Olivia. She takes a bite, wrinkles her slender nose in disgust, and tosses it in the bin.

"I'm going for a run," she says. "Then . . . let's go out for breakfast, shall we? I still don't trust Harper around the stove, and I know for a fact that Cat can't cook."

It is the first true and reasonable thing Louisa has said in weeks.

"Harper's a no-go for breakfast," Cat volunteers. "Too much limoncello."

Olivia shakes her head disapprovingly, all signs of emotional turmoil superseded by her disdain at the idea anybody might not be able to hold their liquor.

"Americans," she sniffs.

Twenty-six

The boys descend after lunch on Friday. With only eight hours left until their return flight to London—direct this time, thank god—Stephen herds them all to a seafront bar he has booked out for the rest of the day, so they can drink to their hearts' content all afternoon, sleep it off when they land in the early hours of Saturday, and be recovered and refreshed in time for the wedding itself on the bank holiday Monday.

Louisa hurls herself at Stephen the moment he enters the establishment, jumping quite literally into his arms and wrapping her legs around his waist as if they have been separated for years, not just forty-eight hours. Hard to believe this is the same young woman who was questioning all of her life choices the night before. Behind him, Freddie Meriweather staggers in cheerfully and calls for a round of tequila, as if he were not presently being held up on one side by Olivia's husband, Harrison, and on the other by Jake. Cat smiles politely at Harrison, marveling at his gall in attending the stag weekend of one of his soon-to-be-ex-wife's acquaintances, before turning to Jake. He deposits Freddie at a nearby table, where he promptly places his head on his arms and falls fast asleep.

"Hi," says Jake, once Harrison has stepped away in search of the bar.

"Hi," says Cat. She finds herself suddenly shy, despite the things they said to each other over the phone last night. The space between them feels charged and thick, like the air before a storm. The last time she saw him in person two days ago, they had just . . .

"Hey there."

Cat almost flinches at the familiar voice. "Ronan?" She gapes as her ex-boyfriend follows the rest of the stags into the bar. "You . . . I didn't know you were here."

"Oh, yeah." He grins. "Ste and me have become good mates. And I'm pleased to say, so have me and Jakey here."

He clamps his hand down on Jake's shoulder in what she suspects is intended as a power move. Jake doesn't stir, just smiles politely, then looks at Cat. His eyes, she imagines, are saying: *This guy? Really?*

"How . . . um. How was golf?" Cat asks weakly. The last thing she ever expected to have to contend with this weekend was seeing her ex and her current . . . whatever Jake is . . . together.

"Jakey and I weren't quite as familiar with the game as Ste and his posh friends," Ronan says. "And the groom spent half the time taking work calls in his room. But we gave them a pretty good run for their money, I think."

"Sure did," Jake says, the corner of his mouth twitching.

Cat can't even begin to envision just how unbearable two days in such company must have been for him. She immediately begins to compose a list of ways to make it up to him, starting with a couple of the ideas she outlined during their call. In fact, she would rather like to start the atonement process right now.

"I was right," Jake says, eyes darting down to take in her dress once Ronan rejoins the other guys.

How fine that line is, Cat realizes. The disgust she has so often felt at being objectified by random men versus the tingle of pleasure when that desire is mutual.

Before Cat can say anything else to Jake, "Bad Girls" by M.I.A. begins to blast throughout the entire bar—Priya has commandeered an aux cable—and Darcy drags Cat away to dance with the girls. Against her admittedly weak protestations, a negroni is pushed into Cat's hand, and one song from their youth mixes into another. Sex and fire, heads that roll, girls who won't go to rehab, and men who don't look a thing like Jesus, all things glamorous and toxic and promiscuous and irreplaceable.

They drink and dance like they're eighteen again, and if Cat squints and forgets the inevitable headache and heartburn this will all lead to, she can almost believe it. Priya fundamentally misunderstands "Dancing on My Own" and uses one of the stags as some kind of stripper pole to show off her moves, doing her part to sustain the time-honored tradition of bridesmaids who will wake up next to a groomsman before the happy couple arrive on their honeymoon. A tearful Darcy and Olivia point their wineglasses at each other like daggers in what has all the hallmarks of an impassioned debate, but when Cat steps closer, preparing to intervene, all she hears is:

"You are so goddamn impressive, do you know that? And if a man is too dumb to recognize that, it's his problem."

"Oh my god, shut up. You're the impressive one. Putting this trip together with like five seconds' notice? I'm astounded."

"*Stop*. You're amazing."

"No *you're* amazing."

"I love you."

"*I* love *you*!"

Glad to see the hatchet buried beneath a case of wine, Cat

leaves them to it. As the lone remaining bridesmaid at a loose end, she means to check on Louisa, but scanning the bar and the beach, the bride is nowhere in sight. At first Cat wonders if she and Stephen have crept off for a premarital quickie, but then she spots the groom making a call out near the water and concludes she's in the bathroom.

At some point Freddie rallies and, buoyed by his second wind, races toward the ocean, unbuttoning his shirt and kicking off his shoes. He paddles in the tide like a child, then tilts back his head and crows at the sky, "Bangarang!" and wriggles out of his shorts, throwing himself into the water.

"Oh my god he *didn't*," Priya exclaims, eyeing the best man now frolicking nude in the ocean with a mixture of shock and awe.

Darcy and Olivia follow her gaze, then look at each other and in their new sisterhood reach an agreement with a single word.

"*Wooooo!!!*"

They discard their shades, sunhats, dresses, and sandals, galloping into the water in their underwear. As if granted permission to give in to their bacchanalian impulses now that the girls have, the other stags take to the water too, splashing and roaring like they are the latest warriors to conquer this precious island and claim its splendor as their own.

And then Jake is standing by her side, and as much as she would enjoy seeing him naked in the water looking like a Renaissance painting, she is in no mood to share the view.

"Having fun?" she asks.

"You tell me." His hand snakes around her waist and pulls her closer, until she feels he could burn through the front of her dress.

"The apartment is empty right now." She's blushing wildly at the sudden pressure against her waist as she says it.

"Is that so?" Jake says, his breath hot in her ear. He leans in even closer and brushes his lips against her earlobe. Cat whimpers audibly, too turned on to even worry about the group's hearing.

"This apartment you speak of," he says.

"Mmm?"

"Make your excuses, then go there. Text me the address. I'll follow in ten minutes."

"Is that an order?" Cat raises an eyebrow. "Now who's taking control."

"Do as you're told," he says, the mirth in his voice evident. "There's a good girl."

He gives her a light pat on the bottom, and she is no longer sure whether she wants him to be joking or not. She feigns a headache to Priya and offers to go and check on the absent Harper, before bolting from the bar. There are so few people left clothed, dry, or remotely sober that she doubts her absence will even be noticed.

She walks swiftly back to the palazzo on unsteady knees like Bambi, reveling in the sunny afternoon and warm air. Skipping from one cobblestone to another with her short designer dress, sunglasses, and increasingly unkempt hair, she feels like the carefree heroine of an Italian film.

Just as she gets to the grand-looking front door to the building, she hears the hum of a scooter pulling up behind her. At first she thinks it is Harper, back from her overnight date with Giovanna just in time to cockblock her, but when she turns around, she sees it is a man perched on the Vespa, his long legs pulled in tight.

"Ja—" she says, but then he pulls off his helmet and shakes his wavy fair hair out of his eyes. "Oh. Ronan. What are you doing here?"

"Priya said you were ill," he says. "I thought I'd come and check on you. I'm surprised your boyfriend didn't."

My "boyfriend" is on his way here now to thoroughly check on me, you oaf, she thinks.

"That's sweet but unnecessary," she tells him. "I'm just tired. I'm going to go straight to bed." She instantly wishes she hadn't mentioned the word "bed" in front of him, but he is momentarily distracted, patting down his jacket and jeans until he locates a pack of cigarettes and lighter.

"Filthy habit, I know," he says. "But I can't get on with vaping. Makes everyone look like a pillock."

"I remember when you smoked rollies," she says, eyeing up the packet.

"Still do," he says. "But they didn't have my brand of baccy here, so I'm making do."

He flicks the carton open, nudges a cigarette upward, and then pulls it out with his lips before lighting it and taking a lengthy drag. The way Ronan smokes is all performance, Cat knows. She used to love the theatrics of it herself, before smoking became less and less cool and more and more expensive. Who can afford a tenner per pack, just to stand outside in the freezing cold making small talk with strangers while the smell permeates your hair and clothes? Eventually the financial constraint became a habit in it-self, to the point where now even a whiff of cigarette smoke makes her feel slightly ill, and she can't believe she ever used to breathe that muck in willingly.

"Want one?" Ronan asks, holding out the pack.

"God, yes," she says.

She grabs a cigarette before her self-restraint, lax after such a prolonged period of day-drinking, can kick in. When she reaches for the lighter, Ronan pockets it.

"Arsehole," she says. "What are you doing?"

He inhales on his own cigarette; the end glows bright orange, and she catches his meaning. "You're a child," she says.

"Come on. For old times' sake."

Cat rolls her eyes, then steps forward, holding the cigarette between her lips and sucking in to light it off Ronan's.

"You never used to mind the tip," he says.

The joke is so offensively bad, and her brain so newly flooded with nicotine, that Cat giggles. She takes another deep puff and places her hand on Ronan's shoulder to steady herself.

"This was a mistake," she says. "I'm either going to be sick or pick up the habit again full-time."

"Would that be so bad?" he asks. "If you started again, not the being-sick bit."

"I've learned it's best not to look back," she says, removing her hand and hoping that her meaning is clear.

"Suit yourself." Ronan finishes his cigarette, seemingly uninjured. He has so much more in common with Louisa and her ilk than he would ever admit. First and foremost, an ego that protects him from almost any harm.

"Go back to the bar, enjoy yourself," she tells him. "I'm exhausted."

"Whatever you say." He brings his hand up to his forehead in a mock salute, then swings his leg back over the scooter. Once he has merrily pootled out of sight, Cat enters the palazzo and begins climbing the steps around the internal courtyard, her head and stomach swimming with a slightly nauseous rush. When she makes it up to the apartment, the walls seem to be swaying—or is that her? She decides a sit-down would be wise before Jake gets here. She walks into her bedroom, leaving the door open so he knows which one is hers, and lowers herself onto the bed.

The next thing she knows, the light has dimmed, and her eyes are crusty with sleep. A sheet has been thrown over her legs. She groans, rolling over toward the window—the sky now a rich orange—and bumping into something. Some*one*. Jake is lying on the bed next to her, seemingly absorbed in Elena Ferrante.

"She's no James Patterson," he says, gently closing the book and placing it to one side, "but I can see why people like her."

"Oh, shit." Cat winces. "I can't believe I fell asleep."

Jake smiles. "You're lucky that you're such a cute sleeper," he says. "And that I had Elena here to keep me from getting too lonely."

"I don't like how close you two sound," Cat rasps, scowling. "I may have to fling her out of the window if this carries on."

Jake tuts. "Jealousy isn't becoming."

"I'll tell you what's becoming," she says. "That tattoo."

She runs her hand up his pleasingly muscular arm, nudging up the sleeve of his T-shirt to reveal the infinity sign.

He sighs and says, "Is there any way we can simply not discuss this?"

"Absolutely not." Cat pushes herself up so that she is at Jake's eye level. "I like it."

"You *do*?"

"Yes! This is good, actually. I was starting to worry that you might be a bit too perfect. Little did I know you had a basic white-girl tattoo."

"Harsh."

"As a basic white girl myself, I'm allowed to say it."

"You are anything but basic, Cat."

"Aw, thanks." Cat kisses his shoulder. "But seriously. How did you land on that particular design? Was it a toss-up between an infinity symbol on your arm and a butterfly on your lower back?"

"Okay. I get the point."

"How about a shooting star on your wrist? I almost got one of those when I was eighteen, but I was a wimp so I got a nose ring instead as I figured it wouldn't hurt as much. Let me tell you, I was *wrong*."

"We all do stupid things when we're young," says Jake. "And we should be allowed some grace." His tone is pointed but his eyes are mildly pleading.

"Fine, fine," Cat says. "I'll let it go."

"Thank you."

"Although I can't promise this won't become my favorite thing about you."

"Your favorite?" Jake frowns. "What about, you know . . ."

"It's like I said. It humanizes you."

Jake smirks. "I guess I should just accept the compliment," he says. "If that means you found me just too confoundingly sexy before you found my one flaw."

"I would hardly say *confoundingly*," Cat tells him sternly. "Distractingly, maybe."

"I'll take that." He rolls onto his side to face her. "And by the way. That little sparkle in your nose? I happen to think it's adorable."

"Well, obviously." Cat grins and pulls him down into a kiss. A second later, he shifts his weight so that she is completely beneath him. She can't believe how good his body on her feels: like it's anchoring her in place, keeping her right where she needs to be. She runs her hands down either side of his face, kisses the full length of his jaw. Isn't that how she's felt ever since they first came up with this crazy plan? That he's the one person she can talk to? That this is where they both belong?

"I missed you," he says. "Is that mad?"

"Wow." She grins. "You're *obsessed* with me."

Jake scowls, and it's the cutest thing, and god, she's in trouble, isn't she?

"Fine, I missed you too," she admits.

"Did you, now?" One of his eyebrows twitches upward, and something in Cat's stomach does a somersault. "What, exactly, did you miss about me?"

"You first."

"All right." He kisses her temple lightly. "I missed your laugh." He kisses her cheek. "Your voice." He kisses the side of her mouth, just barely. "The way you jut out your chin when you're convinced you're right, which is often."

"I do not—"

"You're doing it right now."

He kisses her before she can protest or deny it and then asks: "Your turn. What about me?"

"You are so needy."

"It's called reciprocity. I'm pretty sure our fake relationship had it."

There are so many things Cat could count. The way he fills out a shirt. The way he looks even better *out* of a shirt. The hesitation she felt last night looking at that dress grips her again. Her words slow in her throat. But no. *For once in your life, Catherine, say what you mean.*

"Everything feels so easy with you," she says finally. "It all comes so naturally. At first I thought that was because it wasn't real. That pretending was what made it good. Because I've never really known how to be someone's girlfriend, but I thought I could play the part well enough. That's not it, though. It's you, Jake. Everything feels easier when I'm with you."

His eyes have not left hers the entire time she has been speaking. He caresses her cheek so gently it sends a shiver through her.

If he were to do it again, she thinks tears might spring to her eyes. Then he kisses her, and she closes her eyes, his gaze burned into her retinas like she's been staring at the sun.

The door clicks open, and Jake promptly rolls off her. Without the warmth and weight of him, Cat feels a chill. Louisa stands in the doorway.

"Glad to see you're feeling better," she says coldly. "I heard you had a headache."

"Louisa." Cat pulls herself up into a sitting position. She was never caught with a boy in her room as a teenager, but this is a pretty close approximation, she's willing to bet. "What are you doing here?" Noting Louisa's raised eyebrow, she adds: "I mean, why aren't you at the party?"

"Party's over," Louisa says. "There was an accident." Cat sees now that her tense, icy demeanor is a symptom of something else entirely. Is she in shock?

"What happened?" Cat asks, but Louisa just smooths the front of her dress and continues: "The cars leave for the airport in half an hour. Just thought you'd like to know. So you can get your things in order." She gives Jake an indecipherable look and then walks away, neglecting to close the door as she does so.

Cat jumps off the bed and follows Louisa down the hallway and into her own room, where she is already busying herself packing.

"Louisa. Tell me what's going on."

"It happened not long after you both left," Louisa says, carelessly shoving armfuls of designer clothes into her luggage. "Everyone was in the water. The boys were showing off, splashing around. Freddie decided to impress us all by doing a backflip off the rocks. The sea is so clear here, you would have thought he'd see"—Louisa shudders—"the water below those rocks is full of . . . well, more rocks."

"Jesus. Is he okay?"

"They think he broke both of his arms," Louisa says, "and at least one leg. So, no, Cat, I wouldn't exactly say that he is on top of the world right now. Thank god Olivia speaks Italian is all I can say. She was able to call for help. The poor bloody thing ended up getting airlifted to a hospital on the mainland."

"In a helicopter?"

"No, in a hot air balloon," Louisa snaps. "Yes, of course a bloody helicopter, Cat. Christ." She unceremoniously dumps her bridal gifts from the night before over the heap of clothes, tosses Cat's sketch on top of everything, and slams the suitcase shut. Cat almost flinches, and Louisa takes a breath.

"Listen," she begins, but then the others pile into the apartment in a hot mess of tears and morbid excitement over what happened to Freddie, and Cat doesn't get to hear whatever it is Louisa was about to say.

The boys and girls are separated once again into different cars for the drive to the airport. Harper makes her return just in time to slide into the backseat and stuff her bag between her feet, clearly still basking so hard in the afterglow she is immune to Louisa's glares.

"You look thoroughly shagged out," Cat diagnoses.

"I have no idea what that means," Harper says, grinning, "but thank you." She rests her head on Cat's shoulder serenely. "This is the first time I've ever been to a good old-fashioned bachelorette."

"Really?" Cat frowns. "That doesn't sound right, statistically speaking. We're the same age. I've been to at least one a summer every year since I turned twenty-five."

"I'm not really tight with any of the girls I went to high school with like Louisa is. Most of them stopped talking to me when I came out."

"Bitches!"

"Oh, they *were*. Said they were scared to shower in front of me after gym class. Like they were such trophies? So, nah. I haven't been on the bridesmaid circuit like you. The closest I ever got to this kind of female bonding ritual was a sweat lodge in Joshua Tree with a load of other queer women where we shared our innermost hopes and fears. We had these amazing falafels afterward . . ."

"Sweating and falafels is how a fair few of my hen experiences have ended too," says Cat.

Harper titters beside her. "I'm lucky," she says. "I found my tribe. It took me a while, and I was lonely for some of that time. But I know who my people are. Smart, kind, *deeply* therapized gays. Still. I don't know. All of this"—she gestures at the carful of drunk, sleepy women—"feels like some important girly rite of passage that I missed, that I'm finally being let in on. Like I'm allowed into the girls' changing rooms and nobody is looking at me funny. Does that make sense?"

"It does." Cat lays her head on top of Harper's. "I can't say I will ever fully understand the mentality. A lot of it is total regressive bullshit that I can't believe modern women go in for, and yet all the same, it pleases my unevolved lizard brain to be included."

"Women." Harper sighs contentedly. "We're so complex. I love us."

Twenty-seven

"I need to talk to you," says Louisa. "It's urgent."

They are filing through passport control at Heathrow, having all passed out before the safety demonstration on the plane and woken three and a half hours later, dry-mouthed and bleary-eyed. Cat is so busy dreaming of getting home and into her own bed, and trying her best not to think about the arduous part in the middle where she'll have to traverse London on the Tube, that she doesn't take in Louisa's words until she says: "It's about Jake."

Cat stiffens. What could Louisa possibly have to say about Jake? Other than that she is surprised her perpetually single friend has finally met someone?

"You know it's not my business to pry," Louisa continues, "but something about him just hasn't seemed right from the off."

Fuck. Maybe she hasn't credited Louisa with enough powers of perception. Could she have seen through their pretense at the engagement party? Oh god, what if she thinks Cat has hired an escort to pose as her boyfriend for the wedding celebrations? That would be mortifying. Although not *entirely* inaccurate. At least,

272 • PHILIP ELLIS

initially. Now they're . . . well. Cat supposes she and Jake still need to have a conversation about what exactly they are.

"What do you mean?" Cat asks, keeping her tone intentionally nonchalant.

"Well, at first I thought I was being paranoid, overprotective. You know how I am with my friends."

Cat almost balks at the very notion of Louisa's considering the feelings of other people, but outwardly only blinks.

"But I just had this nagging *hunch* . . ."

"Louisa," Cat says slowly. "Tell me this isn't because he's—"

"Oh goodness, no!" Louisa looks horrified at the implication. "You know I don't see color. I mean, just look at the bridesmaids. I practically have one of each!"

Cat has neither the time nor the energy to interrogate *that* statement, so she simply asks: "Then what's going on?"

They are forced to separate, briefly, into parallel gateways, where they scan their passports and show the cameras their drawn, hungover faces. Once they are on the other side, Louisa beckons her along until they are standing away from the steady stream of knackered passengers. She gets out her phone and swipes. A moment later, Cat feels her own device vibrate in her pocket.

"If this were a film, I'd be handing you a manila folder," says Louisa. "As it is, I've just sent you everything I've managed to dig up about Jake Marlowe."

"Dig up?" Cat looks at her, agog. "Dig *up*? Louisa, did you do a fucking background check on my boyfriend?"

"After a fashion," she says. "I asked Elijah to find out what he could."

The burning-hot rage Cat feels at Louisa's gall, her *audacity*, might threaten to overwhelm her—but at the same time she is filled with a subzero fear of what information Elijah might have unearthed. Does Jake have a criminal record? Did they find links to Vivi? To Sid?

"I am not looking at this," she says. "You're being absurd."

"I really think you should," says Louisa. "For your own good."

When Cat does not respond, she adds gently: "He told you he worked in hotels. He works in *a* hotel, darling. As a bartender."

Trust Louisa to think that anybody with a regular job is some kind of grifter.

"You," Cat says, her voice trembling, "are the worst kind of snob."

"There's more," Louisa says. "He's a criminal."

"I don't want to hear it!" Cat raises her voice. Yes, that's it: get emotional, get defensive, do whatever it takes to end this conversation.

"He's a con man, Cat," Louisa says. She has always had a gift for making her own voice heard no matter what other noise there might be in the room. "Are you listening to me? He's a common thief. He got arrested when he was twenty-one."

"Twenty-one? When *you* were twenty-one, you were doing every class-A drug you could get your hands on," Cat spits. "I don't understand why you're doing thi—"

"Cat, he's *married*."

"No he isn't," Cat says without thinking. "He . . ." She stops herself. *He only wears the ring for show.* But how could Louisa possibly know that?

Louisa nods pointedly to the phone in her hand. Cat reluctantly takes her own out of her pocket and opens her email. A PDF sits in her inbox, the digital manila folder Louisa referred to, no doubt diligently compiled by Elijah in the moments that he wasn't watching them eat gelato and rub sunscreen on each other.

She opens the document. The very first page is, she realizes with growing nausea, a scanned copy of a marriage register, between one Jacob Arthur Marlowe and somebody called Sasha Littleton.

That gold ring. Cat was so happy to hear Jake wasn't taken, so eager to accept his story about only wearing it at work, that she had never stopped to wonder how he came to own a wedding band in the first place.

"I don't understand," she says, although she is starting to. *He's a con artist. A damn good one.* He told her he wasn't married. He lied. And if he lied about that . . .

"I'm so sorry, darling." Louisa folds her arms around Cat in a gesture of succor. In reality, it feels like being jabbed with coat hangers from either side.

"How did you even find this?" Cat asks. What she really means is: *Why didn't I?* So much time and research has gone into this job, and like a fool she took Jake at his word. She had thought his lack of a social media presence made him an asset, all the better to fool Louisa and her cohort. What if Cat was the real mark all along?

"Elijah has contacts," Louisa tells her. "From his military days. They can find out anything."

"I think I'm going to be sick," she says, and Louisa immediately withdraws her arms.

"It's better to know now than later," Louisa says. "This will save you so much heartache in the long run. Trust me."

Cat doesn't say anything. She just continues to stare dumbly down at the evidence in her hands.

"I'm just glad I thought to do this before the wedding," Louisa continues. "Honestly, the thought of that rogue, that rat, in my photos for all time . . ."

"Why did you?" Cat asks.

"Why what?"

"Why did you do this?"

"I told you. I just had a bad feeling about him. I adore you, Cat, but you don't exactly have the best track record when it comes to choosing your own suitors."

"What's *that* supposed to mean?"

"It means you're a thirty-year-old woman and the only successful relationship you have ever had was with somebody *I* picked out for you."

"Ronan? You think *Ronan* was a successful relationship?"

"I think it could be! He's mad about you, Cat, and he's going places. Unlike that beer-pouring scoundrel you're currently so enamored of."

"I don't exactly recall you always having the most discerning tastes, either," Cat retorts. "Didn't I have to go and pick up your antibiotics for you after Gavin gave you chlamydia? For the *second time*?"

"You're upset. I understand. But there is no need to start taking things out on *me*." Louisa bats her doe eyes. "I'm your friend, remember?"

Oh, I remember, Cat thinks. *I remember being your little accomplice. Your scapegoat.*

Louisa tilts her head, furrows her brow, and says, not unkindly: "Why don't you go and put some of that anger where it belongs?"

Cat doesn't know what else to do, and so she simply starts walking, following the flow of human traffic out of the terminal toward the Tube. She has no clue if the others are ahead of her or behind her, can barely keep a single thought in her head other than putting one foot out in front of the other. Then she hears a voice calling her name, and when she turns, Jake is running through the crowd to meet her.

"You're a hard girl to track down," he says with the kind of smile that just minutes before would have filled her with warmth. She's not even sure she can feel her hands.

"And you're married," she says blandly.

Jake's grin falters. "Sorry?"

"Are you?" The rage she felt moments ago with Louisa returns. She grabs it with both hands and says: "Were you ever going to tell me?"

He closes his eyes and bows his head.

"Fuck. It's true, isn't it?" Cat realizes she was hoping he'd deny it all, that he'd tell her Louisa made a mistake. She knows now he will do no such thing.

"That infinity symbol on your arm," she says. "The one that's been drawn twice. That used to be an *S*, didn't it? *S* for 'Sasha'?"

Jake opens his eyes and gives her a pained look.

"I can explain," he says.

"You lied to me. I *asked* you if you were with someone, and you said no."

"I never lied to you," he says. "I just . . . I didn't tell you everything."

"That's bullshit," Cat says. "You *told* me you weren't married."

"No, I said I wasn't in a relationship, and I'm not," he says. "I *was* married, once. Look, I don't know how you even found out about this, but Sash and me, we're through. It ended a long time ago."

"Sash." The diminutive stings.

"We got married young," he says. "We were a couple of young, reckless kids who didn't know any better. We worked a few jobs together, and then . . ." He rubs his hand over his mouth. "She double-crossed me on a grift. Took off with the money. I haven't seen her since."

"I don't believe you," Cat says, even though she feels like she has just been given the final piece of a puzzle she didn't even realize was incomplete. She was sure she was only getting half the story from Vivi, and now she knows. But the hurt, the sting of shame at being fooled, overrides all else.

"I have *never* lied to you," Jake says.

"You said you don't work with a partner," she says. "So, fine. Say this is all true. You prefer to work alone because Sasha burned you. If that's the case, why did you agree to do this job with me, Jake?" She laughs hollowly. "Have you been playing me this entire time?"

It's what she's been afraid of all along. Those moments when she stood alone outside the office block wondering if Jake was coming back. Seeing how easily he can ingratiate himself with people. He said himself he's been palling up to Freddie all weekend. An image has been forming in her mind, and now it solidifies like one of her Magic Eye Monets: of Jake swiping the ring from Freddie outside the church and then running while she waits gullibly inside.

"Have *I* been playing *you*?" He runs his hand up and down the back of his neck. "While you were laughing along with your ex-boyfriend when you were supposed to be meeting me? What was that, exactly? Yes, Cat, I saw you."

"Ronan? He's *ridiculous*."

"Looked pretty cozy from where I was standing. Or were you working an angle with him too?"

Cat shakes her head. "I have been so, so stupid. I was pretending to have feelings for you and managed to convince myself there was something real between us."

Some of the venom leaves Jake's voice. "Don't say that. There is."

"Never underestimate a woman's capacity for delusion, Jake. Imagining we can actually have the things we want is sometimes the only thing that gets us out of bed in the morning. It's like you said—sometimes you start to con yourself. I guess when it comes to love, we're all easy marks. I was even easier than most."

"You know that's not true."

"It doesn't matter," she says. "Not anymore."

"So what, that's it? You hear one thing you don't like and decide it's time to throw it all away?"

"Freddie is out of play. And you won't be allowed into the wedding, not now that Louisa knows you have a criminal record. So, yes. The job's off." She sets her jaw and swallows hard. "It was a good idea," she says. "A great idea. And it so very nearly could have worked."

"Are you talking about the job or us?"

She looks away. Jake seems to exhale all of the air in his body at once and takes a step back, as if he is finally seeing her for who she truly is.

"Do you have any idea what it took for me to trust *you*?" he asks. "To be your partner in this, after what Sasha did? You met my *family*. This entire time, I've been trying to ignore that voice in my head that's telling me it's all going to come crashing down around me again. I made that leap, Cat. I chose to put my trust in you. You . . . you aren't even trying."

Cat blinks rapidly, knowing she only has moments left before her body betrays her.

"I think it's best if we go our separate ways."

Jake scoffs, and his face hardens. "Want to hear what I think, Cat?" he asks. "I don't know if you're cynical because the world has been hard on you or if you make the world out to be harder than it is to justify how cold-blooded you are."

His words glide straight past her clenched jaw and her tight, balled fists, through whatever armor she thought she had.

"Good-bye, Jake," she says, turning on her heel and walking as fast as she can toward the exit marked *Underground*. Her wheeled suitcase thrums over the tiled floor behind her, but she barely hears it over her own heartbeat pounding in her ears. She is proud, at least, to make it onto the train before she breaks down. She sinks into her seat, the hurt coming out of her in wet, aching sobs, and all strength seems to drain from her spine; she slumps forward until she is hugging the suitcase for dear life, sinuses burning, shoulders shaking silently.

Nobody pays her any notice. She isn't the first girl to cry her heart out on a Friday night on the Tube, and she won't be the last.

Twenty-eight

Cat's phone dies somewhere on the Victoria line, and so she has no idea what time it is when she finally arrives home, only that the sun is up and the birds are twittering away like it's the start of a Disney film. It is an idyllic, carefree sound. She suddenly wishes she had a gun.

"The wanderer returns!" Tom hollers cheerfully from the kitchen as she closes the front door behind her, and Cat's finger squeezes an invisible trigger.

"How was the hen weekend?" he asks when she enters the kitchen. He's in his dressing gown and slippers, a steaming mug of tea in one hand, the latest *Radio Times* in the other. It's a weekly ritual of his, flipping through the pages looking for a mention of his name.

"It was fine," she says.

"Just fine?" Tom looks up. "I hear Palermo is gorgeous. I was surprised when you didn't put anything up on Instagram."

"The bride insisted on a social media embargo," Cat says, although she has no idea if that is true. Did the other hens post photos while they were away? They must have. Already, Sicily and everything that happened there are taking on a curious haze, like a dream that retreats farther and farther the harder you try to hold on to the details.

"And isn't the wedding the day after tomorrow?"

Cat nods, and Tom tuts.

"I don't even know where this summer has gone," he says, returning his attention to his magazine.

Oh. Right. Cat temporarily forgot the looming deadline. Tom and Alex gave her until September to find somewhere new to live. Today is August 26.

Splendid, she thinks. *I'll just add that to the growing list of things in my life that are absolutely fucking perfect, shall I.*

"I'm looking," she says defensively. "For a new place. I am."

Tom looks up from his *Radio Times*, confused. "I know you are," he says. "Besides, it's not like me and Alex are going to turf you out if you can't find anything straightaway. London's London, we both know that."

"Right. Yeah. Thanks." Cat looks down at her shoes. She doesn't know if she is just tired or hungover or jet-lagged—can you even get jet lag just from Italy?—but she suddenly feels dazed.

Tom stands abruptly from the kitchen table.

"I am going to make you some toast," he announces. "You look like you need it."

Cat imagines she would cry again at this small kindness if she weren't so dehydrated. Instead, she gives a small nod and sinks into the chair Tom has just vacated.

"Thank you. I'll take some tea as well, if there's any going," she says through a yawn, laying her hands on the table and resting her head on them.

The first thing Cat does when she eventually makes it upstairs, after several rounds of toast and a brief pit stop for a nap on the sofa, is dig her charger from her bag and plug in her phone. The second is to build a bedroom nest for herself out of pillows and a duvet where she can watch *Titanic* in safety. Never mind that it is the middle of the day in August and semi-sweltering, she is in a frame of mind that calls for overrelating to every broad, sweeping plot point in this twenty-year-old film. Rare, priceless diamond? Check. Whirlwind romance? Check.

Cat's not exactly Kate Winslet in this scenario, and Jake is no Leo, but she finds it a comforting enough exercise. Until her phone buzzes, intruding upon her self-imposed wallowing session.

It's Louisa.

> Hi darling. I hope you're all right. I hate it when we argue. Come over for supper tomorrow, you can sleep over. The others all live nearby, it would be so helpful to have all of my bridesmaids there first thing in the morning to help me get ready.

No apology for going behind her back to check up on Jake, but then again, Cat didn't really expect one. She should just be thankful that Louisa's suspicions were limited to Jake and she is still invited to the wedding. Even if celebrating somebody else's perfect relationship is the last thing in the world she feels like doing.

She texts back a curt *See you then*, drops her phone back onto the duvet, and dives back into *Titanic*. Just as the old lady is about to drop the necklace into the ocean—a meaningful but ultimately selfish gesture; that thing could feed and clothe a hundred people—her phone dings again.

Hi

Can we talk?

It's Ronan.

Now's not a good time.

She watches the tiny animated dots on her screen, indicating that he is typing. "Please," she whispers. "Take the hint."

I'm outside

"For fuck's sake," she mutters, pausing *Titanic* and dragging herself up from her bed.

Ronan is leaning against the door frame looking like he has just come off a three-day bender. Which, to be fair, they both have. Cat has never seen him so bedraggled—which is saying something. She met the man at art school.

"I heard about you and Jake," he says. "I'm sorry it didn't work out between you two. But from what I can gather, the man's a scumbag."

Three guesses as to from whom he has been learning all of this.

"What do you want, Ronan?" she asks. "I have lots of bridesmaid things to do."

The truth is that she barely has any bridesmaid duties to speak of—Darcy and Olivia have been entrusted with the heavy lifting, presumably because Louisa perceives the unmarried Cat, Harper, and Priya as uninitiated in these matters—but Ronan doesn't need to know that.

"Hello there," says a voice behind her. "We thought we heard the bell." Tom and Alex have both filed in from the living room. Cat doesn't bother to inform them that Ronan did not, in fact, ring the bell. They really are incorrigibly nosy.

"Which one is this again?" asks Alex.

"That's Ronan," says Tom, poking his boyfriend in the ribs. "The artist, remember? I showed you him on Google."

Ronan eyes them both warily, responding with uncharacteristic reticence to the attention, and then turns back to Cat.

"Can we go for a walk or something?" he asks. Then, before she can protest: "Please?"

Cat sighs. "Fine."

She puts on her shoes and follows him out, shooting daggers at her housemates as she closes the door.

It's later in the day than Cat first realized—*Titanic* is one bloody long film—and the low afternoon sun applies an Instagram filter over all of Islington, making even the corner shop and launderette look like something out of a painting.

Neither of them says anything as they walk, but it's not exactly an uncomfortable silence. Cat can't count how many afternoons they whiled away in pleasant, companionable quiet together, working away at their respective sketchpads. After a while, they reach a small, well-maintained square neatly lined with cherry trees. It is exactly the kind of pocket of London she used to imagine herself living in, back when she was naive and had no idea what it would cost to rent even a single room in one of the houses overlooking this scenic, green oasis.

"What's going on, Ronan?" she asks. "You seem odd."

Ronan sinks onto a wooden bench unspoiled by bird shit or cigarette burns, rests his elbows on his knees, and lays his head in his hands.

"I'm a mess, Cat," he says.

"I was there for your ketamine phase," Cat reminds him. "You're going to need to be more specific."

He laughs, but only for a second. "These last twelve months, it's like I got everything I ever wanted," he says. "My work has legitimacy. I'm getting commissions from people who wouldn't even take my calls two years ago. It's like the drawbridge has come down, you know?"

"I understand," says Cat. "The straight white man is finally getting his seat at the table."

He cracks a wry smile, the same one he used to give her right before he kissed her. For the first time in a decade, Cat doesn't inwardly recoil at the idea.

"That's why you and me work," he says. "You don't take any of my artist ego bullshit. Do you have any idea how many kiss-arses are clamoring to tell me how great I am now?"

"I'd have thought that would be your idea of heaven," Cat says. "Adoration and applause."

"I thought so too." Ronan's smile flattens into a grim line. "But it turns out that's not exactly the case."

Cat says nothing, knowing he's simply pausing for effect, as he is wont to do. For all his many flaws, Ronan is a born storyteller.

"I've spent my entire life working toward cramming my foot in this door," he says. "I was so convinced that if I could just get that recognition, it would all be worth it, and every feeling I've ever had that told me I wasn't good enough, that I'd never make anything of myself, would go away. But instead . . ."

He trails off, and when it becomes clear that he is actually struggling to form his next words, Cat takes a seat next to him on the bench.

"Instead what?" she asks.

Ronan's lips press together even tighter, and for one terrifying second she is sure he is going to cry. Then the muscles in his jaw loosen slightly, and he says: "I'm not happy, Cat."

There was a time, not so long ago, when hearing this may have brought Cat great pleasure. But as she sits next to Ronan now in the lengthening shadows, all warmth from the sun threatening to depart at any moment, she feels no satisfaction. This is, for better or worse, the first man she ever allowed herself to love. She places her hand in his.

"I'm sorry to hear that," she says. She means it.

"I feel like a fool," he says. "Like I've been wasting time chasing the wrong thing. I just keep thinking, if being successful in the one thing I'm passionate about leaves me feeling this empty, maybe I'll never find what actually fulfills me."

His fingers close around hers, and he continues.

"And then I asked myself, when did I last feel truly happy or content? And I racked my brain, and it scared me to realize how long ago that actually was." He shifts on the bench so that he is facing her directly. "It was when I was with you, Cat."

"Me? Ro, that was ten years ago."

"Think about it," he says. "Wasn't everything simpler then? Before we let shit complicate our lives and tear us in different directions. I know, I know," he adds, seeing Cat's raised eyebrow, "but I've got my shit sorted now. We could be together. I could take care of you."

Cat shakes her head. "I don't need anyone to—"

"I love you, Cat," says Ronan. "It took me too long to figure it out, but . . . It's you. It's always been you."

Somewhere deep inside Cat, a much younger woman sinks to her knees and cries great racking sobs at the words she was once so desperate to hear. But now they have an echo. *It's you*, Cat's words this time, spoken in hushed tones in a palazzo that feels so far away it might as well be another world.

"Doesn't it make sense?" he says, clutching her hand between both of his. "Doesn't it just . . . fit?"

When two people have history, it creates a kind of gravity between them. This, Cat reasons, is why she doesn't immediately pull away. It's like a physical force is keeping her on this bench, so she can hear what Ronan is saying and the seriousness with which he is saying it.

It might not be the worst idea in the world, she thinks. Ronan has known her for a long time. If somebody could love her as a messy, insecure nineteen-year-old, then maybe that's the person who can love her now, as a judgmental, neurotic thirty-year-old. Cat imagines herself saying yes, becoming Ronan's girlfriend again, slipping into that world for real. Gallery openings, lunches with Priya and Olivia.

It would be so easy to surrender. And she is so tired.

But Cat can't ignore the way Ronan is gripping her hands so tightly. It is not love or affection in his eyes but need, plaintive and frantic. He is a drowning man, and she is his lifeboat.

"Does it?" she asks. "Make sense, I mean. I'm not sure we ever *did* fit. We were just young and playing Tetris with each other."

"What?" Ronan squints at her, and it has nothing to do with the fading light.

"Tetris," she repeats. "We keep trying to make these pieces fit together, but whatever combination we try, I don't think it will work."

"But," he sputters, "I love you. I just told you I love you."

"And I believe you," she says. "Or at least, I believe that *you* believe you. But, Ronan, it's been ten years. If you'd loved me all this time, I think there might have been some indication before now."

She could make this harder for him, ask him what exactly he loves about her, and watch him squirm and come up with broad, unflattering clichés. Even just a few days ago, she might have. But Cat is no stranger to being lost. The surge of sympathy she feels for Ronan now is possibly even stronger than the love she once had. He is completely, utterly at sea, and she wouldn't wish that kind of despair on anyone. Not even her shitty ex.

The sun is on the verge of vanishing behind the buildings: the trees around them are silhouetted in a blinding gold, every house on the square has its own halo. Beside her, she can feel Ronan's body shaking, and she knows he is seconds away from crying.

"What am I going to do?" he asks, his voice trembling.

"I don't know," she says as kindly as she can. She lays her head on his shoulder, and as if he has finally been granted permission, Ronan begins to weep.

"If even *you* won't have me . . ." He doesn't finish, his words bubbling away under tears.

Gee, thanks, Cat thinks, but she doesn't have it in her to feel slighted. Just like her entire relationship with Ronan, this isn't really about her.

Twenty-nine

Cat arrives at the house on Sloane Square a little after seven on Sunday evening, as instructed, to enjoy a "light supper" with Louisa, Julia, and Harper, who she forgot has technically been Julia and Louisa's houseguest all summer.

Cat has visited before, of course: those trips to see Louisa during the summers between terms at Bristol were how she first came to understand the magnitude of the disparity between their respective lifestyles. She remembers being so tense on her first visit, so afraid of saying the wrong thing or of making too sudden a movement and breaking something priceless, that she came down with a migraine and had to be put to bed in the guest room.

She feels more familiar with her surroundings but no less anxious as she sits in Julia's dining room, which has been redecorated post-divorce, and washes down a kale Caesar with a large glass of Gavi from a bottle that, Harper reveals shyly, was a parting gift from Giovanna. Louisa, uncharacteristically subdued, drinks little at dinner and eats even less.

"Are we okay?" she asks Cat on the first-floor landing after the meal. Louisa is on her way upstairs for a solid nine hours' sleep and has already gotten a head start on her skin-care routine, having taken a sheet mask from the kitchen fridge and arranged it carefully onto her face. The wet membrane hanging from her forehead and cheekbones makes her look like a couture Hannibal Lecter. "We haven't spoken much since . . ."

"Since you had your heavy look into my boyfriend."

"When you put it like that, you make it sound like I'm in the Mafia or something." Louisa's tone is light but forced. She is clearly determined to put an end to this business before she goes to bed.

"We're fine," Cat says. "Honest. All that stuff you found out just threw me, that's all."

"Well, I can imagine," says Louisa. "It was all so *frightful*." She gives Cat a light peck on the cheek, her mask leaving behind a slimy trace that smells like aloe vera and rose water. "Just promise me you won't waste any tears on that man tonight, okay? I can't have you all puffy and red-faced tomorrow." And with that, she bids Cat good night and disappears into her suite on the second floor, leaving Cat to traipse up another set of stairs to the guest room.

"You won't mind bunking in with Harper," Julia informed her when she arrived earlier, no question in her voice at all. What she has forgotten until now is quite how small the guest bedroom is, slotted beneath the eaves, with just enough room for a single bed and, as Harper proudly informs her, an air mattress she has inflated with her own very powerful lungs.

"You can take the bed, of course," Harper says, but Cat refuses. The last thing she wants is for the one kind person in her life to sleep on the floor on her account. She brushes her teeth in the tiny bathroom across the hall and then lies down on the air bed, which lets out a series of gassy sounds that immediately make her new roommate laugh.

"I'm sorry about you and Jake," says Harper, once both the squeaky wheezing and her own chuckles have subsided.

"Thanks," says Cat, staring at the ceiling.

Harper sits up in bed so she can see her properly. "What happened, if you don't mind me asking?"

"Louisa didn't tell you?"

"Oh, I'm sure she was *dying* for me to ask. But I've decided that being a posh gossip isn't for me. I'd rather hear it from you, if you want to talk about it."

"I really don't," says Cat.

"Okay."

"It's just . . ."

"Yeah?"

"You know that cliché that every parent in every film ever says when a kid messes up? About how they're not angry, just disappointed?"

"Sure."

"It's like that. I feel . . . deflated. Like I dared to hope that this might be something, and then it wasn't. More fool me, right?"

"Not at all," says Harper. "There's nothing foolish about hope."

"It's not really my thing, though," says Cat. "I usually accept people the way they are. And more often than not, that's . . . well, a bit crap. But I'm a realist, so that's okay. Wanting somebody to be better isn't going to make them magically transform."

"Honey. That is a very depressing way to be."

"Isn't it!" Cat laughs bitterly. "I suppose I just want someone who shows up for me, who puts me first."

Harper chews her lip thoughtfully for a moment.

"I am going to ask you something," she says, "and please feel free to tell me if I'm being fucking rude."

"Okay . . . ?"

"You say you want someone who shows up."

"Right."

"Do you, though?" Harper asks. "If you really think about it, have you ever given somebody a chance to really be there for you?"

"Of course I have," Cat tells her. "What kind of question even is that?"

"Really? Because it sounds to me like you're the one keeping her eye on the door. Like, if you hold people to a certain standard, knowing that they won't ever measure up to it, then you're protecting yourself from the possibility of heartache or embarrassment."

"Harper."

"Yes?"

"Fucking rude."

Harper just shrugs. "Tell me I'm wrong."

Cat says nothing.

"I have this theory," Harper says. "Want to hear it?"

"I don't know. Does it involve dragging me some more?"

"Tangentially. So anyway. One of my absolute favorite movies is *Practical Magic*."

"What?"

"You haven't seen it? Oh my god, it's the best. Sandra Bullock and Nicole Kidman in all their nineties hotness. Definitely one of the formative works in my early lesbianism."

"Yes, I've seen *Practical Magic*, Harper, just . . . what the hell does this have to do with anything?"

"Just listen! So in this movie, Sandra and Nicole are sisters who are witches, right? And they're raised by their aunts, Stockard Channing and Dianne Wiest, who are *also* witches. But Sandra and Nicole are too distracted by their lives and men and kids to ever get really good at magic. Until one night when they accidentally kill Nicole's abusive shit of a boyfriend, then cast an ill-advised spell to bring him back from the dead."

"Yes, I know," Cat says. "Like I told you, I have seen this film."

"The spell goes wrong, of course," Harper continues, without any indication she has heard Cat. "And the guy comes back as a creepy zombie ghost thing. And when the girls finally own up to what they did and ask their aunts for help, do you know what Aunt Dianne tells them?"

Cat cannot recall the film in the same vivid detail as Harper, and so she shakes her head.

"*'You can't practice witchcraft while you look down your nose at it,'*" Harper says with all the solemnity of a woman quoting scripture, and then flicks her wrist for emphasis, as if her meaning is obvious.

"I am truly, genuinely lost."

Harper sighs impatiently. "It sounds to me like you've been playing at love, Cat," she says, "but you've also been keeping it at arm's length. No wonder your spells are going wrong. Or rather, your relationships."

Cat's cheeks grow hot. She thinks of Jake, with his bruised heart, and the courage it must have taken for him to even start to trust her. It really is crossing a line for Harper to say all this, she decides. It's impolite and altogether far too American.

"I'm not like you," she says. "I can't fall in love every five minutes with whichever tall, dark, and handsome looks my way."

"Well, maybe you *should*!" Harper blows a stray curl out of her face. "Cat, I love you, but you really need to loosen up."

"Maybe you ought to mind your own business," Cat says primly, and she sounds so much like Julia in that moment that both of them burst into fits of giggles.

"I overstep—it's what I do," says Harper. "Just ask any woman I've ever dated. But I'll tell you this, my friend. I'd rather fall in love and get my heart broken once a week than never at all." She reaches to switch off the lamp beside her bed and then collapses back onto her pillow, spent. "That Gavi was pretty strong, huh?"

"Ever the lightweight," Cat says, pulling her sheet up to her chin and closing her eyes. A moment later, Harper is snoring softly, and Cat is left to ponder whether there is any truth to her bizarre theory. Sure, it's true enough that she has been *careful* with her heart when it comes to men, but what girl isn't? She certainly held parts of herself back when she was seeing Ronan, and she thanks her past self now for that caution. And as for Jake . . .

It's not just boyfriends though, is it, chirrups a small voice inside her. Her eyes sting with tears, and she is taken aback by the sudden ache in her chest. When was the last time, before this filterless American entered her life, that she had a real friend? What has kept her from making the kinds of connections with people that others seemingly take for granted? Why *is* she such a loner?

She knows why, of course. Has always known but has never looked it in the eye. Now, lying here in the dark, Cat sits with that knowledge, and it leaves her feeling like somebody has hollowed out her chest with an ice-cream scoop.

After what feels like an eternity of staring at the ceiling, failing to fall asleep, Cat carefully rises from the air mattress, grabs her phone, creeps out of the guest room, and takes a seat against the wall of the landing. Julia's and Louisa's respective bedrooms are one floor below, and so when the person she is calling answers,

Cat is almost able to convince herself that she is keeping her voice low and steady so as to avoid waking them.

"Hi, Dad," she says. "It's me."

"Cat?" In just one syllable, he manages to convey surprise, pleasure, and concern. "It's late, m'love. Is everything all right?"

Just hearing his voice, the Cheshire twang that's so familiar it feels like a part of her, opens a door inside Cat.

"Tell me a story about Mum," she says.

"What?"

"What was your favorite thing about her?" she asks. "What do you miss the most?"

The line roars with static for a second as he exhales deeply. He sounds tired.

"She wasn't just my wife," he says. "She was my pal. Nobody made me laugh like Alice. And nobody laughed at my terrible jokes like her." Cat hugs her knees against her chest as she listens, as if it were possible to curl up inside the safety of her father's voice. "It was her and me against the world," he says. "And then, when you came along . . ."

He sighs again.

"I think that was what took the most getting used to after we lost her," he says. "I was so scared of doing something wrong, of messing you up or letting you down. And I had nobody to talk to about that. Your mum and me, we were a team, you see. There's no feeling quite like that."

"You could have talked to me," Cat says, her throat thick and sore with the sensation of years' worth of pressure finally reaching the breaking point.

"I know," he says. "I know that now. I wasn't good at that stuff back then. I'm sorry, kid. I made some mistakes."

"No, that's not what I meant." Cat rubs her forehead. It's all coming out wrong. "I mean, maybe you did, but you always tried. You were there. You did right by me. You did."

"It's my job. I'm your dad."

"I know. But I . . . I don't think I made it very easy for you, at times."

Static hums in her ear again, and it takes a second for Cat to figure out that her dad is laughing this time.

"You don't love because it's easy, or because you want something in return. You just do it and hope for the best."

"So I hear," she mutters.

"That was always my biggest worry, you know," he says. "After your mum died, I watched you retreat inside yourself. Then you got into uni, and I just thought: *Please, god, don't let her go out into the world believing that letting herself be loved isn't worth the hurt that might come along with it.*"

It's like he knows. He's nearly two hundred miles away, hasn't seen her in weeks, but he *knows.*

"I have to tell you something," she says. "It's something you're not going to like."

The line is silent for a moment.

"All right," he says finally.

Shame, thick and heavy like tar, threatens to slur her speech, and she has to take a breath and speak slowly to get her next words out.

"I sold Mum's brooch."

Nothing again. Cat thinks for a second that the connection has been lost, and then her dad says quietly: "Okay."

"I'm sorry," she says. "Money has been tight. More so than I've been letting on. I went back, tried to buy it back, but it was already gone. I'm so sorry."

"Jesus, Cat!" At first she thinks it's anger she hears in his voice, then realizes it is something closer to relief. "I thought you were going to tell me you've been taking drugs!"

"What? No. No! I just—"

"I gave you the brooch to do with as you pleased. You're a grown woman; you don't need to apologize to me. We all have to do things we don't want to make ends meet sometimes. It's one of the shit parts of being a grown-up. That's life."

"But it was *hers*."

"And I'm sure she'd rather know you're housed and fed than hung up on some trinket. Things are just that, Catherine. Things. It's people who really matter."

"You sound different," she says. "More . . . feelings-y."

"I've been seeing someone," he says.

"What, like a therapist?"

"Ha!" The line explodes again for a second. "No, I have a barber, and that'll do me. I mean, I've been seeing a lady friend." He says it to her like she's five.

"Since when?"

"Six months or so."

"Dad!"

"I know, I know," he laughs. "That's why I've been ringing you, you know. I didn't want to tell you at first, in case nothing came of it. Her name is Josie. I think you'd like her."

"Dad." Her voice trembles.

"It's time," he says. "It feels . . . It just feels right, love. It's been a long time."

"I never wanted you to be lonely," she says. "I'm sorry I stayed away so long."

"Oh, would you listen to yourself! Cat, daughter mine, I love you, but this part of the world didn't cease to exist just because you were no longer in it. I've missed you, and I would love to see more of you, but I do have a life, you know."

Cat laughs, and her sinuses throb. Who knew emotional honesty created so much phlegm?

"I love you," she says. It pains her that she can't remember the last time she uttered the words out loud.

"I love you too," he says. "I always will. Now. What do you need? What can I do?"

"Nothing. I'm good."

"Are you still strapped for cash?"

"It's fine, Dad. Honestly. I'm going to figure it out."

"All right, then. Can I go back to sleep?"

"Sure. Sorry. Yes." Cat wipes her nose with her forearm. "I'll come and visit soon, okay?"

"If you say so, love."

"I mean it. I promise. You can introduce me to Josie, and I'll try my best not to act like a stroppy teenager in front of her."

"That'd be grand. Good night, Cat."

She tiptoes back into the bedroom, where Harper's light snores have deepened into steamship-level honking, and lowers herself back onto the air bed. Sleep still fails to come, and as the night ticks away into the early morning, Cat begins to ponder her next move. She considers moving back home and living in Winsford for a while. But that doesn't feel quite right. It would be like trying to go backward in time. And she doubts her dad would appreciate a boomerang daughter just as he's starting a new phase of his life. But she doesn't think she can stay in London, either.

In just a matter of hours, all of her plans for the future have been obliterated, and she has genuinely no idea what she is going to do next. Her eyes fall on the dress hanging in its carrier on the back of the bedroom door. At least she knows where she can get a free meal tomorrow. She'll worry about everything else the day after.

VOICE NOTE SENT: AUGUST 28, 6:04 A.M.:

Jake. Hi. I just. I'm sorry, okay? I let Louisa get in my head. Actually, no. That's not fair. I got in my own head. And trust me, it's a mess in here. Like, one of those hoarders' houses you see on telly, full of piles of old newspapers and empty aquariums.

This is not going the way I intended. My plans for an apology had involved us being in the same room, but since I couldn't track you down, this is what you get. Apologies, again.

Let's start from the beginning, shall we?

My mum died when I was twelve. And I was sad, for a long time. Really, really sad. And then I got older, and I thought I was over it. Or at least, I learned to deal with it. I didn't realize just how much it affected every single decision I would make for the rest of my life. The kind of person I became.

She was my world. I loved her so much, and she loved me even more. I know you know what that's like. And then one day she just wasn't there anymore. She was gone, and wherever she went, she took that love with her. And my dad, god, he tried so hard, and he loved me so much, but a piece of my heart was missing and that was something nobody could fix. And so I figured, that's fine, you know? I have been loved fully and truly. I know how that feels. And I also know how it feels when that love goes away. Like drowning, but you never actually die. You just have to keep swimming, deeper and deeper, with your lungs full of water. So I think, I just won't let that happen to me again, right? I'll protect myself. Guard what's left of my heart. Fiercely.

And that's what I did with Ronan. Hell, I did it with Louisa. I've spent so many years resenting her, thinking she took advantage of me, but if I'm honest, I think I chose her because I knew I'd always be disappointed. I told myself I expected more from her, but deep down I wouldn't have known what to do if she was a better friend. I was so scared of relying on someone only to end up being left alone that I turned out to be the one to isolate myself.

And then . . . Jake Marlowe.

You said I didn't know what it took for you to trust me, after Sasha. I do. I'm scared that I might not even know how to love without caveats or conditions. How to have any kind of relationship that doesn't come with a price. For the longest time, that didn't bother me. But now . . .

I'm sorry. I pulled you into this mess, cast you as my ideal boyfriend, and you went along with all of it. You agreed to my insane idea and never asked anything in return except for your fair cut. I wish things could have been different. That I'd met you under different circumstances. That it was just a nice, normal girl who walked into your bar. Maybe then things could have been different.

Thirty

The wedding is, as the guests and gossip blogs will all agree later, exquisite. Cat and the bridesmaids arrive in a surprisingly spacious Bentley and are deposited at the bottom of the steps to St. Martin-in-the-Fields on the topmost corner of Trafalgar Square. From here they can see crowds of tourists gather at the bases of the lions, peering curiously at Nelson's Column, which is now occupied by a new sculpture: a wrought iron rendering of two slender figures, one male, one female. They resemble, it dawns on Cat, wedding cake toppers.

"Stephen's wedding gift to Louisa," Darcy says.

"Fuck *off.*" Cat can't resist gaping. *These people!*

"The bride will be here any minute," Olivia says, handing the girls their miniature bouquets and shooing them into formation like baby ducks. Darcy lets her. "Best get a wriggle on."

Cat files up the steps and into the church after Darcy and before Harper, Priya, and Olivia, walking with a slow, practiced pace up the aisle, which has been scattered with cherry blossoms, as if a spring breeze has paved their way with petals. She wonders, briefly, how much it cost to have these out-of-season flowers grown and flown in for the occasion, and then stops herself. Old habits die hard.

The bridesmaids take their places to the left of the altar, opposite Stephen and his groomsmen, who are already stationed to the right and each look like they will be auditioning for the role of James Bond the moment the ceremony is over. Freddie sits at the end of the row in a wheelchair, head held immobile in a foam collar, arms and legs extended out in front of him in plaster casts, posed like a little boy playing race car. He slowly twists his hands to give the bridesmaids a stiff thumbs-up, his entire face enraptured in a dreamlike grin. He must be on the really great pain meds. Or maybe he just loves weddings.

"Stephen looks so fit," Priya whispers, before Darcy shushes her. Cat and Harper say nothing, but she is certain she hears Olivia humming approvingly. They have a point: Prince Charming has scrubbed up even better than usual today, tux hugging his body like half the women in this church wish they could.

"Is it just me," Harper murmurs, "or does he look nervous?"

"He is sweating a bit," Cat agrees, noticing that Stephen's wedding-day glow is at least 50 percent perspiration.

"It *is* August," Darcy says. "Anyway, it's tradition for the groom to be on edge."

"It is?" Cat and Harper exchange puzzled looks.

"It's a power thing," Olivia tells them. "The one time a woman gets to call all the shots is when she's a bride. And even then, it only lasts a day. So you milk it."

"I don't understand," Priya says.

"I kept Harrison waiting twenty minutes before I showed up for my wedding." Olivia's gaze loses its focus as she smiles softly at the memory. "He was convinced I'd gotten cold feet and done a runner."

"My father had our driver do one more lap around the block," Darcy says. "Just to keep Evan on his toes."

"That's mad," says Cat, but at the same time, she thinks she gets it. So frequently, she has silently bemoaned the brilliant, clever women who seem to lose themselves in the minutiae of wedding planning, then the property- and baby-related admin that come after, until they are completely absorbed into the lives of their husband and children like some kind of science fiction hive mind. It *should* be their prerogative to take their time, to treasure those last moments of single life, before that "I" forever becomes a "we."

"But Louisa and Mr. Vincent left the house in their car at the same time as us," says Priya, still seemingly perplexed by the logistics of the thing.

"To be fair," Cat remarks, "Louisa is *never* on time, so this tracks."

As it turns out, Louisa Vincent arrives to her nuptials with uncharacteristic punctuality—only five minutes behind schedule—looking so breathtaking that for an instant Cat forgets she has ever had an uncharitable thought toward her former best friend. The ivory silk hangs from her shoulders and cascades, waterlike, down her body. Her hair, usually bone-straight, sits in luscious waves over one shoulder, adorned with white blooms. Suspended on what must be the finest chain imaginable, a constellation of small bright diamonds is scattered across her chest. The overall effect is as if a river nymph stepped out of a Renaissance painting and onto the cover of *Vogue*.

"Holy shit," Harper gasps. "That *dress*."

"I was with her at the fitting," Darcy whispers, "but this is something else."

"Do you suppose she's even wearing knickers?" Priya marvels.

"Not for an instant," Olivia says.

The bride and her father reach the end of the aisle, and Mr. Vincent gives Louisa an impossibly delicate kiss on the cheek, as if a stray breath might be enough to shatter her. Then he takes his seat next to a stoic Julia, who appears to be wearing half of a taxidermied peacock on her head. Once Darcy has stepped forward to relieve Louisa of her bouquet, the ceremony can begin.

Cat allows herself to tune out at first, painfully aware she is ending the summer as she began it: broke and alone at a wedding. Hearing those same vows repeated now, first by the celebrant and then by Louisa and Stephen, is rather like watching the same in-flight film on a return trip as you did on the way out. It is only when they get to the exchanging of the rings that something in Cat stirs.

"I give you this ring as a sign of my love," says Stephen, turning to where Elijah is standing at the ready with the Tsarina, fulfilling Freddie's best-man duty. Maybe he was always going to be the custodian of the diamond today, and the job was doomed before it ever began. "With my body I honor you," Stephen continues. "All that I am, I give to you, and all that I have, I share with you."

He slides the ring onto Louisa's finger, and Cat feels something that approaches relief. There's no way she could even dream of pulling off the plan now. Not on her own. It's over. She should count herself lucky. She doesn't want to land in a prison cell, sharing bunk beds and a toilet with Britain's answer to Anna Delvey or Elizabeth Holmes.

"I give you this ring as a sign of my love," Louisa recites beatifically. "With my body, I honor you. All that I am, I give to you. And all that I have, I share with you."

It is as if time has slowed down or her senses have heightened. Cat cannot remember how many weddings she has attended, how many times she has sat through some variation of these same vows. But they were always an abstraction to her, she realizes now. Easy enough to let the words wash over you when you're sitting in an uncomfortable pew, wearing a dress bought on credit, wondering how much longer until you get to eat something. She's never let it fully sink in: the promise the two people at the altar are making to each other.

It hits her that Jake has made this same promise before. Jake loved Sasha enough to propose, to offer everything he had to her in front of Vivi and Sid and everybody else he knew. To ink her initial onto his body. There was no scheme with Sasha, at least, not on *that* day. They weren't just playing at being a couple, or tiptoeing around each other's egos, or obscuring their own feelings. They stood up and said it with their chests. What a fool she has been, to have ever mistaken what she and Jake had for the real thing.

Was Harper right when she said Cat wouldn't let anybody close enough to choose her? Or is she missing some key component that everybody else has? Maybe she has simply never been the kind of girl who falls in love for real or for keeps.

Her view of Louisa and Stephen becomes distorted, but she doesn't even clock why until she feels Darcy push a tissue into her hand. She turns and sees that her sister-in-satin is blinking away tears of her own.

"I always cry at weddings," Darcy confesses in a whisper.

"Me too," Cat says just as quietly. They share something approaching A Moment, and then the bride and groom are pronounced husband and wife, and the entire church breaks into uproarious applause. Cat claps along, bringing her hands together until her palms are bright red and sore.

They are still smarting an hour later at the reception in the foyer of the National Gallery. Cat procures a glass of water with plenty of ice and clasps it between her hands, breaking the habit of a lifetime and opting not to hit the open bar as hard as possible.

From where she stands at the top of the staircase, she watches the last stragglers from the church enter through the grand main entrance. Her throat constricts at the sight of a little girl, no older than five, in a poufy dress and sparkly gel shoes, whose eyes widen in amazement as she is led into the vast foyer by the hand of her mother. The woman—a cousin of the groom, she thinks—pulls the girl along impatiently, no doubt keen to deposit her in front of a coloring book or iPad so she can go and get a drink.

If Cat knows anything, it's weddings. She once attended a reception where the bride tripped on her own train and broke her nose sprinting to the dance floor when the DJ played "Mr. Brightside." She begrudgingly admits, to herself if nobody else, that Louisa's is the most beautiful of all the celebrations she has ever been to.

All around her, guests holding glasses of champagne and elegant canapés on tiny napkins mill in and out of the hallways admiring the paintings on display. She doesn't know which is more of a surprise: that the gallery, booked out for the entire day, is allowing people to wander around with food and booze willynilly so close to the paintings, or that Louisa would share the spotlight on her special day with some of the greatest masterpieces of European art.

"*Art is a lie that helps us understand the truth*," her mum told her on their first visit years ago. "*Picasso said that, I think. A horrid little man, or so I read. Loved women, but didn't like them all that much. Still. Broken clocks.*"

"Cat." Ronan's voice does not come as a surprise this time. She glances up from a portion of mosaic on the floor named *Sacred Love* and gives Ronan what she hopes is a genuine smile. Gone is the scruffy, blubbing wreck of a couple days ago. His strawberry blond hair has had a fresh cut and is swept pleasingly back from his face; his jawline is clean-shaven and as angular as ever. He wears the jacket to his plum-colored suit around his shoulders like a cape.

"You look good," she says truthfully. "A little dandyish, but it works."

"You too." He smiles. "Pink suits you."

"I forgot to thank you," she adds. "For *Calliope*. She's beautiful."

Ronan dips his head in what she knows is only a half-arsed nod toward self-deprecation. He would never let anything leave his studio unless he deemed it the perfect execution of what he set out to capture. If he were to ever turn even a fraction of that care to the real people in his life, he'd be one of the most eligible bachelors in London. Cat thinks this with neither longing nor resentment. Ronan McCann puts her in mind of the few occasions when she has attempted to learn how to cook. She will spend hours preparing a meal in the kitchen, but by the time it is even remotely close to being done, she finds she has lost her appetite entirely.

"It makes me happy you think so," he says, taking a sip from a glass of whiskey she didn't even notice he was holding. "No guesses as to who inspired her."

"Okay, enough," she says with a grin. "That muse line worked when we were kids. Don't tell me you still use it."

"It's true," he says. His face is earnest. "I know we're not getting back together, Cat. But that time we had will always mean a lot to me. It was when I figured out who I am as an artist. You played no small part in that."

"If that's the case," Cat says, "I appreciate it. Truly."

"In fact . . ." Ronan swirls his whiskey theatrically, clearly trying to build some anticipation. "It's the core concept of my next exhibition."

"Sorry, what is?" Cat tilts her head.

"Muses," he says. "The inherently female quality of creation. Birth, inspiration, all of that. The divine feminine. And I already know what the crowning piece will be."

"No," Cat says, smile fading. "Ronan, no."

"I need to practice," he'd told her. *"Nobody will see it except you and me. Wouldn't it be special, to create something together?"*

"Some things are far too beautiful to be kept in storage," Ronan says.

He isn't joking. He really means it.

"You are not showing my *vagina* to all and sundry," Cat intends to whisper, but it comes out as a hiss. "Not *again*."

"I never took you for a prude, Cat." Ronan frowns, and Cat feels hot rage prickle across her cheeks like a rash.

"If I were a prude, I would never have posed naked for you."

"Then what's the problem? I thought you'd be pleased."

"Pleased?!"

"To be immortalized!" He tries to put his arm around her, but his blazer drops from one shoulder, and he gives up. "You'd be like my Pattie Boyd."

"I don't care if I'm your Pattie Boyd or your Pat Butcher," Cat tells him. "I won't allow it."

Ronan winces. "The thing is," he says, "you don't really get to allow anything. Me telling you was a courtesy. I honestly thought you'd be happy having your contributions recognized." He shakes his head ruefully. "I mean, it's not like you've done much of anything else in the last decade."

Ronan saunters over to another corner of the gallery, where he is received with hugs and air kisses, and Cat is left to simmer in her fury. This isn't about shame or prudishness, she thinks. From what she remembers of the painting, it's expressionistic enough that nobody would even be able to identify her. It's the fact that once again she feels exposed. Ripped off. She knows Harper is probably right, that it's better to let people in than to keep the entire world locked out, but her track record of choosing who to invite over the threshold is nothing short of a train wreck.

She should have cut the brakes on that fucking Vespa when she had the chance.

Thirty-one

She is sitting on a downturned toilet seat in a stall, taking a moment of sanctuary from the clamor of guests, when she hears two people enter. The first is Darcy, although her voice is conspicuously absent of its usual cheer. The second, she soon ascertains, is Evan, Darcy's husband. And there is trouble in paradise.

"You're drunk," Darcy says. "It's embarrassing."

"Loosen up, it's a wedding," he slurs. Cat hears the tinkle of ice; he has brought his scotch into the bathroom for his scolding.

"I just want today to go smoothly," Darcy says. "It's been a lot of work, you know."

"I know, sweetheart. And I'm sure Louisa and Stevie Boy appreciate your endeavors." Evan's words are kind, but Cat can tell he is very much mocking her. "It's done now, though. Why don't you grab a glass of champagne and actually have some fun?"

"How can you be so calm?" Darcy asks. "With everything that's happening?"

Cat leans forward on the loo, her curiosity piqued. Is this more than a simple marital tiff? She hears the click-clack of Darcy's heels traversing the bathroom and, realizing she is checking under each stall door to ensure their conversation isn't being overheard, swiftly bunches up her dress and lifts her feet onto the toilet seat.

"Nothing is happening," Evan tells Darcy. "Not yet, anyway. And it might not at all. There's no whiff of a formal investigation, just some disgruntled clients taking their grievances to Twitter. It will all get lost in the noise soon enough."

As they continue to bicker, a picture begins to form. Cat isn't exactly fluent in stocks and shares, but even she knows what a Ponzi scheme is. And while she is still not exactly up to speed on what it is that Evan and Stephen's company does, "innovative investment solutions" sounded a lot like snake oil to her when Stephen first explained it aboard the *Maiden*. Now she begins to suspect she was right.

"I don't know what Stephen was thinking," Evan says, "telling Louisa everything. I warned him not to. If I had another go at it, I wouldn't tell you."

"Some men are actually honest," says Darcy with surprising venom. "I know that might shock you."

"Stephen? Honest? Grow up, beloved." Evan takes another gulp of whiskey. "At least the wedding is over and done with. Now, if anything happens, she can't be forced to testify against him."

"Is that why you married me?" Darcy asks, her voice small, and Cat cringes from her awkward hidden spot.

"No," Evan says. "Contrary to what you think, I really do love you." There is a clinking sound as he sets his drink down next to the sink, and a breathy rustle that could be an embrace.

"I love you too," Darcy replies. "I wish I didn't, sometimes. But I do."

"Then let's go enjoy the wedding. Have a drink."

"I'll have a drink if you have a cup of coffee."

"There she goes again." Evan laughs softly. "You drive a hard bargain, but fine."

Cat feels like she's been reading a book that has been translated into English, and now she suddenly finds herself with the facility of language to absorb the original text. Of *course* there was a reason for such a short engagement. Louisa bloody Vincent would never consent to such a thing unless there was urgent cause to do so. Their imminent emigration to Singapore rings truer now too. A tax haven, no doubt. She wouldn't be surprised if Louisa and Stephen set up a lovely show home and bank account there, only to then spend their actual time in some other exotic locale that lacks a rigorous extradition arrangement with the United Kingdom.

They're crooks, she thinks, and a girlish laugh almost escapes her throat. She clamps her hand over her mouth just in time. Is this why Louisa had momentary cold feet a few days ago? Did she flirt with the idea of developing a conscience, then think better of it?

Darcy and Evan leave the bathroom, and Cat waits in the stall for another minute or two before finally easing her feet back down, stretching out her cramped knees, and following them out. The entire celebration now, the ostentatiousness of it all, feels rather grubby. An elaborate lie in plain sight. Or maybe she's being cynical. Maybe the bride and groom really do love each other, and Stephen's financial crimes were just the jump-start they needed to make a commitment.

The worst part, she decides, is that Stephen's family is already richer than God. There's nothing he could ever hope to earn that wasn't already his by birthright. He didn't do this out of necessity.

He did it because he could. Maybe he loves that feeling of getting away with something as much as Cat does. She can't decide if she's sickened or impressed. Either way, if she ever harbored any feelings of guilt about her now-defunct plans to steal the Tsarina, they are gone.

"Cat!"

For fuck's sake, what now?

Priya scuttles over, waving frantically despite already having caught her attention.

"I can't find Louisa," she says.

"Okay . . . ?"

"Olivia asked me, well, told me, to find her. Something to do with the cake?" Priya rambles. "Anyway, I can't find her."

Cat sees now why Priya was never in the running for maid of honor. She is crumbling like meringue under the slightest pressure.

"Relax," Cat tells her. "Breathe. She'll be around here somewhere. I bet you she's just been cornered by some old relative. Or she's fixing her makeup."

Priya sighs in relief at a grown-up taking control and disappears back into the crowd. Cat scans the room: Louisa won't have gone far with this many people around. A bride on her wedding day is like a celebrity: she can't take more than two steps without being stopped by somebody.

Could she? Cat thinks back to that conversation on the balcony. If Louisa really has been experiencing doubts . . . She'd have done something *before* the ceremony, surely, not run out on the reception?

"I swear to god," she mutters, striding through the maze of interconnected chambers, "if you have legged it, I am going to kill you. Pulling a *Runaway Bride* is one mess I can't help you clean up."

She passes fewer and fewer guests the farther she strays from the main event, until finally all she can hear as she marches through passageways is the sharp echo of her own high heels on the polished floors.

"Sorry, boys," she says as she stomps past Van Gogh and Seurat, "no time today."

She slows her pace and is about to turn back, convinced that if the bride fled, it wouldn't have been into the depths of the Sainsbury Wing, when she hears something else: a keening wail. It is coming from a small, discreet door painted the same color as the walls, a staff room or utility closet of some kind.

As Cat approaches the door, the sound becomes clearer. It is like a distressed baby goat, or a dog that has learned to howl along to the television. Cat can't remember the last time she was around to witness Louisa crying, but it certainly has never sounded like *that*. Only as she pushes down on the door handle and swings it open does she recall where she's heard that sound before: through the paper-thin walls of a student house in Bristol.

Louisa is bent over a low cabinet, eyes rolling back in her head, a delirious smile on her face, her dress thrown up over her hips, while Elijah stands behind her, bucking his hips furiously. The entire cabinet scrapes half an inch against the floor with each thrust, then grinds to a halt as the bride and her bodyguard both realize they've been caught in the act. Elijah's low grunting ceases in an abrupt yelp; he carefully extracts his hand from Louisa's hair, which mere seconds ago he held in his fist, and swiftly bends to pull up his trousers. Louisa pushes herself off the cabinet and begins to correct her skirt, her cheeks and chest a flaming red.

"Olivia was right," says Cat, surprised by her own calm. "No knickers."

"Eli," Louisa says quietly, her eyes not leaving Cat, "could you give us a minute?"

"Yes, miss," he says gruffly, walking around her, back toward the door, and then edging around Cat as if she might electrocute him if he gets too close.

"Eli?" Cat says. "Your fly." She glances to his crotch and back. He shamefacedly zips himself up before leaving the room, closing the door behind him.

The room is painfully silent, bar the sound of Louisa's shortened breath becoming more calm and measured, until finally she says: "I need to fix my hair."

Cat lets out a single bark of incredulous laughter. "Are you serious? Louisa, what the hell? You're half an hour into your marriage and you're already—"

"Don't," Louisa says, and her voice wavers. "Whatever you're about to say, just . . . don't. Because I already know, okay? I'm a fuckup; I always have been. Is that what you wanted to hear?"

Kind of, Cat admits inwardly. This is the girl she's been jealous of all these years? *This* is the perfect life? Ten years on and she is still cheating with a bit of rough, only this time on a husband who is, in all likelihood, a white-collar criminal.

"You can't tell Stephen," says Louisa. "You can't. Please. You just can't. I don't know what he'll do. You have to keep this to yourself, Cat. I'll do whatever you want, give you anything. Please. I will owe you for the rest of my life."

I'll owe you. It has been the refrain of their entire relationship, but Cat knows now that being Louisa's emotional creditor is worth nothing. Less than nothing.

Louisa steps forward, reaches out and takes Cat's hand, her eyes pleading. Cat stands there numbly, arm extended like a monarch waiting for a supplicant to kiss her knuckles.

"Gosh, your hands are cold," Louisa remarks after a moment. "I suppose that means you've got a warm heart. Isn't that how the saying goes?"

She's working an angle, of course. Getting Cat on her side, or trying to with everything she has. She's like a toddler who has been caught doing something she shouldn't and is now desperately trying to get back in her mummy's good books. Cat places her other hand over Louisa's and gives it a reassuring squeeze.

"Look at me," she says, and Louisa obeys. "I won't tell Stephen."

Louisa almost collapses with relief.

"Sometimes I wonder what I did to deserve a friend like you," Louisa says, blinking away tears. Cat ducks her head to keep Louisa's eyes on her and, with the utmost care, catches a tear on her pinkie finger before it can fall from Louisa's lash and threaten to ruin her mascara.

"I know it's been a long and weird road for us," Cat says, reaching into her handbag for a tissue and offering it to Louisa, "but I'm truly glad I'm here."

"I'm glad you're here too," says Louisa. "Nobody else understands me the way you do."

"Maybe so." Cat smiles. "I think the same thing about you sometimes. We won't ever again be those messy girls we were when we were eighteen. And only we remember what it was like to be them."

"Oh goodness, stop," says Louisa, fanning her right hand in front of her eyes. "You'll set me off for real."

"I used to hate you sometimes," Cat tells her, shocking even herself.

Louisa stares at her for a moment, then nods. "I know."

"It's taken me forever to realize I have to stop resenting people for having things I don't," Cat says, "and just focus on my life instead. On what I do have."

She helps Louisa tidy her hair and briefly wonders if they are going to hug, but Louisa is already fixing the rumpled neckline of her dress and reassembling the insouciant composure she reserves for the outside world.

"Ready?" Cat asks.

"Ready," Louisa says. "Thanks. I owe you."

Cat laughs, then checks that the coast is clear before leading the bride back to her wedding. She doesn't inquire as to Stephen's less-than-legal dealings or the ins and outs of Louisa's arrangement with Elijah. They are, she figures, none of her business. She escorts Louisa over to her new husband and then seeks out the bar. She's earned a drink today after all.

She sidles up to Harper at the counter. Her American friend has switched her bridesmaid dress for a chic, loose-fitting suit in the same dusky shade of pink and unpinned those garnet curls.

"You look like a cosmopolitan," Cat tells her.

"What are the odds! I feel like one too." Harper asks the handsome server in a waistcoat and dickie bow to prepare the cocktail, and Cat holds up two fingers in a peace sign, indicating she'd love one as well. Usually a little sweet for her tastes, but vodka is vodka.

"Beautiful wedding," Harper says, leaning louchely back against the bar. Cat hums in agreement. "This whole summer has been a real trip," she adds, and Cat snorts. If only she knew the *half* of it. The bartender places their drinks on the counter, and they clink their glasses together.

"Makes me sad to be leaving so soon." Harper sips her cosmo.

"How soon?"

"I fly back the day after tomorrow. Technically I should already be back, but I postponed my flight when they announced the wedding."

"I hope you've enjoyed your time in England," Cat says.

"Are you kidding? I've had a blast getting to know you. All of the 'maids, actually. I feel like an honorary Brit, d'you know what I mean, love?" That last comment is rattled off in a broad approximation of an Estuary accent, which leads Cat to believe Harper has been mainlining *Love Island* or *The Only Way Is Essex*.

"I'm going to miss you," she says. She didn't intend to say it, but she realizes as the words leave her mouth that she means them. Harper looks at Cat in surprise. Her smile is bright and gorgeous.

"Don't miss me," she says. "Come and visit. I can be your guide to the crackpot wonderland that is California."

"I'd love that," Cat says. An image comes to her, of two women in a convertible, driving through the desert, hair billowing madly in the wind like Guy Pearce's cape in *Priscilla*. And why not? What does she have left in London?

"You've got my number," Harper says. "Call me anytime."

"One second." Cat grabs a cocktail napkin and takes an eyebrow pencil from her purse. "Just . . . a little . . . something . . ." Leaning against the bar, she rapidly sketches a head full of tumbling curls, eyes with tiny crinkles at the corners from laughter, a puckish nose and sly grin. Not her finest work—the lines are thick and border on crude—but she hands it to Harper with none of the shyness or self-consciousness she showed at that dinner with Louisa and the others.

"I'll treasure it," Harper says, eyes filling. Cat wraps her arms around Harper and buries her face in her voluminous hair. Without hesitating, Harper hugs her back fiercely.

"Thank you," Cat whispers. She extracts herself from the embrace before she can get even more emotional, knocks back her cocktail, and, with one last smile at her friend, begins to make her way toward the exit, where warm, late-August sunshine is flooding in from outside. It's unbecoming for a bridesmaid, but for the first time in her life Cat intends to leave the party early.

She opens her handbag—the same sequined, slightly battered clutch she brings to most weddings—and discreetly checks its contents: eyebrow pencil and lipstick; a five-pound note so creased it is starting to resemble one of the Dead Sea Scrolls; a pack of mints; a bandage for shoe-related emergencies; and a priceless diamond known colloquially as the Tsarina.

Thirty-two

Now that she is on the brink of making her exit, Cat has to suppress the impulse to hyperventilate. She can hardly even believe what she has just done. If pushed, she would call it a moment of madness. But when Louisa grabbed her hand to beg for her silence, she knew she had an opportunity that would never arise again.

Maintaining eye contact with Louisa and keeping her attention away from the ring was the easy part. The handwork was a different story. Cat was *certain* that Louisa would feel her pulling the ring off her finger, or that she'd feel its absence before Cat was able to retrieve the fake from her handbag under the pretext of getting a tissue.

Cold hands might mean a warm heart, but they also make it a damn sight easier to massage a platinum ring off somebody's finger without their noticing. Cat still can't think of Jake without her breath quickening in hurt, but she has to admit: those lessons with him certainly paid off.

Looking down at the Tsarina, her heart begins to pound. She

has actually gone and fucking done it. Cat realizes that, for all of the planning and talking about the job she and Jake have been doing for the last several weeks, a small part of her never thought they'd be able to go through with it. And here she is, holding just over ten million pounds in her handbag, having pulled the whole thing off entirely by herself.

It is a lonelier feeling than she might have anticipated.

Cat snaps the bag shut and heads for the front doors. If anybody asks, she will claim she needs to get some fresh air. She can feel the sun on her face, when something stops her, and she turns back to take one last look. This will almost certainly be the last time she sees these people, the world she once coveted.

Louisa stands beside Stephen, a practiced, benign smile on her face as they are congratulated by some Tory peer or other. As Cat watches, Louisa begins to fidget, massaging the fake diamond on her left hand, turning it around and around on her finger like a worry bead. A trapdoor in the pit of Cat's stomach falls open. Did the Tsarina ever fit so loosely before? Or has Louisa lost weight specifically in her ring finger over the last couple of days?

She sees Louisa look down at the ring, perplexed, and then extend her hand out in front of her so she can take a proper look at it. Stephen is still deep in conversation with their guest. Louisa turns her hand this way and that, looking to Cat like she is examining how the Tsarinot catches the light.

Time to go.

Why can't she move?

Cat stands rooted to the spot in terror and fascination as Louisa, an expert in nothing if not her own jewelry, arrives at the conclusion she and Jake feared would be the one thing to derail the entire heist. She can tell a fake from the genuine article. In the seconds after making that discovery, her frozen smile mutates into something closer to a grimace. She tugs on Stephen's sleeve, and when that doesn't immediately get his attention, she grabs his shoulder and forcibly turns him to face her, much to the chagrin of Lord Whatshisname.

The happy couple exchange quiet words, and Cat sees Stephen's expression change too. He snaps his fingers and beckons Elijah over to them. Louisa does not even look at him as Stephen apprises him of the situation.

All of this happens in a matter of seconds. Cat could still make her escape, but it would feel more conspicuous now, wouldn't it? Better, surely, to continue playing her part and then slip away later. She only hopes Sid will still be happy to connect her with the buyer. Shit, what if he isn't? This was a huge mistake. What the hell was she even *thinking*?

Louisa, Stephen, and Elijah are scanning the room, as if the ring might present itself upon its absence being noticed. Cat affects an air of pleasant idleness, avoiding direct eye contact. There is no way they can suspect her. To everybody here she is broke, single, and mildly pathetic, but not a criminal. She prays that this perception of her will, for once, work in her favor.

"It's her!" she hears Louisa cry. "*She* has my ring!"

The foyer falls silent, and Cat's blood turns to ice in her veins. She turns her gaze back to Louisa, but to her bafflement, the bride is not pointing at her. Her accusatory glare is directed at somebody to Cat's left. She turns, as does everybody in the room, to the object of Louisa's sudden allegation.

Louisa is pointing at Darcy, who is staring dumbfounded down at her own hand, where the Tsarina sits on her middle finger.

What the hell? What the actual hell?

"No," says Stephen, "it's *there*."

A heartbeat later, murmurs of shock and confusion begin to ripple and echo throughout the vast room, as one by one, the wedding guests find themselves in possession of a Tsarina.

Julia Vincent looks at her left hand as if it is an alien appendage upon discovering a diamond on her divorced ring finger. Stephen's father, Jolyon, almost chokes on the ring that has appeared in his glass of champagne. Olivia and Priya marvel at the way the light plays on the new trinkets nestled in their bouquets. Saffron, Uncle Jonty's companion, admires the ring she has just found on her canapé napkin before casually tucking it into her bra. Harper squints quizzically at hers, floating in her cosmo like a cherry, then tosses it onto a passing tray. A young waiter gets the fright of his life as glittering jewels tumble from the bottle he has just tilted to top up an aunt's wine. Everywhere Cat looks, she sees an array of perfect-seeming diamonds.

"I don't know about you," a familiar voice whispers in her ear as the crowd around them erupts in confused chatter, "but I could really do with getting out of here."

She dares not turn around. Dares not believe this is real, despite the bounty of evidence to the contrary all around her. There is no doubt in her mind, in her heart, as to whose work this is. She feels his hand in hers and, amid the chaos cascading all across the hall, allows him to lead her behind a huge hanging banner, where they can talk unobserved. Only then does she take a proper look at him.

There is so much of him she seems to have forgotten: the tiny creases at the sides of his eyes; the lips so full it almost looks like he's pouting; those black lashes. The way his hands are always so warm they send what feels like a static shock through her whole body. How is any of that possible to forget? Cat Bellamy remembers every insult and slight she has ever endured, has nursed her grief and grudges like hothouse flowers.

She has been holding on to all of the wrong things.

"What are you wearing?" she asks, mentally kicking herself for allowing this to be the first thing she says to him, even as the reason behind his waistcoat and bow tie immediately become clear to her. *Put someone in uniform and they become invisible.*

"You'd be surprised how unobservant these lot are," he says. "You can plant anything on them, as long as you're topping up their champagne at the same time."

"But I told you the job's off," she says, still confused. "How did you know—"

"I know *you*," he says. "Whether you like it or not, Cat, I do. I knew that you wouldn't be able to resist. And I was pretty sure you'd be able to do it on your own. But what kind of partner would I be if I didn't come in with an assist?"

"All those rings." She shakes her head, trying to get it all straight. "We had a ton of decoy diamonds, I know that, but how did you get them all set?"

"Called in some favors and worked through the night." When she says nothing in response, he frowns. The line that forms between his knitted brows is another thing she will never let herself forget again. "If you tell me that I have overstepped your boundaries, I am going to—"

She silences him with a kiss. She kisses him hungrily, letting him feel every ounce of want and need in her, without shame or self-consciousness. He showed up. He showed up for her.

"Jake," she breathes when their lips part, as if only just realizing. "You're *here.*"

He smiles that crooked smile. "I'm still your plus-one, aren't I?"

"Always." She strokes his jaw. "I'm sorry. I'm so sorry. Those things I said . . ."

"Yeah. That was a bit shit of you, to be fair. Maybe I ought to turn you in?" He laughs and makes to pull her out from behind the banner.

"I'm serious," she says. "If I were you, I wouldn't have come. I was awful. I don't deserve you. I don't deserve this."

"There are some very earnest, slightly embarrassing voice notes on my phone that would suggest otherwise," he tells her.

"You listened?"

"Cat." He looks at her fondly, like she is a beloved but rather simple child. "When have I ever not?"

He's right. Jake Marlowe is not somebody who struggles to hear anything or see what is right in front of him.

"I owe you so badly, don't I?" she says.

"You'll have time to make it up to me, don't you worry." His grip on her hand tightens. "But only if we get out of here, like, *now*."

"No arguments here." Cat kisses him once more, briefly, fiercely, and squeezes his hand. "Let's go."

When they emerge from their hiding spot, the wedding guests are all gathered around Louisa. At first, Cat believes this to be the beginning of some kind of investigation, but then she hears Louisa regaling the crowd with her explanation of how the rings were all part of the plan for their big day.

"As many of you know, my darling Stephen proposed to me with the most stunning ring," she is saying. "But what is less widely known is that this ring is actually of some historical significance—not to mention value! I won't go into any vulgar details, but let's just say I actually wear a rather convincing replica most of the time!"

"Just like Elizabeth Taylor," a nearby guest remarks to another, in awe.

"And what more fitting way to thank you all for being here to celebrate with us," Louisa says, beaming, "than to gift our nearest and dearest with a copy of the ring to keep!"

Cat is reluctantly but undoubtedly impressed. Of course Louisa would never submit to the public humiliation of being robbed at her own wedding. Appearances are everything to her. Even now, people are recording Louisa's announcement, photographing their new rings, posting them to Instagram.

"Unbelievable," she says. "Your distraction looks like it's going to go even more viral than mine."

She can't think of a more fitting wedding present for Louisa than a reception that breaks the internet. They back away into the crowd, which has once again resumed the easy buzz of wedding chatter. Stephen still looks stricken, but Cat doubts he will ever tell his family that they have managed to lose the Tsarina for real. Beside him, Louisa gazes out across the throng like a queen surveying her subjects . . . and her glance falls on the handsome Black man in a waistcoat and bow tie holding her bridesmaid's hand. For possibly the first time in her life, Louisa Vincent looks somebody in a service uniform in the eye. Recognition and rage spark on her face, and her stare instantly flits right to Cat.

"We're fucked," Jake whispers.

But Louisa does not speak out, and Cat can see the calculations going on behind those cold blue eyes. Cat realizes, with a delicious glow, that on this occasion, *she* is the one with the power. Louisa does not want her to disclose her affair with Elijah. Nor would Stephen want her to blab about his shady business dealings, if he knew she were privy to such information.

A silent understanding passes between the two women. Cat and Jake will make their getaway, and Louisa will let them. She has, as far as everybody else is concerned, the perfect wedding, the perfect husband, the perfect life. And as long as everybody continues to believe that, Louisa possesses everything she wants.

Cat takes one more look at Louisa, confident that this is the last time she and the bride will ever see each other. She feels a pang in that moment. Not love, exactly, but a close enough approximation that it could pass for the real thing if you didn't know any better.

I'll owe you, she said, all those years ago when they first met. Cat strides out of the gallery hand in hand with Jake, her head held high. It may have taken long enough, but when it finally came time for Cat to collect, Louisa kept her promise and made good on that debt.

They run down the steps like a pair of little kids. Cat just has time to register that the cast-iron bride and groom atop Nelson's Column are already festooned in pigeon shit before Jake directs her toward a waiting black cab.

"Afternoon," Sid calls back to them from the driver's seat as they get in. Cat thinks her heart might actually explode in this moment, and she extends her hand through the break in the plastic barrier to squeeze the shoulder of Sid's weathered leather jacket, before sitting back and turning to Jake.

"I . . . ," she begins, before settling for simply looking at him.

"What?" He grins. *This man*, she thinks, *is pure trouble*. And she would not have it any other way.

"I just can't believe you dressed up as a cater-waiter and still look so . . . *hot*."

He laughs and leans in. "Careful," he says. "You'll turn a man's head with talk like that."

"Then turn it this way and kiss me."

He gladly complies.

When they come up for air, they are crossing the river. The

London Eye glints in the afternoon sun and Cat thinks back to the two people who walked the length of the South Bank together all those weeks ago, passing a lie back and forth between them without realizing it was already starting to come true.

"I'm sorry," she says. "Again. For the things I said."

"I'm sorry too," says Jake. "I should have been more transparent from the off. It's just . . ." He looks up to the ceiling of the taxi, then back at her. "I kept my guard up because Sasha hurt me, and something told me you had the power to hurt me even worse. To break or bribe your way through my defenses, and I would be powerless to stop you. Forget lonely drunk idiots and their wallets, Cat. You could steal presidential secrets if you wanted to. And I don't think you even realize it."

"Stop," Cat says. "You'll make me blush." She's being arch and coy, because earnestness will take time and practice before it comes naturally to her, but she makes sure not to look away. To keep her eyes on this man whose bar she walked into all those months ago and who truly *saw* her.

"I love you," she says. The words come unbidden and true. And she hasn't even finished saying them before Jake says, "I love you too," and envelops her in a crushing embrace.

This. Cat holds Jake as tightly as she can, as if she can convey through touch alone the fierceness with which she loves him, and thinks: *Yes. This.*

"So we make quite a team," she says when they finally pull apart. "Who knew!"

"There are definitely some kinks to work out." Jake smirks. "But I have to agree."

"Remember when my dream job was freelancing for the likes of Mikhail?" Cat throws back her head and laughs. "When it turns out I was a master jewel thief this *whole time?*"

"I am so fucking proud of you," he says.

"I guess I just had to find my passion."

"You certainly did that . . ." Jake does that thing with her earlobe again, and she has to bat him away.

"I've been thinking," she says, "about our next job."

"When?" he asks incredulously. "In the last five seconds?"

"How do you feel about pivoting to art?"

"Cat. We cannot steal those magic water lilies you're so fond of. Somebody is sure to notice. Now, that guy playing 'Wonderwall,' maybe . . ."

"There's a certain promising young artist whose work has recently come under valuation," she says. "A spectacular fuckwit of both our acquaintance."

A knowing expression overtakes Jake's face. "Tell me more," he says.

"There's one painting in particular I'm interested in acquiring," she elaborates. "Its value is more sentimental than anything, but we can nab some pricier pieces while we're at it if you're game."

"Cat Bellamy? Sentimental?" Jake pulls her closer again. "I'd call that growth."

"We can work out the details later," she says, breathing him in. "After we've sold this rock and taken a well-earned holiday."

"Sounds good to me." He kisses her forehead.

"I might also have come to the conclusion," she adds, "that I could, possibly, benefit from some therapy."

"Well, you *are* rich now. I hear therapy is a rich-person pastime." Jake's grin is sheer wickedness. He rests his forehead against hers and his voice softens. "Have I mentioned I love you?"

"You can keep telling me; I won't get tired of it."

"Maybe I should be more sparing. Wouldn't want it going to your head."

"We just stole a ten-million-pound diamond. If you're worried about my ego, I regret to inform you I am going to become insufferable for the foreseeable future."

"That's my girl."

Something about the way he says it makes Cat want to clamber into his lap, and she is about to when she remembers Sid, who to his credit is whistling softly in the driver's seat, keeping his eyes strictly on the road. She falls back into her own seat, certain her skin has flushed the exact lewd color of her dress.

There'll be time for that, she tells herself. *So much time.*

Jake's hand slips into hers, and she links her fingers between his, overcome with pleasure at how perfectly they fit: a key unlocking the door to a place she knows now is her home. She raises his hand to her mouth and kisses his knuckles tenderly.

"Still thinking a desert island?" he asks.

"Maybe. But I'd like to make a quick stop somewhere first." Cat gives Jake an affectionate peck on the very end of his nose and asks: "Have you ever been to Cheshire?"

Acknowledgments

I started writing *Love & Other Scams* during the cold, depressing, seemingly unending lockdown of 2021. I originally had the idea a few years earlier after an especially expensive summer of attending friends' weddings, and had been saying for my entire adult life that I was going to write a novel, but it wasn't until I found myself trapped in a tiny flat with far more free time than I was comfortable with that I finally sat down and started doing the work. With a decade and a half of rejected short stories under my belt, I figured it would be a productive coping mechanism if nothing else, but I could never have expected the ride it would end up taking me on. All of which is to say, this has been a long time coming, so please bear with me because there are a *lot* of people I would like to thank.

First and foremost, Vikki Burns, who spent many evenings throughout the pandemic "gossiping" with me about Cat, Louisa, and Jake as if they were real people. I figured out at least half of the plot during our FaceTimes, then later while hanging out on your patio with Marley, who made his way into this book in the form of Raymond the black Lab. Laura Blake and Gemma Milne, who would sit and write with me, exchange voice notes about our respective projects, or even just text me saying *Put down your phone and write!*—I wouldn't have even finished a first draft without you.

My author friends who already had books out in the world when I started this journey, who offered me support and advice and showed me it was possible: Nate Crowley, Jordyn Taylor, R. Eric Thomas, Adam Sass, Caroline O'Donoghue, Kate Young, I learned from watching you!

My agent, Florence Rees: you changed my life when you slid into my Twitter DMs. None of this would have ever happened if you hadn't taken a chance on me. The same goes for Maria Whelan at InkWell, Daisy Watt at HarperNorth, and Kate Dresser at Putnam. I couldn't have asked for a better team to champion this book, and I can't wait for us to do this all over again.

Unlike Cat, I am lucky to be surrounded by loving, supportive people here in the Midlands who lift me up and are only too glad to help me celebrate my wins: Lez Navarro, Sapreena Kumari, Mark Hipwell, Leo Buckley, Laura McEwan, George Elsmere, Becky Weaver, Vicky Osgood. As Taylor Swift herself said, it's nice to have a friend.

It might not come across as such in the book, but I genuinely do love a good wedding, and it has been an honor to be a part of so many special days. This book wouldn't exist without the many couples whose nuptials I have happily attended, but I want to name-check three brides in particular. Chloë, Zlatka, Adele, I met you back when we were all messy teenagers like Cat and Louisa, and I am proud to know you as the incredible women and mothers you are now. (Let it be known that your weddings were *so* much more fun than anything depicted in this book.)

Thank you to all of my friends and colleagues at *Men's Health*. Great writers, even better people.

A special shout-out to every coffee shop, restaurant, wine bar, pub, and hotel lounge where I spent hours writing: Abi Connolly at Arch 13, Aman and Sophie at 40 St. Paul's, Hotel du Vin, the Pineapple Club, the Grand Hotel, 200 Degrees, Diplomats, Wayland's Yard, the Wolf, the Exchange, the Rep. I basically stopped cooking for the year I worked on this, so cheers for keeping me alive.

My mum, Sue, and my stepdad, John: Where do I even start? I know words are my thing, but they fail me sometimes. There are also those who are no longer here but whose hands I constantly feel guiding mine over the keyboard: Dad, Hazel, Tom, Granny, Catherine. Thank you. I love you.

And finally, to anyone who has ever been single at a wedding, the only queer person on a night out, the last remaining friend who hasn't had kids or bought a house or landed their dream job or figured their life out, I would just like to say: I believe in you, and you look fucking amazing.

Love & Other Scams
Reading Group Guide

1. *Love & Other Scams* offers up grandeur in the form of a big wedding and its imposing havoc. Discuss whether you noticed any silent signs of chaos surrounding Louisa's wedding, outside of Cat and Jake's involvement. In what ways can disorder and elaborateness go hand in hand? Given the multiple events Cat mentions having attended at the start of the novel, do you think such repetition can cause even the most lavish of weddings to lose its spark?

2. Cat is a big lover of the visual arts. How does the splendor of art contrast or align with her approach to life? How do you think her passion for art plays a part in her reactions—if at all—to fine experiences like the trip to picturesque Palermo, wearing rich textiles, and attending the wondrous boat event?

3. Cat's hobby lifting wallets means she's no stranger to scheming. Discuss the range of feelings you might experience if you were to steal from someone. Which of these emotions would you expect to overlap with Cat's? For Cat, which impulse prevails?

4. Cat and Louisa have known each other since their college days. Despite their different backgrounds, why were they drawn to each other? How do Cat's feelings about Louisa when she first imagines the heist differ from when they first met? How does this progress when she and Louisa have a quiet moment on the balcony in Palermo? What about at the wedding itself?

5. To pull off such a scheme, one needs the strength of acute observation. Do you think Cat is observant? Or do you think she tends to see what she wants to see? What do you notice about Jake's powers of perception in contrast to Cat's?

6. Author Philip Ellis subtly pokes fun at the lifestyle of the wealthy. What "posh" trait stood out to you as the most bizarre? Which did you find yourself surprisingly relating to? Who in the story is the greatest caricature of the upper classes?

7. Louisa's bridal party includes a range of personalities. Of all her bridesmaids, who would you connect with most and why? How would you have handled Louisa's "bride mode"? Have you ever been a bridesmaid? What did you consider the most important duty?

8. Discuss the theme of authenticity and inauthenticity in *Love & Other Scams*. Who do you consider the most true-to-themselves character? The least?

9. Cat and Jake's Bond-esque endeavor unavoidably requires deceit and manipulation. Despite playing for the same team, how does this context impact their trust of each other? What role does

meeting each other's friends and family play in how they understand each other?

10. The role of mothers in this story is significant to our understanding of Cat and Jake. Describe the various ways in which author Philip Ellis illustrates a mother's impact. To what extent can we attribute Cat and Jake's compatibility to respective upbringings?

11. Cat and Jake discuss how they'll use their earnings from the heist. How would you split ten million pounds (or dollars), and what would you spend your portion on? Who would be your partner in crime?

Tam Bernard

PHILIP ELLIS is a contributing editor for *Men's Health*, covering relationships, pop culture, and LGBTQ+ issues. His work has appeared in *British GQ*, *Teen Vogue*, and Repeller, and his short fiction has been long-listed for the Commonwealth Short Story Prize. He lives in Birmingham, UK.

🐦 Philip_Ellis
📷 philipellis

Praise for
Love & Other Scams

"I went into *Love & Other Scams* expecting a fun, witty, sharply observed romp. Not only did it deliver on all fronts, but it also packs an emotional punch with a pair of complex main characters I cared for deeply. This book stole my heart!"

—Ava Wilder, author of *How to Fake It in Hollywood*

"Ellis's sharp wit and masterfully drawn characters completely sucked me in from the first page. A true rom-com in every sense of the term, it's a pure delight!"

—Falon Ballard, author of *Lease on Love* and *Just My Type*

"If you've ever had your weekend ruined and your budget broken by a so-called friend's over-the-top wedding, *Love & Other Scams* is the book for you."

—Katherine Heiny, author of *Early Morning Riser*

"Fresh, fast-paced, and funny with a wonderfully warm cast of characters—it's everything you want and more from a book about diamonds, deceit, and desire. I adored it."

—Laura Kay, author of *The Split* and *Wild Things*

"Mischievous, magnetic, and heaps of fun. No matter how you're feeling, the pages instantly cheer you up."

—Emma Gannon, author of *Olive*

"With a sharp eye for detail and some of the funniest dialogue I've read in a long, long time, Philip Ellis has managed to give me the debut I didn't know I needed: a heisty romp of rom-com that brilliantly skewers marriage, class, and love. He's the real deal, and so is his brilliant book."

—Grant Ginder, author of *The People We Hate at the Wedding* and *Let's Not Do That Again*

"Two con artists. A scam. A cat-and-mouse game. And yet the real heist here is debut author Philip Ellis's ability to so fully capture a reader's attention with vibrant characters and the seasoned skill of a pro. I was laughing from page one and I already can't wait to read what he writes next."

—Steven Rowley, author of *The Guncle*

"*Love & Other Scams* is such a blast from start to finish, reminding me of some of my favorite things: the movie *Heartbreakers*, Sophie Kinsella novels, and finding someone you can talk trash with at a wedding. By some sleight of hand, Ellis had me increasingly invested in Cat and Jake's relationship even while I was legit laughing out loud at their hijinks. I loved every minute!"

—Alicia Thompson, author of *Love in the Time of Serial Killers*